PENGUIN TRAVEL LIBRARY

The Grand Irish Tour

Peter Somerville-Large comes from the same family as Edith Somerville, co-author of the 'Irish RM' stories. He was educated in Dublin, and after leaving Trinity College spent a decade working abroad. Journeys to North Yemen and northern Iran gave him material for his first two books. In addition to *The Grand Irish Tour* he has written four books about Ireland: *The Coast of West Cork*; *From Bantry Bay to Leitrim*, which followed the flight of O'Sullivan Beare; *Irish Eccentrics*; and *Dublin*, which has been described as 'the best general work on Dublin in print'. He has also written four thrillers. He lives in Dublin with his wife and daughter.

Peter Somerville-Large

The Grand Irish Tour

PENGUIN BOOKS

Penguin Books Ltd, Harmondsworth, Middlesex, England
Viking Penguin Inc., 40 West 23rd Street, New York, New York 10010, U.S.A.
Penguin Books Australia Ltd, Ringwood, Victoria, Australia
Penguin Books Canada Ltd, 2801 John Street, Markham, Ontario, Canada L3R 1B4
Penguin Books (N.Z.) Ltd, 182–190 Wairau Road, Auckland 10, New Zealand

First published by Hamish Hamilton Ltd 1982
Published in Penguin Books 1985

Made and printed in Great Britain by
Cox & Wyman, Reading

Filmset in Monophoto Photina by
Northumberland Press Ltd,
Gateshead, Tyne and Wear

To Catherine. In memory of J.S.L.

Contents

WINTER

SPRING

GALWAY
Slieve Aughty Mts.
Gort
L. Atorick
The Burren
Scarriff
L. Derg
Lisdoonvarna
L. Inchiquin
CLARE
TIPPERARY
Cashel
Fethard
Limerick
Carrick-on-Suir
Tipperary
Kilsheelan
L. Cur
Bruff
Kilrush
Shannon
Suir
WATERFORD
LIMERICK
Mt. Melleray
Loop Head
MUNSTER
Cappoquin
Buttevant
Doneraile
Kerry Head
Kanturk
Blackwater
Mallow
Youghal
Magharees or
Seven Hogs
Rough Pt.
Tralee
Ballydesmond
KERRY
Cork
Mt. Brandon
Killarney
The Paps
Dingle
Killorglin
Ventry
CORK
Loo Bridge
Kilgarvan
Kenmare
Cahirciveen
Sneem
Glengarriff
Bantry
Bantry Bay
Schull
0 5 10 20 40 miles
10 20 30 60 km

I
Newgrange · Loo Bridge · Kenmare

Before going to Munster I went to Newgrange on the shortest day of the year. By eight in the morning of the 21st of December, when the dawn was beginning to make the Boyne visible and the cattle browsing beside the river's water meadows, the small crowd gathered before the locked gates was showing signs of desperation. Most people had driven down from Dublin in the dark to be in time to see the sun strike the altar.

The man beside the gate said again: 'Papers!'

Wails. 'We weren't told about papers. They just said in England we could come.'

'Sorry. There are people here with papers.'

Above on a gentle slope the Neolithic edifice, as big as a hill, had been newly plastered by archaeologists with patches of shining white stone which managed to make the massive mound look municipal and suburban. The man continued to keep the gate locked while we stomped, trying to keep warm. I was properly prepared, having taken the precaution of getting a note from the Board of Works in Dublin. Only a handful of others could hand the tyrant gatekeeper similar passports. We were let through one by one while the rest waited in anguish. Many had serious reasons for being there.

'Last year I saw the light creep along like a living creature.' Today the sun was covered with a belt of cloud. Inside we pushed down the low narrow passage until we stood wedged together in semi-darkness beneath the corbelled roof of the small chamber. I touched an ancient spiral carved on a stone and waited to witness a mystery of the renewal of the seasons.

'If you get down on your knees perhaps you'll see something!' A good many of the privileged were too arthritic to obey, but I knelt and squinted down the sixty-two-foot passage towards the light at the far end which was fuzzy, grey and shadowless. No magical movement would come out of that, no sunbeam trickling up and caressing the altar stone like a spent wave.

'Irish weather.' Enough light filled the chamber now to see faces.

A roar echoed down the passage. 'Will you come out? There's another party waiting.'

We trooped out and down the slope towards those who had been kept out, a young crowd mostly, concerned with Druid cults, ley lines and the like. They were furious and anguished. Some were delighted that the moment of sunrise had not been much of an experience for us. It must have been like this often enough at the time when the solstice was vitally important. Did those attending ancient ceremonies which invoked the lengthening of days consider such cloudy December dawns inauspicious? Was this inauspicious for my journeys?

On another overcast winter day I arrived in Killarney by the Dublin train. I had come down just before St Brighid's Day, the first day of spring, to witness old traditions that survive in Kerry.

A shrine on the platform proclaimed 'God wishes to establish in the world devotion to the Immaculate Heart (Our Lady of Fatima)' above the official notice ALL CHANGE HERE FOR TRALEE AND CASTLEMAINE. In the Gents, each cubicle was topped by rows of ferocious spikes like spears to keep out invaders. I went over to the comfortable and decorous Great Southern Hotel and sat on a sofa in the pillared lobby to drink coffee. I recognized the hall porter whom I had known years ago. His uniform flashed with silver and gold under the chandeliers. Among the green velvet sofas we remembered mutual dead acquaintances.

'Oh, he's long gone . . .'

'The children didn't come to much . . . a couple took to the drink . . .'

'God rest . . .'

'Drink took him . . .'

'Ah well, he was a nice man.' There was no gloom in the sweet melodious Kerry voice.

The scent of chips wafted down the street where outside the cinema a queue formed in the rain to see a film called *The Black Bitch*. There was evidence that St Brighid's Day offered opportunities for commerce. In souvenir shops St Brighid's crosses were attached to cards full of explanation. 'St Brighid's feast is at Candlemas when the days are so much longer that a candle can be dispensed with . . . The days are then a cockstrike longer, the footsteps of a cock on a gentle evening when his crop is full . . .' What did it mean? Could a tourist – if any existed in February – make sense of it? Outside the chip shop a group of small itinerant children dressed in gaudy clothes stood in the rain. A boy in a blue dressing gown, his face blackened, wearing the suggestion of a mask, huddled beside two girls in bright pink dresses and crumpled leather boots. Across their noses was pinned yellow gauze.

'Something for the Biddys,' they whined.

'Those kids hunt in packs,' the shopkeeper selling crosses complained. 'They take advantage of the saint. The Council should do something . . . it's bad for business and gives a bad impression to visitors.' Beside him a notice for the Biddy Ball offered BAR FACILITIES and a prize for the BIDDY OF THE EIGHTIES.

The bus took me to Loo Bridge where brown hills were scattered with grey rocks and spotted yellow gorse and amber water roared and frothed under the bridge. There were a few farmhouses, some old tobacco signs and herds of wet cattle belonging to hill farms hidden in sticks of winter fuchsia. Dominating the place were two rounded hills, the Paps, Da Chich Anann, the breasts of Anu or Danu, Celtic goddess of plenty, responsible for the fertility of Munster. Her sister deity, Brighid, was Celtic patroness of poetry and learning. Brighid's Christian namesake took on ancient mythology and ritual. Her feast day, the 1st of February, coincides with Imbolg, the pagan festival of spring. She was born at sunrise, neither within nor without a house, was fed with the milk of a magical white cow with red ears, and used to hang her wet cloak on the rays of the sun.

Under the breasts of the goddess of plenty Mrs Lynch was supervising the celebration of the first day of spring. She was dressed in a belted mackintosh and a black hat and scarf and her face was painted. The pagan schoolhouse was packed with Biddys. Everyone was dancing to music provided by an accordion, a mouth organ and a tin whistle. There were a good many children with masked faces, boys and girls dressed in pinafores and scarves. A man from Radio Telefis Eireann making recordings was also dressed up, in an old coat with a silk scarf draped across his face. He held the microphone to a girl who sang in Irish in praise of Brighid. Next a boy in a skirt sang like a linnet, Brighid's own bird, a song about Irish resistance to English perfidy. Then there was more dancing, arms pressed to sides, thump of feet before the fire.

Outside a full moon rose over the Paps. 'It's a good Brighid's evening. That will mean a good harvest.' The people love St Brighid round here, added Mrs Lynch, who had been to hiring fairs as a girl and could remember the time when crooked rush crosses were made to protect man and beast and not to be sold to tourists. Born in the sixth century, Brighid united the pagan and Christian worlds. The little cowherd ousted her pagan namesake, the stern patroness of divination, prophecy, healing and the smith's craft.

All the Biddys were outside now. A boy dressed as a girl carried a collecting tin and the brideóg, a large pink doll wrapped in an orange shawl wearing a mitre decorated with St Brighid's cross. They were getting into cars to follow the saint's wanderings around the countryside. The first farmhouse they came to was empty, but at the second they were welcomed in. The woman of the house watched the group dance while the RTE man made his recording before they were given tea, bread, butter and cake and coins were thrust into the tin. Then on to the next farmhouse and more dancing, more waves of music from the musicians, more tea. The dancers romped on the concrete floor; a dog barked, hens cackled in their runs and St Brighid's night passed away into another year.

When I left them the rain had begun again. In need of different refreshment, I went into a small pub where a solemn group of men sheltered in a dimly lit bar. Two old farmers in gumboots played cards while over the hills the Biddys were still dancing. A voice would be raised about the price of cattle or fox pelts or the elusive red deer that strayed over the mountains from Killarney or men who had made good.

'He threw up sixpence and down came a pound. If he fell in the muck he'd come up with fivers stuck all over him.'

'What's the use of being rich? A millionaire do eat the same as we do.'

Or Dutchmen.

'They'd skin your grandmother for the price of a drink.'

'You want to watch before they'll have all the farms bought.'

'And wouldn't you leave Ireland, Denis, if the government gave you a handout of thirty thousand like the Dutch government do?'

'Glad to be rid of them.'

Here was more the atmosphere of a pagan rite – sparse Kerry words, the sparse Kerry reply, the clock ticking, rain on the windows and pints downed. No one watched me leave.

I slept at the old railway station which had been converted into a youth hostel. The platform and rusty buffers survived together with the waiting room where passengers had sat around and warmed their knees. As a child I had often travelled on this line from Headfort to Kenmare in little carriages with damp plush seats, bevelled mirrors and tulip light shades. At Loo Bridge the train would stop for water and the passengers went into the pub. The railway has totally disappeared, its path buried under the long hedge of willows and alders, the route marked by an occasional broken bridge or gate with a rusty sign, G.S.&W.R., warning people of forty shilling fines, and water towers decaying like old castles.

'It was great company the old train. It went at one o'clock and we knew it was time for dinner, and at four o'clock when it passed the wife put on the kettle for tea.'

I walked through Kilgarvan's crooked street which was lined with brilliantly painted houses. Potted geraniums in brass holders, still luxuriant in February, behind net curtained windows added to the colour. At one end of the town a brace of abandoned Morris Minors lay in a field and at the other the statue of Christ presided over the graveyard. 'Thy Kingdom come' – the headstones made a foreground to mauve waterlogged hills.

The old terminus was at Kenmare where passengers caught their first glimpse of the sea. The train's arrival would be greeted by small men in puckered cloth caps with sheep dogs and bright orange donkey carts. They would be waiting together with the station master and the porter from yet another splendid Great Southern Hotel. Arriving visitors used to follow his burly figure in red tunic and blue cap as he pushed a creaking cart with their baggage up the wide main street.

At Kenmare I recognized the Lansdowne estate office with its walled-up window that blinked disapprovingly at the Catholic church. There was the bakery where just after the war we had our first taste of white bread in five years and tore it to pieces in our eagerness to cram it into our mouths. Opposite stood O'Brien Corkery's, the emporium remembered for its long wooden counter, the advertisements for emigrants travelling by White Star to America and money sailing up on wires to the cashier in her signal box to pay for boots, bacon, shaggy suits, a new outboard engine or whatever. The long counter was still there and you could still buy almost anything.

It was twenty years since I had been in Kenmare and there were changes like the vegetarian restaurant near the unisex hairdresser and the Dutch bistro where I sat eating pork chops in garlic sauce and drinking white wine. But the Lansdowne Arms on the corner opposite the Carnegie Library was exactly the same, and indeed had looked like the perfect country hotel long before my time. The tourist handbook for 1852 has an illustration showing it looking very like it does today. Its great moments were in the days of coaches and Bianconi cars, when visitors passed through on their way to Killarney.

The success of the Lansdowne Arms reflects the nineteenth-century development of Kenmare. Two hundred years before, the town – location rather – then known as Nideen, was in the possession of that versatile Cromwellian doctor, Sir William Petty, who obtained most of the neighbourhood by marrying a Fitzmaurice heiress. Nideen, almost inaccessible, was not much of an acquisition. When Arthur Young came down this way there was no road over the mountains and he and his fellow travellers felt 'agitation and suspense' at the various 'horrid, grotesque and unusual forms in which the mountains rise and the rocks bulge'. Their chaise had to be moved over the rocks with levers and ropes by six stout lads provided by a local landlord. Things were not much better sixty years later in 1838 when Henry Inglis had to walk much of the way while his coach was heaved along with rotten rope.

Even then, however, the amazing Scottish engineer, Alexander Nimmo, was building the road we know today which changed the hair-raising journey to a tourist's diversion. A tunnel full of echoes joined Cork and Kerry. Asenath Nicholson, an eccentric middle-aged American missionary, went through the tunnel in 1842 relaxed enough to 'give full scope to my voice and in singing' so that she could observe that 'the echo was tremendous'. When Thackeray made the same journey in an overloaded car 'one man sang on the roof, another waved a pocket handkerchief from a pile' while the jolly yacht's crew included among the passengers 'made a pretty howling'.

In 1778 Arthur Young saw a tiny hamlet with 'three or four good houses' including one for Lord Shelburne's agent which still stands disdainfully beside a new housing estate. The new road, and the patronage of the Lansdowne family, changed Kenmare into a model town with barracks, hospital, the first suspension bridge in Ireland, a poorhouse, orphanage and model schools. In 1852 Dr John Forbes, a physician to Her Majesty's Household, visited the 'National Boys and Girls school and an Industrial School for girls ... and the girls were all neatly dressed and very tidy'. He noted the amount of teetotallers in the town, for Father Mathew's influence was still strong. How reliable were the impressions of a man who praised Lord Lansdowne for 'his general liberality and generosity in promoting emigration from his estates'? His Lordship got a bad press after hundreds of his tenants walked to Blackwater Bridge from Kenmare workhouse, to ships anchored off the pier bound for Quebec and New York. Lord Lansdowne meant well. Emigration was a measure to relieve distress and when his agent offered tenants free passage and a few shillings over he insisted that 'not the slightest pressure was put on them to go'. The offer was considered generous by his peers, since tenants could hardly expect compensation for the hovels they were leaving. Lord John Russell said, 'You might as well propose that a landlord compensate the rabbits for the burrows they have made.'

Dinny O'Shea told me how his great-grandfather had seen bodies floating off Kenmare pier after a quayside riot over the distribution of Indian meal. Murty Larry O'Sullivan, the Gaelic poet, remembered 'thirty dead bodies lying on the road at the edge of the town between Dr Mayberry's house and the Bell Height'. Dr Mayberry's memorial in Kenmare's Protestant church tells how 'he tended the sick and dying throughout the years of famine and distress'. In New York the wards full of sick emigrants from the area around Kenmare were nicknamed Lansdowne wards.

The Lansdowne Arms, whose establishment was an immediate result of Nimmo's road, weathered the famine, 'a great vacant house ... Castle Rackrent style with blustering, blundering waiters in the rambling rooms'. Countless travellers have stepped out from here in their mufflers, tall glistening top hats and crinolines, to climb into coaches and long cars, surrounded by beggars and idlers. They drove off with a splash, or, if they were extremely lucky with the weather, in a cloud of dust, towards Killarney where the first glimpse of the lakes would be a highlight of their Irish Tour.

You can imagine the daily scene as a Bianconi car known as a 'Bian' – pronounced By-ann – is led out in front of the Lansdowne

Arms, the harness of the horses silver-plated with the initial B on back straps and blinkers. Most likely the horses are fifteen hands two inches high, the size known in the army as 'troopers'. Bianconi favours this uniformity which simplifies the supply of harness and enables quick changes to be made at the stages. He is reckoned to own more horses than the Khan of Tartary and knows every one of them. His way of talking about them is famous. 'Who says we must take Miss Moll off the Mitchelstown road? She'll do for the Fethard road ... Tartar is on his legs again and will be fit to work next week ... Tim Healy says he has no trouble with Badger ... he goes like a lamb.'

Bians from Kenmare used Mr Nimmo's new road. I went in search of the old road, the one used by these early aristocratic travellers, the Chevalier de Latocnaye and Prince von Pückler-Muskau. The *Post Chaise Companion* correctly described this route as 'nearly serpentine'. Today it is a track, zig-zagging upwards from Kenmare to the Gap, then twisting down by the two lakes. I followed it as it snaked off the new road through reeds and rocks, occasionally tracing the stone edges of the old paving. When I came to the Gap I could view the lakes and the Kenmare estuary on either side of a range of mountains and try to feel the thrill expressed by Arthur Young. 'There is something magnificently wild in this stupendous scenery, formed to impress the mind with a species of terror.' The first rhododendrons, Killarney's Triffids, leapt out of the dead grass. They concentrated around ruined houses, dark leathery patches of green against the winter brown. In a couple of months they would flower abrasively all over the mellow landscape.

Before the ice age rhododendron flourished in Ireland and pollen investigations have found frequent traces in deposits two hundred thousand years old. The ice killed it off some one hundred and seventy-five thousand years ago when it was driven eastwards by cold beyond Europe to the Black Sea. Geographical barriers held it in Asia Minor until it was reintroduced. By 1800 it was still a comparatively rare garden species, but it was like a genie in a bottle. Suddenly Ponticum discovered it had come home and the acid soils of Ireland suited it perfectly. It bounded over estate walls and has rampaged ever since, threatening the native forests, squeezing out light from other plants and covering the landscape with what an earlier generation described as housemaid's mauve. All over Killarney men are cutting down plants and rooting them out, but defoliates, sprays, poisons and axes fail to stop the vulgar menace.

At Clogheen church the old road ended where the oak forest began. The bare upper branches of the oak trees combined in a tawny mist while their roots were dipped in the brilliant green of ferns and mosses. The rhododendron clumps assumed gigantic proportions. Surely nothing climbing the Himalayan hillsides could be as vast as this huge round shrub or that one forming a gloomy bank between the road and the lake? Here was the police barracks built like a castle – 'to keep the natives in awe', wrote the German Johannes George Kohl in 1842, 'and only a police sergeant and eight men controlled the desolate mountains far and wide'. Here was the tunnel carved through rock familiar to generations of tourists. Here was the rain again. The pall of cloud that had hidden the Reeks and Mangerton overtook me and spilled down my back as I walked towards Killarney town.

2
Killarney

'Kerry rain was as tedious as a suit in Chancery,' observed one disgruntled nineteenth-century traveller. 'Pour, pour, pour unceasingly,' wrote Mrs Hall in 1842 from the shelter of the Herbert Arms where she and Mr Hall were compiling their guide book packed with detailed advice on guides, hotels and prices. 'The noble trees of Muckross absolutely bend beneath the weight of waters. The cock who crowed so proudly yesterday, and carried his tail like a banner has just tottered past, its crested neck stooping and the lone feathers trailing in the mud.' A guide book of 1822 telling of twenty-six 'viewing stations' and the dangers of 'unrestrained use of spirits by the boatmen' mentioned sadly that 'strangers often quitted this wonderful district without enjoying a single fine day'. A favourite word in travellers' descriptions was 'melancholy'.

Yet travellers came in hordes to view 'the Lakes'. Mrs Delany sketched them. In 1786 Dorothea Herbert saw 'a party of Spanish grandees come purposely to see the Lake and its environs'. Sir Walter Scott and Maria Edgeworth were rowed on the Lakes – the boatman revelled in the honour, and when he was rowing Lord Macaulay twenty years later told him that it was a compensation for having missed a hanging that took place that same day. Queen Victoria was here.

As soon as it became fashionable to admire romantic scenery Killarney became popular. The period when the region began to attract visitors can be gauged by Richard Pococke's two visits. During his second visit in the summer of 1758 he observed, 'I saw this place ten years ago, a miserable village, and now there are good Inns, Lodgings and Accommodations for Strangers who come ... mostly during the months of July and August.' This is confirmed by Charles Smith's *History of Kerry*, published in 1756. 'A new street with a large commodious inn are designed to be built here; for the curiosities of the neighbouring lake have of late drawn great numbers of travellers to visit it.'

There were other ways of reaching the beauty spot apart from the exhilarating journey over the Windy Gap. Pococke rode in one August day in 1758 on a route from Listowel and Tralee, a distance of forty-seven miles. Others travelled from Limerick, like Sir John Carr in 1802, who stopped at Castleisland and enjoyed some wine and water while the horse was being changed. He noted a funeral procession, listened to the Irish 'howl' and admired 'blue and purple mountains which arise from a sea of vapour' among which were the lakes of Killarney. Many, like Thomas Carlyle, came direct from Cork along the Millstreet road. Carlyle's breathless staccato impressions place him among the most vivid of travel writers; the pity is that he spent so much time on Frederick the Great. 'Rain; Hay-y-p! down hill at a rapid pace, happily we get away ... Desolate, bare, moory country; hanging now in clear wet; much bog, mainly bog; treeless and swept over by a harsh moist wind, ugly and very cold ... a fierce rain where we changed horses ... wretched people cowering about look at us and beg ...'

By the time travellers arrived in Killarney they tended to be peevish. Carlyle found 'a chaos of hungry porters, inn agents, lodging agents – beggars storming round you like ravenous dogs round carrion ...' He wrote in 1849 and his notes are pervaded with the horrible aftermath of famine. But beggars have long been a feature of Killarney. The anonymous Sportsman who complained in 1838 of 'hundreds of men, women and children ... all seemed bent on one determined purpose ... that of robbing the unfortunate traveller' spoke for generations of irritated visitors. In addition there were hucksters, the equivalent of modern souvenir-sellers, like the man who approached John Barrow trying to sell him arbutus seeds.

The next problem was finding a bed. Sir John Carr's inn was crowded out, the landlord protesting that he had not even a vacant chair. He made his way to another inn which was comfortable enough, except that he had to fasten his bedroom door with 'an old pair of snuffers'. In 1849 Carlyle lodged at Roches, 'a long row of half cottage-looking buildings' where the bedrooms were 'the smallest ever seen'. The one assigned to him 'reminds me of being tied up in a sack'.

The Lake Hotel had its share of criticism. In 1865 another visitor walked up its avenue dressed in a 'walking tho' not exactly tourist suit'. He had a light knapsack, a leghorn straw hat to wear in fine weather and an umbrella to use in wet. Mr Barry, proud to call himself an Englishman, was on a walking tour of Ireland. He carried his indispensable *Murray's Handbook for Ireland* and his experiences and opinions would be turned into a book.

'If you wish to see a country thoroughly and to acquire correct impressions of the manners, habits, and customs of the inhabitants ... and to know something of their inner life and the way they treat strangers ... walk! ... walk! ... walk!'

But walking in the rain even with an umbrella made him bedraggled. When he arrived at the Lake Hotel his appearance did not appeal to the other guests or to the proprietress who looked at him 'suspiciously' and told him there was no bedroom. Only when he said he would go instead to the Muckross did she allow the ancient Boots to bring him to an unsavoury room with a feeling of dampness about it and, he thought, the proximity of a sewer. But the Boots, who had worked at the Lake Hotel for eighteen years, had exceptional powers of persuasion. 'Indeed I think on a warm summer evening he could persuade a traveller to sleep on a dunghill. "With a blanket under you, Sir, and a sheet above you, you will sleep as quietly as on the best bed we have in the house."'

I chose to stay at the Lake out of sentiment, since it used to be a regular stop-over for my family. My mother would arrive with a car full of hens and dogs and baskets containing a cat or a rabbit, for all of which the kindly hotel staff found accommodation in one of the sheds at the back. Blind eyes were turned when the rabbit or a privileged dog was taken into the bedrooms. The shabby, slightly musty atmosphere that mixed with the comfort in those days has gone and things are a lot more modern now. But eating bacon and eggs beside windows overlooking the lower lake and the mountains is an unchanging pleasure.

Over the years Killarney breakfasts have soothed fretful spirits. Crofton Croker, who had a bad time in 1831 and quoted Arthur Young's remark on an Irish hotel ('Preserve me from the fate of such another!'), could comfort himself with the reflection that 'an excellent breakfast may be had, made upon potatoes, butter, eggs and milk by men who have walked amongst the mountains'. Another traveller shouts, 'Hello, Gorham, breakfast all in a hurry, if you please; tea, coffee, bread, butter, toast, eggs, hams, honey, salmon, all very good ... is everything ready, Gorham?' (Gorham is never mentioned again in this particular book; footmen and waiters made poor copy compared to garrulous boatmen and guides.)

As breakfasts were consumed plans were made for the day. The tourists observed by John Barrow in 1838 in the coffee room of the Kenmare Arms were typical with their 'maps, a well-thumbed guide to the Lakes and just plain talk'. Visitors gave themselves more time in those days. The Halls recommended five days for their crowded itinerary while Kohl thought six or eight days were necessary 'to enjoy all the charms of the neighbourhood of Killarney'. When the weather was fine, the atmosphere was cheerful. Here is the Kenmare Arms on a warm spring day in 1850. 'There were strangers from all parts of the world to be found on the pavement, lounging at the threshold of the house or reading newspapers in the coffee room' and 'waiters ... running to and fro, packing up hampers with cold fowls, tongues, hams and constant messages to the confectioner's shop'. Lunches could be eaten on the lakes to the sound of bugles.

In Muckross Abbey, dominated by its ancient giant yew admired for centuries, I found the monument to Lucy Gallwey, wife of Lord Kenmare's agent, erected by the inhabitants of Killarney as a testimonial of grateful feeling. John Barrow had also looked at it, together with the ossuary of skulls and bones nearby which he considered a 'disgusting exhibition of the remains of poor mortality'. Dorothea Herbert, a prey to Gothic horrors, trembled on seeing them during a forbidden visit by night: 'We ... groped our way to a tall Melancholy Avenue of Elms ... We entered the Enclosure ... and drew back with horror whilst the Bats and Owls clap'd their wings around us ... the outside of the Abbey is adorned with battlements of human Skulls and Bones ... a most terrifying Spectacle indeed ...' The 'human skulls in hundreds and bones in thousands' were cleared away after they had offended many visitors, including Sir Walter Scott.

Opposite the gates of Muckross Abbey is the Muckross Hotel, one of the most famous and long-lived of Killarney hotels. Unlike the bland new tourist palaces it recalls the past with its old-fashioned dining-room, stag-horns in the hall and a photograph of Bernard Shaw lounging outside the door in 1923. Jack O'Shea, a dignified octogenarian whom I came across in the bar, still remembered his visit. He also remembered the first motorcar that came into Killarney in 1910. In the pre-motor world the majority of tourists scorned the train and preferred to come by coach from Glengarriff.

When he was a young man Jack had worked as a valet in Muckross House in the days before it had electricity and was lit by lamp and candle. The charmless Victorian mansion is now the property of the State. In the grounds signs direct you to Monk's Walk, Lovers' Walk and a mossy Arthur Young Road. Muckross used to belong to the Herbert family. The Herberts and Kenmares divided up Killarney between them, each family getting about the same proportion of picturesque bits. The pre-Georgian Muckross House was considered most delightful in its setting: 'a most uncommon mixture of large rocks, shady valleys and opening lawns,' commented William Ockenden, approvingly quoting Bishop Berkeley who had said that Louis Quatorze might make another Versailles, but only the hand of the Deity could make another Muckross.

The high-spirited Herbert cousin, Dorothea Herbert, travelled down here with her parents from her home in Carrick-on-Suir in 1786. Her father, who had spent his childhood at Muckross, 'felt his youth renewed and acted the child weeping and laughing for joy . . . See here Mrs Herbert . . . look at that Mountain Miss Herbert! Do you see the Lake now Young Gentlemen?' There were few of Killarney's beauties that Dorothea did not visit – Teamis, Ross, Innisfallen and Dinish where the company ate a 'meal of cold meat in a cottage'. They sailed past the Eagle's Nest to 'the wildest part of the upper lake shore' where 'we spent the day in the utmost glee only interrupted by My Cousin Fanny Herbert losing one of her shoes in a Quagmire and Mrs Cherry Saunders and one of the Scotch officers tumbling headlong in the same as they attempted a leap over it lovingly together'.

From Muckross you could look down on the waters of the lower lake. 'Lake clear, almost black,' Carlyle wrote, 'slaty precipitous islets rise frequently.' The young French Royalist Chevalier de Latocnaye who had come to Ireland during the Revolution had also admired the same scene: 'One of the finest I have seen on account of the chequering of woods and plains.'

Going on the lakes was an essential part of the Killarney experience. The Halls itemized expenses of boats and their crew, guides and buglers. Most of the larger hotels had their special boat and crew. Guides were an optional extra, but people usually hired them for their excessive blarney and the lurid legends they told. They were as important as the hampers and ponies, and, on the face of it, more so than the buglers. And yet buglers and often other noise-makers were invariably there. Dorothea Herbert saw 'a Multitude of Boats cover'd the lake with French Horns and other Instruments'. The nine guineas Sir John Carr spent on hiring Lord Kenmare's boat included 'the charge of the boatman, French horns, victualling them, powder for the pettecro' (a small cannon).

Setting out from Ross Castle by boat, Carr enjoyed echoes which he thought remarkably clear. In 1839 Henry Inglis expressed his delight because he had managed to hire 'the prince of Kerry bugle-men'. They blew in the passes and deep valleys, they blew in the lakes, they blew while tourists ate their picnics, and again and again visitors remarked on their wonderful echoes. The second most famous listener to these sounds was inspired to write: 'Blow, bugle blow, set the wild echoes flying . . .'

The most eminent visitor to Killarney came in the summer of 1861. Both the Kenmare and Herbert families competed to entertain Queen Victoria – it was rumoured that the expense ruined the Herberts. But she stayed at Kenmare House. Lord Castlerosse had a royal barge brought over from London to ferry the Queen, Prince Albert and four of their children on an exhaustive tour of the beauty spots on the upper and lower lakes. According to the *Morning Post*, 'Her Majesty exhibited unceasing interest in the scene about her, and frequently expressed to Lady Castlerosse her sense of its almost sublime character. The Prince Consort also was specially pleased with the new scenes to his observation.' It was a happy day to be remembered as one of the last occasions that Prince Albert enjoyed himself. Four months later he died.

The Queen was spared the cruel spectacle of a deer hunt, once a regular sight for visitors. 'The deer are roused from the deep woods which skirt the lake by hunters used to the sport on foot, as horses are useless.' The hunted animal would be driven into the water while hundreds of spectators looked on from boats or from the shore. Thackeray drew a picture of watching tourists sheltering from the rain under umbrellas while barelegged girls sold them plums, whiskey and goats' milk.

Although deer hunts have long ceased, the red deer are threatened now by Killarney's other decorative menace. Like the rhododendron, the Japanese Sika deer are a nineteenth-century introduction. They browse on shoots and young leaves and gnaw away at young native trees, ignoring the rhododendrons. In 1860 Lord Powerscourt brought down a small herd to Killarney from Wicklow which not only multiplied but began to inbreed with the native red deer. Hybrids abound as the Sika invade the territory of the lofty red deer and steal their does.

The true pure-bred red deer have to be kept far away from their Sika cousins. Some people think that it is only a matter of time before the Sika find them, and that will be the end of the pure native stock. The red deer found in other parts of Ireland have been reintroduced from Scotland, and only here in Kerry are they truly Irish. I went to look for them with Dan Sullivan of the National Park. Dan is in the tradition of old nineteenth-century guides and knows Killarney and its surroundings with a lifetime's familiarity. In his job as warden he has to supervise more than twenty thousand acres of hillsides and lakeside, hard constant work. He took me around Mangerton, along the vast open area of mountain that stretches all the way to Kenmare and Dungarvan – partly over the same ancient track that brought me back from the Windy Gap. This country, once filled with people, is deserted apart from the sheep and deer. Dan pointed out an old lime kiln surrounded by heather; at Crinnagh were some broken walls and at Friar's Glen a family had been evicted long ago. 'A man was paid to play one note on a fiddle and get them to leave . . . for the old landlords preferred the deer to people.'

'Who owned the land?'

'Herberts.'

Were the Herberts like that, the charming cousins of Dorothea and her clergyman father? Would the people who picnicked so gaily by the lake and played cards and flirted and danced in rainy weather go to the trouble of evicting a family from a small wild holding?

The morning passed before I saw deer for a second, five does and a stag, a fleeting impression, very ghostly, grey rather than red. Then they were gone, dissolved into mist.

'True Kerry red deer,' Dan said. I did not tell him about Lord Grandison's gift. In 1725 Lord Grandison presented Lord Kenmare with a small herd from Dromana in Waterford because they took up room at a time when he was ploughing up his park land. But, even if they have Waterford blood in their veins, at least the shadowy beasts I had seen were descendants of Irish deer and not the Scottish interlopers elsewhere.

I followed Dan's bulky figure about the mountainside, up screes and past drifts of smoke where tussocks of bleached molinia grass were being burnt to allow for new spring growth. Across the upper lake loomed the Eagle's Nest where eagles did indeed nest – there and elsewhere – until the beginning of this century. At one time there must have been scores. In 1760 William Ockenden was rowed out on the lakes and recorded a sight that will never be seen again. 'We rested upon our oars to watch the flight of numerous eagles.' In modern times you can get something of the same delight from watching gannets.

The eagles declined steadily during the nineteenth century because they were treated as vermin. Robbing nests of eggs and young was a recognized sport. John Barrow noticed a boy in the yard of the Muckross Hotel 'playing with two fine eagles and lifting them without the least fear of their formidable talons'. Ten years later in 1845 Asenath Nicholson mentioned how young eagles were kept as pets in Killarney, and in between Bible readings she went out and watched a nest being robbed. So did Johannes Kohl around the same time. The nest of one pair of eagles had been robbed annually for twenty years. Kohl was rowed out to see it pillaged yet again and watched through a telescope. A man was lowered in a basket from rocks high above the nest. 'He has already planted one foot on the ledge and is bending down, partly to make himself complete master of its young . . . one of which he has already grasped by the throat.' With unusual compassion for a man of his time Kohl pondered the ethics of this robbery. 'The faithful love of this old pair returning every spring, and their sorrow . . . every summer for twenty years is a touching reflection.' He did not contemplate the possible extinction of the eagle.

Back in Killarney town I visited Mr Counihan's stables opposite his shop in the main street where lines of jaunting cars freshly painted in a livery of black, blue and red waited for the spring influx of visitors. They were handsome vehicles, but Mr Counihan was pessimistic about their future. Costs were going up all the time, the traffic was worse and worse and nowadays it was impossible to hire good drivers.

I left him for Annabeg beyond the town where the boggy land begins again, the landscape Carlyle described as 'like a drunk country fallen to sleep amid the mud'. He would have liked to see the regimented transformation brought about by green rectangles of firs and Sitka spruce changing the scene in an orderly fashion that contrasts with the predatory take-over by the rhododendron. These firs are also alien. The only conifer native to Ireland is the Scots Pine which became extinct, and like the red deer had to be reintroduced from Scotland.

In spite of the big new hotels and the wash of tourism the Gap still impresses in the old Kerry-romantic way, a gash in the mountains with the clouds circling low and, usually, rain. 'High rugged black cliffs . . . wild grey damp sky, and damp sky and showers still scudding about' was the weather when Carlyle came. It was exactly the same now. Rain in Killarney is as natural as sun in the desert.

Here visitors used to arrive in their pony cars, dismount and make their way by foot and pony down to the lake, again to a musical background. The sounds of bugles and exploding cannon helped the landscape to 'possess the imagination to the highest pitch of frantic enthusiasm'.

I had a drink in Kate Kearney's Cottage. When Carlyle did the same in 1849 this was a sad place, and his notes reached a crescendo of gloom. He and his companions set out from Killarney along a moor road that reminded him of his old Scottish retreat at Craigenputtock. Beggars waited to ambush them, running beside the car, ignored by the passengers. One particular persistent or desperate man, however, who ran for '2 or perhaps 3 miles' 'does get coats to carry, and a shilling, I suppose'. They went to Kate Kearney's Cottage which they called the Dunloe Hotel. This was a joke. 'Squalid, dark empty cottage, where with a dirty table and a bench, without fire visible, food or industry of any kind, sit two women to press upon you the "dainty of the country", whiskey and goat's milk.' One was Kate Kearney's niece who 'if lifted from her poverty . . . might be a handsome woman'. The two were representatives of the Gap Girls who persisted at Dunloe until the turn of the century, getting their living from tourists. The National Library has a grim series of photographic portraits of Gap Girls, bare-legged and shawled, taken in the 1880s. Carlyle tasted his drink – 'a greasy abomination' – handed over sixpence and fled. 'Poor wretches after all; but human *pity* dies away into a stony misery and disgust in the excess of such scenes.'

I sipped my Paddy in the cosy bar behind the shop with the tourist cases and the postcards and thought about all the people in Caesar Otway's words 'hurrying along like a gang tied to fashion's chain from the Giant's Causeway to Killarney'. Many of them found the lakes and mountains did not fulfil their expectations. 'On the whole

Killarney disappointed us all,' Lockhart wrote after Walter Scott's visit, 'so much the greater should be the damnation of all the guide books and tour-makers.' Others – the majority – were so exalted by the views or irritated by the drawbacks, that unlike Carlyle they did not try to take in the 'dilapidation, beggary, fatuity' or comprehend the misery. It was pleasant not to be faced with such moral dilemmas. I looked out through the rain at the elaborate hotels serving the modern tourists, not mockeries of hospitality like the old Kate Kearney's Cottage, but welcoming and comfortable, if ugly. Carlyle would have approved of them.

3
Ring of Kerry

A very small proportion of those who flocked to Killarney took the trouble to go further into the wilds of Kerry. The concept of the Ring of Kerry as a tourist attraction is recent. In the nineteenth century it was remote and unvisited and people considered it had few attractions. Many of the inhabitants spoke nothing but Irish, and according to Asenath Nicholson they had the reputation for being 'of a cunning disposition and inquisitive'.

Mrs Nicholson had been tramping round Ireland for eight months by the time she came to Kerry. Her mission had brought her over from New York in the *Brooklyn* during the summer of 1844. She was of evangelical New England stock and her Christian name is mentioned once in the Bible as belonging to the wife of Joseph. She had a call from God to distribute Bibles to the Irish, to go to their homes, live and sleep among the people and read portions of the holy book to them. It was a lonely and difficult task. She found things particularly troublesome when she got to Killarney because a previous missionary had been scattering tracts that attacked the Roman Catholic Church with more venom than usual. The local bishop had told the people that 'we must not touch a Protestant book'. Often her Bibles were indignantly returned to her, even though they were the Douai version. As usual, everywhere she went she was pursued by beggars.

Leaving Killarney she had set out west for Cahirciveen, walking the first ten miles. 'My feet were soon blistered, the road stony, the rain threatening.' Well after darkness she reached a 'stage-house' near Killorglin, a large thatched cottage with a pile of manure outside the door. Inside were eight men drinking, the landlord, his wife, three daughters, two teamsters, geese, hens at roost and a cow. The cow annoyed Mrs Nicholson, but the landlord explained that it had a new calf and was warmer in the house. Then in front of ten male witnesses – the eleventh was too drunk to take interest – one of the daughters of the house washed her feet in 'the pot which had been used for boiling the potatoes'. The mother insisted, urgently whispering, that this was a duty to a 'wairy stranger'. Mrs Nicholson found a biblical parallel. 'The washing of the feet of strangers and guests is, in these mountains and glens of Ireland, a literal and beautiful illustration of our Saviour's example ... So ought ye to wash another's feet.' She was led by a burning splinter of bog wood to a bedroom which contained three beds – one for father and mother, one for the three daughters and one for herself. Another daughter attended her and helped her to undress, also according to ancient laws of hospitality.

Looking out from the bus window I seemed to see Asenath Nicholson after she left the stage-house the following morning, trudging along the same road, a small determined figure carrying her carpet bag full of Bibles and tracts, singing loudly as the sun came out and shone on the sea. Her outfit for travelling around Ireland consisted of a coat covered with polka dots which were fashionable during the 1840s, a big bonnet, a parasol and a large black American bearskin muff which tended to frighten children.

There was the first glimmer of the sea and the sands of Castlemaine. The bus tumbled into the long main street of Cahirciveen where in many places that atmosphere of the past persists. A Railway Hotel and a Railway Bar recall the trains that stopped here decades ago. Dark interiors contain old-fashioned brown bars, long wooden counters and the occasional brass scales or brass measuring rod nailed to the counter. I was looking for the establishment where the anonymous Sportsman who made a fishing tour of Ireland stayed in 1838. It had been an inn owned by a cousin of Daniel O'Connell, 'comfortable with excellent beds and a snugly furnished room'. The owner was a 'wine and whiskey merchant, store-house keeper and general dealer' who had a large unglazed print of his famous cousin hung over the mantelpiece.

I may or may not have found the right establishment – the proportions and age of the building were right, if not the decor. I woke early to Sunday somnolence, empty bottles on the counter and little round plastic tables beneath a large photograph of the Pope smiling over the empty lounge. Hours later I ate my fry – the traveller's breakfast, the trinity of two slices of bacon, sausages and an egg arranged in an identical pattern in every hotel and guesthouse in the country.

'There's half a gale there yet,' pronounced the proprietor when I was stepping out into very hard rain. The wind moaned through telegraph wires as I went south-west from the town along a road beside a threatening grey sea. I walked by dried banks of fuchsia, which in summer would be scarlet and blue, while the occasional car passed heading for church. No one stopped for me. Hedges dripped and a bog stretched to the mountains. I passed a cat newly killed by a car and told myself that this was the Kerry I loved. It was winter, and rain was to be expected, but throughout the year there isn't a moment without the threat of a downpour. How many summer regattas had I seen with men in their soaking best suits, standing under downpours on packed piers watching for boats hidden in torrents or in mist?

Waterville has attracted fishermen since the time when every stream and lake in Ireland teemed with fish. The Sportsman came here direct from John O'Connell's pub in Cahirciveen intent on catching trout and salmon in the surrounding rivers and in Lough Currane. Although Waterville already had a reputation for magnificent fishing, it was still a small place, 'a cluster of cottages' without an inn. The only vacant room he could find belonged to the priest. To vary a diet of trout and salmon, the Sportsman bought a lamb off the mountain for three shillings and sixpence. But it became a pet and never got eaten.

Besides listing his exploits with rod and line, the Sportsman included other details in his narrative, like his moving account of a funeral when the long lugubrious cry of keening accompanied the dead man as he was rowed over Waterville Lake to an ancient burial ground. Or his description of an outdoor meal: 'First a large iron pot, slung by three sticks over a clear turf fire; well washed but not skinned potatoes; a fowl split and well-seasoned and a crimped trout of eleven pounds, hot even unto burning; plenty of lake water, clear as crystal; and finally an infusion of the best Cork whiskey.' Eleven pounds was a good weight for a trout, even at a time when monsters were caught frequently.

In the hills behind Waterville his companion shot a large eagle. He thought that when erect the bird must have carried his head between three and four feet from the ground. The 'rock-king' was very old, undoubtedly over a hundred years old, the Sportsman was told, and for years had been carrying off chickens, salmon and the occasional baby. His demise was greeted with glee.

'"Hurrah," exclaimed Segueson, "done at last. St Patrick, and he's an ould offender; row on, row on, take care of your legs." A wounded eagle of the largest size lay screaming on the ground; there was life enough left to render him dangerous as he crawled, or rather jumped towards us, flapping his enormous wings and with revenge and mischief in the furious expression of his eye.' He was killed with stones, the butt end of the gun and oars. When they carried him back to Waterville, the whole village turned out to look at him. The Sportsman thought of having him stuffed, but no one local knew how, and he had to be content with keeping his claws, which were later mounted in silver and became handles to bells and ropes. So the carcase of 'the noble marauder' was given to Mr Butler's dogs.

This Mr Butler must have been an ancestor to Ted Butler who was at school with me. I hadn't seen him since, but I knew that the Butler family had once owned most of Waterville, in addition to the Skelligs whose pinnacle rose out of the sea to the south. The Butler Arms hotel was called after them.

'Does Ted Butler still live here?'

'He's down the road at Caherdaniel.'

The wide estuary of the Kenmare river lay by the road with lines of mountains on the far side under a fleecy sky. The rain that threatened did not fall. Ted had been a farmer and a fisherman before coming to Caherdaniel where he had a small bar. It was a comfortable place on the road leading down to the pier and Derrynane.

Tied along the pier was a boat which he had just sold. The man who had bought it was hoping to visit the Mediterranean, but there was work to be done and bolts, spars, and coils of rope were sprinkled around with other evidence of the mariner's springtime activity.

I shared pints with him beside a turf fire in the pub. He was as easygoing as I remembered him. He seemed to have enjoyed most things in his life, the farming and the obsessive fox-hunting in Tipperary, the fishing for lobsters around the coast, and now boats and the enjoyment of his cosy haven. Did I feel envy?

Caherdaniel is not as quiet as it might be since a perpetual trickle of visitors comes down the roadway to see among palms and daffodils Daniel O'Connell's slate-covered house which is filled with mementoes and effects. During the years he lived in Dublin he would pay regular visits to Derrynane, using the place as a holiday home for relaxation. The Sportsman describes the Liberator setting out with friends and dogs for a hare hunt in the mountains. He made a four o'clock start from Derrynane along the road I'd just walked. When the hunt was over he was entertained to breakfast. 'First a large bowl of new milk which instantly disappeared; then a liberal allowance of cold salmon soaked in vinegar – a very common dish – of this he ate heartily; after which he finished a bowl of port wine, then took leave of his entertainers, and set off to walk six miles to his home.'

During his lifetime visitors used to come and inspect the house. A housekeeper was in charge. 'Its furniture was plain, but there is a hearty welcome to every sojourner,' wrote the Sportsman who went there fresh from the killing of the eagle. Asenath Nicholson was not so lucky. When she arrived in November, she was shown around and inspected the library with its lives of saints, law books and Waverley novels. The housekeeper gave her bread and cheese. Outside, darkness was falling and it was raining. The two middle-aged women looked at each other across the expanse of table inlaid with round towers, Celtic harps and wolf hounds.

'I said, I dread the walk, and should the storm increase upon the mountain as there is no place to lodge, what shall I do?

'"It will be bad for you," rejoined the housekeeper, a vulture in female form, as she showed me out of the house.

'I said, I will do as much for you if you call on me.'

The night was the worst Mrs Nicholson ever experienced. The wind was so strong that in places she had to walk backwards. She encountered a weary horseman going in the opposite direction, and when his hat was blown off was able to transfix it with her umbrella. Then she continued her fight against the wind. The physical hardship was nothing compared to the shock of inhospitality. Admittedly she was usually badly treated by the well-to-do who regarded her as an eccentric soliciting charity, and it was only among the poor that she could be sure of a welcome. But she had expected more from the connections of the Liberator. 'And is it from the house of Daniel O'Connell that a female stranger has been driven this perilous night? Is it from the house, which, above all others, I had been told in my own country was a welcome resort and tarrying place for every stranger in every clime that I have been virtually turned out to perish, if not saved by little else than a miracle?'

Houses in the Kerry Gothic style displayed gables, curling wooden eaves and fretwork bargeboards, their narrow windows hiding dark damp interiors. In their gardens rustling palm trees rose among the fuchsia hedges and clumps of arum already in bud. I could see the strand of Westcove to which we once sailed on a hot summer's day through a glut of mackerel to fish for pollock off the rocks. I picked out islands in the Kenmare river, Sherkey, Garinish and the two Pigeon islands. At the top of the pass I talked briefly to an old man. Behind was his farm in rushy fields distinguished by a line of dead-headed hydrangeas. He had farmed and fished in the area all his life under the brown ring of Staigue Fort. I had last been here when the fir plantation on the hill was newly planted. Among the bleak lines of trees I could hear the whine of a saw.

Sneem lay in a green bowl, garish as a circus. This year must have been Sneem's turn to paint its houses, and the brilliant colours parodied the tones of nature – the mauve of heather, blue, lime green, ox blood red and bright yellow like gorse. The river that divided the town in two cascaded under the bridge, nearing the end of its journey to the estuary. Across the bridge, the waist of the figure of eight of buildings that made up the village, the copper-green weather vane shaped like a salmon shook in the wind like a wet dog above the small Protestant church. The little green where I could remember grazing geese and cattle was now carefully railed off. A new Dutch hotel. Winny Hurley's place was still there, Christianson's, J.J.'s and the butcher where carcases used to hang outside, crows perched on their steep sides pecking at the meat.

The postman put me up in his house in the top square, and we talked about the old days and people dead. Winny Hurley had only died recently and the place would never be the same without her brooding dominant personality. She had the air of an abbess as she commanded her bar, now turned into an amazingly smart restaurant. J.J. Sheehan had been gathered so long ago that even I could remember him going. They don't have shops like his any more, full of women's coats in puce and Kelly green, pastel-coloured dresses, hobnailed boots, and gumboots and sticky black mackintoshes that had to be torn apart, all hanging from the ceiling, while every corner got crowded out with spinners, books, coils of wire and rope, sides of bacon, tins of galvanizing paint, creosote, Elsan disinfectant, John West's salmon and hunks of smoked ling. J.J. used to sit in the snug behind the shop wearing his crushed brown hat stuck with fishing flies and giving us the latest gossip. Smoke from his Gold Flake curled up to the ceiling as we learned about the fire at the Dunravens' garage and the latest exploits of the divorcee staying at the Great Southern.

I borrowed a bicycle and set off for Rossdohan. At the turn to the Oysterbed I could still trace among the reeds the concrete square laid out for dancing. Half the people assembled on summer evenings would be engaged in dignified jigs to the squeak of a fiddle, feet tapping on concrete, while the other half sprawled on the grass watching or went away and courted. It wasn't until the 1940s that this particular assembly was found to be unwholesome and the clergy stopped it.

At Rossdohan I sought out Dinny O'Shea who used to work for my parents. Here was his small house with its familiar interior, the bright polished black and brass stove and the view of the sea and the island of Illaunslea from the window. I ate Lizzy's ample tea and listened to Dinny's soft complaints. This used to be a wild heathery sort of place with the sea lapping the rocks, but now the Dutch had come with their big bungalows that surrounded Dinny and Lizzy.

'Didn't that cost £40,000? And then they bought another? They never give a man a day's work. Do everything themselves. Mean people, I tell you. I miss the English.' Wasn't it better to hear Dinny going on about Dutchmen than reminiscing too much about the dead?

At the Oysterbed the dank landscape opened out to the pier and another view of the estuary gloomy and beautiful as ever, with streaky mountain ranges rising on the far side above the white cliffs of Ardgroom. To the right was wooded Garinish Island, a good anchorage for yachts. At one time it belonged to Lord Dunraven, a yachting man always trying to do better than Sir Thomas Lipton. His family laid out Garinish with coral paths and planted one of those gardens that flourish in warm damp with tree ferns, acres of camellias and species rhododendrons and the smell of rotted humus.

The Dunraven boathouse reflects the proper preoccupations of an international yachtsman, and is a vast building like a church. It was made from Norwegian pine and Norwegians were imported to build it – the Christiansons in Sneem were their descendants. I could see the sloping roof beside the pier where we went conger fishing at night under starry skies, using big metal hooks baited with mackerel guts. The odd monster was pulled out of the darkness beneath the piles, six foot long with a head as big as a horse and a strength that made killing it a feat of dragon-slayers.

Ahead was Illaungar, a small lozenge of land taken by rabbits and seabirds. I remembered the otter that swam off the rocks. In spring, seals curled up and sunbathed, the babies woolly and white, the adults mottled like slugs. Certain hot summers were heralded by shoals of Portuguese men-of-war, each carrying its section of knotted bead curtain. One summer six dolphins played about the bay in front of the Oysterbed pier. In those days there was less publicity about dolphins and we were rather frightened of them. They were bigger than our rowboat and jostled it as they swam underneath us. Or they would leap from the water to look at us for a second out of a piggy eye before plunging back in. Later, they would wait for us in the morning and come rushing up to the boat like tame dogs. At night they would escort us back from the pier, leaping about the bows, hissing as they breathed, covered with rippling phosphorescent water.

Another summer was the year of the killer whales, which behaved very like the dolphins, rubbing their bodies against our boats. But they were too big to admire in the same way, their tails as big as sails and their heavy bodies surfacing for air with a threatening clumsiness that nearly capsized us many times.

Behind Illaungar was Illaunslea, an eighty-acre island, almost square. When my father bought it in 1933 it consisted of rocks covered with heather and gorse rising from little boggy valleys. My father already possessed a large uncomfortable property close to Dublin, but an island at the far end of Ireland offered a challenge.

Drains had to be dug, thousands of trees planted and paths hacked through the undergrowth. Two piers were constructed, then a suspension bridge and several boathouses. My mother planted a garden whose progress my father recorded in a diary. Six apple trees were obtained from Watson's nurseries and after them came azaleas, bush roses, rhododendrons and two little eucalyptus trees in tubs. Trees and flowers were followed by a vegetable garden. A Kerry cow and a donkey arrived. The tennis court was made out of coral and carried over in sacks. The swimming pool was meant to be filled by the tide, but never worked well. Yachts and boats accumulated. The *Tern*, a four-ton Bermudan-rigged cutter, was sailed down from the Clyde. The *Kingfisher* was smaller. There were large rowboats, the *Memphis* and the *Sudden Death*, dinghies and *Shira*, a thirty-ton yacht we bought from the Dunravens. They looked imposing when they were at anchor.

The house was designed by Michael Scott to accommodate the effects of a rather small ship. The bunk beds were very narrow and a steep ladder led aloft. Lighting was provided by oil lamps and a Tilly. Guests were given collapsible washing tubs filled with water from a cistern which had to be hand-pumped. The Elsan was located down a path hidden by shrubs except for the railway signal to be raised when in use.

In the early days the simple life was simplified further by a maid standing in the little kitchen passing mackerel and tea through a hatch. There were nannies who panicked several times a day, fearing that their charges had fallen into the sea. Jimmy and Dinny looked after the boats, dug the potatoes, weeded the paths and washed up breakfast on the mornings we departed for Dublin. When we came down Dinny would be waiting at the Oysterbed to greet us after the long journey. The dogs would leap out into the boat shivering with excitement. Everything had to be carried out of the car – the crate of hens, the food, the cat or rabbit in a basket. Everything had to be handed down into the open boat. The rain would start, but often not the engine. Dinny would pull away with the string, but when there was no response we were doomed to sit on cold wet seats and row. Sometimes it would be windy, sometimes calm enough to hear the slow swish of a heron's wings. The clean sheets for beds would be carried in torn brown paper parcels and the bread, newly bought in Sneem, would get wet. When the boat reached the island the dogs would leap for shore first. Then everything else had to be lifted out and carried across the slippery slatted pier over the pitted water, up the wet rocks, through the rhododendrons and up to the house.

We were expected to enjoy our Spartan life and to scorn the luxury represented by the Great Southern Hotel whose bulk was just visible further up the Kenmare river. Guests were supposed to conform. There were dozens of them, invited down all summer long and put to work clearing undergrowth and mixing cement for the latest project. They bathed in the cold sea and went sailing in rain or storm. If they carried a flask of whiskey to alleviate their sufferings, they were banished to the bow to drink it. Life was either heaven or hell depending on temperament and the weather. It rained about forty per cent of the time. It would clear in the evening to beautiful sunsets whose light swept over soaking shrubs.

The little bunks so ingeniously fitted into cabin-like rooms were damp and brought on backache. Some guests would run out of cigarettes, others would long for newspapers. One weakling fled to the Great Southern where he was spotted lounging in a deck chair. He was considered an imbecile. Plenty could not wait for the gales to die down so they could take to the boats and make for the mainland. But others, particularly children, thought it was the most beautiful place in the world.

The island is sold and the house is now uninhabited. I rowed over to look at it, a little house in a jungle. Rhododendrons have massed in an almost impenetrable tunnel. The fir trees planted so painstakingly have become huge and dark and the two eucalyptus seedlings are eighty feet high. The tennis court is a thick cushion of undergrowth. I recalled the time when there were views of the sea from every window. I remembered the housewarming. More than seventy local guests from Sneem and round about were ferried over. A travelling fiddler brought his bike in one of the rowboats. There was a marquee, trestle tables and a little platform for dancing. Forty-two dozen bottles of stout and ale were provided, together with several kegs of whiskey.

My brother and I, who were small, were given the job of cutting with a pair of silver scissors the red ribbon that stretched from the veranda. Then, according to the *Kerryman* who had sent along a reporter, 'the visitors ... inspected the house, after which they adjourned to the dance platform where refreshments were liberally served throughout the evening, when dancing and singing and the best of good fellowship prevailed.' The party went on all night before the guests were ferried over to the mainland on a calm morning with many singing choruses and splashes. My father observed in his diary for June 1935: 'Not one man could have drunk another bottle . . . only twenty bottles remained unopened ... we had only just beaten the maximum capacity of Sneem.'

4
Glengarriff · Bantry · Schull · Cork

At Bonane near Kenmare I traced another old route over the Caha Mountains. This was the ancient road to Glengarriff. Let Thackeray and other Victorians shout and echo their way along Nimmo's new roads and tunnels and remark on the grandeur of the prospect. Tourists have been following those new routes ever since. But here was a way across the mountains that must be very ancient and very likely known to the man who put up standing stones and built the ring forts on the lower hills. It was an ambling track leading into the mists past bubbling streams. After a good while it seemed to end under the dividing hills beside Pat Sullivan's lonely farmhouse where hens scratched in the manure outside.

Pat and his sister lived here and farmed in the old way. He thought nothing of getting up early and walking his cattle the twenty miles to Kenmare and then walking home again. He had no neighbours for miles around. Old? Seventy, perhaps. He pointed out where the path began again over the hill to Glengarriff. 'Keep to the side of the rocks, man!'

I plunged into the Caha Mountains and was soon lost. The mist brought trouble, only moving briefly to reveal patches of snow, a looming collection of boulders or a forestry plantation. Then the curtain parted to reveal Bantry Bay big enough to accommodate Wolfe Tone and the French fleet, the whole British navy, or the wretched oil tankers. In their time they were the biggest in the world, each with the grace of a giant pencil swinging through gales round Sheep's Head, slopping oil all over the place.

Any view of Bantry Bay is like a painting by Claude. He struggled to achieve his glorious effects both by painting from nature, and experimenting with different planes and coulisses that led the eye through his pictures to far perspectives. Often he used a waterway with light behind, like Bantry Bay, a shining highway to a luminous distant sea. If he had come here he need not have exercised his imagination and ingenuity at all. Today in the sudden sun the bay offered a representation of his Golden Age.

The rain came down again at Glengarriff. When Thackeray got soaked here he felt that 'the inhabitants should be inured to the weather and made to despise an inconvenience which they cannot avoid'. After it cleared I visited Garinish Island which is now the property of the nation. There is a confusion about the Dunravens' Garinish Island in the Kenmare River and the Bryces' Garinish in Bantry Bay, also called Ilnacullin. Annan Bryce, a northern business man, bought his island beside Glengarriff in 1910. There was nothing on it except rocks, heather and gorse and a Martello tower. The terrain must have been just like our Illaunslea. Like my father, Bryce had to have drains dug and shelter belts planted, but on a vast scale. He called in an architect called Harold Pinto to design the garden and gave him an unlimited budget. Pinto oversaw an army of men building a series of walled gardens, pavilions and a clock tower. Too much effort and a failure in taste took the spirit out of the place. While the Dunravens' gloomy paradise at Kenmare is beautiful and mysterious in the conventional Kerry rain forest style, Pinto's municipal park is vulgar and cloying.

I was given a lift to Bantry after the driver spotted me reading the Motorist's Prayer pasted on the back window of his car.

Before we take a place
Behind this wheel we pray
Oh Sacred Heart
Guide us on our way,
Virgin Mary, Morning Star
From every danger guard this car.

'A hell of a lot of good she's been,' he said as we drove to Ballylickey. She hadn't been able to stop a lorry backing into him causing two hundred pounds' worth of damage. He felt he might take the poem down. We skirted the sea; over at Whiddy the black *Betelgeuse* had entombed fifty men. 'The inquiry's been great for the hotel business. Without the accident there's some would have had to close down.'

He dropped me in the middle of Bantry near the statue of St Brendan the Navigator given by Gulf Oil when the company first moved into town. The saint looked down towards Whiddy with his arms outstretched. Did the gesture always seem to be one of grief and futility?

I stayed at Vickery's – in the old days the name would have been enough. The Bians and the mail coach from Skibbereen changed horses outside, while passengers climbed down to glasses of hot punch and lavish meals. Recently, half the building was sold to Gulf to house computers looking after tankers. The other half clings to the past. In the inner hall a chandelier, gilded mirrors, a piano, a half life-sized china swan and steel engravings of scenes from Shakespeare. Eccles Hotel at Glengarriff had similar engravings, perhaps because of the efforts of an enthusiastic Victorian salesman. The two ladies who ran the hotel were standing close to the fire.

'If there are more than five guests you can turn on the central heating.'

But I was the only person staying that night. A wet mist settled over the town and through the bedroom wall I could hear Gulf's computers clicking away.

Next morning I looked up Ed Sheswell-White who had recently inherited Bantry House. What a legacy! The decay and grandeur is positively Moghul. Ed has to keep up the Rose Room with its Gobelin tapestries, the great blue dining room with its damp, twenty-foot plaster sideboard and gigantic copies of Alan Ramsay's portraits of George II and Queen Caroline in thick gilded frames. Hardly any land went with the house – it was just a big red and white building with many empty rooms surrounded by a few acres of steaming wild garden. A heavy wisteria, bare and grey in winter, a sweeping veranda, lines of steps tangled with grass and weeds, combined with dripping trees and sweeping views. Stone storks with crowns around their necks – part of the family crest – looked across a balustrade to another Claudian view of the Bay. The middle plane of the landscape is Whiddy where pieces of the *Betelgeuse* were still visible, suggesting a tragic theme – the Fall of Troy, perhaps. Would Ed dedicate his life to this tumbledown entry into the world of the imagination and spirit? Every day brought problems – problems with the roof and its valleys and gutters, problems with dry rot, perpetual leaks, flaking stone and general maintenance.

He was camping around, making bits of the place into a home. This evening a fire was lit in the study for the first time in years. He invited me to stay the night. We were in the library that overlooked the steps and the terraced garden when the alarm sounded with a shrillness proportionate to the size of the rooms.

It seemed someone must be after the furniture which had once adorned the Petit Trianon, the paintings, perhaps the old regimental colours or the Byzantine ikons in the hall. The alarm, a recent innovation in the age of technology, presented another problem. It continued shrieking. Ed checked the fuse boxes and switchboxes. He rang the Garda in Bantry.

'Are you alone, Sir?'

'I've a friend with me.'

'How do we know he isn't holding a gun to your face?' Pause. 'Are you sure nothing's been taken, Mr White?'

'How can I be sure?' He rang off, checked again. There were plenty of places where a thief could be lurking. He couldn't possibly leave the house and come into Bantry for a meal as we had planned. I thought it best to forgo the pleasure of sleeping in a four-poster bed in a tapestried room and return to Vickery's for another night beside the computers.

When I went to see him in the morning the sun had come out and the hall echoed with Strauss playing on his hi-fi. He had figured that the fire he lit in the study must have broken the circuit.

At the foot of Mount Gabriel lay Roaring Water Bay on which the islands had been dealt out like cards on a table. Mrs Hall praised them with a quotation:

> Sea-girt isles
> that like to rich and various gems inlay
> The unadorned bosom of the deep.

Right under Mount Gabriel, tucked away in the corner of a big natural harbour, is Schull. The main street has changed little in the years I have known it and the names of the shops are familiar, Barnett, O'Keefe, Regan, Newman. But outside the town strangers come and go all the time. Foreigners, English mostly, but Americans, Dutch, and Germans as well, are constantly moving in, buying farm-houses, redecorating them and staying for a while. For a few years, writing, pottery, batik-making, running restaurants and guest houses and pot-smoking keep them going. However, there are strains.

'It's a disaster area for marriages,' an Englishman told me, meaning expatriate marriages.

Eventually these strangers flee, abandoning their lovely outposts, and others move in. The winter defeats most of them. The old absentee landlords must have felt the way they do. Having observed the waves of newcomers for a long time I would put their average stay at around five years. Of course there are exceptions. Perhaps Smokey Joe and his community will be exceptions.

I came across Smokey Joe in the post office. 'I know your face,' he said firmly. I hesitated. Surely I would have recognized this tubby figure in yellow oilskins and blue yachting cap, that great white beard with sun rays of nicotine stains around the mouth, the glasses held in place by string?

I found him again in Barnett's with his friends – two natives of Long Island, an Englishman call Kim who was a member of a commune established on the same island of which Smokey Joe was a patriarchal figure. Joe was holding forth between pints and puffs. 'If I was king for a day I'd make people only have the possessions they could carry on their backs ... The problem with money is how to get rid of it ...' He was gentle and mild-mannered and talked ceaselessly. A Dublin man. No wish to live there again. His lifetime experiences ... photographer, running his own club, getting through money. He was happy to live on Long Island and be his own man. His wife was there now.

Later we all embarked in a shaky-looking clinker-built rowboat, the two Long Islanders singing away. The voyage, powered by a Seagull engine, was not a long one, but choppy. 'Seasickness is entirely due to fear.' We turned west into the wind up Long Island sound and I was reminded of old sailing days in Kerry.

Long Island or Inisfada must be one of the dullest gems in the ocean's bosom, a strip of land running east and west a mile and a half long and half a mile wide, treeless and featureless apart from a little strand and at the west end the blue scars of a copper mine. At the turn of the century the island had a large population which spoke its own distinctive dialect, a blend of Irish and English. The numbers of people are indicated by the lines of cottages of a distinctive two-windowed design which were erected by the old Congested Districts Board to help the struggling inhabitants. The population has steadily dwindled. But in the last decade a number of poorer good-lifers have been induced to settle here. The land may be exposed, but the soil is fertile. The Congested Districts Board built well and the little houses have sturdily put up with almost a century of gales. They are cheap, even if you take into account the effort of bringing over materials to do them up. A fair amount of strangers have settled, giving the population an unexpected boost. It is not easy to gauge how they get on with the locals and unwise to make judgements. Smokey Joe's community had been there for five years.

We tied up the boat and the singing Long Islanders vanished instantly. Loaded with supplies Smokey Joe, Kim and I walked past the pier, the wind in our faces, Joe audibly appreciating the changing light and the freedom.

'That's still derri,' he kept saying, pointing to various cottages we passed. He meant 'derelict' as opposed to 'done up'. Those that were in the possession of the new order were recognizable by the gardens. As we went along signs of industry were apparent, piles of seaweed stacked for manure, vegetable plots, tethered goats and the occasional wind charger.

We paused at Joe's house which was not a Congested Districts cottage but made of wood. It looked like two wooden packing cases tied together, the wind charger behind sticking up like a bow. The usual meticulous vegetable garden surrounded it. Joe left his box of groceries there, but did not invite me in.

'We'll go on to Kim's ...' Kim, who had not been saying much, assented with a monosyllable. Since his house was nearly at the east end, this meant a further walk in the wind along the treeless spine of Long Island.

Another garden plot was laid out with little patches where newly sown seeds were sprouting. Potatoes had been planted weeks ago. Strings of home-grown garlic hung outside the door. The inside of the house contained a number of children, a spinning wheel and some rag rugs. A Harris loom was squeezed into a small upstairs room. Kim's wife was at work using natural wool to knit a Guernsey. She did not seem to mind that Kim had been over in Schull for most of the day. It appeared that all along Long Island women of the commune sat like fisherwomen of old, knitting lumpy expensive pullovers to be sold to tourists on the mainland. I was reminded of Azerbaijani tribesmen putting their families to work making carpets. I knew that many people who had lived in West Cork all their lives disapprove of communities like Smokey Joe's because they cannot understand how people should voluntarily seek out the poverty which they have spent their lives trying to escape.

In Schull I learnt that the Rectory had been sold. After two hundred and fifty years the Church of Ireland was letting it go and the new owner had plans to demolish it. It was a long narrow house on a lawn dropping down to the sea. A plaque above the pillared front door gives the date 1721 and the initials J.L. This was John Limrick, a landowner in the neighbourhood who tried out his skills as gentleman architect and built the 'very good parsonage house on a pleasant bay called Skull Harbour' noted by Richard Pococke in 1758. In 1827 Caesar Otway paid a visit to the Rector and wrote: 'My friend resides in an ancient glebe house sheltered down on the shore in a sunny nook halfway between the church and the village. It is under the guardianship of a protecting hill, and some old sycamores in solitary magnificence seem to say, We are here to show that no one shall be as comfortable as a good minister.'

The sycamores are still standing and the atmosphere does indeed suggest tranquillity enjoyed by a succession of good ministers. But this is West Cork, not some quiet parsonage in England. The man who succeeded Otway's friend was the Reverend Robert Traill, grandfather of the playwright John Millington Synge. He became rector in 1832. He has left a diary covering the years 1832 to 1838, revealing himself to be a lonely bigot engaged in bitter parochial quarrels. Of the Methodists who poached his congregation he wrote, 'I verily believe that Methodism is gnawing away the very vitals of real religion in the land.' An estranged wife preferred to live in Dublin. His baby son died. His bishop thought him over-zealous and did not advance him.

In addition, Traill had to face contemporary problems. His appointment to Schull coincided with the bitterest period of the tithe wars. 'One clergyman within 30 miles of us has been murdered, and another most narrowly escaped with his life by taking refuge in the house of the priest.' Traill had no doubts that he was entitled to the dues he could not collect. 'The ungodly are rising up against me, and these poor deluded Roman Catholics are caballing to deprive me of my tithes. Alas! what wickedness is this? Is it not resisting the powers that be?'

In the 1830s when cholera crept along the coast his cousin and the wife of his curate were among the victims. It was difficult to know what caused the disease, but the hand of God was evident. In July 1833 Traill wrote how 'the very Saturday subsequent to O'Connell's profanation of the Sabbath the cholera was found in Cork, and it has already swept upwards a thousand to the grave'. More logically he believed that one old man was stricken in Ballydehob after sitting up in the evening watching a garden where the dews had fallen heavily, since it was well known that cholera was induced by dews.

He wrote details of his rugged daily routine. He worked very hard, journeying to distant parishes on horseback to address surprisingly large congregations. He preached in a remote valley at the back of Mount Gabriel to 'my dear flock in that secluded place'. He caught cold after riding in the winter rain and inhaled vinegar to relieve his chest. Since the diary ended abruptly at the sorrow occasioned by the death of his mother, we do not have details of later experiences. He found time to translate Josephus's *Jewish War* in a version that became a standard work. It is strange that one of the most vivid passages in Josephus is the horrible description of deaths from starvation in beleaguered Jerusalem. Such deaths Traill was to see for himself in 1847 in famine-stricken Schull. He could have retired to Dublin, but stayed in his parish to work among the sick and the starving. He died in Schull of typhus in 1847.

His favourite Bible passage was said to be from St Paul's Epistle to the Thessalonians:

'For yourselves know perfectly that the day of the Lord so cometh as the thief of the night.

'For when they shall say, Peace and safety; then sudden destruction cometh upon them as travail upon a woman with child; and they shall not escape.'

I went out to Cape Clear in Denis Daly's boat, leaving Schull pier in the gathering dusk, slipping past the old *Fairweather* and waving to Jimmy Reilly, the harbour master. The chugging diesel took us out beyond the point and the Amelia buoy where the sweep of the Fastnet light shone on Long Island, Carthy's Island, Horse Island, the distant Skeams and Sherkin on the port bow and the Three Calves straight ahead. Motoring on a calm evening was a tranquil way of traversing Roaring Water Bay, a contrast to the rowboat with shouting oarsmen who carried voyagers across in the nineteenth century. Traill paid regular visits to the island, like his predecessor who told Caesar Otway, 'I am the vicar of Cape Clear Island where I have no Protestant parishioners except about twenty of the waterguards.' The waterguard tried vainly to prevent smuggling.

This was before the vexed period of souperism which began on Cape Clear in 1847 – cruel timing – when the Protestant Island Society supplied funds to have a Protestant church and school built. For two decades a clergyman and then a schoolmaster, reputedly drunken, struggled as fishers of men. But once the shadow of the famine was lifted the islanders returned to the faith of their ancestors. The men of Cape were 'fine, honest, guileless and lived mostly on the harvest of the sea'. They were a nation to themselves, strangers, a challenge to mainlanders. 'Oh, boys,' shouted Pat Hayes in the boat that bore Caesar Otway home from the north harbour on a stormy day, 'we will never be able to stand in Schull if we let these Capers have the laugh over us – we are done for ever if we put back to Clear . . . We may as well when we get home go spend the rest of our days in Judy Mahony's cabin knitting socks, if we let these duck-footed fellows cut capers over us . . .'

This evening Cape Clear was in darkness, a humped whale-shaped island whose people remain Irish speaking and have always contained themselves and their secrets beyond Ireland. Beside the harbour near St Ciaran's Holy Well and the Gallan-Ciaran, the pagan pillar-stone Christianized over a thousand years ago by the mark of two crosses chiselled deep into the granite, I stumbled against a Gents Portaloo. Tourism had arrived at the place where Christianity dawned in Ireland.

In the morning I went to the bird observatory founded fifteen years ago to watch the migrating land- and seabirds who pass Cape Clear in their millions. Colin Rhind who works noting rare species has seen the changes of the past decade. In summer roads and pathways all over the place are knee-deep in sweet papers. The island is a terminus for numerous hitch-hikers from all over Europe. Some go to the youth hostel; others camp. In August the little place swarms like an ant-heap. Visitors disobey elementary country rules, leaving gates open and breaking down walls. The chaos concentrated in a small area becomes an annual shambles.

Pad Cadogan thought: 'In a few sharp years everything will be finished.' The island would perish; the declining population, the flood of visitors and blackguardism would destroy it. His misfortune was that his farm stood in the way of the ruined castle of Dun an Oir, the golden castle. Everyone who arrived at the north harbour made their way to it, since it stood nearby and was handy for those who landed from Baltimore and from Schull and were too idle to walk the rest of the island. He had lost cattle through his walls being broken down and his fields had become a public byway without a word to him. He had put up signs that ten years ago would have been inconceivable – TAKE NOTICE, NO TRESPASSING, KEEP OUT, PRIVATE PROPERTY! Other farmers had to do the same, a terrible new thing in their lives. And who took a blind bit of notice?

The ravages of tourism are seasonal like the passage of locusts. Today, in early March, the sun shone and the mountains on the mainland stood out clear to the north. I took the steep little road which Colin designated the M1. Robert Traill and his curate had walked up this hill in their long black capes and hats. 'Having looked a little about us and examined a stone which is worshipped by the poor ignorant Roman Catholics, we proceeded to the lighthouse, and having collected as many as could attend, we first sang a hymn, I then prayed, and afterwards lectured for about three quarters of an hour.'

Below the spot beside the old lighthouse where Traill had shouted over the wind to the little group of lighthouse keepers, sailors and revenue men, I found John Sawyer's farmhouse. I had met the Sawyers briefly in Dublin before they deserted a more mundane lifestyle. Cape Clear seemed to have numerous good lifers, possibly because those intent on self-sufficiency pick it out on the map for being as far away as they can get in Europe. Their newly renovated cottages and gardens were dotted about on the island, more picturesque than those of native Capers.

In four hard years the Sawyers' tussocky eight-acre farm had been cleared and reclaimed. Where there was once a furze garden was now a good field. Around the house was the evidence of how the great escape had become a practical reality, ducks, hens, pigs brought over from the mainland and a sign saying B&B. The porridge they served their wistful guests came from their own oats.

'I could play you a tape on how many times I have explained the problems of survival to other would-be escapees.'

The beaches were scoured for bits of wood and floats from Russian trawlers which were exchanged for fish. They maintained an ancient Land Rover. They said that the wind and rain did not bother them. All they had to do when they sat back and listened to the storm was to think of Cornelscourt and Ballybrack and the other suburban wastes of south Dublin from which they had escaped.

Back on the mainland I took a bus fifty miles to Cork. Thackeray had arrived there in a green coach driven by four bay horses which attracted crowds of beggars. His observations of the city are detailed and sometimes curious, like his enthusiasm for the lunatic asylum – not the present Gothick extravaganza – where 'everything was conducted with admirable comfort, cleanliness and kindness'; or the county jail, 'this palace of a prison . . . so neat, spacious and comfortable that we can only pray to see every cottager in the country as cleanly, well lodged and well fed as the convicts are.' Asenath Nicholson, making a similar grisly round of sight-seeing, also approved the county jail with one reservation: 'the barbarous relic of a treadmill is a standing testimony that Christian nations who practise it need to learn the first principles of civilization.' She was more sensible, too, about the Ursuline Convent which excited hysteria in Thackeray at the thought of pretty nuns immured. She noted 'the company of healthy and cheerful looking nuns, affable and intelligent, teaching a school of young ladies and poor children'. It was Ash Wednesday and she was given a dinner of pea soup and toast – 'for me a rich treat'.

Both Mrs Nicholson and Thackeray met Father Mathew in Cork at the height of his powers, 'a stout handsome honest-looking man of some two-and-forty years'. Thackeray drew him in his top hat receiving homage from his admirers; later, he encountered him sheepishly after he had wined and dined too well. Mrs Nicholson, an ardent teetotaller, went to his house which had a room 'entirely devoid of ornaments except cautions to the intemperate' where 'the lame and deformed, the clean and the filthy, the well-clad and the tattered kneel and take the pledge'. A clerk registered their names. He told her that at that time in Ireland there were an amazing five million, four thousand who had renounced drink, and Father Mathew's campaign still had momentum.

I walked down Patrick Street thinking how the statues of those beloved crowd-gathering contemporaries, Father Mathew and O'Connell, dominated the streets of Ireland's major cities. Past the statue, over Patrick Bridge towards the Metropole Hotel, red brick and ornamental, erected in 1892. The idiotic turret promised an interesting Gothic interior, but inside it had been modernized in a singularly drab way. I would have liked to have stayed at the vanished Imperial, that old gathering place for travellers which Inglis had considered 'a most excellent and splendid establishment' and *Murray's Guide* called first rate. When Carlyle came to Cork his destination was the Imperial as his coach bowled down beside the Lee and he looked out, gathering his quick impressions. 'Cold, dusty, windy, steep height now on our left . . . clothed with luxuriant wood, nice citizens' boxes nestled there . . . Cork itself, white-houses through the twilight vapour . . . Lee Bridge sharp on left, fine crowded street . . . "Wo-hp!" porter of Imperial is waiting . . . I get letters, washing, mutton chops for dinner.'

I made an effort to consider modern Cork and its recent expansion and prosperity. My absorption in nineteenth-century travellers coated my impressions with the varnish of the past. I found that the traffic snarl-ups, the acres of new suburbs, the new glass County Hall, the new hospital, the hamburger heavens and chain stores could not disperse the shadows lingering among shabby terraces of Montenotte or the narrow climbing streets of Shandon. In this 'one of the most inconsistent cities in Ireland' – the words are from *Murray's Guide* – 'a mixture of noble streets and broad quays with the very dirtiest and illpaved lanes, the whole being set off by a charming frame of scenery that compensates for many a defect', a large portion of my family had once flourished. Merchants, clergymen and men of law in beaver hats and nankeen trousers lived comfortably here in big servant-filled houses on South Terrace or beside St Luke's at the same time that Thackeray was visiting. The bones of some are in the vaults of Shandon church beneath the bronze fish on the red and white stepped tower. They may qualify me as an honorary Cork man. I have qualified for the modern definition of a city's native. 'You can't be a true Cork man until you've had a traffic accident on Watergrass Hill.'

5
The Blackwater · Mount Melleray

The spectacular right turn of the Blackwater at Cappoquin is a complicated geological puzzle. After its abrupt changes of direction it flows down a wooded gorge where the geologists trace four anticlinal sandstone ridges. Whatever about them, it is a noble stretch of water, expansive, with trees hiding estates.

I stayed near the river in a rambling tranquil house at Villierstown which was called Bleach and was once a flax mill. Two hundred years ago Lord Grandison, who created Villierstown as a model landlord's village, tried to introduce weaving and flax-growing into the area. His plans did not work out but remnants of the endeavour are the name Bleach and the reedy ponds below the lawn of the house which were once pools for washing flax.

When Pococke came here Lord Grandison, who was at his busiest as an improving landlord, took him on a tour in a chaise to point out the plans for Villierstown, the inn and seven houses already built for 'Necessary tradesmen', the Charter boys apprenticed to the Weavers, the chapel he was about to erect and the bleach yard down near the river. They returned to Dromana, Lord Grandison's seat, a former Fitzgerald castle and home of that venerable countess who fell out of a tree. Pococke admired the hanging woods and grounds, the terrace that overlooked the river and the splendid mansion, 'sitting on a rock over the Blackwater'.

Nearly a century later Carlyle, whose weakness was snobbery, was 'received with real hospitality and a beautiful quiet politeness'. He found no occasion for dyspeptic remarks about Irish slovenliness. He was reminded of England all the time, soothed by his bedroom overlooking the river 'begirt with mere silence'; by his bed – 'O the beautiful big old English bed!' and by Lord Stuart, 'quite English in style with the good-natured candid-drawling dialect (à la Twistleton) that reminds you of England'. On 'the pleasantest morning of all my tour', after a simple breakfast, 'all in excellent order (tea *hot* and as you find it rarely in a great house)' he went with Lord Stuart on a tour of inspection very like Pococke's. It was entirely satisfactory: 'fantastic ... all trim, rational, well ordered here'.

The estate was kept rational and well-ordered to within living memory. Mrs Ormonde who lives beside the Lodge can remember the place immaculate before the Land Commission acquired it. The stables the Commission knocked down were 'one of the finest in the world'. Everything was carefully maintained. 'If a daisy pushed its head out of the ground a man would get the sack.'

The Hindoo Gothick gate lodge at the other side of the estate looked like a cutting from Brighton Pavilion. Over the drawbridge the forestry people had taken over, their presence signified by the red stumps of the avenue trees they had felled. In the winter mist the gardens revealed themselves as a lot of young nettles and broken greenhouses. But the 'hanging woods' at which Carlyle gazed from his bedroom window, noting how they plummeted to the wide band of the river, were as lovely as they had ever been.

Mrs Villiers-Stuart, a member of the family, bought back the old house from the Land Commission for a thousand pounds which included a few acres and the church at Villierstown which is now open for ecumenical services. It was a gesture that arose from duty, since the Fitzgeralds and their collaterals, the Villiers-Stuarts, had lived here since the twelfth century. She simplified to some extent the problems of roofs and gutters by demolishing the Georgian part of the house which left her with only thirty-six bedrooms. But maintenance costs were soaring ... a film company was interested in leasing the place for an historical picture ... just the right atmosphere ... what did I think? We went upstairs to view the trees mirrored by the river, the distant Comeraghs, and directly beneath the foundations of two towers lying among layers of rubble.

'Do you feel anything? The ghosts? Do you find them malevolent?' Lord Barrymore had shot himself in the small room overlooking the river because of his gambling debts. Many people wouldn't sleep there nor in the other room where a blackamoor had been incarcerated and had perished. Her old gardener heard from time to time the rustle of long dresses on the empty lawn. She herself always felt a warm presence every time she returned to the house. Perhaps the spirits were grateful that she continued to provide them with a home.

Johnny Murphy took me fishing on the Blackwater. It is a most elusive river, difficult to find; only the odd road or track leads down to its banks and then it lies behind thick banks of reeds. On the old pier I met a woman whose husband had worked the ferry at Villierstown when coalboats tied up near her house and the captains came inside for a cup of tea. These Welsh or English coalboats were the vestiges of a once-flourishing river trade. In the nineteenth century the Blackwater was a highway filled with barges, sailing ships and steamers ferrying goods and travellers between Youghal, Dungarvan and Cappoquin. Other smaller craft went further upstream to the quays at Clonmel.

The empty river has lost its traffic, the coalboats, the vessels bringing salt to the bacon factory at Cappoquin and the old passenger steamers. It is also in the process of losing its salmon.

'The men are scarce and so are the fish,' Johnny said. Four of us crowded in a small boat embarked at the first dawn light into a still calm surface – it was amazing that the river could be as calm as a lake. The swans hooped and flapped their wings. As we waited Johnny chronicled the salmon's decline. The shoals enter Youghal Bay where they face a series of formidable obstacles – the drift nets at the river mouth, the fish weirs at Ballintrae, drag net fishing which was what we were doing, poaching and the rarefied legitimate pleasures of fishing at the Duke's pool. If any fish managed to get far upstream, drawn by smell to the headwaters and the one and only place where they spawned, the eels were waiting to get the eggs. And anywhere there was the chance of picking up the disease. The disease was like ringworm in calves and their eyes melted out of their heads.

The tide had fallen enough to reveal a bank to fish from. Here we were in the mud waiting for the fish to show. The mad scramble to cast out the net preceded the slow rhythm of pulling it in.

'Jesus, there's a few all right.'

For seconds the fish gleamed silver threshing the water before vanishing in mud. Dark shapes struggled until a sharp blow on their heads killed them. Our first netting caught nine; the next drag brought in two small trout and the third, before the tide forced us off the bank, yielded half a dozen more salmon. An average morning, Johnny said. The fish were washed to get the mud off, thrown into a plastic sack and brought back to Villierstown, gourmet material. Every year Johnny and the others found it harder to scratch a living. How long was it since boats used to be weighed down to the gunnels after a catch? Or gentlemen, tired of salmon steaks, threw chunks to the dogs under the table? In far older times there was a folk connection between the flesh of salmon and the pink decay of leprosy. The medieval traveller, Gerard Boate, wrote how 'this horrible and dreadful disease' originated 'through the fault and foul gluttony . . . in the excessive devouring of unwholesome salmon'.

Above Cappoquin, Mount Melleray spread across a mountain side. The monastery was built from 1831 by Cistercian monks of the Strict Observance who had been expelled from Melleray in Brittany. Sixty-four monks, most of them Irish, set about turning the mountain land into an abbey and a farm. They had been given six hundred wild acres by a local landlord, Sir Richard Keane, at an annual rent of a shilling a year per acre for twenty-one years, then half a crown an acre for ninety-nine years. Local men made a boundary wall with their spades and mattocks. Asenath Nicholson was told how

> on the appointed day the people assembled and formed a procession at Cappoquin with the monks at their head carrying a cross. A band of music escorted them up the mountain and the provisions and implements of cookery were carried in carts, the woman following to cook the provisions. Thus commenced the wall, and so continued daily, the band going up at night to escort them down, and ascending with them in the morning.

In a very few years the 'rocky sterile unpromising spot' was transformed. The efforts of the struggling community tended to arouse hostility among those imbued with a Protestant distrust of monkery. Henry English, who spent a day at Mount Melleray in 1838, was undeniably impressed, but could not help deriding the misdirection of human energies and the prevalence of superstition. By comparison Carlyle was objective. He glared at 'hooded monks actually in brown coarse woollen sacks that reached to the knees – Irish *accent* from beneath the hood as a brother greets us'. He inspected the 'dormitory very large, wholly wooden and clean; bakehouse, poor library, nasty *tubs* of cold stirabout (coarsest I ever saw) for beggars' – he was an authority on porridge – 'silence; each monk when bidden to do anything does it, folds hands over breast, and disappears with a *large* smile and a low bow; – curious enough to look upon indeed!' He concluded the account of his stay with a gleeful sneer, describing how the Prior had discovered some of his monks 'surveying the Youghal-and-Cappoquin steamer, watching its arrival, from their high moor as the event of *their* day; and had reprovingly taken away their telescope: ah me!'

Mrs Nicholson showed cautious respect towards the monastic routine while resenting the male chauvinism. 'We saw a monk approaching in his gown and cowl and hoped that he might be coming to meet us. But he passed in silence, not casting a look upon the prohibited article, *women*.' Today women are not allowed to stay in the main guesthouse, but have their own hostel located a decent distance away.

Thackeray skipped Mount Melleray altogether. 'I was very glad we had not time to see the grovelling place; and as for seeing shoes made or fields tilled by reverend amateurs, we can find cobblers and ploughmen to do the work better.'

Mount Melleray must have continued to have a trickle of disapproving Protestant visitors over the years since Thackeray passed it by, during which it has quietly flourished. It weathered the famine when the monks had to sell their poultry and 'their fine organ (a pious gift)'. In the 1920s its expansion was aided by the purchase of Mitchelstown Castle, a grandiose building modelled after Windsor Castle, the property of the notoriously cruel and eccentric Earls of Kingston. When it was burned during the troubles, the fine cut stone of the ruin was carted over twenty miles to Mount Melleray and used to enlarge some of its buildings. Is there any irony or sense of triumph meant by the framed picture in the dining-room that shows Mitchelstown Castle in its prime? Or is it simply a record of achievement?

The Brothers farm their six hundred acres meticulously by the most modern methods. 'Sir Something's waste land' has become a superb model farm, its lush green fields edged by plantations of trees. I watched a Brother set off towards a plantation to exercise a couple of dogs – a rare moment of pleasure. Every visitor has commented on the beehive industry of the place and the farm buildings display the most up-to-date techniques. I wondered about the battery hens. Surely the cruelty of the system conflicted with Christian principles? Not at all. Denials from farming monks are indignant. Vatican II has changed the religious life and introduced factory farming. Monks must practise the scientific approach to agriculture. No picturesque medieval Books of Hours methods here. 'We can't live in a museum.'

Mount Melleray dispenses traditional hospitality and has done so since its inception. It is free, but only churlish Popery-conscious

Thackeray-minded guests would fail to leave a thank offering equivalent to the price of bed and breakfast. There is a lot more to be experienced. The notice inside the guesthouse reads: RISE 7.30. MASS IN PUBLIC CHURCH 8 O'CLOCK. BREAKFAST 9.00. DINNER 1.30. VESPERS 5.30. TEA 6.00. COMPLINE 8.00. RETIRE TO ROOMS 8.30. IN ADDITION GUESTS ARE ENCOURAGED TO BENEFIT FROM DIVINE SERVICE, RECITATION OF THE ROSARY, SPIRITUAL READERSHIP AND MUCH DISCUSSION.

'How long will we have you for?' Brother Bonaventura asked. I weathered just two days. The guesthouse was centrally heated and the food was good. In February few casual visitors came – at the time I was the only one. The others were studying for holy orders or were on a retreat. They included a young Seminarist, a couple of Divine Word missionaries, a Professor of Theology and a batch of middle-aged men studying to be priests. It was easier to make a late entry into priesthood than into a contemplative order. 'You want to get into those good and early while you're a young man,' a late entrant told me. He was finding the transition to religious life a lot more difficult than he had anticipated. He had been an army sergeant and getting on when he made the decision, so at least he was used to strictness and routine. I told him that often here in Mount Melleray I was reminded of army life. 'What order are you in?' an aspiring priest asked across the breakfast table, and he could almost have been asking what regiment. There was an atmosphere of rank and discipline that suggested an officers' mess.

Some experiences at Mount Melleray were very good. Any outsider must be moved by the services in the Brothers' own lovely chapel which can be watched from a small public gallery. (Asenath Nicholson: 'The sight of nearly 100 monks dressed in priestly robes with all the accompaniments of grandeur cannot fail to impress a credulous people.') But time passed slowly. In an atmosphere of formal religious companionship I was spiritually outdistanced. I walked up and down the gravel paths or circled the cloisters past their secretive doors – ENCLOSURE. NO ADMITTANCE – gazed at the hills, sought solace in my room and visited the small burial ground. When Mrs Nicholson was here already twelve monks were buried with wooden crosses at their head and feet. Occasionally I felt the need for a drink. Other visitors have felt the same. The nearest pub was miles away at Cappoquin. On Sunday which is open day when people come from all over the neighbourhood I wandered among the lines of cars parked in front of the big grey buildings. The public chapel was filled with worshippers and there was a throng of people in the shop buying coloured pictures of the Pope, sheaves of rosaries, books and holy medals. Everywhere among them were the Brothers fluttering their brown robes.

Cups of tea, more walking in the garden. Church bells ringing again. I had already been to early mass. Was I up to another? Some of my companions were back on their knees. A discussion about spiritual difficulties. Talk about prayer.

'The best time of all for praying is in the early morning . . . A priest needs a good block of prayer before the day starts . . .' Brother Bonaventura sitting at a red baize-covered table directing a discussion group, expertly fielding questions. It had been a strange experience being soothed, invigorated and bored at the same time. The soul may have been toned up after its sojourn at a spiritual health farm.

6
Carrick-on-Suir · Cashel

Carrick-on-Suir is faded, old-fashioned and provincial, in the words of *Murray's Guide*: 'A small straggling town which need not detain the tourist.' A bottleneck fouling traffic opens to the main street. Across the river Tom Ormonde's sixteenth-century manor house survives unfurnished, its ornate stucco decoration incorporating medallions with profiles of Queen Elizabeth whom Black Tom admired, kept warm and protected from damp by two small heaters.

Across the old stone bridge spanning the sleek coil of the River Suir I searched for Dorothea Herbert's house. Once I thought I had found what I was looking for when I came across a battered eighteenth-century building beside a tannery with stone pillars topped by pine-apples, false symbols of prosperity. Could it be the 'villa', Dorothea's home, which had 'three large Parlours, 2 large Halls, 7 large Bed-chambers' and 'a great low Garret, a perfect Wilderness of Antique construction that made the blood run Chill with Horror'? Was the slaughterhouse beyond the tannery situated in the Herberts' 'Pleasure Garden', and did the tannery overlay the garden, the 'Wilderness of sweets'? What about the view? It was wrong, even given the passage of time. The sweep of the Suir from here was not the real prospect she described in such detail as visible from her 'Pretty Wilderness'. I had to conclude reluctantly that this handsome slum was not her family home and that her father's rectory had disappeared. But she must have been familiar with the house, for whoever lived here would have been part of the 'Carrick Set', the small town society of which she was a part. It may have been the house of 'Mr Coughlan a Clergyman' or Mr Anderson and Mr Young, Dr Carshore, Mrs Dobbyn, 'three families of Smyths' or some other genteel family who helped to make up the 'uncommon well stock'd Neighbourhood'.

Dorothea wrote her reminiscences in the first decade of the nineteenth century when she was middle-aged, heartbroken in love and on the verge of going mad. They were entitled dolefully *A Help to Memory or Retrospections of an Outcast by Dorothea Roe*. When John Roe, the man she loved, married another woman, she deluded herself that she was his true wife. But, although her writing has an underlying tragic note, there is more humour than sadness and the *Retrospections* are a touching, funny eccentric autobiography of great charm.

She was born in Carrick in 1770, the eldest of nine children of a well-connected couple, the Reverend Nicholas Herbert, rector of the town, and Mrs Herbert, a sister of Lord Desart. Mr Herbert was a younger son of the Herberts of Muckross where Dorothea had visited and thrilled at the gloom of Muckross Abbey. She and all but one of her siblings survived a rugged childhood with 'first a bad Nurse, 2dly a Mad Nurse and 3rdly a sickly Nurse'. In childhood she was taught to dance by 'Mr Tassoni whom she plagued heartily' and to play by 'a blind drunk French Music Master named Monsieur Dabeard'. These teachers were succeeded by fat Mrs O'Hara who instilled in Dorothea a passionate love of music, and Madame Bondagée, a Royalist refugee, 'an old French woman' who 'came begging to us cover'd with Rags and Sores – my mother took her out of Charity and bought her two Cotton Negligees – She taught us all French capitally and as capitally taught us how to make mushroom soups and Soupe maigre.' Like Mrs O'Hara and Monsieur Dabeard she 'turned out drunken'.

When Dorothea was eighteen and enjoying the balls, romps, marriages and diversions with the military that occupied Carrick society, the family was directed by the local archbishop to spend a part of each year at Knockgrafton, Mr Herbert's most remote parish, situated between Cashel and Cahir. A mile away from Knockgrafton Parsonage is Rockwell. At the time Rockwell was owned by a family named Roe, and the handsome son of the house, John Roe, was loved desperately but vainly by Dorothea. Instead of marrying her he 'joined himself in execrable Union with a Common Drab of the City – a mere street strolling Miss – Daughter to one Counsellor Sankey of Dublin.' Dorothea could not face the reality of the 'final End to all my long fostered Hopes'. 'I shall always regard him as My Husband though his renegade Amour has placed a Barrier of Vicious Obstacles to my Claims ... No surreptitious Wedlock can invalidate the just Claims of the Miserably unfortunate Dorothea Roe.'

The deaths of her father and brother and the events of 1798 when her father's proctor was murdered at Knockgrafton helped to bring her closer to insanity. Her middle years, according to her, were years of persecution and isolation. She was confined, and bullied by her family and always pining for her 'husband'. And yet this was the period during which she wrote her *Retrospections*. In the later chapters the gaiety is increasingly replaced by more sombre passages until finally the autobiography becomes a pathetic diary. '1809. 23 August. Nothing new, Mr Nick dined abroad, Mr Phelan dined here. 17th Sept. Day spent as usual, lonesome and stupid enough. Mon 28 Attack'd on all Sides by the Damnd family below.' In that year the *Retrospections* ceased. We know nothing further about her except that she died unmarried aged fifty-nine in 1829.

Her family kept the manuscript of the *Retrospections* and they were published in two volumes in 1919 and 1930. It is difficult to convey the flavour of her writing without lengthy quotations from passages like the description of the Herbert girls' régime of beauty care or the great winter of 1783 when the family spent forty-seven days wrapped in greatcoats over two fires in two parlours gambling with cards for roasted sprats which were driven in shoals up the Suir by the weather. Or the visit to her cousins at Castle Blunden where the ladies and gentlemen slept in dormitories and the gentlemen spied on the ladies with loud tittering and giggling until the ladies' pot-de-chambre overturned and 'the whole Contents meandered across the Lobby into their Barrack'.

Perhaps if she had been an Englishwoman her *Retrospections* would have gained more attention and would have placed her in literature as a representative of the rural diarist school worthy to be compared with Parson Woodforde. But in Ireland *belles-lettres* are less admired than works of the imagination and Dorothea Herbert has vanished into obscurity once more.

I walked into Curraghmore ten miles from Carrick to call on Lord Waterford who lives behind beeches, limes and oaks. The bare branches filled up the landscape to the horizon, the same wall of trees noted by Arthur Young. Up this avenue in 1797 through the four stone gateposts decorated with urns trudged the young French Royalist refugee, de Latocnaye, who arrived at the great front door 'tired and breathless' expecting the courtesy of a bed. He was travelling round Ireland with his necessities in a bundle on the end of a stick.

They included spare silk stockings and powder for his hair so that he could demonstrate at any time that he was a gentleman. In addition he had his essential letters of recommendation which had proved so useful on his tour that he was hardly ever obliged to stay at an inn.

At Curraghmore things were different and the usual hospitality did not materialize; he got a meal and nothing more. He was angry when he was told there were no available beds, for if Curraghmore did not have spare beds, what other house did? He walked back down the long avenue plunging through the mud in his white stockings, followed by Lord Waterford's man. At Portlaw he went to the inn, where he was told once again that no accommodation was available by 'an ugly looking domestic, and it was only Lord Waterford's name that made him suddenly relent'. But de Latocnaye, too, had changed his mind. 'They ran after me begging me to return. "I would rather pass the night in hell," I said.'

It began to rain and only the generosity of a poor family saved him from a dreadful night. 'I placed myself on the hard bed of misfortune.' He lay down surrounded by 'half a dozen naked children, a pig, dog, two hens and a duck', consoling himself with a maxim of Lord Chesterfield's. 'Those who travel needlessly from place to place observing only their distance from each other and attending only to their accommodation at the inn at night, set out fools and certainly will return so.'

A smattering of landed gentry continues to live in the rich valleys of Waterford. I had seen a number of elderly examples in the sparse congregation at Cappoquin church, enough to prove that they have not yet vanished like golden eagles. Elsewhere in Ireland they are extinct; there are many places where they have disappeared from the scene for so long that they are a folk memory. Invariably they have left wicked reputations. Objectionable many of them were and yet one cannot help feeling pained when eccentric or miserly or generally difficult relatives and connections are lumped with the Lord Lucans and classified as ogres.

The Beresfords are survivors in a family where ogres have abounded. Legend burns bright overlaying memories of wickedness and tragedy that live on in stories of the murdered footman, the seven generation curse, the young heir fallen from his horse, the countess dead in childbirth and the 3rd Lord Waterford killed in a hunting accident.

This 3rd Marquess painted the hooves of a parson's horse with aniseed and hunted him with bloodhounds; painted a policeman bright green and tied him to some Mayfair railings; sat on the hats of a London milliner and squashed them flat; swept glasses off counters on numerous occasions; jumped into an old woman's crockery basket and smashed everything; shot out the eyes of the family portraits in a house that he had rented. It was said in his favour that he paid for the damage he did. After he married he settled down to hunt and hunt – he seldom returned from a meet until ten o'clock at night. When not hunting he evicted. Hunting killed him and he was carried back lifeless on a hurdle at dead of night to his lonely lady at Curraghmore. The locals sang:

> . . . O Lord Waterford is dead
> With the devil at his head
> And 'tis hell will be his bed
> Says the Shan Van Vocht.
>
> They won't put him in the pit
> Says the Shan Van Vocht
> Where the common sinners sit
> Says the Shan Van Vocht.
> But he'll get a warrum sate
> Up beside the special grate
> Where his father bakes in state
> Says the Shan Van Vocht.

The present Lord Waterford seems mild and pleasant enough. His house is amazing. Past the lines of pleached chestnuts the forecourt is an architectural extravagance with stables fit for Pegasus on both sides, two-storeyed, pedimented and decorated with rusticated Doric columns and arched doorways where moulded architraves are topped by lunettes. St Hubert's stag, the de la Poer family emblem – a de la Poer heiress married a Beresford and brought him Curraghmore as her dowry – sits on top of the central block which is the original twelfth-century castle tower with structural alterations that have given it a baroque face-lift. The antlers supporting the cross are genuine stag's antlers. The architect responsible was a Waterford man named John Roberts. It seems likely that he must have been familiar with the buildings of Vanbrugh, since you have to go over to Blenheim to find a similar effect of symmetry and theatrical grandeur. And the gardens are supposed to be laid out from a plan of Versailles.

Outside, Lady Waterford exercised a horse. Inside, I was faced with a pleasant example of country house chaos. On the hall table were emblems of the chase, whips, riding hats and a stuffed fox. In a corner polo sticks overflowed from a dried elephant's trunk. A Beresford must have hunted other game besides foxes. An enormous group portrait looked down at a glass case containing three lions in pampas grass. The great formal rooms, some painted by Zucchi, Angelica Kauffmann's husband, had a wintry look. Accompanied by an ancient maid, Lord Waterford took me to the staircase of the original castle tower, to the billiard room over the old hall. Not every billiard room has plaster decorations supervised by James Wyatt and pillared doorways surrounding the green baize. It is a conversion.

'This was the old ballroom.'

In spite of the table and the framed rules on the wall for pool and billiards, the noble room should be associated less with gentlemen in shirtsleeves holding cues and more with the sound of fiddles and lutes and the sight of formal eighteenth-century dancers. Dorothea Herbert was here one winter evening in 1788 for the great ball held to honour the Duke of Clarence. 'Everyone was invited.' The Carrick set and the neighbouring gentry came to see 'The first of the Brunswick Race who has Visitted [sic] our Isle'.

Dorothea and her sister, Fanny, took a lot of trouble with their appearance. They sent off to Kilkenny for 'New Hats and Feathers, Chapeaus being then the rage'. Their dresses were resplendent, 'Gawze over Fanny's blue and My Pink silk Linings – They were all trimmed all over with black Velvet Biasses . . . and no Eastern Queens ever cut such a dazzling Appearance.' The girls were like 'two resplendent Suns Glittering with Diamonds'.

And so to the ball. 'We went peppering to Curraghmore' and the great forecourt filled with horses and carriages and lit by flaming torches carried by footmen. First there was tea, after which 'the Dancing began to a very fine Band and other Music'. The Duke of Clarence, showing himself a true Hanoverian, danced with 'most of the prettiest Females'. After supper when they returned to the

Dancing Room 'His Royal Highness honour'd each one of them with a Kiss as they pass'd, guarding the Door that None should pass out unblest, which affronted some very much, while others thought it was a high Honour.'

It began to snow just as the time came for departure. 'The Day after . . . The ground was cover'd with snow which fell in large flakes during the Night . . . Some carriages going had stuck in the woods all Night and their owners were obliged to remain in the Mortifying Situation without any Prospect of getting out of it – Of those who were returning . . . some lost their shoes, some their Caps and Not a few their Hearts.'

I went back to Carrick to the house by the tannery where effluvia from the slaughterhouse stank, pieces of torn plastic were scattered by the wind and rusty cans showed brown among the weeds. The panelled hall was permeated by a sour smell emanating from the crowd of empty milk bottles and in a flat upstairs a woman was shrieking at her children. On the return of the heavy wooden staircase I saw Dorothea's ghost. She was dressed in gaudy clothes, something like her shepherdess fancy dress – 'a picturesque Short Jacket mitr'd with blue – the mitring quill'd with white Love Ribbon'. On her head a 'small white chip Chapeau' was decorated with a bunch of 'Natural Flowers'.

She stayed with me as we walked out into the spring sun. It was easy to pick out the buildings she would have known – the pub now called the Duke of Ormonde, the Carbury Cleaners which was surmounted by an old slated front, the ochre-covered belfry now striking the hour which appears in the watercolour she painted of the town.

Provincial Irish small town life at the end of the eighteenth century is not easy to recreate in the imagination. But you can find out nearly everything you need to know about Carrick-on-Suir in 1799. Not only is there the detail in the *Retrospections*, but a census for that year has survived in the British Museum. From this you can learn that Carrick had 10,907 inhabitants, Catholic except for 298. (Dorothea gives the names of about fifty of these Protestants.) The census lists the numbers of persons engaged in trade, all men over sixteen. They include thirty-three breeches-makers, sixty-nine brogue-makers, sixteen hatters and eleven chandlers; forty-one smiths, one inoculator, three stay-makers, three snuff-grinders, five musicians and one dancing master, very likely Mr Tassoni. The list makes clear that in spite of the navigable transport flowing through the town most everyday objects were made locally – candles, breeches, coaches, beer, combs, boats. Seven builders found employment supplying local river traffic. The *Retrospections* have a list of their own which supplements the census – the Herberts' tailor was Old Leary, their staymaker Old St John, their Butcher Old Hervey and their shoemaker Tom Phillips.

This morning the river touched the arches of the old bridge and the brown water reflected the fields, hills and sky. The Suir, tidal as far as Carrick, used to be a river highway like the Blackwater, its traffic passing between Waterford and Clonmel. In Dorothea's day barges and sailing boats passed through loaded with wood and coal, and she would have listened to the cries of sailors and dogs barking as the traffic drifted on past the 'hanging woods and the dome of Slievenamon'.

I traced the towpath behind ruinous warehouses and long-disused stone piers, and followed it through briars, young nettles and barbed-wire fences. This river path was once described as 'one of the most pleasant that the tourist can meet in Ireland'. Dorothea's ghost stayed with me. We detoured round a factory that blocked the route where horse barges had pulled their load and made our way past two small weirs and some water meadows. Across the river Coolnamuck still flourished, 'a beautiful place near a romantic Glen'. The hills were still wooded, though with the dead green segments of forestry plantations.

Near Kilsheelan we came across two broken arches by the river. Dorothea reminded me that here was Linville, home of poor Ned. Her cousin, Ned Eyre, a strange yet attractive eccentric spendthrift bought Linville in 1786 'after searching out every old ruined seat about (for such only would he take)'. He lived 'in a most romantic retirement with half a dozen favourite servants and two very large spotted spaniels of the Leopard Breed which he called Miss Dapper and Miss Kitsy and adopted as Daughters and Co Heiresses'. What is left of Linville consists of the old boathouse and an avenue of eight lime trees standing by themselves in a line in a field above the river.

Ned Eyre was 'the greatest Oddity in the world'. He wore bright silk or satin, often women's clothes. 'His hair was dress'd like a Woman's over a Rouleau or Tete, which was then the fashion amongst the

Ladies.' He sometimes carried a muff, sometimes a fan, and was always painted up to the eyes with the deepest carmine; a sort of eighteenth-century drag. He played cards constantly and bought two hundred pounds' worth of lottery tickets each year. Extravagance ruined him and he and his mother fled their debts to go abroad; they died impecunious in Flanders to the sorrow of their cousins.

It seemed sense to call at the nearby castle and ask about Linville. A yapping dog followed me through the yard towards a flight of steps, leading up to the heavy wooden door which was open, with the sound of a radio coming from inside. A long wooden table surrounded by high medieval-type chairs was set for dinner. But no one was about, only the dog which made a lunge. I gave it a swipe with my umbrella.

I went on to Kilsheelan to a pub where I asked my questions. The woman behind the bar told me Kilsheelan was the cleanest town in Ireland, the castle was called Poulakerry and had recently been done up, and if I wanted to find out about local history and the like I had only to ask Mr Mandeville.

Mr Mandeville was a retired clergyman who lived in a Georgian cottage up a muddy lane. He was spare-looking, wizened by African sun, and under his jacket he wore an embroidered Ghanean waistcoat. In his sitting-room a grand piano took up most of the space and there were books, Victorian watercolours, ferns and vases of daffodils. His sister brought in tea and sponge cake. He knew all about Linville, Ned Eyre and Dorothea Herbert.

'I am related to her.'

In 1804 Dorothea's sister Sophy had married 'a very pretty Young Man with high expectation' named John Mandeville. Their son, Nicholas, married a daughter of John Roe, Dorothea's beloved. My host, Maurice Mandeville, was the great-grandson of this pair, and had inherited the manuscript of the *Retrospections* which lay among the flowers and books preserved under a glass bell. The even copperplate was faded but clear. I examined the writing peppered with capital letters, distinguished by her individual spelling and topped by her elaborate chapter headings adorned with verse. 'A Squandering Heir. Chapter 61. A Smart little Lover. Love like a cautious fearful Bird ne'er builds, but where the place Silence and Calmness yields.' There were also her watercolours including a self-portrait showing a plump dark young woman with black eyebrows and long curling hair. Her ghost was still beside me very like her picture, smiling at the coincidence.

Fethard is tumbledown with a castle, the survivor of five gates and the old barracks for the alien military. Many of Dorothea's acquaintances were officers from regiments stationed all over Waterford and Tipperary.

Next day I walked through the soft green Tipperary countryside beyond Fethard. The winter fields were full of fat grazing cattle, crows wheeled in the sky or landed softly on the road to pick at cowpats. It began to rain, and shaking squalls rattled on my umbrella. A halt beside an IRA monument was time to learn of glories in the days when 'terror stalked the proud land of the Gael'. A blast of wind shook some corrugated iron with a roaring that sparked off the crows and made them scatter across the sky like ashes. The trees bent sighing, there was more roaring, this time of traffic. I had reached the Newinn crossroads on the main Dublin–Cork road.

The house that had been Knockgrafton Rectory was right beside the road, a grey three-storey building with a mass of daffodils under the trees. Mrs Downey, an admirer of Dorothea, took me around the small hall, with the staircase cutting across the window, the parlour and the kitchen. Maurice Mandeville had shown me Dorothea's painting of the Rectory which was two-storeyed in the days when the Herberts spent their summers there. She depicted the Rector, his wife, and a female figure, probably Dorothea herself, standing in front of the house receiving gifts of wheat, poultry and fish from parishioners. This agricultural produce was given in lieu of tithes.

The tithe system, so outrageously unsuitable to Ireland, was supported by the powerful Protestant clergy which depended on it for income. Contemporary pamphlets from ecclesiastical sources argued that tithes could never really be oppressive since they depended on the actual produce of the land. However, it was stated in a debate in the Irish parliament in 1787 that a peasant, who was in all probability a Catholic, might be working for sixpence a day, and yet had to pay eight or twelve shillings a year in tithes to the local Protestant clergyman.

Opposition to the system became organized with the Whiteboys movement. The *Retrospections* refer frequently to the Rev. Nicholas Herbert's troubles with Whiteboys raiding the land and burning the hay. Tithe proctors, who were agents for the gathering of tithes, were among the Whiteboys' chief targets, and Richard Shortis, Mr Herbert's proctor, together with his wife, was murdered savagely at this very rectory on the eve of the 1798 rebellion.

In happier years the Herberts came to Knockgrafton every summer for three months. The house had perspectives looking towards Cashel and towards Rockwell, the home of the devastating John Roe 'where I spent the happiest and most miserable Hours of My Life'. The Roes were Dorothea's father's parishioners, not quite in the same social class as the Herberts. Rockwell has turned from the 'Head farmer's style of house' into huge Rockwell College, and schoolboys walk down the avenue to the lake 'where John Roe was yearly enlarging'.

'Sure no Woman had ever such strong Claims to any Man's Love as I had to John Roe's . . . for no woman was ever so wrapped up in one man or so ruined by him.' He was her Heathcliff. 'The fire of his Eye, his expressive Countenance, the bewitching Sound of his Voice impassioned the Heart and forced the Mind to Admiration.' It is painful to read of Dorothea's obsession. In the spring of 1798 after John Roe's marriage when she was twenty-eight she was attacked with 'one of the most frightful Nervous fevers that any mortal got over . . . brought on entirely by grief and Despondency of Mind . . . at the first onset I was taken with a violent fit of Screeching and continued that way delirious for some Hours, from that I fell to singing, psalms . . . so piteously as to draw tears from Dr Barker . . . I felt as if Soul and Body were sinking for ever and ever in some bottomless Abyss.'

I did not like to leave her like that with all the gaiety and laughter extinguished. I went on to Cashel where she had pleasant memories. She wrote of her visit to the races with a party of friends. The Herberts journeyed from Knockgrafton in their new bottle-green coach and 'four of the handsomest young Bay Horses in the Kingdom'. Ned Eyre accompanied them in his glass vis-à-vis rouged to the eyeballs. In the evening at the rout in the assembly the Herbert girls wore pink lutestring and black silk bodices with white plumes in their hair. Their dresses were a present from Ned Eyre who outshone them wearing the same pink lutestring, his suit decorated with paste diamonds so that he was 'One blaze of Brilliants from Top to Toe'.

I found the racecourse which functioned up to a few years ago. The concrete stand surviving stubbornly in the empty field was a link with the eighteenth century. Behind, the Rock stood out. The building on the summit would have looked the same to Dorothea since Archbishop Agar stripped the cathedral roof in 1749. Her mind was too full of courtship and amusement, since, although she had a fashionable liking for ruins, she never mentioned the mighty edifice looking down on damp green fields.

7
Lough Gur · Doneraile · Kanturk

Frost sparkled in the morning sun and the puddles were opaque under a cloudless sky. A double rainbow hung over the lake which curved round the hump of Knockfennell. This is limestone country. Mankind, attracted by the fertile pastures around Lough Gur, has settled here since prehistoric times leaving traces of ancient farms, crannogs, field systems, tombs, ringforts, castles and a wonderful stone circle. The evidence of history makes the lake mysterious even without tales of the ruined city beneath and the Earl of Desmond riding on the waters.

The area round is packed with things for archaeologists to look for.

'What do you think you will find?' Sissy O'Brien asked a couple of them as they dug into the soil over a century ago.

They told the little girl: 'Butter and bones, perhaps a four-headed sheep or a long-nosed pig and fireplaces, perhaps bodies, perhaps treasure.'

Sissy's memories were made into a well-loved book, *The Farm by Lough Gur*. She was born here in 1858 and after a happy childhood married a young farmer named Richard Fogarty and moved away. Later she dreamed of the past.

'There is a hill in the County Limerick called Knockfennell whose southern slopes fall steeply into Lough Gur. On a green ridge above the lake stands the old farmhouse where I was born.'

In 1904 when she was living in Bruff, not far from here, she met Mary Carbery. Lady Carbery, born Mary Toulmin, was an English-woman who after a privileged Victorian childhood married Lord Carbery from Castlefreke in West Cork. He also owned land in the neighbourhood of Lough Gur, and this brought his wife to County Limerick and her first encounter with Mary Fogarty.

The two women renewed acquaintance in old age when Lady Carbery, an authoress and poet, realized the unique value of Mary Fogarty's detailed memory and asked the old woman to record her life story. The association was fruitful.

'While Mrs Fogarty in Ireland was remembering, I, in England, was trying to weave her notes as I received them into a continuous narrative, here and there filling inevitable gaps . . . In this way Mary Fogarty's story came to be written with her and for her by her friend Mary Carbery.'

The result is a skilful and sensitive compilation of old memories that forms a haunting recreation of Sissy's girlhood. It was published under Mary Carbery's name. Perhaps when the two women briefly met in Greystones in the 1930s, and planned the enterprise, this was decided upon. One assumes that the idea and encouragement came from Mary Carbery. Mrs Fogarty was supplying the raw material, but her noble co-author was turning it into literature. *The Farm by Lough Gur* has been reprinted many times, always under the name of its substantial ghost writer.

Flocks of starlings swarmed over a ploughed field and above them wheeled seagulls far inland. Sissy's old home framed the view, a long low farmhouse with ivy-covered walls and neat windows that still suggested solid prosperity. Her father had been a strong farmer. When I walked down to it the air of affluence proved to be illusory. Cattle grazed the lawn, briars grew in the flowerbed and the house looked uncared for. 'Our farm was like a little colony, self-contained where everyone worked hard and all were content and happy.' The O'Briens had four maids and employed labour for outside work. Compared with the majority of their neighbours they were privileged.

But now the staircase had gone, the old hearth and fireplace – 'the pride of the house' – had been bricked up and the rooms in which Sissy's family lived seemed small and dingy. It was an effort to imagine the women sitting at the table, the cat lying on the window sill, the jug of clotted cream, the pair of boots beside the door and Sissy and her mother making cream cheese with 'thick cream which was just on the turn mixed with a pinch of salt and a little dry mustard'. Pleasanter to look out of the dusty windows on to the lake. 'When I think of home I see Lough Gur . . . like a bright mirror on which are reflected blue sky, bare hills, precipitous grey rocks and green pastures dotted with sheep and cattle.' On the grass where Sissy and her sisters had played ring-a-ring-o'roses I could see the weeping ash planted by her mother and the two arbours of beech and hawthorn where the girls had courted.

I found the present owners of the farm, also called O'Brien, working in the yard. They had little time for the book or the author. The original O'Brien family at the farm 'didn't step down very much. They lived very big and weren't what they claimed to be – almost landlords.' Later, when I met Sissy's nephew, he sympathized with this attitude which is locally prevalent.

'Aunt Bessie was a thin woman full of charm and culture. But she could also be fault finding.' He considered the O'Briens of Lough Gur dreamers and snobs in what he called 'a cap-touching age'. It may have been Mary Fogarty's snobbery that allowed the book to be published without her name as co-author. Aunt Bessie had remembered her rural background when she was old and living in a Dublin suburb, which may have accounted for her only recalling the beauty of things and not the harsh dismal side of everyday life of the period. She conjured up a rural idyll – the kitchen with its long oak table where the men sat down for tea after work, her mother's model dairy, the small room where the family gathered to sew and read books, Dickens and Scott, authors associated with the English middle classes. Her father farmed two hundred acres belonging to the de Salis family and the young Count de Salis was a good friend. In comparison to her golden picture the harsher realities of a small farmer's life in nineteenth-century Ireland seemed like the other side of the moon.

When she was eighteen Sissy married, after a farmer's courtship, old-style without romance. The proposal was delivered by a stable lad. 'I took the letter ... a plain straightforward offer of marriage unadorned by any word of love or line of poetry. I answered quite simply, accepting the offer. Then I went to my mother.'

Before the wedding she went away in a special landau, a bouquet of chrysanthemums in her lap.

'God bless you, dear Miss Sissy, and send you happy.'

There were loud cheers from the yard, dogs barked, the greys pranced and the coachman cursed. 'We are safely past the sandpit, the alley, old Malachi's orchard and Dooley's cottage. The wind is buffeting the lake and throwing spray at the carriage.' In Sissy's imagination – or was it Lady Carbery's? – her coach was drawn by the Black Mare of Lough Gur and Lord Desmond's silver-shod horse.

The route of Sissy's landau ambled down the hill from the farmhouse, past the meadow where her father kept the yearly bulls, down to the Neolithic Amenity building, a patch of vulgarity like a spore in a dish, with flowerbeds, sloping Neolithic roof and car parks for tourists. Knockadoon Castle, hidden in trees, rising from a machine-strewn farmyard, is not yet tidied up. Known as Black Castle, castle and farm still belong to the de Salis family. From here Sissy and her friends raced up to the top of Knockadoon and Eagle Rock to stand with Lough Gur spread below them and listen to a man playing a cornet.

Sissy went to a dance at the Castle with her future husband. Neither the Japanese lanterns strung through the trees nor the wax candles which lighted the rooms moved him to sentiment or romance. 'He watched me dance with other men without jealousy and remained calm when other youths shouted with enthusiasm over the fine violin playing of old Mr Regan and Thady his fiddler.' They danced until the sun came out and outshone the lanterns.

Like others round about, Mr Ryan who now farms the land about the castle was critical of the O'Briens' pretensions. 'It wasn't all that hot. The people around Lough Gur didn't like it at all.' He meant Sissy's book. There was the old sense in it that they were superior to the rest. The story of how Mr O'Brien would read the paper to his men just wasn't true. As for the tales of the convent in Bruff where the girl went to school, they upset the nuns. Waking up with a pull of the bedclothes and the words 'Praise be to Jesus' and all that criticism. And she said that the church here at St Patrick's Well was 'stark and bare in its poverty'. Local writers are seldom popular.

Sissy described going to St Patrick's church one Easter day with the family, the girls wearing brown lustre gypsy bonnets with brown ribbons to match. 'The hedges on the way ... were full of primroses, lamb's tails dangled from hazel boughs sending tiny puffs of pollen into the sunshine; from the sky fell the song of larks. The clip-clop of Beauty's hoofs, the whistle of the whip, the ding-dong of the chapel bell were the only sounds.'

Today was another church festival when the bells made similar sounds and a heap of cars gathered at the crossroads with people tumbling out wearing sprawling tufts of shamrock pinned to their jackets. Just inside the gate I noticed the grave of John O'Brien of Lough Gur, Sissy's father. In the crowded church listening to Mass in Irish my attention wandered to the bearded statue of St Patrick looking down from beside the altar and the milk churn filled with holy water standing on the altar steps.

After mass everyone went down the road to St Patrick's Well. A line of children and old people walked to the small recessed archway under an old tree where the lintel round the dark well had been decorated by Mrs Dineen with primroses and daffodils in jars and a saucer of shamrock placed before a small image of the saint in a glass box. When the round of pattern and prayer was over, bottles which had contained Powers, Coca-Cola and Fanta were filled with purgative holy water. Holy water keeps well – I remembered Mrs Lynch at Loo Bridge showing me a bottle that was taken fifteen years ago. Now I was told that water drunk at St Patrick's Day was particularly efficacious, known to cure rheumy eyes, sore throats, cancer and arthritis. The crowd stood in the sunlight and quaffed it. The well water was the best. Hadn't this one and that one been saved from illness and dying? It might be best to take a drink of both. That way you wouldn't go wrong.

At Friarstown, St Patrick's was being celebrated with the best beagle hunt of the season. Men in green hunting coats and shorts carolled round the field behind the stalwart figure of Michael O'Brien-Kelly who was controlling his Oakfield beagles with the help of a huntsman, chief whip, two assistant whips and foot followers in waterproofs, tracksuits and wellies running here and there under a dripping Limerick sky. 'I tore my old britches going over the ditches on St Patrick's Day in the morning.' We caught no hares. No one seemed to expect them to be caught, neither the Master nor his earnestly trotting hounds, nor the followers looking forward to tea and cakes in the old sitting-room at Friarstown House.

In Doneraile Canon Sheehan stood on his plinth in the wide main street where names on the shopfronts were Norman – Fizelle, Birmingham, Tidbridge. Beside the old gates into the Doneraile estate stood St Mary's church, bereft of the golden weathercock and the flags that had danced above the riders in 1747 when, blessed by the clergyman, they departed for flood, bank, fence and mud, towards the spire of St John's church in Buttevant in the world's first steeplechase.

Inside the gates stands Doneraile Court. The original castle was acquired by Spenser when he arrived over from Wexford to make his big Cork land grab. His son sold Doneraile to the St Legers. A house was burnt and a house was built; this surviving shell was erected in 1730, a few years before the steeplechase. Two very odd episodes happened here. The story of the lady hiding in the clock to spy on

Masons is well known. The second happening was recent – the case of the missing heir.

Doneraile Court is an empty block standing ready to enter the knacker's yard of Irish ruins. I found one man living there, Arthur Montgomery, who had carved himself a flat out of the emptiness. He conducted me through the bare pillared hall to the curved rooms that overlook the main lawn, the panelled study where Elizabeth Aldworth's clock had been located and the skeleton of the winter garden where Harold Nicolson sat listening to summer rain and fountains among ferns and smelling the tuberoses.

Elizabeth Bowen thought Doneraile 'a lyrical place' and big house owner herself – Bowen's Court, seven miles away, was built by the same architect, William Rothery – she ruminated over continuity in a famous passage of writing. 'What runs on most through a family living in one place is a continuous semi-physical dream. Above this dream level successive lives show their tips, their little conscious formation of wish and thought – with each death the air of the place has thickened as if it had been added to.' And yet she destroyed her own wavering three-hundred-year-old dream. Bowen's Court perished and haunted her memory. A few stone walls, ironically signposted by the Tourist Office, are all that remain of her old home. By selling it she killed it as deliberately as if she had taken a beloved old pet to the vet to be put down. She comforted herself 'it was a clean end'.

By contrast Doneraile Court is dying slowly, stripped of its furniture, the flesh of its bones. Twenty years ago it contained some pleasant country house kitsch – dark Irish tables, Nelson's sword, a set of chessmen carved by French prisoners of war, Armada chests, Tippu Sultan's flag and Elizabeth Aldworth's portrait – she was pleased to have been made an honorary Mason and she had herself painted in Masonic garb. All that is left of the interior fittings are a few reminders – some chimney pieces, an Art Nouveau stained glass window in the hall and the illuminated address the dealers didn't want. Beneath a picture of Lord Castletown as a uniformed Boer War hero the lettering makes a neat display of the despised virtue of loyalty. 'We hope that you and Lady Castletown, the daughter and worthy successor of Lord Doneraile to whom all were so much devoted, may reign happily for many years at Doneraile Court. Signed on behalf of your Lordship's sincere friends and tenants.'

About half a century after this address was presented the 7th Viscount died. Very often when the head of the St Legers departed this life a coach with headless horses sped up the drive. On this occasion there was no coach, but when the doctor came out of the house after attending the deathbed, Lord Doneraile's herd of red deer were waiting, gathered in a silent semi-circle outside the front door.

Soon afterwards a young American turned up claiming the title of Lord Doneraile together with the house and its contents. On Sunday, 27 July 1969 his ownership was to be fully recognized by the American Ambassador in Ireland. Arthur Montgomery showed me a newspaper cutting announcing the event and describing how the house 'contained numerous antiquities ... a fine collection of guns and spears from all over the world'. Everything was ready and invitations sent out when news came that the House of Lords disclaimed the newcomer's right to call himself Lord Doneraile. The party was cancelled. The missing heir, thrown out by the trustees, returned to America and there was no one to take his place. A foolish sale followed when the dealers fell on the house. It is said that the subsequent resale price of one table equalled the total paid for the rest of the furniture. The Land Commission acquired the demesne while the Georgian Society took over the house and continued to have a glum interest in it.

Arthur is the Society's representative. I spent the night sharing his small flat which was the only warm place in the building. He had painted up the hall and hoped to repair the broken banisters of the staircase that could accommodate three women walking abreast wearing crinolines. He planned to turn his attention to the guttering, window frames, floor boards and in time to some of the leaks in the roof. He took me out of the flat into the cold to look at some plaster-work. 'I can gaze at it for hours.'

In the morning when he went off to Mallow I let myself out of the empty hall and explored the servants' quarters. Since the Georgian Society sticks to its title literally and largely ignores post-1830 buildings, the flagged kitchens, sculleries, dairies, larders, butler's pantry, the curious octagonal room with a wheel for hanging meat and the lines of stables and outhouses were all extremely decayed. The garden was less depressing, brightened by banks of daffodils beside the Awbeg. Somewhere here the young Harold Nicolson sat with Lord Castletown who persisted in talking about 'You English'. In the old gardener's cottage live Ruth and Megan Morgan who are trying to do for the garden what Arthur is doing for the house, clearing flowerbeds, making paths through matted vegetation and pinning back fruit trees to brick walls. I made my way past the spot where one of the St Legers used to hide in the bushes to leap out and ravish female servants, and went back to the gate.

I set out for Kanturk. 'It's a long wearisome road,' a man told me as if I was walking to Jerusalem. The morning was dank and misty. I stamped my feet and walked under an avenue of trees. A car gave me a lift for a few miles, careering along alarmingly because the driver had a hangover. He set me down at Ballyclogh where a castle looked down on the village from a surrounding farmyard. Saplings had sown themselves on the steps, and under the roof a stalk of ivy grew like fan vaulting. The farmer who owned it watched with surprise as I ferreted around the remains of the rooms. Those days were past, gone with the devil and the last cannon ball. And so had the landlords. He was hot against the local landlords who had departed a good while ago. Very wicked. The little church where they had worshipped had become a store.

When I stopped for a Guinness in the village the publican was amazed. 'By Jesus, you're a desperate man. Do your legs never get tired?' No countryman walks a yard if he can help. He quoted me 'twenty, youth ... thirty, strong ... forty, gone ... and no more a man.' He was so sorry for his ancient customer that he followed me in his car and gave me a lift to Cecilstown. This was another little village dominated by a castle, a magnificent tower called Lahort that stood out over the countryside like a factory chimney.

Lahort is a fifteenth-century MacDonagh MacCarthy stronghold built in the middle of a ringfort. After a Cromwellian battering it was reprieved and lived in by the Earl of Egmont. It continued to be a private residence which was most unusual, since the gentry usually avoided the old tower castles and built their houses elsewhere. In 1876 it was done up lavishly and an elaborate machicolated gateway added. Mr Hogan lives in it now, and he is suspicious of strangers. Arthur told me how he had paid a call, but all attempts to see the inside had been repulsed. He caught a glimpse of Dutch blue tiles in the kitchen before the door shut in his face. Other tourists, medievalists and curious people like me have been no more lucky.

In front of Lahort was strung a line of washing, and a TV aerial stuck out of a small window. Cattle browsed beside the Victorian gateway as Mr Hogan stood outside his medieval front door watching me closely. I talked about the castle's beauty, how unusual it was, and how I had heard that the 1876 repairs and oak furnishings had cost £20,000 which would have been something like £200,000 today. Could this have been possible? Mr Hogan interrupted me. 'I must get back to the machine.' He turned and ran inside, slamming the nail-studded door behind him. I knocked, but there was no answer, I looked up at the false parapets, but saw no sign of movement. I did not find out what the machine was, and my knowledge of the interior of Lahort remains confined to the 1831 description in the *Gentleman's Magazine*. 'The ground floor is now a dining parlour and above this is the drawing room. We then rise to the State Bedroom, besides which there are six others. From the battlements an extensive prospect is commanded ...'

Walking into Kanturk I hit the main road and traffic, a policeman on the bridge checking licences, old women in doorways and a creamery. The Dalua and the Allow rivers meet at Kanturk and flow united through the town. Outside, the sun filtered through the empty stone windows of Kanturk Castle, the fortified house built by the MacDonagh MacCarthys, Lords of Duhallow. It is smaller than it should be, because the Privy Council, like modern county councils, refused full planning permission on the grounds that the proposed building would be too large for a subject.

The Commercial Arms was full, since there was a cattle market the following day. The talk in the bar was of pigs and cattle. In the morning, buyers and farmers crowded into the dining-room, sitting around two lines of tables, their pints of stout and their fries in front of them. Last night we ate boiled bacon, turnips and potatoes in their skins, and now was the time for rashers, egg and sausage washed down with Guinness.

By seven o'clock fish was being sold in the square from the back of a van and a Pakistani trader had laid out a trestle of clothes. A little distance from his pullovers and underwear, two soldiers with guns stood at the ready outside the bank and a garda smoked a cigarette in a waiting car watching out for possible hold-ups. The Mart was just opposite the hotel where the dealers and sellers assembled among pens of cattle and sheep that had come out of lines of lorries from all over the country. The men in belted coats carrying their sticks had bad memories of the days of the old cattle markets when they had got up long before dawn on winter mornings and driven their beasts in many miles for sale. They recalled the sharp practices, the luck money, the dealers like raging wolves, the long hours standing huddled in the rain and the filth everywhere. The sales ring was better in every way.

The calves were prodded into the ring and the auctioneer's voice rattled as their future was settled. 'Sit down, lads . . . let the others see,' he called to the men with chiselled country faces and greasy macs. A farmer beside me in an old blue dustcoat whirled his hands as another batch of cattle blinked their eyes. Later, he offered me a lift to Ballydesmond.

The rain began to fall as the soft Arcadian landscape was abruptly replaced by reedy fields and hills. The Kingdom of Kerry was approaching, marked by the bridge at Ballydesmond. 'We think we are in the most miserable and wet part of Ireland,' my companion Richard Leader said. The old hotel where travellers used to stop before going on into Kerry was closed and shuttered, the lettering above the door peeling. But in the cosy parlour behind Richard's shop I was given a meal and a seat by the fire and offered a bed for the night.

Richard's farm looked towards the undulating Paps, and behind them the Killarney mountains, suffused in mist, hovered above a scrawny countryside that could break a man's heart.

A farmer, singing to himself, was scything rushes, while back at his house his wife was engaged in providing food for the Stations. Each family in the neighbourhood took its turn in preparing bowls of trifle, sandwiches and cakes to be eaten after the priest said Mass. Across the road in the pub a score of bachelor farmers were enjoying themselves with rebel songs and talk.

I drank with Timothy O'Sullivan the postman, who knew every corner of the land after fifty years of cycling the roads. He told me the original Gaelic name for Ballydesmond meant Place of the Rushes – more appropriate than the later name of King Williamstown. That could have been after King William all right, but more likely it was after the planter hereabouts, Sir William Pelham. All that had been largely shot out of memory. He recited a local poem about the source of the Blackwater.

It rushes forth with its incarnation
Through rocky cascades it rushes down
And ceases not its agitation
Until it reaches King Williamstown.

The brook flowing under Ballydesmond's stone bridge became the wide waterway I had explored below Cappoquin. I looked for the source in the direction of Mount Eagle and Knockanefune in a wilderness of tossed clouds and bogs where a small clear pool bubbled up between rocks and a stream tumbled down at the beginning of the run to Youghal and the ocean.

It rises on the border of Cork and Kerry
Among the moors and the mountains high
With heather clad hills and bluish berries
Stains the heart with a purple dye . . .

Coming down the track I met a forestry worker who invited me to his house. Almost before my feet were inside the door his mother was making me my second huge breakfast of the morning.

Tis the haven home for the hunted stranger
With its valleys fair and hills sublime;
There the noble Desmond from debt and danger
Once found a refuge in Meenganine.

The land of rushes, maintaining the old tradition of hospitality, had welcomed me as if I had been the noble Desmond himself.

8
Paps · Dingle · Shannon

On the last day of April I followed a side-road into the Paps which led to a penitential station. A shrine to the Virgin stood in an ancient ringfort that looked out from the mountain slope back to Ballydesmond and the hills that held the secret of the Blackwater's rising. This was the same part of the Kerry where I had seen St Brighid's Day celebrated. There was also a farmhouse in the ring which was about a hundred yards across, and the old man who came out to watch me setting up my tent was the latest and very likely the last to struggle for existence in a place that had been settled in Neolithic times. His name was Tim O'Sullivan, the same as the postman at Ballydesmond. He had a collarless buttoned-up shirt, a grey jacket and carried a pitchfork.

'Are ye opening a bar?' he asked. 'Are ye selling anything?' The sight of my activities stirred memories. It was many years since he had seen a tent here. He could just recall days almost gone out of memory when a world of people from all over Cork and Kerry used to come to this sacred spot. But didn't they still? I asked him. I wanted to be here on May morning to witness their arrival.

'You'll have a share of people but no entertainment to hold the crowd.' It was not at all like the old days when booths and tents were crowded into the ring and all May Day there was merriment.

I climbed a rounded shoulder – not the right word – of one of the aggressively symbolic Paps and tramped over the wind-blown body of the Goddess. Other deities besides Anan stirred in these parts, mocking the Christianity that had conquered them, leaving their signs, standing stones and dolmens scattered among the fields and blazing spring gorse. Blackfaced sheep and lambs grazed on the spongy slope facing the distant reflections of the Killarney lakes.

In the morning the sides of the tent were wringing wet and outside the mist was low over the ancient ring. I squatted in the tent preparing breakfast with a wobbling gas burner, while the rooks cawed and the sun struggled to break through the clouds. In the next few hours a trickle of pilgrims came to the shrine. A family drove up the boreen in an ancient Morris Minor and while the children put a bunch of flowers in a jar below the Virgin's statue – they called her Criobh Derga – the parents prayed. Since the grandmother was cured of bad hips by the water they had been coming here every year. Their journey was in the true nature of pilgrimage because their home was far off at Ballyvourney on the other side of the Derrysaggert mountains. Here was a man from Millstreet kneeling on the broken steps, a woman with a rosary hanging from her hand and others filling up bottles. This water was good for cows about to calve, and for other animals too, when you had lost patience with the vet. It cured unexplained aches when the doctors shrugged their shoulders and took money from you for doing nothing. In all about a dozen people sought the benefits of the blessed water. Mostly they were old. The leaping around with sprigs of green rowan, or 'green', and young people dancing and bounding with joy were long over.

'The first big break in the festival came with the first world war,' Tim O'Sullivan said. 'It was the shortage of tents that killed it.' He was poised on a ladder painting his corrugated roof. His house in the ring was very small, the little windows looking over the grass to the statue of Our Lady standing above her flowers like the Goddess Anan. Later when all the pilgrims had gone I had a cup of tea inside in front of the open hearth with its blackened crane swinging over the fire. We sat under the devotional picture, myself, Tim and his friend Jimmy Cronin who had come in to cut his hair. They reminisced about the old days, the drinking, singing and dancing. And how from the first of May for the next sixteen days people came to pray and take the water. The old local name for the shrine was 'the city' most probably derived from the word cahir or fort. They cackled and chortled when I told them I was travelling on to Killarney.

'They'll skin you there.'

But after leaving them I did not linger in Killarney, still waiting for the tourist season to open. I managed to get a swift lift out to the Dingle peninsula. At Dingle fishing boats rested in the harbour, *Star Immaculate, Roving Swan, Silver Light.* On the road to Ventry the hawthorn was coming into bloom with the first fuchsia flowers that would soon thread scarlet through the west. Beneath them the bank was covered with primroses.

At Ventry harbour I took off my shoes to walk along the golden strand, curved like a torque, where the men from the Armada died. At Slea Head were the towering cliffs that Synge found overwhelming. 'They seemed ten times more grey and wild and magnificent than anything I had kept in my memory.'

Synge acknowledged the grandeur of nature in West Kerry which is reflected in the fine faces of local people. Before him, fastidious visitors found little to enthuse about and usually felt that they had come on an unnecessary trip to a savage place. Typical was a delicate traveller called Lydia Jane Fisher, who ventured to Dunquin in 1845, found her sensibilities disgusted by the dirt and rats, and referred to the people in a fearsome phrase as 'the limpets or aborigines of Dunquin'. 'Dunquin is the wildest place in the whole world ... the women dress like men and the men like women indiscriminately.' The weather did not help. Her cries of woe were spelt out in her *Letters from the Kingdom of Kerry*. 'It is pouring rain; a wet Sunday in Dingle; can anything be more doleful ... we had intended to have gone to Ventry to church, but here we are ... confined ... crabbed ... what is it to us that the Atlantic is near? We cannot see it, we cannot hear it. What is it to us that we are surrounded by mountains? They are shrouded in mist.'

One wonders if Miss Fisher encountered Asenath Nicholson who in the summer of 1845 reached Dunquin with blistered feet having walked from Dingle. Mrs Nicholson was taken to a rock known as Nancy Brown's Parlour and sat on a seat like a stone settee watching the women on the strand, some with jugs and some with seaweed, and the children picking shells. As ever on her encounters with the poor she was impressed by their simplicity and kindness, and here at Dunquin by the beauty of the women. 'When I looked on these Kerry girls I thought shall I pity such loveliness? The mountain breeze is ever fanning their dark hair; they know nothing and heed nothing of the vain show of the world, but are content when at night they have herded their flock to lie down in their cabins till the early dawn shall again summon them to the mountains.'

Although she was forever trying to draw the Irish people nearer to her God, she nevertheless respected their faith. At Dunquin she had nothing but admiration for the old priest whom she met 'sitting by his fire ... surrounded with Latin authors ... and antiquated looking books in Hebrew, Greek and Latin ... Never in Ireland had I spent an hour where so much real knowledge had fallen on my ear . . .' Her spirit was truly ecumenical. In general on her travels she was critical of the evangelism then prevalent through the West of Ireland. She sought out missionaries and men of God all over the place and judged them rather like a representative of a food guide visiting a restaurant nowadays.

Remembering the poverty and degradation that lingered into my own lifetime, I tried not to regret the smartness and the new bungalows. But oh, to have been here in Synge's time before the tourist buses and strings of cars. No notices offering accommodation and arrows pointing to beehive huts. No big white crucifix looking out at the Blaskets, no golf course or craft shops.

The spirit could not help feeling uplifted the further Dunquin was left behind. There were the views and the sky filled with larks. From time to time I passed a field with an ancient stone building. I watched two men on the bog cutting the fibrous red bank and loading up a sleigh; in a nearby field there was a ploughman digging the lines of sod with two bay horses. At Morestown I met Ed Hutchinson who builds currachs. After driving lorries in the daytime for the Kerry Co-op he trains crews in the evening to race in regattas around the coast. This year for the first time he was training girls. Boys and girls in jeans carried the long 'canoes' with their gleaming black skins down to the water to Ed's orders in English and Irish. The girls were nervous and plainly aware of the facts contained in Edith Somerville's observation that 'the currach has no keel and a sneeze is rightly believed to be fatal to its equilibrium'.

I watched the black craft flying across Ballydavid harbour. I sat on the beach near the bloated remains of a dolphin and a shark and a boatload of freshly-netted salmon far more abundant than the rewards of the men on the Blackwater. Across Morestown I could see Mount Brandon and determined to climb it.

The road from the village led straight towards the big brown mountain which dominates the sky the way the Blaskets dominate the sea. St Brendan's lonely oratory was a fleck near the top. I rested on a stone wall near a field of iris while John Francis of Shanakeel, who was bringing back two empty churns from the creamery, halted his rattling milk cart and offered me a lift. I climbed in and we jogged along, the sun in our faces, the air full of the sound of larks singing over the bog. He told me his pony was fourteen years old and wouldn't be going on much longer. The harness was just about impossible to replace and it was hardly worth decking the old fellow in a new outfit.

Near Ballybrack among some old farm buildings he pointed out the Casan na Naomh, the beginning of the Saint's road, the pilgrim's route up Brandon. The old pattern day of June 26 had been changed – 'they threw it out'. Now it was May 16 in a few days' time. I would miss it, and climbed alone.

Very little remained of the track. But visibility was clear and I made the long climb without difficulty to St Brendan's cell which gives a special focus for pilgrimage. No one can fail to be moved by the thought of the lonely contemplate crouching here in wind and mist, or, when God swept the cloud away, gazing at a view that cleansed worldly desires. The sea glinted from the sandy isthmus to the north round to Dingle and Slea Head, always the Blaskets, and in the distance the cones of the Skelligs where St Finan, Sweeney o' the Skellig, Elann of Skelligs, Balthac, Cormac the anchorite and other holy men found an even more spectacular sanctuary from the vanities of secular life. But to the west the sun was an enticement and you could believe that St Brendan descended from his cell on an impulse to embark on his fabulous voyage.

Getting down the north side of Brandon would try any saint. Notices in Irish indicated the way or told of precipices – which? AIRE! CNOC CEAR painted on a worn and rusty red triangle was plainly a warning, but of what exactly? Who cared if the non-Gaelic speaker took the wrong path and plummeted to his doom? Cliffs loomed, the perpendicular track fell down into a tangle of lakes and rocks while the wind tormented me and threw me off balance. And yet this side must be considered the easiest since the saint's road by which I had climbed is the less popular route for pilgrims to climb. Or do those choosing this side seek martyrdom? 'Bishop Casey did it twice,' John Francis had told me, comparing the fortitude of the higher clergy. 'Bishop MacNamara didn't.'

Above me loomed the escarpment leading to the Conair Pass. I was glad to reach the bottom. I walked by Lake Cruttia and picked my way off the rocks into bogland with Cloghane at my feet. A lane swept me down towards the sea.

'Are ye a Dublin jackeen?' a man called after me. There was no malice in his voice, but he was reminding me that I had been unwise.

No one should climb Brandon alone. Almost every year some foolhardy person is caught in cloud.

The bare mountain splendour was behind me and here again were thick fuchsia hedges and lush vegetation. A farmhouse painted Madonna blue and another Tahitian pink heralded Cloghane, a little faded place with a thin main street and a muddy strand. The old long-closed shoemaker's shop with its faded lettering is ruinous, while the church next door sprouts grass and weeds. There are those who can remember the priest taking Mass in Irish there, but the language has died out. At Morestown Irish is still strong; the old lady who sold me sweets in the morning had sold them in English and counted her change in Irish. But, although Cloghane is officially in the Kerry Gaeltacht, Brandon acts as a language barrier. 'We'll do anything but speak Irish here.'

Cloghane has other clerical ruins like the lonely shell of a Protestant church where coastguards sang 'Fight the Good Fight' and sheep eat the grass among the tombstones. A few yards away Crom Dobh gazes out from the wall of a ruined medieval church with a look of ferocious dismay. He was bested not only by St Brendan but by St Patrick himself, who tamed the famous wild bull. Crom Dobh became a Christian with some regrets, according to the expression of this battered ancient head with its missing chin and protruding disgruntled eyes.

At Fermoyle beach I took off my boots and began walking. The beach around Ventry had been a sandpit compared to the eight-mile expanse before me. The hard sand was under my feet; the case of a crab glowed like brick in a wreath of seaweed. I was lucky. Behind me a cloud had fallen over Brandon and the saint's oratory, and today the yawning precipices and the views were curtained off.

A seal slipped off a rock as I reached the road. I had a drink at Fahamore's pub before walking to Kilshannig. Beyond Rough Point I could see the Magharees or Seven Hogs scattered on the sea. St Brendan chose the mountain for his retreat and a hermit called St Seannach selected one of these little islands where his prayers fell among fishes and birds. Was there competition for these outposts, rivalry among ascetics for the most lonely, comfortless and exhilarating parts of the wilderness? When Arthur Young visited the area these islands were famous for their crops of corn and people lived on them happily. But they have been deserted for a long time, and now only the cattle, landed there for pasture, watch the fishermen pull lobster pots as they toss in the dark sea behind them.

At Castlegregory I had the largest breakfast of my life – toast, two eggs, six sausages, slabs of hairy bacon, tomatoes and black pudding, washed down by very strong tea. I felt like a Japanese Sumo wrestler as I devoured it, watched by the owner of the house who was eating a solitary boiled egg. I was well fortified to walk the long straight road from Castlegregory to Tralee. But I had got a lift and was driven away from Lough Gill and its swans and rushes and the spectacle of houses floating above the flat sandy landscape.

In the nineteenth century Tralee was much used by travellers who stopped there on the way to or from Killarney. The town has rows of houses 'built in the height of English fashion' which made it a last outpost before the more adventurous sought out 'all that was wild and uncultivated in Ireland'. Some visitors got a great welcome. When Prince von Pückler-Muskau came he was taken for Napoleon. 'Long life to Napoleon, your honour,' shouted the throng who watched his coach making its way through the dusty streets. When Henry Inglis arrived he sat beside the coachman. The streets were thronged with carts and people, a little boy marched before blowing a trumpet; while the driver, with an air of extraordinary importance, bawled out the 'boys' and the 'gintlemen' to make room for His Majesty's Mail Coach.

From Tralee I went by bus towards the Stack mountains. Occasionally a farmer down on the road held up his hand for us to stop or a woman with a shopping bag climbed in panting and settled herself in her seat with a sigh of satisfaction as if she had been before a blazing fire. I got out at Ballyheige and walked towards Kerry Head, a rocky ten-mile hammerhead of land and rock reaching out into the Atlantic and guarding the mouth of the Shannon.

Near the ruined church of St Erc an old man watched his terrier scratch for a rabbit.

'Sit down beside me on the bank and take your breath. Your legs will be crushing you on the road.' I basked in the sun beside a patch of bluebells and looked back south to Mount Brandon, and the Magharees low and black in the water. My companion talked of his eighteen years in England including the war years. He had worked with a group of fellow Irishmen on an RAF airfield and the bombs raining down. Only the Irish prayed. He'd stayed on for a bit afterwards. 'I'll tell you something. I could have married thousands of times, and there were plenty of women.' He had preferred to remain alone and return at last to the peace of his farm overlooking the sea.

The sun went abruptly, the fringes of light vanishing behind cloud. Drops of rain fell. 'Blast it, won't it ever make up its mind?' The fickle weather changed instantly and the sun returned to recharge the bright colours of grass, hay, gorse and even turf, glowing like brown velvet, as well as the long houses above fields that melted into the sea which were decorated with shells and bands of pastel paint and topped with thatch held down by rope.

When the road came to an end I walked past luminous patches of gorse to view the watery expanse from Kerry Head to Loop Head. Just visible across the Shannon, perched on the river's edge, was Carrigaholt, a roofless castle with a savage history. When de Latocnaye first caught sight of the Shannon he decided to go for a swim at its mouth. 'He is not truly an Irishman who has not yet plunged into it, and as I desired to do always in Rome as the Romans do, a plunge into the Shannon was my first operation here.'

Where did he take his dip? How did he get down off this headland? A cutter told me that there were some places where you could climb down to the sea. They were dangerous. A few years back three people were washed off a rock and the currents were something fierce and to remember. De Latocnaye must have been directed down to the water where he would have put down his bundle and removed his wig, hat, silk coat, pantaloons and black stockings before plunging naked into the chilly magnificent water.

The Shannon used to serve passengers as well. It is not so long since 'you could go by steamer to Limerick for half a crown with a bar thrown in'. Today the ferry that crosses the bulging river, in so short a time that passengers stay in their cars, is the vestige of the elaborate service that once plied up and down. But there is enough time to view the lovely scene, and perhaps, like John Forbes, who crossed in a steamer in 1840, to consider its sublime nature. 'No one could contemplate this grand mass of water sweeping calmly and silently onwards without feeling that he is looking on something more than beauty.' A tanker clawed its way towards the Amazon-wide mouth and the undulating water gleamed in the evening light round Scattery Island pierced by its Round Tower.

9
Limerick · Slieve Aughty · Burren

At Kilrush I gave a quick look at the old quays and the impressive main street dominated by the monument of the Manchester Martyrs 'judicially murdered by a tyrannical Government' before retiring to Crotty's Bar. A wait beside the long wooden counter sipping stout preceded the bus to Limerick. The Georgian period is so much associated with Irish city architecture that one is inclined to forget that the bulk of Limerick, like Cork, and indeed Dublin, had been until recently a sadly run down Victorian town. When Thackeray viewed the vibrant colourful bustling streets full of apple women selling green fruit, of dragoons and carriages filled with pretty girls, he wrote, amazingly: 'I never saw a greater number of kind, pleasing, clever-looking faces among any set of people.'

By the time Robert Graves arrived for garrison duty with the Welch Fusiliers the tumbledown buildings formed his lasting impression of Ireland. 'Limerick looked like a war-ravaged town . . . many of the big houses seemed on the point of collapse. Old Reilly told me nobody built new houses . . . when one fell down the survivors moved into another. He also said that everyone died of drink in Limerick except the Plymouth Brethren who died of religious melancholia.'

From early times the town has inspired oddly grotesque comment from visitors like Monsieur de la Boullaye le Gouze who reported after visiting the stews in 1644 that 'Limerick is filled with a great number of profligate women . . . which I could not have believed because of the climate'; or Sir John Carr, who in 1802, after eating some excellent cow beef, went off to inspect the house of correction. His prosaic narrative – for Carr was a notoriously boring writer – suddenly became lurid and terrible with his descriptions of naked madmen standing in the rain, prostitutes in chains dragging around heavy logs, squatting idiots and starving, half-naked, half-famished diseased women shrieking for covers against the cold.

So it's a relief to see modern Limerick as a pleasant developing provincial town knocking down its ancient heritage and putting up office blocks, chain stores, and such like. Old landmarks linger like the Protestant Young Men's Association, and Cruise's Hotel has been transformed from my childhood. The highlight of the journey from Dublin to Kerry was always a sojourn in the dining-room full of gilded mirrors and heavy sideboards stifled by Sheffield plate. (Thackeray: 'A very large and complete establishment, certainly one of the best in Ireland.' Carlyle: 'Cruise . . . a lean eager-looking little man of forty . . . ambitious-bad dinner, kickshaws (sweet breads, salmon etc.) and uneatables.')

I had come to Limerick to follow the fortunes of John Stevens, the English Jacobite, an earlier visitor who saw the city at its most desolate moment. Stevens was a fervent supporter of the exiled King James II and came to Ireland in his army resolved to 'follow him through all hazards in the hope of being instrumental in regaining his just rights'. Stevens wrote a dispirited account of his experiences as a defeated soldier, first at the battle of the Boyne and the rout that followed, then as a member of the besieged garrison at Limerick. His experiences during the siege were dreadful. The soldiers were supposed to camp in the neighbourhood of the town, but all the tents had been lost at 'the unfortunate day at the Boyne' as was most of the army's baggage.

During the winter of 1690 Stevens had the greatest difficulty in finding provisions for himself, since like the rest of the Anglo-Irish Jacobite army he had been paid in brass money which shopkeepers refused to accept. Exasperatingly, King James's French allies were paid in silver coin. A captain's subsistence, which was a crown a day, 'would yield but a quart of ale and that very bad'. When brass money ran out there was no pay at all. The barefoot and ragged soldiers endured terrible hardships, starving in torrents of rain while they tried to defend the old town from a strong disciplined Williamite army. In due course Limerick was destroyed. 'When first I saw this city about four years before, it was inferior to none in Ireland but Dublin and not to very many in England, and I have lived to see it reduced to a heap of rubbish . . . such are the effects of war, and such the fruits of rebellion.'

After the siege Stevens retreated northward over boggy country towards Galway. He reached Scarriff and then plunged into the wilds of the Slieve Aughty mountains. I picked out his route at Scarriff on the south-west of Lough Derg. You would not expect much of Scarriff after reading about it in Stevens's memoirs or from Carlyle ('dim extinct-looking hungry village') or from Edna O'Brien whose home town it is. But the town was buoyant and prosperous this sunny day in May, benefiting from the sleek Shannon cruisers roaring through and the Merriman festival. Near the Merriman Inn a small casino filled with one-armed bandits welcomed screaming excited children.

The Slieve Aughty mountains reach down to Lough Derg where Mountshannon, a pretty landlord town ('a very Prod looking city', Edna O'Brien's mother described it), and nearby Holy Island, Inis Cealtrac, the island of churches, are civilized and beautiful attractions for tourists. But few visitors leave the lake to explore the hills behind which in some ways are only a little less wild than when Stevens found them.

When I walked into them I was immediately lost in mist, and stumbled about until I came to a farmhouse where I could ask the way from an old man and his sister sitting in front of their open hearth. They were no use at all. They did not seem to have moved much for fifty years. He needed new glasses and couldn't read my map.

'If you don't know the mountains you'll never come out of them. They're all bog.'

At so short a distance from the new-mown lawns, tubs of flowers and the Chinese Dove Tree at Mountshannon I followed a path of sorts over little brown rolling hills covered in mist. Centuries ago they were heavily forested, forming part of the great oak wood of Suidan cut down long before Stevens arrived. Now when the mist blew aside I could see the occasional patch of conifers like a hair transplant. Not a soul seemed to live here. There had once been a community because I found an abandoned school, a long room set in the middle of a bog with a fireplace at each end. Name and date were chiselled on the entrance, Gunrakely National School – 1845. National schools like these were first established in 1831. By the time Gunrakely was built there were about three thousand, attended by over three hundred thousand children. The irregular, uneven, eccentric, sometimes marvellous, sometimes terrible hedge schools that taught Virgil, Horace, *Paradise Lost*, the poems of Ossian, the Life and Death of Robert Emmett, the History of Freeny the Robber and other miscellaneous subjects to the ragged young were destroyed, their masters driven to drink or sent to the workhouse. The famine more or less eliminated classical education and something more basic took its place. I sheltered by the flaking wall chewing a sandwich and thought of the children of Gunrakely learning the three R's and religious instruction given separately according to faith.

On my map I noticed Lake Atorick which seemed a possible place to camp. Instead of making straight for its waters I began to look around for one of Dermot and Grania's numerous stony beds, and lost my bearings from Gunrakely in the mist. Then coming down over the brow of the hill I found a pool of black water surrounded by more hills and bogs with a plantation of trees on the far side. The green and red bog mosses around it were suddenly brilliant in sunlight and the water sparkled like jet.

I camped beside some black rocks and a bed of reeds. Yesterday the surface of Lough Derg had been blown and scattered by a south-east wind, but tonight was dead calm on Lake Atorick. I cooked my dinner on a wisp of sand. Sounds were heard clearly in the stillness, the plop of fish rising all over the lake, distant sheep, a cuckoo and water birds. A heron pounded across my vision and a couple of ducks rose frantically.

John Stevens blundered somewhere along his way, his musket and bag on his shoulders. I seemed to see him exhausted from his long march, his clothes torn and mud-soaked – his ragged shirt, his eighteen-pound brass money suit ('the button holes wrought with worsted') and his pointed shoes ('five pounds brass'). He considered himself 'a signal sufferer for his religion, his King, and for Justice and Loyalty' and it appears that most of his suffering came not from fighting which was hard enough, but from discomfort that culminated in the retreat from Limerick. 'At Scarriff begins one of the most desert wild barbarous mountains that ever I beheld and runs eight miles outright, there being nothing to see upon it but rocks and bogs, no corn, meadows, houses or living creatures, not so much as a bird.' The weather drowned out birdsong. Throughout his time in Ireland, from his arrival in Bantry to the dreary winter in Dublin, then the retreat from the Boyne followed by the forced march to Limerick and another horrible winter, the weather had been terrible. When he came to the Slieve Aughty, 'this day we marched about four miles of the mountain, a violent rain falling most part of the time which made the way extreme toilsome afoot, the long sedge twisting about the feet, and the bog sucking them up, as that which immediately draws to the water, being naturally soft and yielding. For our comfort at night we had a bare bog to lie on without tents or huts or so much as the shelter of a tree, hedge or bank. The rain held most part of the night.'

He spent the night near here stretched out on the boggy morass beside his exhausted companions. Lying with his head burrowed in his tattered cloak, the rain soaking every part of him, he must have reflected that he was never meant to be a soldier. He had been Collector of the Excise at Welshpool. But he was an adherent to the old religion and the accession of William of Orange disgusted him. In January 1689, he left England to join James II at St Germain near Paris and become 'a voluntary exile for love of his prince'. Then he had been sent to Ireland to the miseries of a defeated campaign.

The long range of hills was deserted except for the odd lonely farmhouse. I walked slowly, my rucksack heavier than the day before because of the rain that had fallen on the tent during the night. Since leaving Scarriff I had come across no settlement or shop, and even when I hit the main road to Gort I found the same emptiness. I passed a forestry plantation scorched by fire with blackened stalks of trees and pools of grey ash through which sprouted bright green growth. Some miles on a farmer gave me some milk. He was standing outside his small house cutting reeds. Nothing would get rid of them, he said. The ground was like a man's face; the reeds came up strong like a new beard after shaving.

At Moyglass I found a post office with funeral wreaths propped in the window and pipe tops threaded through with string. I drank four bottles of fizzy orange juice before pressing on. 'You must follow the cows,' a man said leaning on a gate. They ambled on the curling mountain road that danced ahead through more hills. Sometime in the late afternoon I reached a small stream and an arched stone bridge. Below was a ruined cottage with a broken roof and walls where an ash seedling had sprouted.

Again I needed milk. Hill farming country was around me, and yet neither the woman near the bridge nor the old man at the thatched cottage or the women way beyond in the lonely house with its attendant ancient Morris Minor and barking dog had a drop to spare. I returned to the stream and pitched my tent, watched by another old farmer who was on his way home.

'I wouldn't sleep there if they gave me all Ireland.' Later I was standing on the bridge talking to him, when the woman I had approached earlier came up on a bicycle. In one hand she held a whiskey bottle full of milk.

'This is for you. There's a parcel under the bush,' she said before riding off. When eventually the garrulous old man trailed away I looked up to where she had pointed and found a brown paper parcel which contained a large slab of cake. I drank tea with milk and ate fruit cake beside the stream flowing through a field of cowslips.

When I came out of the tent in the morning a hare was waiting which ran off at the sight of me. I went to thank Miss Spain – she had given me the cake – and took a photograph of her standing before her door. Beyond her house was another empty school which had a horse tethered to what used to be the bicycle stand.

After walking all morning I began to see signs of cleared farm land. I had walked three days from Scarriff following John Stevens and only one small shoulder of the Slieve Aughty was before me. Beyond was the main road passing the concrete slab where they used to do the dancing, and a granite gate belonging to some old house with four smiling lions looking down. Here is what John Stevens said about the end of this stage of his journey.

'We marched to Loughrea six miles ... all the country hitherto is wild, mountainous and in my judgement may be called barren, but some people are blinded with affection that they will not allow the worst soil to be called barren, because it produces fern and wild sedge which the miserable cattle are forced to feed upon.'

He was a mild enough man, 'a very honest young man', Tyrconnel called him when he recommended him for a commission. After the flight over the Slieve Aughty to Loughrea he fled out of Ireland and retired as a soldier. Eventually he came to terms with the changes in England and settled in London where he took to scholarly pursuits. He had spent part of his youth in Spain and Portugal since his father had been in the service of Catherine of Braganza. Now he translated a number of books from Spanish and Portuguese as well as Bede's *Ecclesiastical History of England*. His reminiscences of his Irish experiences written long after his rebellious youth had passed were described as *A Journal of my Travels since the Revolution containing a brief account of all the War in Ireland, impartially related and what I was an Eye-Witness to, and deliver upon mine own knowledge distinguished from what I received from others, with an account of all our marches, and other memorable passages wherein I took a part, since first I had the honour of a commission in His Majesty's Army in Ireland*. It remained unpublished – Jacobite literature was not popular in the London of his time – until the manuscript was rescued and edited in 1912.

Last time I was in Gort, Glynn's Hotel was distinguished in a startling way by a big glass case full of scarlet, orange and black tropical birds. They had come from Coole at the time it was pulled down. Witnesses of the dance-like glory that those walls begot, they had the indignity of being removed, first from Lady Gregory's old home and then finally thrown out of Glynn's. I dedicated a moment's memory to that laurelled head and rejected the idea of a drink from the ample bar that had been shovelled out from Glynn's interior.

The heat made Gort Mediterranean and people were sitting outside. I sat on a bench beside a woman sipping orangeade outside the Stirrup Bar. The sun invaded arthritic limbs so that an old man who came by greeting her courteously had a sprightly step.

'Madam.'

'Yourself. He's eighty,' she murmured as he turned the corner. A horse and flower-bedecked cart trundled past bearing a long-haired family looking like well-organized tinkers.

'English ... are they right or are we?' Dirty little children climbed down, their arms full of flowers. She had been to a party given by that type. The pinewood dresser was beautiful and she had admired the stereo. She hadn't liked the meditating bit. They were all over County Clare.

I had another pint inside. 'We're in for a spell of hot weather,' the man behind the bar said, his face perspiring, his tie unloosened, a touch of panic in his voice. Like many countrymen he regarded a heatwave with the dread inspired elsewhere by a hurricane. His forebodings were fulfilled, for next day, too, the sun shone. It was Ascension Day and the church sucked up people like a vacuum cleaner leaving the sunbaked street empty. I tried the Church of Ireland to find that it had been turned into a public library with bookshelves instead of pews. No one had the heart to take away the memorials. George Hugh Gough, died March 1900, third Viscount Gort, late Governor of Ceylon ... Lady Gregory's husband. Most likely he had brought back the tropical birds.

Thwarted of prayer I retired again to the bench outside the Stirrup

Bar and read Carlyle, savouring the moment when he thundered down on Gort.

> Bog round us now; pools and crags; Lord Gort's park wall, furze, pool and peatpot desolation just outside; strong contrast within ... poor Lord has now a 'receiver' on him ... approach to Gort; Lord Something-else (extinct now, after begetting many bastards) it was he that planted these ragged avenues of wood – not quite so ugly still as nothing; – troublous hugger mugger aspect of stony fields and frequent, nearly all, bad houses on both sides of the way. Haggard eyes at any rate. Barrack big gloomy dirty; enter Gort at last. Wide street sloping swiftly; the Lord Something-else's houses – quaintish architecture is now some poor house ... dim big greasy looking hotel ... to bed; snoring monster in some other room; little sleep; glad it was not wholly none.

I could think of no other writer who conveyed the sad period with similar immediacy. Would the reminiscences have been so vivid if he had visited at some less terrible time? He used stream of consciousness long before Joyce put thoughts into Leopold Bloom's mind. From here he took the Limerick–Galway coach ('stones, stones – with greenest islets here and there'). While he puffed and blew his way to Galway I left sun-drenched Gort for the Burren.

I had a drink in Ballyvaughan among the tourist cottages in a bar decorated by a print of Dr Bryden making for Jallalabad. Then I spent the night in a hotel called the Ritz. It was one of a collection of shabby hotels which is Lisdoonvarna.

'Do you want to buy one?' a man in the street asked me. Chairs were piled under glass balconies where dried-up geraniums stood on dusty window sills. The Imperial and the Savoy were empty and I had the Ritz to myself. The new dance hall waited for the opening of the short season. May was too early for the formidable pop festival whose excesses have become legendary, or the smooth September season traditionally associated with simpering nuns and bachelor farmers.

The hotels, built over a hundred years, are now too many for the visitors who come. The tremendous hulk of the Thomond rotted visibly, window frames sagged and floors were scattered with fallen plaster and wormy boards. But the turreted Spa still did business, and now the pump room was open. The sick and hypochondriacal could walk past Ellison's Patent Rush Preventive turnstile to take the waters. (They would have to wait a couple of months to dip into the old wide enamel baths aided by pulleys and chains with wooden handles.) According to the old notice in the pump room the eggy water which I sipped from a thick glass contained sulphuretted hydrogen ten times more powerful than the equivalent at Harrogate. It was good for the bowels. The pump was dated 1892, but invalids had been drinking the clouded liquid for years before that, when Lisdoonvarna had a well-established reputation for gaiety, match-making and relaxation for holidaying clerics. 'A favourite resort of Irish priests,' noted *Murray's Guide*, adding that 'English visitors may see much of Irish Life and character in the evening parties that are temporized at the Lisdoonvarna hotel'. The appeal of Lisdoonvarna had been to Irish people. When the Walking Tourist toured the Spa in 1865 (in carpet slippers because his feet were sore) he noted it to be 'still in a rude state' and thought that 'if it is to be wished to attract English visitors it is essential that springs should have their proper surroundings'. But English visitors never came in any number, nor foreign tourists. The attractions of Alpine flowers and sulphuretted water were too specialized and even when the big hotels were built the Spa, tucked away in barren limestone hills, had none of Killarney's appeal.

I went to the Carran depression which is a huge turlough, a lake that rises and falls with the seasons. Under water in winter, in May it was a smooth green expanse of grass like a steppe. I searched out the University centre which had been established for the study of flowers, insects, rocks, reptiles, ferns, pinemartens, turloughs and other things to be seen in the Burren. I found Francis Bonham who was researching into the habits of feral goats. Although goats in Ireland are domesticated, there are a number of herds which consist of animals that have reverted to the wild. Their numbers are added to by further escaping domestic animals. Two such herds live in the Burren on remote mountains, as agile and timid as chamois. There is fear that they may be doing damage to the unique flora of the region as they range over the limestone plateau and hills. No one has yet seen a wild goat with a gentian sticking out of its mouth, but if a gentian came its way it would eat it. Fran's task was to investigate the range and diet of these creatures and to monitor the destruction wrought by their grazing habits.

He took me to Lough Gelain, another turlough, its rim an orange crust, its centre, blue as an eye, diminishing day by day under the hot May sun. Above the water rose Mullagh More, one of the most distinctive mountains of the Burren with a limestone terrace ascending in a helix to a flattened top which makes it look like a mountain in a medieval painting – Dante's Purgatory or Brueghel's Tower of Babel. Mullagh More, a name of evil association, means simply, a large hilltop.

The sun shone down on slabs of stone like coffin lids that tinkled as we walked on them. In the crevices between were patches of grey grass sprinkled with small rare flowers. In the turlough mud itself grew a pale violet, and round its edge were silvery green bushes with a few yellow flowers of a rockrose that likes to have its winter dip in the rising waters. We walked by flowerbeds containing mountain avens like creamy daisies, gentians, and a score or so of dull pearly little orchids that were the rarest of the rare. Round the base of the mountain were hazel woods where we waded through garlic, a flower that has lost its reputation for beauty like a lovely lady with B.O. The sloping terrace of Mullagh More gave views towards Lake Inchiquin and the Burren's edge of stony landscape silvered by small lakes, patches of hazel scrub and limestone patterned like lizard skin. Every now and again Fran would point out juniper trees that his goats had nibbled down to topiary.

Towards the summit he looked for the animals of which there was no sign. He collected some turds, put them in a box and inspected enclosures that he had wired off to study what happened to vegetation untroubled by goats. He swept his binoculars round the curving mountains with the horrifying suggestion that we should ascend another one. Then I watched him making gestures as he pointed to the next mountain where a number of animals were moving like lice. He said he could tell each goat apart by its markings and had named them after his friends. It was hardly the close relationship between man and beast as demonstrated by those handsome girls in Africa who get grants to go and live with gorillas.

I left him to wander over less formidable landscape. Not all the land was flat rock by any means – much has been cleared and now the pasture was vivid green like young wheat. Fields and lanes were edged with hawthorn that was occasionally tinged with pink. At Castletown three fat geese strutted across a bright green field. There was the stump of a castle among buttercups and rusty farm machinery. I talked to a man leading in a mare and a nine-day-old foal.

'I don't know if there is any history attached to the old castle, but I suppose there is.' He hated the fine weather. 'We need rain every few weeks because of the light soil.' Sunlight shimmered over the Carran depression; here was a dolmen and another view of Mullagh More and Lake Inchiquin, here was a cowtrack leading down to a pool bubbling out of the rocks called the Seven Streams. Orange-tipped butterflies and a brimstone flicked near it, while water beetles scampered across its surface. Above me beside a gorge stocked with hazel a large ninth-century fort known as Cahercommaun once housed a community of farmers, craftsmen and ironsmiths. Now it is an impressive Zimbabwe sort of ruin far from any road and only a path leading to it. In the evening silence I pitched my tent inside the stone walls and sat for a while greatly satisfied.

'Hello there!' said a voice, 'enjoying yourself?' A round red face wearing glasses peered through the tent flap. 'Do you mind if we take photographs?'

Just because I had followed another route I had deluded myself that the signs indicating Cahercommaun were too obscure to lead people here. But the old fort with its unchanging atmosphere had become another cosy snapshot in an album back home. After the friendly old pair of tourists had left, my night in the wilderness was far from the mystic experience I had hoped for and became merely uncomfortable.

De Latocnaye mused about the strange scratched landscape of the Burren: 'It would seem that this country had been swept by the ocean in some great convulsion of the globe, and that the covering earth had been in this way removed. Here are to be seen plains of seven or eight miles without the least vestige of soil and without verdure other than that of a few hazel-nut bushes which grow in odd corners of the stones.' He exaggerated since the green verdure is there among the rocks. Like Lough Gur the Burren is scattered with reminders that men preferred fertile pastures untroubled by trees that have to be felled. Over the years, farmers, shepherds and warriors scattered their traces, dolmens, crosses, raths, enclosures and castles. Leamaneh at its crossroads, extended into a fortified house with stone-cut windows, is the most prominent, but I preferred the remoteness of Gleninagh Castle facing the sea with a holy well and a deserted garden full of lilac beside it. Up the stone staircase a pair of choughs had built a nest in a window niche which was full of scarlet-throated young wailing for food.

SUMMER

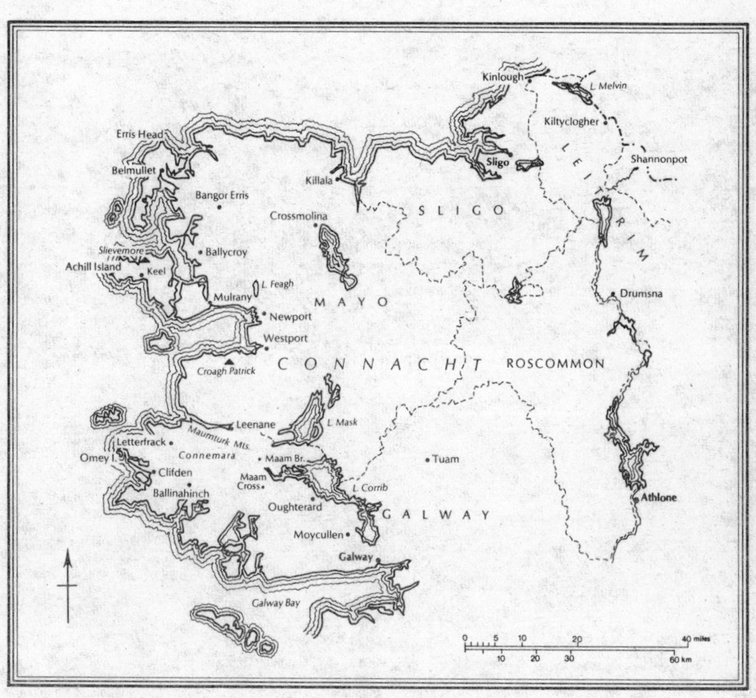

Kinlough
L. Melvin
Kiltyclogher
Erris Head
Belmullet
Sligo
Shannonpot
Killala
Bangor Erris
SLIGO
Crossmolina
Slievemore
Ballycroy
Achill Island
Keel
L. Feagh
Drumsna
Mulrany
MAYO
Newport
Westport
CONNACHT
ROSCOMMON
Croagh Patrick
Leenane
L. Mask
Maumturk Mts.
Letterfrack
Omey I.
Connemara
Maam Br.
Tuam
Clifden
Maam Cross
L. Corrib
Ballinahinch
Athlone
Oughterard
GALWAY
Moycullen
Galway
Galway Bay
40 miles
60 km

10
Galway · Ballinahinch · Clifden

The bus from Galway carried me past a suburban string of bungalows straining for a glimpse of Lough Corrib that lies to the right of the road. Beyond Moycullen I could see the square bulk of Ross House through the trees. Thackeray may have noticed it when he viewed 'shabby gentlemen's seats' from the Clifden car. I got down at the old entrance gates where the Martins of Ross kept their soup kitchen during the famine. The hungry people who flocked to it also followed to its resting place in Galway the corpse of Thomas Martin of Ballinahinch who died of famine fever. The procession of ragged mourners took two hours to pass these gates. That was suitable for a member of a family which considered itself the uncrowned monarchy of Connemara.

The Martins were Anglo-Normans who settled in Galway and became powerful. In the sixteenth century Robert Martin, High Sheriff and Mayor of Galway, obtained a large tract of land west of the town and established Ross as his country seat on the site of an O'Flaherty castle. From this point the Martins moved further westward and consolidated themselves at Dangan, Birch Hall and Ballinahinch. The branch of the family at Ballinahinch prospered the most, gathering to itself 200,000 acres of Connemara.

The Martins of Ross had more modest possessions because they remained Catholic and Jacobite until the mid eighteenth century when one of them married a Protestant neighbour for love. Their big grey house stands beside curving Ross Lake from which these Martins took their name. Behind this little lake through the sequestered trees shimmer the open waters of the Corrib.

One member of the Martins of Ross was Violet Martin, the friend, cousin and collaborator of Edith Somerville. The reputation of Somerville and Ross has held its corner of Anglo-Irish literature. Violet Martin wrote about her home affectionately and comprehensively. She described it as 'a tall unlovely block of great solidity', adding that 'a man is never in love till he is in love with a plain woman, and in spite of draughts, of exhausting flights of stairs, of chimneys that are the despair of sweeps, it has held the affections of five generations of Martins'.

The present Ross House, built in 1777 after the first burned down, is like a fortress, and Martin considered that the idea of defence was not absent from the builder's mind. Although the rebellion of 1798 did not put it to the test, it survived the great storm of 1839 which was known as 'The Big Wind'. 'My grandfather gathered the whole household into the kitchen for safety, and looking up at its heavily vaulted ceiling, said that if Ross fell, not a house in Ireland would stand that night. Many fell, but Ross House stood the assault, even though the lawn was white with spray borne in from the Atlantic six miles away.'

In an essay called the 'Biography of a Pump', Martin conveyed the atmosphere of a big house in the nineteenth century when 'vast and simple cooking operations' were conducted on an open grate four feet long. 'Vats of meat pickle lying in cellars where the light came greenly through ivied windows; cauldrons of potatoes and possibly cauldrons of punch; these formed the highest claims on the water-supply before the dynasty of the bath.' All over the house the turf boys, 'necessitated by an establishment where coal had never been seen and an armful of turf burned away in an hour', wandered barefoot between turf house and the kitchen and fireplaces of the house carrying either baskets of turf or buckets of water. They quarrelled endlessly with the cooks and housemaids. Martin described a New Year's Eve party in the coach-house when they filled a hip bath with hot whiskey and water. 'Then minutes later the bath was empty and a ring of boys radiated from it at full length lapping the last drops and even licking the enamel, while the dancing was resumed with startling emphasis.' In her disconcerting way she turned instantly from farce to something like poetry.

> Outside a light snow was on the ground, the North wind blew dark in that bitter midnight, and the ice on the lake uttered strange sounds – hollow musical shocks with the voice of the imprisoned water in them. Every tree in the woods stood separate in white silhouette, the rime sifting through the branches in a dry whisper. Upon this subtle mood of winter came forth from the open doors of the coachhouse the light of lamps with tin reflectors, the shrewish scream of the fiddle as Pete-een bawn jerked his white head in accord with 'The hare in the corn', the aroma of punch and cider and of clothes seasoned in turf smoke . . .

Such scenes were part of Violet Martin's early childhood. When her father died in 1872, 'the curtain fell for ever on the old life at Ross'. Her brother became an absentee and went to London. His choice was partly the result of political changes that affected the position of big landlords. We are assured that the Land Act of 1870 made no difference to Ross since evictions never occurred there, and the Martins had already evolved a system of tenant right. Like many people of her class Martin defended the old ways: 'the mutual dependence of landlord and tenant ... was a delicate relation, almost akin to matrimony, and like a happy marriage it needed that both sides should be good fellows.'

In 1872 there was an election in Galway when a Home Ruler was supported by the priest at Oughterard who was a fervent Nationalist. James Ross, Violet's father, naturally supported the opposing candidate and urged his tenants to do likewise. For the first time the people on the Ross estate did not follow the dictates of their landlord. On the day of the election, 'my father ranged through the crowd incredulously asking for this or that tenant, unable to believe that they had deserted him. It was a futile search; with a few valiant exceptions the Ross tenants ... voted according to the orders of their Church.' Undoubtedly the family felt deeply the destruction of the old balance of benevolence and trust; James Ross, believing he was betrayed, appears to have died of a broken heart. The tenants keened as they followed his coffin and the Martins of Ross departed.

Violet Martin, her mother and her mad sister returned to Ross sixteen years later. The house, ravaged by caretakers (ironic word), was in disrepair; their agent had embezzled funds and they had lost most of their land and their importance as landlords. Martin brought back the house from the brink of ruin almost entirely by her own efforts, spurred on by the terrible dutiful love that only an old house can inspire. Like Elizabeth Bowen she was aware of the 'semi-physical dream', that is the result of continuity and tradition. In a letter to her cousin Edith Somerville in July 1888, she exulted in the 'wonderful sleeping beauty palace air about everything, wildness and luxuriance and solitude'. According to Edith Somerville, she 'sacrificed herself to the Lares and Penates of Ross'. Almost alone she struggled with restoration, helped by a few people on the estate who remembered past glories and still had affection for the family. 'Her letters became full of house paintings, house cleanings, mendings, repairs of every kind.' The outside offered a similar challenge. The old yard where 'despairing creatures' had sheltered during the famine was waist high in weeds, and the rest of the garden had returned to nature. With Anglo-Irish vigour, Martin set about gardening. 'My hand is shaking from working on the avenue ... I mean cutting the edges of it, which will be my daily occupation for ever, as by the time I get to the end I will have to begin again, and both sides mean a mile and a quarter to keep right ... the tenants have been very good about opening and working here for nothing except their dinners ... It is of course gratifying, but in a way very painful.'

That letter was written over ninety years ago, and it was sad to see so much work and love gone to waste and Ross for all its solid appearance reverted to half-ruin and suffering badly from the lion and lizard syndrome. Still, it was an enchanted place, a dream house by its sickle of lake. This was just the sort of 'pensive evening' when Edith first saw Ross 'still and grey with a yellow spearhead of light low in the West ... with the brown mountain, Croach-Keenan and the grey sky. The woods of Annagh, of Bullivawnen, of Cluinamurnyeen, trail down to the lakeside, with spaces of grass and spaces of hazel and spaces of bog among them.' A pity about the large new suburban bungalow on the edge of the lake stridently combating the surrounding romantic tristesse.

In Oughterard Keoghs the grocer offered Green Drakes, Hackled Greens, Cock Robins, Bloody Butchers and Green Olives. The man in front of me asked for four flies and four pints of milk. A lone voice cried down the street: 'Have you any mayflies, lads?' Out from the rhododendrons at the pier stretched the cool grey waters of the Corrib with the distant towers of Ashford Castle visible beyond the islands and boats trawling busily. At sunset fishermen returned to their guest-houses and proudly laid out their trout. A guest read aloud from a newspaper: 'Corrib ... fair mayfly hatch with some boats taking three or four pound trouts in the day ... Oughterard area 134 trout, 164 lb in 78 rod days.'

Sporting fishermen have been coming to Oughterard for about a hundred and fifty years. When the Sportsman arrived in 1839 complaining about the 'Detestable vermin perch' which infested Corrib he was a pioneer. Previously the town was better known as a spa. Maria Edgeworth, who saw it in the autumn of 1833 at the first stage of her Connemara tour, found that 'the place has a kind of desolate look mixed with *pretensions* which a watering place out of season always has'. She had agreed to accompany her rich philanthropic English friends, the Cullen Smiths, who planned to tour Connemara. A year or so later she wrote a lively account of her adventures to her brother Pakenham Edgeworth out in India.

She and her companions arrived at dusk from Galway in the Cullen Smiths' lavish coach. They found their hotel 'half covered with overgrown ivy, damp, forlorn, windows broken, shattered look all about it! out came such a master and such a maid! and such fumes of whiskey punch and tobacco ... Sir Cullen got down from his barouche-seat shaking his head and telling us in French that it was quite impossible.' They tried the clergyman, magistrate and police and would have been hard pressed to find accommodation but for the kindness of a Mrs O'Flaherty who threw her sons out of their beds and gave them a room.

Later visitors or travellers walked around the town pursued by beggars. Thackeray was enraptured: 'a more beautiful village can scarcely be imagined.' As the nineteenth century advanced, increasing numbers of tourists flocked to the pretty spot. In his fulsome little *Tour of Ireland* published in 1892 Sir Reginald Hotes invited inspection of 'Oughterard ... termed the entrance to Connemara, pleasantly situated by Lough Corrib with its picturesque bridge, marvellous transparent stream, handsome constables and handsome church.'

It was to lampoon writers like this that the cousins Edith Somerville and Violet Martin set out from Oughterard in 1890 on their own idiosyncratic tour of Connemara. They wished to condemn gently the chatty tone of many current guides, particularly one which a friend had sent them 'written as it were in description of a tour made by an ingenuous family party'. Jack, very manly; the young ladies very ladylike, a kind and humorous mother, etc. Jack is much the most revolting. What disgusted Martin particularly was the way the book stressed 'the disappearance of the Martins from the face of the earth, and deplores the breaking up of the property "*put together by Cromwell's soldier*"!'

The two young women had begun their literary collaboration with the two novels, *An Irish Cousin* and *Naboth's Vineyard*, and were about to embark on their masterpiece, *The Real Charlotte*. Meanwhile, supported by a magazine called the *Lady's Pictorial*, they wrote a series of light-hearted travel books, one of which *Through Connemara in a Governess Cart*, complements Maria Edgeworth's equally lively letter about Connemara written half a century before.

The Cousins were determined that their own account of travels in the west would be aimed at 'those who do not require either mental improvement or reliable statistics'. Their journey began in London and they travelled down to Oughterard from Galway past Ross House which Martin was in the process of restoring. Like most respectable visitors they stayed at comfortable 'Miss Murphy's'; Murphy's has become Egan's. They searched the village for a suitable horse-drawn vehicle and found 'the trap of our brightest dreams ... a governess cart that would hold just two people and a reasonable amount of luggage' together with a temperamental jennet named Sibbie, 'a long-legged long-eared brown animal'. The stable where Sibbie spent the night has become Egan's bar, and the rest has been modernized. The Cousins left no detailed description but would surely recognize the eating room from an account written forty years later of 'a gloomy apartment of Berlin wool anti-macassars, plush chairs, cases of stuffed pike and an enormous picture of Grattan's Parliament'.

Next morning they set out. The governess cart, scrubbed down until the varnish glistened, was carefully stowed with 'a portmanteau, a dressing bag, a luncheon basket and a large and reliable gingham umbrella'. The contents of the luncheon basket included bottles of wine.

Thinking of them bowling along past 'trim covered villas' I wondered if I could hire something of the sort myself and follow them through these pleasant suburbs and out into the bogs and mountains. Near the old station, now a carpet factory, I saw an advertisement for a riding school and applied to it, mentioning Recess and Clifden. Impossible ... today's traffic ... the hard slippery tarmac ... the distance ... still tomorrow they would do their best.

Next morning I waited outside Murphy's-Egan's near the spot where so many had departed in sun, wind and rain for the wilds of Connemara. Writing in the 1860s with the smugness that came from an era of improved transport and communications, the Halls expressed their horror at the state that region had presented half a century earlier: 'the wildest and most unknown part of the civilized world ... the British law was inoperative there as in the centre of New Holland; there was scarcely a road over which wheeled traffic could pass; nothing resembling an inn to be found; the owners of its soil reigned almost supreme as the petty despots of Swabia.' By the owners of the soil the Halls meant landlord princes like the Blakes of Renvyle and the Martins of Ballinahinch.

It was to visit the Martins of Ballinahinch that Maria Edgeworth set out from Oughterard in 1833 with the Cullen Smiths in their ample coach with its outriders and postilions in blue coats. Maria, carrying her books and reticule with spectacles, was afraid of horses and sat with her back to the driver so that she couldn't see them. She was always good company, talking and laughing all the time, with an endless flow of anecdotes. She knew that the gate lodge outside Oughterard marked the beginning of the longest private avenue in Europe, some sixty miles long, leading to Ballinahinch Castle.

I heard the clip-clop of a horse against the sounds of traffic. Here was a dog cart driven by Mark Geoghegan threading its way down the main street. I climbed in and we set out down a quiet lane swaying between hawthorn bushes and catching the scent of gorse. Each twist of the road brought a whiff of meadow grass, a glimpse of fir trees or a swathe of rhododendrons, until we came to the edge of Lough Corrib and a view of mountains and tufted islands. Mark was over eighty and had spent his life here; his horse, Sheila, was thirty. He could remember Miss Murphy who owned the hotel when Martin and Edith stayed there, various 'half gentlemen' and the eccentric Chevalier who bought Ross from the Martins. The Chevalier was a great patriot, was put in a play by Brendan Behan, walked round Oughterard in a saffron kilt and talked only French or Gaelic (although as a favour he condescended to address his Anglo-Irish relations in Albion's hated tongue). Mark reminisced affectionately, raising his whip or his very old bowler hat to the people we passed. You could never travel in the cart on the main roads now, it would not be fair on the horse. Now, we were around the lake and the road stopped; the dog cart could go no further. I got out and watched it drive back towards Oughterard, Mark sitting straight up in the seat and the old Connemara mare flicking her tail, trotting along the hawthorn-scented lane.

Following the old man's direction I skirted the lake and made the mountain crossing to Maam Cross where a roadhouse and shop and the old station, now turned into a seaweed factory, cluster about the roads that meet here – one from Ballinahinch and Roundstone, another from Clifden and another from Maam and the Maumturk mountains. You'd think it a forlorn sort of crossroads in the midst of nowhere but there was nothing forlorn about the guesthouse where I spent the night and the folk group that made the walls tremble with song. Next day I walked the few miles over to Maam, in search of Nimmo's lodge.

Alexander Nimmo was a remarkable Scot whose work has been largely forgotten. He is only tangibly remembered by a pier named after him in Galway. And yet during his short career as an engineer – he died in 1832 aged forty-nine – he transformed Ireland. The serviceable roads he constructed included the steep hilltop roads between Kenmare and Killarney and Glengarriff and Killarney, and the first road from Galway to Clifden. He built numerous piers and harbours and was a railway pioneer. One of his early railways ran to Ballinasloe to take horses away from the fair. His interests included modern languages, astronomy and draining bogs. He founded the town of Roundstone and imported Scotchmen to live there, many of whom are buried near him in the graveyard there.

He chose to live at Maam Cross where the views of bog and mountains and the gleaming west end of Corrib may have reminded him of his native land. After his death his home, Corrib Lodge, was taken over by his Scottish servant Mr Rourke, and turned into a highly successful hotel which over a century and a half has accommodated such diverse people as the Sportsman, Lord Leitrim and Patrick Pearse. Mrs Keene, the present proprietor, recently came across Pearse's name in an old register.

Among the first guests was Maria Edgeworth's party. 'Corrib Lodge is a neat, bleak-looking house which Mr Nimmo built for his own residence when he was overseer of the roads, now turned into an inn kept by his Scotch servant . . . he gave us bread and butter and milk, moreover hare-soup such as the best London tavern might have envied.'

Thirty years later the Lodge was visited by the Walking Tourist. Mr Barry did a walking tour of Ireland wearing a bright knickerbocker suit. (We have glimpsed him before, arriving at Killarney in disarray.) Mr Barry was an endearing traveller (in spite of his Gilbertian protests about nationality his name suggests an Irish ancestry). He landed at Belfast on 11 August 1865 and began an anti-clockwise journey round the coast. He tells us that he had digested all the books he could find on Ireland without taking notes. 'I only allowed the information just obtained to pass through my mind without making any attempt to find a resting place for it.'

When he stopped for the night he was usually 'overwhelmed with friendly advice and kindly interest' from the moment the boots took his small bag up to his room. In diverse coffee rooms other guests would crowd around asking the usual questions. 'How many miles do you walk in a day? Do you carry an umbrella? Have you a black silk hat with you? What shirts do you wear?'

He averaged fifteen or twenty miles a day. When he arrived at Maam, the Lodge was run by a tenant of the notorious Lord Leitrim, Mr King, who was not such a good cook as Mr Rourke. The Walking Tourist noticed that chicken served up the night before was presented to guests for breakfast disguised as grouse. He had been given Lord Leitrim's bedroom and spent a good deal of time listening to stories of his Lordship 'who seemed to be of a generally selfish and eccentric disposition'. Two years before, Lord Leitrim had perpetrated his famous tease on his enemy, Lord Carlisle. The foppish Lord Lieutenant was touring the west in state accompanied by a sumptuous entourage. Lord Leitrim ordered Mr King by letter to crowd out the hotel with tenants so that there could be no possible accommodation for the Lord Lieutenant's party which had to blunder on through the night towards Clifden thirty miles away. According to a contemporary account, 'poverty and pigs for a time were exchanged for unwonted cleanliness and unlimited whiskey, and the amazed labourers and workmen were found ready to quench every spark of manly feeling, and to combine in a paltry conspiracy against one of the most amiable of men'.

Corrib Lodge was an oasis in the midst of a rain-sodden desert crowded with people living at subsistence level. In spite of his good dinner Henry Inglis looked out of his bedroom window in the summer of 1834 at the rain 'while a thousand images of appalling misery and hopeless poverty crossed his mind'. 'God knows I feel acutely for the people of this unhappy land,' he wrote in the preface of his book.

At Maam, Inglis was told about a pattern held in the nearby mountains, and set off accompanied by Mr Rourke, the proprietor of the Lodge, to see the fun. I followed their route up into the Maamturk mountains. 'You take the first turn to the left and just continue walking until you exhaust the road,' I was told. 'Then continue walking.' The day was hot and the spectacle of a middle-aged man sweating along an uphill road brought me the offer of a cup of tea. 'Enjoy yourself and take it easy,' the woman said. 'What's the rush to get up that mountain?' I asked her about the pattern and she said there had been talk of reviving it. 'But it'll only bring in tourists. It's Sunday today and we go to Mass and isn't that just as good? We all live as well as we can.'

From her home a side-road led to the old pilgrims' track and the mountain shoulder. When Inglis walked up here the track was filled with pilgrims. 'Far up the winding way for miles before us, and for miles behind too, groups were seen moving up the mountainside ... the women with their red petticoats easily distinguishable; some were on foot, some few on horseback and some rode double.'

A ten-foot-wide path could still be seen leading to a saddle between two hills. That was the old pilgrims' way. Here was St Patrick's Bed and a small round lake hidden under rocks. At this place scores of tents and a throng of pilgrims greeted Inglis as he came over the brow of the hill. He wrote a detailed account of the proceedings, people camping, people drinking, people praying, people making the rounds, people fighting. He admitted: 'I have been honest enough to wish to see a regular faction fight.' He got his wish and watched the Joyces, 'a magnificent race of men', fortified by poteen dealing with their opponents.

A stoat came out and scampered around the rocks. I climbed the black curve over St Patrick's Lake and the whole magic world of Connemara stretched at my feet. This was literally a heightened aspect of the 'much admired view' of the lakes and Twelve Pins stretching to the Atlantic. It is not easy to describe. It defeated Thackeray. 'The best guidebook that was ever written cannot set the view before the mind of the reader, and I won't attempt to pile up big words in place of the wild mountains.' Forbes emphasized that all his statements were made on the spot 'so that the reader wasn't cheated'. High above Maam he rested gasping and wrote down his exact impressions of what he saw: 'The whole landscape spread out before us consisted of a cluster of mountain tops black and barren, rising up on every side in a hundred different shapes.' Kohl came up with a good phrase when he described Ireland as 'the richest cloudland in Europe'.

I left the solitary men in frock coats to their meditation and spent an easy evening by the dark lake. The little grating sound of grazing sheep and the thump of rabbits were the only noises I could hear as I lay down in my tent watching the sunset. Next morning I climbed down the other side towards bog, an easy descent into a liquid brown landscape and Nimmo's road.

Somewhere along this road Violet Martin and Edith Somerville stopped for their first picnic. 'We pulled up under the lee of a low bank and spread out our eatables on the seats of the cart.' The Cousins described in ecstatic detail 'the unpacking of the spirit lamp and its glittering bride, the tin kettle, the dinner knives at sixpence apiece, the spoons at twopence halfpenny; the potted meats, the Bath Olivers, the Bovril and the Burgundy'. They enjoyed picnics and described them with gusto. 'There is in the matter of picnics no middle course endurable. If they cannot attain to the untrammelled simplicity of the savage, they require all the resources of civilization to justify them.' Another truth which they isolated was that 'packing up is the dark feature of the best picnic'. Replete, they climbed up behind Sibbie and trotted on to Recess.

I followed them through Recess and towards Ballinahinch along the shores of Glendollagh Lake. When the Cousins were here they were on the look-out for the home of Martin's remarkable connections, 'a long lake in a valley, a long line of roofs skirting it, and finally on a wooded height, the castle ... a large modern house with its battlemented top, very gentlemanlike and even handsome, but in no way remarkable'. That description would pass today. The change from the romantic to the prosaic had taken place in the 1850s when the impoverished Maria Edgeworth, last of the Martins of Ballinahinch, let her estates pass into the possession of the Law Life Insurance Company.

Previously the Martins flourished here as eccentric and lonely monarchs who dispensed legendary hospitality to any traveller who penetrated the wildness. De Latocnaye tramped through the bog in the summer of 1797 to pay his respects to Humanity-Hairtrigger Dick Martin and get a free night's lodging. 'I have never been in the house of a rich man who appeared to care so little for the things of this world.' Here was the owner of an estate sixty miles long and forty miles wide and his new house had to be stopped for lack of funds. However, de Latocnaye considered that 'a palace would certainly seem to be an extraordinary thing in the middle of the mosses'.

Later visitors were contemptuous of the simplicity of Martin's house, 'a large plain-looking building' according to Barrow; 'a wretched white farmhouse' in the words of the Sportsman. Inglis who came here after his climb to St Patrick's Bed found a similar anomaly between Richard Martin 'who was quite a sovereign' and 'his hardly baronial house'. Since it was called Ballinahinch Castle, something imposing was expected. In fact it was named after a small sixteenth-century tower built by Donal of the Combats O'Flaherty on an island in the lake, before the arrival of the Martins.

Maria Edgeworth and the Cullen Smiths set out for Ballinahinch from the inn at Maam. Mr Rourke warned them that, as his late master Mr Nimmo's road was not yet finished, they would have to take the old bog road. 'It would be wonderful if we could get over it, for no carriage had ever passed nor ever thought of attempting to pass.' However, obstinate Sir Cullen insisted that travelling by carriage was the only way. His party could hardly dart over the bog on foot or go on horseback – in any case Miss Edgeworth was afraid of horses. So they set out. 'The first bad step we came to was indeed a slough ... the horses sank up to their knees and were whipped and spurred and they struggled and foundered ... and the carriage, as we inside passengers felt, sank and sank.'

Inglis, who had been forced to take the same uneven road, had been extremely indignant about its condition. 'Shameless ... it is impossible for any vehicle unless with the assistance of half a dozen men to carry it or at least to assist in its progress.' He added, 'When I say vehicle ... I mean an Irish jaunting car of the strongest build.'

But the Cullen Smiths had chosen to travel in a massive coach which needed an army of men to help it circumnavigate the ruts and holes of the 'region dolorous' they had to cross. Here was the portly figure of Sir Cullen pushing with the others while Maria was being carried in the arms of a giant called Ulick Burke 'as he might a child or doll'. Sometimes through the jolts and suffering while the helpers 'dragged, pushed and screamed the carriage over' they could see Nimmo's new road 'looking like a gravel walk often parallel to our path of danger, and yet for want of being unfinished there it was, useless and most tantalizing'.

When they reached Ballinahinch the house was on fire. However, once this was sorted out the Martins offered their customary hospitality which was needed for an unexpectedly long time. Lady Smith became sick and unable to travel, so that they were forced to spend three weeks at Ballinahinch: time for Maria to record the particulars of 'the *tail* of a feudal estate'. Thomas Martin, son of Humanity Dick, was the ruler. There was his wife and his extraordinary daughter, Maria, aged seventeen, fair-haired and, in Maria Edgeworth's opinion, looking like a Leonardo painting. (Fifty years later the Cousins met an old woman who remembered her as 'beautiful and white and charitable, only she had one snaggledy tooth in front of her mouth'.) Maria Martin knew Latin, Greek and Hebrew and had been taught engineering by Nimmo. Her French and a course in 'fortification' had been learned from an officer of Napoleon who instilled in her a passionate admiration for the Emperor. When she walked outside the castle her father's tenants streamed after her and she treated them imperiously. 'Je sais mon métier de reine,' she told Sir Cullen Smith. In later life she took another guest up a neighbouring mountain and told him that everything he could see belonged to her.

The castle was 'a whitewashed dilapidated mansion with nothing of a castle about it except four pepperpot towers. It had broken panes, wood panes and slate panes, and in the ceilings and passages terrible splotches and blotches of damp and wet, which we were bound not to see as we passed with Mrs Martin.'

During Lady Smith's convalescence there was time to sketch, talk to Maria Martin and eat huge meals of lobsters, oysters and game of all sorts washed down with wine and champagne. Thomas Martin sat at the end of the table shouting out orders and instructions: 'Molly here ... plate, pepper ... champagne to Lady Smith ... Miss Edgeworth ...' When Maria Edgeworth retired to her room the windows rattled and the whole place seemed damp and cold. But then next morning how magnificent it was to gaze out at 'an immense lake and mountains of prodigious height ... and two bare-footed short-petticoated women under my window carrying a tub between them down to the lake'. At breakfast she was offered hot rolls, coffee, tea and ham. There was only one teapot in the house – 'the maids were always obliged to wait for breakfast till we had done with the teapot'.

In due course Maria Martin was to die penniless in America and Ballinahinch was taken over by the Law Life Insurance Company which was responsible for the castellated building disparaged by the Cousins. It passed through the hands of the Indian cricket player, Ranjit Singh, before becoming today's luxury hotel. It gives no idea of Thomas Martin's lavish yet rough and ready life-style, but half a mile away down by the lake there is some evidence of Martin prodigality. Little is left of the stables which cost Colonel Martin £15,000 to build and were paved with alternate blocks of green and white Connemara marble – only a shell is to be seen, many troughs and patches of cobblestones where grooms walked out with the Martin horses.

11
Clifden · Omey Island · Letterfrack · Leenane

Two hundred years ago the land around Clifden was covered with trees. A Victorian traveller wrote how 'a peasant assures us that he remembers Lettery mountain lying in shade and the road from Clifden to Streamstown passing through woods in which the trees were so close that a man might walk upon the top of them'. In the woods and in other parts of Connemara the red deer still wandered freely; at Ballinahinch Maria Edgeworth was offered venison.

At Clifden sore feet and an aching back from carrying my bulging rucksack all day from St Patrick's Bed sent me into the first guesthouse I came across. Welcome, said the landlady, and John F. Kennedy and Pope John Paul II looked down benignly. In the dining-room among tartan mats and pieces of Belleek china sat two American girls who were hitching around the world. As they chatted about Egypt and other global high spots I thought of the Cousins in their Clifden lodging house, 'on greasy horsehair-seated chairs in the parlour, while the bubbling cry of the rasher and eggs arose to heaven from the frying pan, and filled the house with a grey fog'.

It was here at Clifden in 1891 that Madame de Bovet ate what she considered 'at least in Irish terms ... a memorable meal ... among the most joyful souvenirs of my life'. Because of bad weather that had held up their arrival, twenty-two guests 'dripping like fountains and as ravenous as wolves' crowded into the dining-room of the Mullarky Hotel where a big square table covered with damask was piled with dishes. First there was an abominable soup of pepper and cloves ('the secret is shared between England and Ireland') followed by the main courses which consisted of two legs of mutton ('altogether an Irish triumph') which were the highlights of the meal since the four boiled fowl were 'dishonoured by a white paste and chopped parsley'. There were potatoes served the usual way, boiled in their skins, and then the sweets, biscuits, celery and cheeses, each guest hacking out his own portion. Madame de Bovet concluded her account of the meal eaten to the sound of rain lashing at the windows with a treatise on Irish cooking. 'The mutton is sometimes replaced by an excellent duck with quite a vile flavour, spoilt by stuffing and aromatic herbs. On feast days you get two or three places of fish, fried, boiled and roasted, salmon, mackerel or most kinds of big sole.' Lunch, usually served à la carte, was almost always chops or steaks.

Madame de Bovet thought little of the salmon which during the summer was offered as hamburgers are now. There could be too much of it and indeed of fish in general. Samuel Bayne, an American who toured Connemara and Donegal in a jaunting car in 1902, complained of 'an aquarium style of living' in one hotel where he was offered 'salmon boiled and salmon broiled, cold salmon, salmon steak, salmon croquettes, salmon cutlets and stewed salmon, interspersed with white trout, black trout, yellow trout, brown trout, sea trout, speckled trout with gillaroo'.

But enough about food. Outside, Clifden waited in the sun. 'A dear little place,' a man cutting turf near Derrylee lake had commented, amending his remark at my surprise to 'an expensive dear little place'. Clifden has welcomed tourists since its inception. The visitors crowding into giftshops with their rucksacks are successors to Asenath Nicholson who walked into the town in the rain of May Day 1845 smelling lilac and apple blossom and observing people dressing a maypole with flowers. Others jogged in from Galway on Bians or Royal Mail Cars, swept by winds, blinded by dust or rain and dazzled with scenery. Old photographs depict the scene, showing long cars straddling the main square, bowler-hatted men lolling by gilded shop fronts, and the two church spires, Catholic and Protestant, confronting each other. The way each strove to dominate the town used to be significant, for Clifden was a notorious location for the 'reformation movement' and the 'stirabout creed'. John Forbes was told that out of forty converted children in the Protestant Mission School between the ages of fourteen and eighteen 'only one had "jumped" back to Catholicism'. Seventy years later in 1909 Stephen Gwynn could still refer to the 'rival' churches and describe how each Saturday Protestant missionaries stood in the main square preaching the gospel.

Clifden as the chief town in Connemara was a natural geographical centre for such goings-on. It was very new; at the beginning of the nineteenth century it did not exist. Some time before Nimmo began importing Scotsmen to Roundstone a man named John Darcy acquired an estate on the Atlantic seaboard and began to encourage the growth of a town nearby in a place where there was scarcely a road or cottage. He gave cheap building leases to contractors and quite soon 'a very neat town' grew up with a hundred good slated houses, three good streets, a fever hospital and 'an enormous orphanage'. Darcy lived at Clifden Castle on the coast road above the town, a stark grey Gothic house according to old photographs, the sort that tended to get turned into a school or religious institution. The alternative is a good comic opera ruin, which is Clifden Castle's fate. A man cutting grass in the field outside the Gothic gateway told me how the roof was pulled off in 1919 and the land divided up. He had heard nothing good or bad about the Darcys.

Up the hill a coastguard station looked down on the bay where English men-of-war once tacked up and down and tars had come ashore to exchange their cocoa and rum rations for eggs, milk and butter. The building had gone the way of the landlord's castle. On the other side of the road a thatched cottage had weathered the years better than either. Hens scratched in the yard under a pile of turf among a few yawning dogs and a donkey cart.

I followed the route taken by Asenath Nicholson from Clifden past Streamstown beside the sea to Omey Island which is separated from the mainland by a stretch of sand that is regularly flooded by the tide. I traced her path over the ribbed strand and then to the west end of the island across exposed fields by a reedy lake. Down on the shore St Feichin's Church was being rescued by archaeologists from the sand; before they started only a gable had stuck out. Wind blew sand over the graves in the graveyard. 'In memory of Martin from your workmates in England.' In fields full of thyme and yellow trefoil scattered ruins and thin green lines of potato ridges told of the times when the population was numerous. Which ruin was the house where Mrs Nicholson stopped and found 'sixty-three living and moving beings with calves, pigs, hens and ducks'?

Before retiring to a clean bed she gave her hostess a piece of her mind. 'I told her plainly I came to Ireland because I had a right to come; that they were daily sending loads of beggars and abused emigrants to us, and I had even come to see what they could be at home.' The next day when she crossed the sands at Omey she had great difficulty. There were no signposts as there are now and she got lost. 'I found myself entangled in rocks after crossing the strand, and was a full hour climbing and creeping to get out.'

I obtained a lift to Letterfrack beside Ballinaskill Bay topped by a wave of mountains, Altnagaighera, Doughraugh, the Twelve Pins and the distinctive profile of Diamond Mountain. I sympathized with the Victorian artist who 'manfully confessed that he could do nothing with Connemara'. But the Cousins dismissed the 'tall crudely conical mountains' around Letterfrack as 'such a landscape as a child would draw'. And Edith was no mean painter.

When the Cousins drove into Letterfrack they stayed at 'Mr O'Grady's fuchsia covered hotel' which evolved from Carson's Hotel recommended by *Murray's* in 1878. By the time of the Cousins' visit fuchsia had become widespread, but twenty years earlier it was still rare enough to draw comment. Murray's piece on Letterfrack recommended that 'the tourist should note the luxuriant fuchsia hedge skirting the lane leading from Carson's to the foot of the mountains', and the same hedge was there to greet me more than a hundred years later.

The hotel, a plain whitewashed building in old photographs, survives as a private house together with the derelict stables where the Cousins lodged their governess cart and Sibbie. The Walking Tourist stayed at Carson's, sitting in the large coffee room over an open fire thinking of 'that pretty girl dressed in blue I saw in the coffee room at Leenane' and watching a waiter preparing whiskey punch, a potion that has yielded somewhat to Irish coffee: 'two or three lumps of sugar . . . then pour in some hot water and dilute . . . then pour the whiskey into the rummer and fill up three parts with hot water, stir well and the whiskey punch is made.' In the same coffee room the Cousins gazed out 'as the mist blew softly against the French window and swept past on the road like a procession of ghostly ball dresses'. They were disappointed by the prosaic comfort of Connemara hotels. When they came to writing their book they had to invent some scenes of 'comic squalor that is endured gladly for the sake of its literary value'.

Like so many centres in the west, the village of Letterfrack started off modestly, very modestly if Henry Blake is to be believed. He described it at the beginning of the nineteenth century as a small grubby insignificant hamlet where 'the miserable cabins were all in ruins' and 'the rattle of carriage wheels was a sound quite new to the natives and they peeped out of their lowly dwellings with an aspect barely human; their long black hair tangled over their necks and shoulders and their bright black eyes but just discernible through the half-opened door'. A landlord himself, Blake blamed this poverty on the lack of any resident landowner, 'the absence of a fostering hand'.

The fostering hand appeared briskly soon after. As Clifden was developed by Darcy, Letterfrack was transformed by Mr Ellis, an English Quaker. He built up a new village with a shop, 'the wonder and comfort for the country around', started a non-sectarian school, built 'pretty cottages' and drained the land round about so that it became 'a green smiling island amid the dark desert of moors and bogs around it'. Travellers had nothing but praise for Mr Ellis and his efforts which resulted in such a 'general look of neatness and comfort'. He took care of his adopted people during the famine and 'saved a whole population from utter ruin, nay from death itself'. You could not help admiring the purposeful Quaker effort whose only trace now is the orphanage which the Christian Brothers took over and turned into a Remand Home.

I climbed Diamond Mountain for the glittering view and a glimpse of the towers of Kylemore which are a proof of Mr Henry's love. 'How I should like to live here!' Mrs Henry said, looking across at mountains where eagles still soared during one of the most expensive fishing holidays ever taken. Mr Henry set about with quarried stone to convert an old fishing lodge of the Blakes into these towers and battlements and to fill the great hall with potted palms, love seats and carved woodwork. All the interior fittings had to be brought across the bog. A chandelier would come down from Galway on an ass and cart.

Mr Henry's gift to his wife was completed in 1860 but it did not bring happiness. A few years later, they stayed in Cairo where Mrs Henry died of fever. She was forty-five. He brought her body back to Connemara to be buried. The nuns who run the school that the castle has become showed me a touching portrait of Mrs Henry in a silver dress, and the brick mausoleum half-buried in vegetation where you can read in greenish moss-filtered light the inscription about her death and his, after lingering on for half a century in his lonely castle.

Near Tully Hill, a heather-covered ridge, I looked down on Renvyle and the Atlantic beyond. A stump of a castle faced the sea; inside the walls were piles of lobster pots and stacked turf on which perched a large black hen that had just laid an egg. This castle was in Blake country. Like the Martins, the Blakes, descendants of an old Galway family, had acquired and ruled a large tract of Connemara. In the 1820s, Henry Blake, the current head of the family, took to writing. When Barrow and Thackeray came to Ireland, the author of 'those beautiful amusing *Tales from the Irish Highlands*' published in 1825 was still living at Renvyle in his old sixteenth-century house 'within a stone's throw or wave's dash of the vast Atlantic'.

At the time of the visit of Maria Edgeworth who wrote these words, Renvyle like Ballinahinch was a sanctuary in a roadless wilderness. She came straight from Ballinahinch with the Cullen Smiths after Lady Smith's partial recovery. 'I spare you a repetition of sloughs.'

The Blakes' old house at Renvyle between the rocks and the sea offered a surprisingly comfortable anchorage. It was much more luxurious than Ballinahinch. 'We could not help sighing with the wish that our late hospitable host had half these comforts of life.' Renvyle with its ancient black panelled rooms was more like an English manor house. Although Henry Blake happened to be away, the party was lavishly received and Maria Edgeworth retired in comfort, listening to the wind outside and the roar of the sea. When she gazed at 'that magnificent awful shining November view' she may have thought of Letter One dated January 1825 of her host's collected letters. 'Henceforward you are to consider us cut off from the ordinary routine of society, leading somewhat of a patriarchal life, or rather living in the style of the old feudal barons, enjoying proud solitude, the grandeur of our rocks and mountains.'

On a summer's day in 1890, sixty-seven years later, the Cousins drove up in their governess cart to the shingled 'long, grey two-storey house ... with low Elizabethan windows and pale weather slated walls, wholly unexpected and altogether unique as far, at all events, as this part of Ireland is concerned'. Behind the iron-studded hall door were the low oak-panelled rooms that had greeted Maria filled with aged country house trappings – oaken props for guns and fishing rods, long black oak chests and a gilded four-poster bed to sleep in, in short 'everything old fashioned, even medieval, dark and comfortable ... nothing in the least suggestive of a hotel'.

But hotel Renvyle had become. Like the Martins, the Blakes were eventually overwhelmed by debts. Even in Thackeray's time the decline was coming. Viewing the Blake estates he complained how 'the spectacle of a country going to waste is enough to make the cheerfullest landscape look dismal; it gives this whole district a woeful look indeed'. In addition, during the 1880s the current owner of Renvyle, a tough old widow, got into trouble with the Land League. Mrs Blake's subsequent relationship with her tenants gained her misery and notoriety, and it was only by a matter of timing that she did not add a new word to the language and we do not talk of blakeing rather than boycotting. The Cousins, who had little sympathy for the Land League, imagined her 'with her refined intellectual face and delicate physique taking a stick in her hand and going out day after day to drive off her land the trespassing cattle, sheep and horses that were as regularly driven on to it again as soon as her back was turned'. When they looked out of their low-panelled bedroom window, they saw that the donkey that collected the grass mowings from the lawns in panniers had no ears. Passionate animal lovers, they were horrified to be told that these appendages 'was cut off in the time of th' agitation'. It was not their purpose in their light-hearted travel book to investigate the causes of the antagonism expressed so savagely by its mistress's tenants.

So Mrs Blake, down on her luck, turned Renvyle into a wonderful hotel. The Cousins enjoyed their lobster soup and excellent coffee, watched a peacock strut past their window, wandered in the garden with its borders of brilliant flowers, browsed in the dark-panelled turkey-carpeted library which Maria Edgeworth had inspected approvingly, noted the contemporary copy of Raleigh's *History of the World* and a treatise on torture, and ventured out to Grace O'Malley's castle. Mrs Blake gallantly persevered to make her hotel a success. Near the noticeboard in the hall she had put up some journalist's expression of the benefits of tourism. 'The more the English go to Ireland and the more they understand the Celtic nature, the better for both nations. Experience shows that when they mingle they coalesce.' But the Cousins knew that this wasn't true.

Although Mrs Blake struggled on, the family eventually lost out. Oliver St John Gogarty acquired the house, loved it passionately and grieved, as we all should, that it was burnt in the Civil War. The building put up in its place is a pastiche. Once again Renvyle House is a hotel. I listened to the piped music, glanced at the television, peered into the great bar and walked away from Renvyle with its caravan park, new thatched cottages for renting and flotsam of tourism.

At Rossroe Pier I faced Mweelrea mountain, its green slopes tipped by the cloud that darkened the grey barrel of Killary. Travellers usually compared Killary to a Norwegian fiord. 'There is no scene in England of the same character and on so grand a scale,' Inglis considered. Thackeray was transfixed. 'Let the reader imagine huge dark mountains in their accustomed livery of purple and green, a dull sky above them, an estuary silver bright below . . . a pair of seagulls undulating with the waves over the water, a pair of curlews wheeling overhead . . . and on the hillside a jingling car with a cockney in it, oppressed by and yet admiring all these things.'

He was on his way to the inn at Leenane at the end of the Killary. Today it is the Leenane Hotel. It began as a hostelry during the early part of the nineteenth century, the place where Big Jack Joyce entertained and became a legend. Everyone knew of Big Jack and many wrote about him. His family had been wealthy middlemen, but according to Blake he was 'nearly reduced to the level of the common peasant' as a result of 'extravagance and mismanagement'. When Blake came over from Renvyle by boat and sailed down the Killary in search of material for his book, Big Jack entertained him regally. After Blake had written about him other travellers sought him out and he became a celebrity. The Cullen Smiths coaxed their cumbersome chariot along the shores of Killary Bay, and while they waited for the tide he entertained them with chicken and glasses of port. Henry Inglis was intrigued, describing him as 'near akin to a giant', 'a shrewd intelligent plain spoken man'. They enjoyed each other's company, sitting down to a gargantuan meal of salmon and potatoes washed down with whiskey. Here was the romantic savage at his most dignified. 'For my part I could not have addressed a King of the South Seas with more respect.'

A few years after Inglis's book was published another traveller penetrated to Killary and called in on Big Jack. John Barrow saw him as 'a stern looking man of enormous muscular power with an arm like Hercules'. They sat beside a big fire talking of Inglis's book; Big Jack thought he had been made too much of. Then they had a sensible conversation on religion; 'we agreed that it would be most desirable that Protestants and Catholics would shake hands and be friends and not interfere with each other's people'. When Barrow went to bed he took further notes about the household. Apart from Jack, the family, which included a son over six foot in height, only spoke Gaelic. He described the kitchen with the wild game hanging from hooks in the ceiling and the schoolroom with four huge beds 'each capable of holding nearly half a dozen people if occasion demanded'. Finally he noted the industry of the dozen or so girls of the family employed in spinning and weaving, the wheels constantly 'making a buzzing noise not unlike that of a large blue bottle fly'.

But Jack Joyce's world was vanishing. Later visitors regarded his life-style with a colder eye. In 1839 Caesar Otway could decry 'the romantics of Connemara' like Inglis and Barrow. 'There is nothing strange or extraordinary in this group of mountains . . . nothing in the appearance of the people.' The figure of Jack Joyce himself had been exaggerated out of all recognition. ' 'Tis true I met with Big Jack Joyce . . . but one well-fed bacon eating man or family has no right to fix unreal magnitude on a whole people.' Otway considered you could find similar Jack Joyces in all the tap rooms between Liverpool and London.

Joyce and his giant brood vanished. By the time the Halls wrote their guide books Killary had become part of the plebeian and ordinary world. They quoted the prospectus of a Mr O'Reilly of Leenane, 'Late of the coastguard station who begs leave most respectfully to inform travellers, tourists and the public in general that he has taken the house lately inhabited by Mr John Joyce at the head of Killary Bay and fitted it up as a hotel.'

Mr O'Reilly's prospectus marked the end of the old wild Connemara. Mr Nimmo's new roads had opened up the west. According to Maria Edgeworth, he had built a bridge across Killary against Big Jack's advice. He built it three times, but each time it was swept away by the wind and sea. 'We saw the ruins of it on the sands.' Apart from Maria's note all memories of this bridge have vanished.

The hotel prospered. It seems that the only visitors to Killary who did not pause and stay were King Edward VII and Queen Alexandra who in 1903 drove down the edge of the bay from where the royal yacht was moored. By then the Leenane Hotel was under the rule of a character almost as colourful as Jack Joyce. Major McKeown – the rank was honorary – besides being proprietor of the hotel, was postmaster and storekeeper, rented out rivers and lakes to fishermen, shipped salmon to London and owned ten thousand acres of shooting land in addition to a sheep mountain which liberally supplied his hotel. The American, Samuel Bayne, complained 'we had on succeeding days . . . roast mutton (hot and cold), stewed lamb, boiled leg, roast saddle, minced lamb, mutton cutlets, broiled kidneys, lamb chops, Irish stew, suet pudding, sweet breads, French chops, sheep's head and mutton broth'.

Stephen Gwynn, in search of Gaelic culture and enticed by the hotel lights, sulked at the composition of guests. 'We have become tourists.' He complained about the almost universal use of English and, worse, the Unionist newspapers. 'I looked for any of the Nationalist papers . . . but I looked in vain.'

This was because the majority of visitors was English. The Cousins, sitting in the dining-room watching three curates in blazers and white trousers, sadly reviewed travel in Connemara in 1890.

> At this hotel – as indeed, at all the others we stayed at . . . we were almost the only representatives of our country, and casting our minds back through the haze of English faces and the Babel of English voices . . . two painful conclusions were forced upon us – first that the Irish people have no money to tour with; second that it was the Saxon influence and support alone that evoluted the Connemara hotels from a primitive feather-bed and chicken status . . .

Ninety years on there was still a fair sprinkling of English, those intrepid enough to ignore the IRA, together with French, Dutch, Germans, and some jolly Swiss Germans who kept me awake most of the night with their songs and laughter.

12
Achill · Newport · Ballycroy

Beyond Leenane where the mountains enclosed the fiord like wet green towels, stood Aasleagh, a rectory and church cocooned in rhododendrons. Like so many little Protestant country churches this one was closed except at the actual times its withered congregation attended a service.

Martin Joyce, who had the key, showed me round the plain stone building in which I found the monument to Captain William Houston, late of the 10th Hussars whose 'unfailing rectitude of conduct, whose high personal endowments with liberality towards all creeds and kindness towards all who had served here will never be forgotten'. Mrs Houston had erected that to her husband. She was the author of a vivid and unhappy book, *Twenty Years in the Wild West*, which described her experiences in this area during the nineteenth century.

I asked Martin Joyce if he knew about Mrs Houston, and he remembered 'she had cut up the place in her book'. Every Sunday afternoon she and the Captain came here to worship. Behind them would be a sprinkling of converts and a few Scottish shepherds that the Captain had enticed over from Ross-shire, perhaps a half-dozen souls in all, gathered to listen to 'a very red haired zealot whose surplice was usually unwashed and in holes' who preached violently against the errors of the Church of Rome. He described the Virgin as 'a sinful unrighteous woman' and the cross 'a blasphemous emblem' . As for the Irish 'they were hopelessly doomed (they being liars and idolaters) to everlasting burning'. Mrs Houston's own faith was simple and tolerant and her Catholic tenants and neighbours did not understand it. 'It was something gained to convince even one among them that I, a Protestant, believed in a merciful Saviour and recognized the Holy Virgin as "Blessed among women".'

Keeping an eye on the Pandora's box of a sky, I climbed the shoulder of Ben Gorm from where I looked down on Killary and watched the silver light on the water filtered by the darker shadows of the wind. Here among these sharp treeless mountains Captain Houston grazed his 'herds of horses, sheep and fat kine innumerable' according to a local guide, on 'an immense mountain property'.

The Houstons lived at Doo Lough, which is a few miles north of Leenane beside Delphi. To this remote and beautiful place they had journeyed to tame the wilderness and make their home in the spirit of later settlers in Kenya. Today, the ruin of their house is hidden in rhododendron, but when they arrived for their twenty years of rain and loneliness the view to the surrounding mountains and the black lake was open.

Mrs Houston subtitled her book 'A True Story of a Modern Exile'. Her husband's reasons for coming here were vigorous, 'a determination to settle on a large unreclaimed estate amidst bogs and moors scarcely reached by roads, and associated with the wish, too romantic and sanguine as it turned out, to benefit the area'. He would bring in trained people from England and Scotland and, if necessary, evict. 'Eviction,' wrote Mrs Houston, 'is often on the landlord's part the truest mercy towards the poverty stricken ones.'

They came just a few years after the famine, trailing their baggage along the ill-kept road to their newly bought property. They journeyed 'in a kind of non-descript vehicle which was slowly drawn through the muddy roads, and up and down many a hill, by a pair of lean ill-fed horses, and through the roof of which the raindrops trickled'.

You may disapprove of the Houstons' intentions, but you must feel for her sinking heart as she approached her new home. 'As we drove along the last four miles of the defile on which, owing to the height of the mountains, the sun never shines, while the wind cuts through it like a tunnel . . .' she first caught sight of the house, an old fishing lodge of Lord Sligo's, 'in all its isolated dreariness . . . its unredeemed native ugliness'. The wild uncultivated moorland reached to the front door.

How could anything have gone right? Even the water in the lake was too cold to have a swim or a 'tubbing' as she called it. Her book is a litany of misery involving contacts with beggars sitting in the kitchen asking for food, priests, Fenians and the terrible preacher in her own church. Crops planted on the reclaimed moors never seemed to ripen. 'In nine seasons out of ten the sheaves of oat and barley stand . . . melancholy monuments of useless industry on the rain-soaked bogland till the grain grows in the ear and the crop is useless save for forage.' People around did not like the imported shepherds and the evictions. They stole sheep and someone poisoned the dogs. 'Every dog was dead ... six bodies in all they were ... stark and swollen ... poor dear creatures ... some grudge by a local man ...'

'You see that far hill?' a farmer near Doo Lough told me. 'They built a house up there for a shepherd, right on the summit and the poor man had to go up and spend every night there and watch over the sheep that they weren't taken.'

'How can I bear this life?' Mrs Houston often asked, 'and the answer was always the same ... what has been given you to endure you must endure ...' There were a few compensations. She took up fly fishing, admired the glorious scenery and was occasionally uplifted by a moment of beauty like the sight of eagles chasing 'six milk-white swans' across Doo Lough. But when her husband died suddenly on 3 October 1872, she did not stay. She left gladly. 'Never again on my return from a short sojourn in sunnier climes would I be met at the entrance of the sunless Glenmura valley by the weird welcome of pitiless black and driving rain.'

The Walking Tourist came down this road from Delphi and watched the mailcar go by. 'The drenched passengers were looking thoroughly uncomfortable, particularly some young ladies who were burying their faces in shawls to escape the driving misty rain.' I passed him going forth from Doo Lough – we were fated to walk in opposite directions – into that part of West Mayo that consists of quiet country lanes, golden beaches and Croagh Patrick.

'Like a mountain of purple coal,' one traveller described this banner thrown in the sky to St Patrick, while another, viewing the 'lofty almost regular pyramid' on the last Sunday in July, felt 'the devotees creeping up the side gave an appearance of motion to the whole mountain'. Asenath Nicholson climbed Croagh Patrick not in July, but at the end of May. She climbed by herself and was soon 'lost in miry bog and intricate windings of deceitful paths for two hours. I lost a beautiful Testament which had been my companion for many a mile; and when looking for it a man called out "Ye arn't thinkin' ye can go up the mountain tonight? Darkness will be on ye ... and ye'll perish there".' But he didn't know Mrs Nicholson, who, instead of reciting pater nosters as she climbed, counted islands in Clew Bay, fifty of them, until she reached the summit and admired the view, 'picturesque and dazzling'.

The pilgrims who continue to climb Croagh Patrick on the last Sunday of July are celebrating Garland Sunday which had evolved from Lughnasa, a pagan festival, marking the end of summer. Today they had come on bicycles, in cars, on foot and by busloads off the Dublin trains to Westport. Past the chips caravan at the mountain foot, men in gumboots carrying sticks, looking more like drovers than pilgrims, Dublin housewives, thin priests, plump Americans and boys with transistors held against their ears ascended slowly. It was a hard sweaty journey to the top and torture for those who insisted on climbing barefoot. They slipped and bled up to the last shaly bit where the small oratory stood in a curl of mist with the sound of the priest coming out of a glass booth. No sparkling view this Garland Sunday.

I got a lift to Westport and from there took a bus out to Achill where Slievemore is another mountain that dominates a whole area of Mayo. I wanted to see the small village of Doogort situated under Slievemore which is the settlement created by the Reverend Edward Nangle. His rule here which lasted for over a century is the most remarkable of all missionary efforts on the west coast of Ireland.

Nangle began his campaign of 'Christian heroism' when he went to Achill in 1831 – partly for his health and partly to take potatoes to the inhabitants who were suffering from famine and typhus. At that time the island was separated from the mainland and Nangle came with all the fervour of St Patrick to relieve the isolation and poverty. 'Woe is me if I preach not the gospel' were words that drove strong spirited men against Rome. The settlement was run on Moravian lines with the aid of another missionary and three scripture-readers. The collection of hovels under Slievemore was soon transformed into 'five stone slated buildings, of two storeys, houses which have never been seen on the island'. This nucleus was soon added to by a 'cheerful-looking square of plain white houses', three schools, the inevitable 'orphans' house' and a hospital. The focus of the settlement was the new church of St Thomas where 'the noble hearted missionary' preached his sermons. Round about the people were encouraged to cultivate fields and gardens. Nangle taught the men trades, particularly building and sign-writing, and many of those who emigrated to America – they went mainly to the mid-West – obtained good jobs. He helped his flock through famine as is evident from the cauldron behind the houses.

He was very tall, according to John Barrow when he visited him in 1835, 'pale and dark with finely formed features and expression so mild and so pensive that you could not think he could utter a harsh word or raise his voice beyond the reading of a prayer'. Some admired his work very much. 'Like another Luther is Mr Nangle on Achill,' considered a contemporary, 'preaching twice a day against Popery, exposing the craft of the priest.' The Reverend Mr Fitzpatrick who visited Doogort just before Nangle's death went to the infant school to listen to the children singing to the tune of 'The White Cockade' a hymn composed by the Apostle of Achill himself.

> And we'll remember the days of yore
> the friends who we loved but may ne'er see more
> the old sea shore which our young feet trod
> And the house where we gathered to worship God.

Not only Achill, but the outlying districts, received the benefits of Nangle's mission. Fitzpatrick went out to the island of Inishbiggle where 'it was charming to us that in this remote part of Mayo where the church of Rome reigns and where rebellion and lawlessness are rampant, these poor converts are accustomed in obedience to Apostolic command and the language of the Church of Ireland to pray for our gracious queen'.

The church of St Thomas still stands serenely facing Slievemore and the little white houses. It has a plain interior with pinewood benches. A modest tablet tells of the 'Reverend Edward Nangle, Founder of the Achill Mission who died September 9th, 1883 in the 83rd year of his age'. The visitors' book is filled with remarks like 'Inspiring! How Peaceful!'

In fact there was little peace in the progress of the colony which encountered much opposition. There were Protestants who disapproved. From her lonely valley at Doo Lough Mrs Houston observed how 'the Bible Christians marched, and taking advantage of the bitter distress which reigned supreme in the heart of Achill's mountains . . . commenced their operations with a fervour and zeal which too often outran discretion'. *Murray's Handbook* cautioned : 'It may not be out of place to warn every tourist in the West of Ireland that he must be prepared for extreme statements whether from Protestant or Catholic, and for lack of religious charity which each party would do well to discard.'

Nangle was soon in conflict with the parish priest of Achill, Father

Conolly – but the most concentrated opposition came shortly after the founding of the colony from that formidable firebrand, Archbishop MacHale. The Archbishop of Tuam visited Achill accompanied by thirteen priests, together with a band and banners on which was written 'Down with the schismatics'. 'Scald them, hunt them, shout after them, persecute them to death and pull down their houses over their heads' were general instructions with regard to jumpers. For a time the new schools had to be closed down while Nangle went around accompanied by an armed guard. He sought legal sanction for his safety and resumed his work.

'A theological scrap,' Cyril Gray considers MacHale's visit, 'no more than that.' Cyril's family had lived and worked here for many years, and as a retired schoolmaster with an interest in Achill he had started a small museum. It was the same old story. In due course the jumpers jumped back. Like missionaries everywhere Nangle brought a measure of good, relieving a desperately poor part of Ireland.

One of Nangle's fiercest critics was Asenath Nicholson, who came to see for herself this 'oasis where the wilderness had been converted into a fruitful field'. Already in 1845 Nangle's work, together with that of his unpaid curate, Dr Adams, was famous in ecclesiastical circles. Mrs Nicholson gives a vivid picture of the colony, the white cabins, the infant school, the female school, the school for boys and the handsome dining hall in which a hundred orphans were fed, clothed and taught to read and work.

But her own personal experiences were disastrous. As so often happened to her, she faced a curt refusal of accommodation so that she, a teetotaller, was obliged to spend an unspeakable night in the cabin of Molly Vesey who made her living from selling whiskey. Dr Adams refused her breakfast, while Nangle and his wife more or less ignored her when she went up to the schoolhouse to interview them. The visit began badly when the Nangles' children 'laughed in a low vulgar way' at the sight of her, and things got worse when she mistook Mrs Nangle for 'an upper servant of the house'. Mrs Nangle icily presumed that one of her letters of introduction from a clergyman was the work of a Jesuit. Mrs Nicholson retaliated by criticizing the Nangles' method of reading the scriptures to adults rather than teaching them to read, before taking a glacial leave.

The truth was that her eccentric appearance allowed her to be taken for 'some outlandish American pauper seeking charity'. After her visit when she got to Dublin she was shown a copy of a news-sheet called the *Achill Herald* which was put out by the Nangles. To be fair to them, they had a good deal of trouble from unwanted visitors. The *Achill Herald* attacked Mrs Nicholson with a venom that might have been reserved for Archbishop MacHale. 'It appears to us that the principal object of this woman's mission is to create a spirit of discontent among the lower orders and to dispose them to regard their superiors as so many unfeeling oppressors.' She was, the paper concluded, probably 'the emissary of some democratic and revolutionary society'.

She had her revenge when she wrote her book. After stressing the hospitality she had received from some non-converts in the area who lived in appalling primitive conditions high up in the nearby mountains – 'never could be seen a more miserable group and never was more kindheartedness shown' – she considered Nangle and his work. While acknowledging that 'much had been done and well done to make a barren waste a fruitful field' she attacked the concept of keeping people to a dingy subsistence on eightpence a day. 'These converts, turned from worshipping images to the living and true God, as they are told, holding a Protestant prayerbook in their hands which they cannot read, can no more be sure that this religion, inculcated by proxy, emanates from the pure Scriptures, than did the prayer book which they held in their hands when standing before a Popish altar.' She followed this with the words of 'a reformed priest attached to the colony' – one would like to know more about him – 'there is a great deal of religion in the world, but very little piety, and after all, probably the Mahometans are the true church.'

I had a last look at Cyril's little museum and gallery and his garden filled with bright rain-sodden flowers. Nangle's colony looked just as it did in the illustration drawn by John Barrow in 1835 except that the potato ridges and reclaimed land had gone wild. Slievemore, dominating the little square of buildings, rose steeply from the sea.

Eagles traditionally nested on Slievemore. Arthur Young reported how 'eagles abounded very much in carrying away lambs, poultry, etc., they also catch the salmon'. Doogort in the shadow of the mountain was particularly vulnerable to their predations. William Maxwell wrote that 'when the wind blows from a favourable point the eagle sweeps through the cabins and never fails in carrying off some prey'. The coastguards living directly under the cliffs where the birds nested suffered most from what Mrs Houston called 'these splendid Arabs of the air'.

Climbing up Slievemore and looking over the edge of the sea and the entrance to Blacksod Bay, I forgot about missionary preoccupations. Not only did the mountain attract Bible thumpers, but sportsmen as well. The most famous sportsman in Ireland came here, a small man burdened down with guns and equipment, accompanied by a couple of long-haired dogs that could have been spaniels. William Hamilton Maxwell, old India hand and veteran of Waterloo, came to the West of Ireland, fished and slaughtered game and wrote about his experiences in an exhilarating and bloodthirsty book that was published in 1829. *Wild Sports of the West* enchanted such an unlikely reader as Maria Edgeworth among thousands of others. Its popularity, together with that of Blake's *Tales from the Irish Highlands*, introduced a wide public to Connemara and Mayo and started the stream of visitors who came to inspect their beauties.

Looking out across the sea, I enjoyed Maxwell's description of a summer day's hunting on Slievemore. At dawn near the coastguard's house where he and his companions stayed they had a swim in a deep transparent rock pool, then a hearty breakfast which was followed by preparations for the day's sport. 'The dogs were duly coupled and sundry disengaged gentlemen of the village whom we found lounging at the door, were being invested with shot and game bags, when roused by an exclamation of the keeper, we witnessed a curious scene.' It was the pesty eagles, flaunting themselves high above their eyrie with their brood and teaching the young birds some of their skills. 'The old birds tore up turfs from the mountainside, rose high in the air, and dropped them' for the young eagles to catch.

The sportsmen and their dogs duly wandered over Slievemore and after a good 'exterminating day' returned to Doogort, their game bags stuffed with fur and feather – thirteen brace of grouse and seven hares. The eagles had a reprieve. Maxwell looked down the great fissure in the cliff that contained their nest and viewed the evidence of their diet: 'the bones of rabbits, hares and domestic fowl were not numerous . . . but those of smaller game and various sorts of fish were visible among the heap.'

In pursuit of Maxwell I went north from Keel and Keem Bay, taking a bus to Achill Sound, through Mulranny and on to Newport which Maxwell had called 'the ultima thule of civilized Europe'. From this squalid cluster of houses he journeyed to 'terra incognita, the wilds of Moy and Erris and the lonely Mullet over which the winds blew and the waves drenched the sands in spray'. Newport was built up and improved after his time to become what it is now, a pleasant little seaport with its heart in the nineteenth century.

Maxwell wrote that the way from Newport to Bangor Erris was by the New Road which passed over Lough Furnace and Lough Feeagh and crossed the mountains. I inquired about this New Road, but no one had heard of it, until I met Mrs Mulchrone whose son knew a man who had come down that way last year. She offered to drive me to the place where it started near a castellated ruin known as Shawne Lodge. There was a dotted line on my map which did not seem to be duplicated among the bogs invaded by rhododendron, the patches of forestry and the yawning empty mountains through which I intended to walk. According to McParlan's *Statistical Survey of Leitrim and Mayo* written in 1802 the New Road was 'rough and devious as those of the Alps or Mount St Bernard. In the course of thirty miles from Newport to the Mullet this Alpine road is intersected by about twenty rivers.' I found that McParlan is still accurate to a fault.

The New Road was visible as a scar in the turf. Sometimes pieces of carefully placed rock appeared or some corbelled edging snaked along for a few yards before vanishing. Beyond the plantations was the saddle or pass leading towards Nephin Beg. The great brown bog of Erris is studded with lakes to Blacksod Bay. The moorland was far lonelier now than it had been in the old days ... no one to meet on foot or horseback trudging across the hills to Newport Fair. This bog had been another home for red deer and the last one was not shot until 1922. Richard Pococke wrote that deer 'are a very indifferent food, being ever the hunting of them affords great diversion to those who traverse the mountains on foot, but they frequently escape the dogs'.

After walking about fifteen miles I camped beside the walls of a ruined mountain booley under the hump of Nephin Beg. The sun hit the scars of old water courses running down its sides, making them shine like satin. One waterfall still slipped down. Below me the bog stretched to the horizon. Pococke must have stayed in a house like this one when he stopped for the night as he jogged this way on horseback towards Erris in 1752. He was given a stool near the fire, 'the smoak rising up and condensing above'. He ate eggs, butter, new milk and oat cake from wooden utensils by the light of twisted rushes. His guide called for an egg, 'broke off the top and emptied it into a scallop shell'. When they entered the people of the household had been boiling a goat. 'I suppose it was not very good as they industriously concealed it from me.'

Next morning was misty so that the track from the ruin was harder than ever to make out as it crossed the next line of empty hills. Pococke explained very well why it was a waste of money to build a road on a bog. 'It makes a course for the water, and rain washing away the earth, leaves it a very stoney rough road.' More and more wild bog. Then very suddenly civilization appeared beneath me. Below the boggy plateau where I had stood was a river where I could see two men walking their dogs beside the bank. There was a ridge of potatoes, a few iron sheds, and further down on my side Bridy Lenihan's solitary house. Dogs and children watched me coming, and when I reached it I was given a glass of milk and told that recently a party of cyclists from Bangor had come the same way as me. How the hell had they managed it?

Now instead of the boggy trail I was walking easily on the footpath beside the brown Owenduff river. In the distance I could see Slievemore on Achill with a ruff of cloud around its peak. After half an hour I came to a lonely house among trees and knocked to inquire the way. To my surprise the door was opened by a friend from Wicklow. A few minutes later I was sitting down to a massive meal with a group of people whose one purpose in coming here was to fish.

This was Lagduff, once a revenue officers' barracks as some rifle racks in one of the bedrooms indicated. Now it was dedicated to the piscatory arts. Engravings of trout decorated most walls and all round were more racks for rods, tins and flies, reels and nets. The household had caught twenty-seven salmon in four days and expected more. There was a smokeroom at the back to smoke the sides so that no one had to suffer from eating an immediate surplus of salmon. The Owenduff flowing outside the lodge was regarded as one of the best rivers in the west for fishing. Each stretch, each small pool, had its own name, the Rock Pool, the pool called after a forgotten Brigadier, and Pul Garrow known so well to the author of *Wild Sports of the West*. He fished up and down the Owenduff.

'Nothing, my dear George, can be more beautiful than the play of a vigorous salmon. The lubberly struggles of the fish-pond are execrable to him who has felt the exquisite pleasure that attends the conquest of the monarch of the stream.' Passages in Maxwell's book enticed people like the complaining English Sportsman to come to Ireland to try their luck. What fisherman would not be attracted by the description of a day's fishing as enjoyed by Maxwell? The day, for example, when he took 'seven capital fish, including a salmon of thirteen pounds seven ounces' weighed on the cook's scales at Croy Lodge? Or the time when 'from half a dozen white trout fresh from the sea I received excellent amusement; and at six o'clock returned to dinner gratified with my sport, pleased with myself and at peace with mankind'?

From my bedroom I could hear the Owenduff running down to the sea from its birthplace in a boggy hole in the mountains that I had crossed. By ten o'clock next morning Lagduff had emptied and members of the household had dispersed with enthusiasm that bordered on panic to their various pools and stretches of river. Would they be anything like as lucky as Maxwell?

'I sent the fly across the water with the lightness of the thistledown at the moment the breeze eddied up the stream and curled the surface deliciously. A long dull ruffle succeeded – whish! span the wheel; whish-h-h-h whish! whish! I have him!'

I thought of Edith Somerville and Violet Martin, who throughout their tour of Connemara treated the ill-success of anglers as a running gag, giggling at 'the invariable fisherman catching the invariable nothing'.

Croy Lodge, which had been Maxwell's fishing headquarters, stands on the final arm of the Owenduff estuary where it meets the sea. It is still a very lonely place. A long straight stretch of road across a bog, then a closed gate, a sketchy avenue, and there it is beside bogs and sea, a shore line of sand dunes and a view of distant mountains.

'You must imagine a low snug building, and in good repair,' wrote Maxwell. 'The foam from the Atlantic breaks sometimes against the window while a huge cliff seaward defends it from the north-west.'

It was here that the restless slayer of fish and fowl found a measure of happiness. William Hamilton Maxwell came from the north of Ireland, from Newry in County Down. After his varied military service the tall, good-looking soldier entered holy orders. He was never a good clergyman. In 1820 he was given the rectory of Ballagh in Connemara which had no congregation to speak of. But there was plenty of game in the area for him to destroy. And not too far away in the wilds of Mayo was his retreat at Croy Lodge where he arrived overburdened with equipment, 'three books of fishing flies, rods, baskets and a thousand and one useless etcetera from a city's tackle shop'. Here he went fishing and wrote his books. His first novel, *O'Hara*, was not a success, but it had some importance because it initiated the rollicking style of Irish fiction which Charles Lever improved upon and which reads so badly today. Then, *Wild Sports of the West* brought him fame. This was followed by a number of other books, including reminiscences of his military past.

His literary career was more successful than his ecclesiastical, and in 1844 he was deprived of his living for non-attendance. A brief marriage was unhappy. He died after years of ill-health and pecuniary distress in Edinburgh in 1850: an unsatisfactory life whose crowning achievement was written here beside the Atlantic storm.

The old thatched lodge he knew has changed to a slated two-storey building. Its fall on hard times has been recent. Not a ruin yet, it is neglected and empty, the doors locked, the windows barred, the little porch battened down with wood against storm and through a dark window a room full of broken furniture.

I camped in the porch, enduring a night of hellish rain such as Maxwell had experienced. 'The storm came on apace; large and heavy drops struck against the windows; the blast moaned around the house; I heard the boats' keels grate on the gravel as the fishermen hauled them on the beach.' That was the night a dead seal was washed up outside the porch.

The rain passed and the morning presented a world of calm reflections and lazy clouds where each small sound was magnified, the cry of gulls, a woman's voice rounding up cattle on the far side of the estuary and the rustle of heron's wings. I walked on the deserted golden shore around the small bluff of land that falls into Tullaghan with the wide sweep of Blacksod beyond. In Maxwell's time this place abounded in fish. He is full of descriptions of boatloads of mullet and salmon, sand eels, lobsters, crabs, and turf baskets filled with oysters costing sixpence.

The tradition of abundance continued to within living memory. Today the run of salmon might satisfy the anglers of Lagduff, but it is nothing like the past. James Cafferkey who lived beside Croy Lodge told me he had spent a lifetime pulling the lads out of the sea. Among memories of bad times and poor people he could recall the carts that came out from Mulrany to collect the salmon at Croy. You could catch sixty or more with a single cast of the net. He pointed out all the places along the water where there were poles from which the nets used to be hung out to dry. Now even the plebeian mackerel were getting scarce.

13
Bangor Erris · Belmullet · Killala

The road curled across the bogs in the direction of Bangor Erris. The flowers on the turf were tinted chintz and mauve. I was reminded of the countless watercolours of Percy French decorating the innumerable rectories and respectable suburban houses. We had been taught to despise them, but now I could see that his genteel palette was more exact than Paul Henry's beefy mountain landscapes.

'By Jesus, aren't you an awful man carrying that load,' an old man working on the bog called out. Beside him was a turf stack and a dog lay panting at his feet. He owned a smallholding which was just big enough to provide turf for his family. But holdings like his were vanishing fast. We could see the mechanization at work where we stood, huge machines with long tubular steel arms gobbling up the bog and leaving it 'smooth as a pig's arse'. The old man didn't like them at all; money poured into harvesting the turf could have been better spent. He didn't mention the ugliness that the machines left behind them, but he felt it. Here is Blake writing to a friend in January 1823:

> This is indeed the country for the botanist, one so indefatigable as yourself ... you would be well rewarded for the labour of springing from one kind of rushes to another, by meeting with the fringed blossoms of the bog beans ... the yellow asphodel ... the pale bog violet and the beautiful English's fly trap spreading its dewy leaves glistening in the sun ... not to mention the numerous ferns, lichens and mosses which is beyond my botanical skill to distinguish ...

Caesar Otway who passed near here where we sat drinking our tea would have approved the work of the machines devouring Blake's bog flowers. 'Perhaps under the mechanical and chemical improvements of the coming times the bogs may be made to supply the waste of the coalfields of the Empire ...'

I walked over the skinned landscape, botanically barren, nothing but a friable soft brown dust. Ahead was Bangor Erris which I reached late on Sunday evening. Crows perched on the ESB wires and men sat in lines of cars. I was lucky to get a bed.

'Five pounds,' the child who showed it to me said.

'Should I pay your father?'

'I deal with the rooms.'

'Can I get a meal?'

'We don't serve meals.'

In the town the café offering COFFEE AND AMUSEMENTS was closed. I postponed the problem and walked down to the bridge over the Owenmore river decorated with BRITS OUT. Further along was the musical bridge which was cursed – every man who built it was killed – and the place where in 1817 a shaking bog carried away some cottages containing the shrieking O'Hara family and two visiting soldiers of the 92nd Highlanders. I walked back into Bangor Erris past the garage piled with rusty cars and a locked building signposted in the most unlikely way CABARET. Back at my lodgings my pleading was triumphant and I managed to raise a fry. And so to bed with its orange coverlet below a cracked mirror, a plastic Virgin in the corner, a glass ashtray full of cigarette stubs at her feet.

At breakfast a pair of Dutch cyclists were staring out of the window at the grey houses and bog. They were eating their fry methodically – continentals insist on getting their full value in the way of Irish breakfasts – but were in an obvious temper. Why had I been charged only five pounds for the night while they were charged six?

'You came early,' the proprietor said, his finger pointing accusingly. 'And this man,' indicating me, 'came later.'

They found it hard to work out logic in a foreign language. Intimidated, not caring to argue further, they departed, watched by the proprietor's entire family and me. They had fourteen speed gears on each bike and never got off on the steepest hills. Bottoms up, heads down, they rolled out of Bangor Erris into an empty silent land.

I followed more comfortably since I got a lift from a young couple from Dublin home for the holiday weekend. They had no desire to return and live here. The winters were terrible. It was winter, not poverty that drove people to schizophrenia and emigration. If you were down here in November you could feel the depression building up. Summer was well enough. They left me at Blacksod pier at the far end of the Mullet where a pair of caravans contained French families. The boys were fishing and folding chairs were placed around a little table full of food. The scent of garlic-tinged cooking and good coffee floated across the water.

From the headland the views encompassed stately mountains and sea, Achill draped in clouds, the Inishkea islands and the Black Rocks where the seabirds used to be so tame they could be caught with nooses on poles or knocked on the head with sticks. They were uneatable, but their feathers were used for stuffing mattresses. Eggs, however, could be eaten, and were important in a barren land; a local pastime was watching men being lowered over the cliffs to collect them. 'Daring aeronauts,' a traveller wrote in 1836, 'however fearful this practice seems to be, yet by custom they think very little of it.'

The Mullet is a long sandy finger pointing southwards into the sea, what old travellers called a gut of land and assigned the name Mullet because it resembled the fish of that name. So Otway claimed – he could find no other etymology. The fields were hedgeless and I looked out for trees. 'There is not a whole tree in the Barony of Erris,' Carr wrote in 1802, quoting an earlier traveller who heard a farmer's son expressing surprise when he saw his first tree near Killala. 'Lord, father, what is that?' There were very few now. 'We've tried everything,' a man at Aghleam told me. Most trees got uprooted in storms. Any that survived remained stunted. The bush of fuchsia opposite me had been the same size for years.

Down near Elly Bay I found the remains of Binghamstown Castle which Otway had seen turreted and castellated, 'to give a half-military appearance'. In Dublin I had been shown a watercolour owned by a descendant of the family; in the old days it had a greenhouse, a chapel and a bathing box beside the sea. Now it is what you would expect – a grass mound and pieces of broken wall.

'It had to go,' the woman who lived in the adjoining farm said. She remembered it well.

The Binghams were people of tenacity and eccentric vision. Part of the family settled in Castlebar and got a bad name as Earls of Lucan. A Major Bingham arrived in these sandy wastes around 1823 long before Erris boasted a road. He began to construct a track capable of bearing two-wheeled carts in order to get his castle built. He was also the founder of a miserable little village called Binghamstown which was unkindly christened Beggarstown by contemporaries. Even

Murray's Guide had no good word for Binghamstown: 'A collection of wretched huts.'

It began to rain and under my umbrella I followed the line across the field that marked the old avenue. There was not the slightest sign of a tree. 'I cannot well conceive what Major Bingham's motive was for this location,' another traveller wrote, 'on a property where the sea was everything and the land comparatively nothing.'

But Binghams stayed on until 1926 when the castle was prosaically auctioned. The blend of scenic magnificence and abundance of game may have held them.

In contrast to Binghamstown, Belmullet is patently the work of an improving landlord. The Barony of Erris was owned by a handful of men, including the Bishop of Killala, each of whom claimed enormous tracts of bog. One of them, William Henry, who possessed about a third of the area or 47,500 acres, set about bettering his estate in 1824 by building Belmullet which prospered in a way Binghamstown did not. By 1838 it was a place 'where you could see industry in all its stirring shapes ... large and well built stores ... masts of ships lying at the ends of the principal streets'. By 1877 there was a regular passenger service to Galway.

From the main square where Synge had watched a crowd of shouting boys throw up firebrands in celebration of St John's Eve you could see Blacksod Bay and Broadhaven Bay at either end of the street. Across the small bridge that links the Mullet with 'the continent' was an endless low landscape full of sand dunes and empty beaches where houses stood out against the skyline like castles. The Annagh peninsula was green on one side and gold on the other where the dunes touched the sky. Rabbits, thick as fleas, ate the grass.

The bus to Crossmolina went over great floating bog lands along the road which some have considered the bleakest in Ireland. We drove on through the boggy wastes to where Nephin starts forth from indistinctness like a grey phantom. So thought Caesar Otway in 1830 when the only traffic was the occasional cart or horseman. He stayed at Crossmolina upon which he heaped a lot of invective. A condescending Victorian portrait of an Irish whiskey house ... 'filthy beer pots, tumblers grimed with last night's punch, or the froth of porter, all in confusion covered a counter; and where tobacco pipes, bits of blue soap, mouldy bricks of bread, and damp squares of salt garnished the window'. Otway describes how he was offered 'white bread, butter, tay, eggs and rashers of bacon by a drab of a woman leaning against the half open door' who later brought him upstairs to his bedroom. But there was another incumbent lying asleep there ... 'a pair of legs protruded beyond the bedpost, being launched with a body attached to them in the middle of the floor'. The woman seized the ends of the legs, 'cursing and reproving all the while', and Otway who renounced any further idea of lingering in Crossmolina escaped in his jaunting car.

I followed him out on the Killala road. At St Mary's church I sat down for a rest, fumes of Empire circling my head. A monument to Sir James Jackson inscribed PENINSULA. Henry Charles St George who died serving his regiment in 'Birmah'. Lt Col William Orme who lost his horse in the charge of the 16th Lancers at the battle of Aliwal.

Outside, the dome of Nephin graced the distance and nearby the waters of Lough Conn were clear and lovely. Along this road on a summer's day in June 1732 Mrs Delany had travelled from Crossmolina. Her companions had been Mrs Ann Donellan, called Sweet Phil – short for Philomel. They were on their way to Killala where Bishop Clayton was in residence. Mrs Clayton was Mrs Donellan's sister.

Mrs Delany had been Mrs Pendarves then. She came over from Chester the year before with Mrs Donellan and they spent the winter in Dublin. Now their summer journey across Ireland was full of pleasant incident. At Dangan, the home of Mr Wesley, there was 'music, draughts, dancing, shuttlecock and prayers'. At Castlegar Mr Mahon organized fishing and a lavish picnic on an island in a lake. The frequent stops helped to relieve the hardship of the journey in a carriage which lacked springs for a smooth passage on the atrocious Irish roads.

Hay was being brought in from the fields on top of tractors that squeezed through narrow gateways and left hedges tousled with golden wisps. The first sight of Killala was the Asahai complex, a lot of big grey sheds spreadeagled across a hill, chimneys that rivalled Killala's round tower, a vast parking area crammed with cars and a golf course.

In a pen beside the road a farmer was dosing sheep. 'Did you ever see a maggot?' He showed me. Then he poured liquid from a jam jar across a sheep's back. 'This stuff will kill them dead.' I asked about the factory and he said that the workers were on a three-day week.

'If all else fails it will make a good cattle shed,' I commented.

'You're not the first person who said that.' He gazed reflectively at the complex. 'When they were building it one of the boys working on it said, "There'll be cattle in it yet" . . . I think he was right.'

The Japanese presence was indicated with oriental delicacy by a notice that stood out like a kimono at a parish dance. 'These small trees THUJA PLICATA have been planted here with love and care that all may be able to enjoy them and watch them growing to beautiful trees 30 metres high.' I looked for small yellow men but there was no other visual sign of the new invasion of Killala.

A bellringer was summoning the town's handful of Protestants to morning service. Bishop Clayton's old cathedral had been demoted to a parish church. Mrs Pendarves would have said it deserved no better. 'You would not dream it was a cathedral.' In her day there was no organ or choir and 'a good parish minister and bawling of psalms is our method of proceeding'.

The barn-like appearance of the interior was emphasized by the lines of old-fashioned wooden boxes on each side of the aisle. In Bishop Clayton's time a throng had packed these pews and he had sat on his throne benevolently regarding the fashionably dressed congregation, 'an eminent scholar of commanding deportment who united the dignity of an ecclesiastic with the ease of a fine gentleman, sumptuous in his mode of living and munificent in charitable works'. He offered living proof that the jest 'as poor as the Bishop of Killala' was ironic. Did his sermons from that pulpit have the strain of heresy that marred his later career? Unlikely, since in three years' time in 1735 he would be promoted Bishop of Cork.

Today was hot and airless and I napped in my pew. You could do what you liked within the protective wooden walls of these boxes. One of Mrs Clayton's children smuggled in a puppy which had to be removed by a vestryman. Mrs Pendarves sat facing the Bishop wearing a blue satin dress specially brought over from England with a petticoat 'broidered in the manner of a trimming woven in silk'. Beside her sat Mrs Clayton rouged beyond modesty.

Twenty years later Richard Pococke, still a humble clergyman, although on the brink of his own episcopal career, preached from the same pulpit. And later still Arthur Young occupied one of these horseboxes, having waited on the bishop of the time and conducted an improving talk on draining bogs and weaving.

De Latocnaye, a Papist, did not attend divine service. His visit was a strange portent of disaster, since he arrived in Killala in the summer of 1796 two years before his fellow countryman, Humbert, sailed in. His presence caused consternation. Who was this Frenchman in the long black coat clutching a red cambric handkerchief? The bishop in residence at the time was Bishop Stock, who would soon be almost beggared by the burden of entertaining French officers come to fight on Irish soil. He made inquiries about de Latocnaye and was satisfied. Here was Jacques Louis de Bougrenet, Chevalier de Latocnaye, an aristocrat from Brittany. This French Royalist officer who had been forced to become an émigré in 1791 was far removed from revolutionaries and their dangerous talk. Mrs Stock invited him to dinner, but first he walked across to the round tower to take a prospect. 'It seemed rather to have been built as a sort of signal tower for ships at sea rather than as a bell tower or building in connection with the church.' Perhaps that idea occurred to him afterwards when he heard about the invasion. That summer landing by the French at remote Killala was the faintest of possibilities. The year before, their ships had struggled into Bantry Bay and been dispersed. West Cork was fortunate; Humbert brought only misery to the men of West Mayo.

The tragedy of Humbert's invasion contrasts sharply with the jolly experiences of Mrs Pendarves forty-six years before. It is hard not to accuse her of frivolity. True, on her journey across Ireland she made one comment on the Irish condition: 'the poverty of the people as I have passed through the country had made my heart ache – I never saw greater appearance of misery.' But such reflections did not prevent her from having a holiday in Killala of considerable gaiety. In that poor wild country among leaking thatched cottages and ragged people her presence seems as out of place as that of the Japanese now.

She and her friends stayed in the feudal state of the Bishop's Palace. It was not an imposing building – 'old and indifferent enough' – but the setting was fine. 'The sea so near us that we can see it out of the windows; the garden which is laid out entirely for our own use is pretty with a good many shady walks and forest trees.' The Palace has gone, the gardens overlaid by a council estate. The rustle of her dress, her quick infectious laughter and drolleries are hard to invoke in a world of TV aerials and dustbins.

'We rise at eight, meet together for breakfast at ten, after that we set down to work ... we dine at three, set to work again between five and six, walk out at eight and come home in time enough to sit down to supper by ten. Very pretty chat goes round till eleven, then prayers and so to bed.'

The bishop provided mountains of good food. On one occasion Mrs Pendarves and her friends went fishing on the Moy and returned with a load of salmon and trout. 'What was best of all the salmon was dressed for our dinner ... we might have eaten beef, pig, lamb or goose, but we stuck to fish and left the flesh for vulgar mouths.'

'Work' consisted of drawing or letter-writing or decorating the grotto. No one remembers anything about this grotto which was very likely the first in Ireland. She covered it with local shells and others more exotic from the bishop's collection. She revised her schedule and took advantage of the long summer days of June and July 1752.

'We go every morning at seven o'clock to that place to adorn it with shells. Phil and I are the engineers, the men fetch and carry for us ... and think themselves highly honoured.' The 'work' was relieved by pleasant day-long expeditions out to beauty spots or to an island off Killala Bay. Perhaps their pleasantest outing was to Downpatrick. I followed the company's route by way of Ballycastle and out on the road to what Caesar Otway described as a greensward of headlands with views of the cliffs and headlands of north Mayo leading back to Broadhaven Bay.

Mrs Pendarves and her party of around twenty people set out from Killala with a coachload of provisions. 'We left home about eleven and went for miles in coaches and chaises, then we all mounted on horses and went to a place called Patrick past the oratory blessed by St Patrick.' Mrs Pendarves and the younger members of the party looked for shrubs and shells for her grotto. They climbed to the top and marvelled at Doonbristy, the broken fort. This is a sandstone pillar that rises a hundred and fifty feet out of the sea, topped with a patch of grass on which can be seen the remains of a building. Centuries ago some family with a liking for perilous living had farmed at the very edge of the ocean. Then storms had broken off the fragment from the mainland isolating the homestead on the top of the great cylinder. Was it abandoned, or were these people suddenly cut off from safety, shrieking above the noise of the wind?

Mrs Pendarves described Doonbristy enthusiastically, 'nothing but the ocean and a vast rock ... green grass grows upon it and there is the remains of a wall . . . it is so perpendicular that none would climb it . . . the day was so windy as to make the waves roll most beautifully and dash and foam about the rocks. I never saw anything finer of the kind, it raised a thousand great ideas.'

Meanwhile the bishop's servants prepared a great fire and put a sheep on a spit. The menu was 'swilled mutton, that is a sheep roasted whole in its skin, scorched like a log'. Smoke from the fire could be seen for miles around. The main party of older people sat in their carriages sipping claret and eating off pewter plates stamped with the bishop's crest. The bishop chewed his chop with both hands, his wife nibbling more daintily and holding a handkerchief. The young people sat on the grass with a rock for a table. 'I never ate anything better; and though there was a grand variety of good cheer, nothing was touched but the mutton.'

Back in Killala they prepared to enjoy the fair. 'Tomorrow, Madam,' Mrs Pendarves wrote to her sister, 'we are having dainty things. Tis Killala Fair Day. There are to be the following games viz, two horse races . . . a prize for the best dancer, another for the best singer, a third for the neatest drest girl in the company. Tobacco to be gained for by old women, a race by men in back, and a prize for the best singing boy.'

The fair duly took place with a good deal of noise and fun.

> . . . about eleven o'clock Mrs Clayton, well attended in her coach drawn by six flouncing Flanders mares went to the strand. Three heads the first race, the second gave us much sport, five horses put in the best horse to win, and every man rode his neighbour's horse without saddle, whip or spur. Such hallooing, kicking of legs, sprawling of arms could not have been seen without laughing immoderately. In the afternoon chairs were placed before the house where we all took our places in great state . . . the dancing, singing, accompanied with an excellent bagpipe, the whole concluded with a ball, bonfire and illuminations . . . Pray does your Bishop promote such entertainment at Gloster as ours does at Killala?

For the Killala festival two and a half centuries later a marquee was erected very near the site of the old palace. Amplifiers were turned to full pitch. In the afternoon I listened to the children's bands that had to compete with them, and a group of vocalists who had been singing at the Fiddler's Green and were now performing from the back of a lorry.

'Please . . . what is that?' A Japanese, the first I had seen, wanted the duck race explained to him. Suddenly the town was full of Japanese training their long-lensed cameras on an unfortunate duck which was being chased by a couple of rowboats. My inquirer next took a series of pictures for his album of men embarking on the slippery pole to the spirited accompaniment of the performers on the lorry. A trawler was taking out people at a pound a head, and a gun went off announcing the start of the Ladies' Swimming Race. There was much of the casual gaiety that Mrs Pendarves had experienced. But the noise . . . who would not long for the crackle of illuminations in exchange for the music that cascaded all night over the roof tops of Killala and the round tower? It was just short of daylight when merciful silence followed the playing of the National Anthem.

14
Sligo · Lough Melvin · Shannonpot

Festivals were part of the summer scene. Another one had taken place at Ballysadare. I had always associated that sober town with milling and merchants, Polifexens and Yeats. But henceforth I would see it as suffering the aftermath of its pop festival, scattered with litter so wildly that it looked as if a river had rushed through the main street. Unshaven youths were hitching their way down the Sligo road. On the bus solid farmers and their wives were observing with disapproval two young Germans kissing and holding hands, oblivious to their surroundings. The man wore glasses which he did not remove as he mumbled away at the girl.

In Sligo yet another festival – the Yeats Summer School – was in full swing. Pubs, guest houses and hotels were crowded as academics and scholars trooped to seminars. The centre of activities was the Imperial Hotel where I was persuaded to attend a two-hour lecture on Celtic mysticism. After that I felt I had earned a few drinks. I ended the evening stretched on a sofa in the hotel lounge. I had lost my key and found it again, but at three o'clock it no longer fitted the keyhole to my room.

I took another bus northwards into Sligo County towards Streedagh Strand. Here was an abrupt change of mood. In the drizzle I could not see where the grey slaty sky joined the grey sea. I could hear the crash and roar of waves as they broke over the rocks beside the place where I pitched my tent. From here I planned to trace the route of Don Cuellar, the Spanish Armada survivor who was wrecked on Streedagh Strand. After many terrifying experiences he escaped from Ireland, and after he reached safety related his adventures to a friend in a letter that was discovered and published three centuries later.

Benbulben was a vaguely threatening shape hidden in mist. The rocky headland of Streedagh Point stood up like a tooth as I walked on the curved sweep of 'fine sand' inspected by Lord Deputy Fitzwilliam in the autumn of 1588 when it was covered with ship's timbers, cables, boats and corpses. Don Cuellar and his comrades were wrecked here in a September gale, 'so great a storm on our beam with the sea up to the heavens so that the cables could not hold nor the sails serve us'. He could not swim, but when his ship, the *San Juan de Sicilia*, foundered, he was saved with the help of a loose hatch and a prayer of our Lady of Ontañar whose shrine was near his home in Segovia. She sent four waves to wash him on to the beach where he lay covered with blood and bruises. All around him were corpses. There were live men too; 'enemies and savages' wandering up and down stripping the living and the dead of their clothes. Don Cuellar lay in the darkness beside 'a gentleman ... a very nice young fellow, quite naked'. At one point two looters came up and covered them with rushes and grass before going off to break open chests. Don Cuellar awoke to see crows and wolves attacking the dead and to find that his companion had perished.

In the distance the outline of Classiebawn Castle recalled more recent tragedy – the death of Lord Mountbatten. I walked to Staad 'Abbey', an overblown name for such a tiny building, two miles south-east of Streedagh. When Don Cuellar saw it he approached with some idea of finding sanctuary. The little cell was dedicated to St Molaise, one of whose miraculous attributes was ironically the ability to walk on water – he had once walked out to the island of Inishmurray. Don Cuellar found nothing but more horror when he reached the building, 'forsaken, the images of the saints burned ... and within were twelve Spaniards hanged by the English Lutherans'.

Dazed and lost he made his way back to the beach where the wild scenes of pillage were continuing. He wandered off and ran into a settlement from which four people were on their way to the beach to plunder – 'an old savage', two young men, one English and one French, and a very beautiful 'savage' girl. Although they robbed him of his possessions including a gold chain and the girl stripped him of his holy relics, she still gave him some help – a meal and a poultice for a wound he received from the Englishman. He was then sent on his way, directed towards the Dartry mountains twenty miles distant. He had to avoid a village which has been identified as Grange. In his time there was a castle standing on what was a highway between Connacht and Tyrconnel. Today the highway still goes through, with a roar of traffic.

In the sixteenth century this area was thick forest, hiding the view of Benbulben that rises out of the watery fields like a Maya shrine. In this forest Don Cuellar had a piece of good fortune, finding a scholar who understood Latin, a mutual language. Again his wounds were dressed, he was fed and provided with a horse and a boy for a guide to take him over the first mile of road. But his temporary well-being only lasted a short time. He had the misfortune to meet another group of about forty 'savages' or 'Lutherans' who beat him and left him naked. He covered himself in bracken and continued walking until he came to a settlement of huts beside a lake which appeared to be deserted. Entering one of them he found to his terror three men naked as himself who turned out to be more Spanish survivors. 'The poor fellows rejoiced and they asked me who I was. I told them I was Captain Cuellar. They could not believe it because they felt sure I was drowned and they almost killed me with embraces.' In retrospect the idea of four proud Spaniards mother-naked except for Don Cuellar's bracken draperies struck him as funny. To his correspondent he admitted, 'As the narrative is ludicrous and true as I am a Christian, I must proceed to the end with it in order that you may have something to laugh at.'

The village of thirty huts where he and his naked companions spent an uneasy night and another day hiding from passing marauders under sheaves of straw appears to have been on the shores of Glenade lake. It was near the place where I struggled to pitch camp and beside the still water on which the rain drummed furiously. Oh, that remorseless rain. How could Jack Yeats have written of its attractions? 'The rhythmic squelching of the water in and out of our shoes ... savour it ... you will find that the rain has lost its spiteful qualities ... you are one with the clouds, the lakes, the falls and the full smiling rivers of a friendly land.' In the Middle Ages Gerard Boate's eccentric ideas about medicine attributed dysentery and ague to rain; the 'looseness' was said to have come from the wetness of the air.

Rain was less a problem to Don Cuellar than bitter cold as he and his companions, still naked as far as the reader can make out, journeyed round this lake and across the mountains to a village under the patronage of Brian O'Rourke of Breffni. O'Rourke was a scourge of the English – they later hanged him – who took under his protection more than seventy helpless Spanish survivors. He himself was away, but the women and children of the village cared for them charitably.

At this point Don Cuellar's story becomes confused. He left within a party of fellow countrymen to find *La Duguesa Santa Ana* which hovered off the coast waiting to take up survivors. For some unspecified reason he did not reach her, unlike his companions who were to perish in her when she foundered in yet another of the fearful storms of 1588. Perhaps his wounds kept him back. 'It pleased God that I alone remained of the twenty who went in search of her, for I did not suffer like the others.' Right up to the end of his adventures he was an amazingly privileged survivor, repeatedly one of the tiny minority who escaped death.

He was now directed by a friendly priest to a castle of 'a native chief, a very brave soldier and a great enemy of the Queen of England'. This was McClancy, a minor chieftain owing allegiance to O'Rourke, who still held a precarious independence from English rule. His kingdom was tiny, only about eighteen square miles, but strategically important because it was remote, tucked away in the Dartry mountains and difficult for Elizabethan invaders to reach. In addition it bordered Lough Melvin which provided the site for two castle refuges. One of these, built on an island, is Rossclogher and historians guess that Don Cuellar repaired there.

I followed his route along the barrel-shaped Glenade valley lined with limestone cliffs. On the way he had been waylaid by a blacksmith who kept him prisoner for more than a week and made him work at the forge. Its site could well have been one of the abandoned cottages in the hills which I passed on the back road to Kinlough. Three small windows, a low dark room with weeds growing out of thatch and beside it a stream for cooling metal suggested the place where Don Cuellar 'worked at this miserable trade in affliction and sadness' until rescued by his acquaintance, the priest, who arranged his transfer to McClancy's castle.

At Kinlough the lady at the post office pointed out the 'blue rocks' on a neighbouring hill and said that every time a McClancy died a piece of blue rock falls. The farmer who directed me to Rossclogher had no time for the past. 'I'm a bad hand at history. I've enough to do with cows and calves.'

A few pieces of stone among ragweed indicated where McClancy's village had stood in forest beside the lake. Here was the ruin of a small church where Don Cuellar and his compatriots – McClancy had ten Spanish soldiers, shipwreck survivors, in his train – heard Mass. The shell, floating in weeds, retained a small window; a sycamore grew out of a wall. I had been told that the former owner of the land took away stones to make a shed, but none of his cattle came out of it alive. He should have had more veneration and sense.

The castle, wrapped thickly in ivy, was on a small island, possibly the site of a crannog. It was not very far out and there may have been a causeway in the sixteenth century. When I swam to it, a few strokes was all I needed to reach it, and naked, like Don Cuellar, I explored the ruin which was very small, twelve paces from wall to wall. Heaps of cut stone from the fortification had fallen into the lake. McClancy, his villagers and his guests must have spent most of their time on shore while the castle was used for defence rather than for habitation.

Don Cuellar stayed here three months, living at close quarters with the McClancys and telling the fortunes of McClancy's wife and the other women. From his experiences in this village he made his famous observations on Irish life.

> They live in huts made of straw. The men are all big and handsome and as active as roe deer. They do not eat oftener than once a day, and this at night, their usual food being oat bread and butter. They drink sour milk ... On feast days they eat some half-cooked meat without bread or salt. They dress in tight hose and short jackets of goat's hair; over this they wear a blanket and their hair falls low over their eyes ... They sleep upon the ground on rushes newly cut and full of water and ice.

The life-style of his hosts may have been basic but their hospitality was evident. Irish hospitality continued to be remarkable. Half a century later Le Gouze, also travelling in perilous circumstances, noticed how a stranger 'had merely to give a person a sniff of snuff to be assured of a good meal, the best they have to eat'.

In December 1588 Sir William Fitzwilliam, the Lord Deputy of Ireland, invaded the west. The idea of a winter's campaign was novel in sixteenth-century warfare; Mountjoy would take full advantage of it ten years later when he descended on Kinsale. Fitzwilliam went to Streedagh where he viewed the Armada wreckage. Then his troops veered towards the Dartry mountains close enough to McClancy to make that petty chieftain nervous.

On a Sunday after Mass in the little church beside the lake, 'the chief with dishevelled hair down to his eyes ... burning with rage, said that he could not remain and he decided to fly with his villagers and their cattle'.

The nine surviving Spaniards who had taken refuge at Rossclogher decided to remain and fight the Lord Deputy's men from McClancy Castle. 'We would defend it to the death. This we could do very well ... for it is founded in a lake of very deep water, which is more than a league wide at some points and three or four leagues long.' So Don Cuellar and his fellow Spaniards watched McClancy and his followers streaming away into the hills driving their cattle before them. The Spaniards were given six muskets, six crossbows and holy relics from the church. They had to face an army of something like eighteen hundred men.

I camped within sight of the castle on ground which is good pasture now, but then was 'breast deep' in mire so that only those who knew the area well could find their way by secret paths. The little ivy-covered castle was faithfully reflected in the calm waters of the lake. In the distance was Rossfriar where the Lord Deputy's men had floundered.

Next morning I returned to Kinlough and passed the thin line of tourist houses above the lake to explore Rossfriar. Here was dank weed and mud and water up to my thighs. Fitzwilliam's men had struggled just so. The commander found himself in a dilemma since the island was beyond the range of the artillery he carried and there were no available boats. The English lingered for seventeen days. Nothing was accomplished except for the hanging of two stray Spaniards and the regular sounding of trumpet calls across the water to Don Cuellar and his friends with shouts that if they left their castle their lives would be spared. They shouted back to the trumpeter 'to come closer to the tower as we could not understand'.

'Finally our Lord was pleased to help and deliver us from the enemy by sending dreadful storms and heavy falls of snow.' Snarling and muttering threats, Fitzwilliam retreated. Such was his discomfiture that he did not mention the siege in any state papers.

I had not realized that Rossclogher Castle scraped the northern border and that part of Lough Melvin was actually in Northern Ireland. Next morning I set off to try and find the Black Pig's Dyke. I left Don Cuellar arguing with McClancy who had returned after the English were gone. By now the Spaniard was a valuable ally, and the chieftain had even offered him his sister in marriage if he would stay. But 'so much friendship was not to my liking' and ten days after Christmas 1588 Don Cuellar set out for Antrim. No one knows the route he took 'through the mountains and uninhabited regions', only that according to his testimony he journeyed for twenty days to the northern coast and the rocks where the *Girona* had sunk. For the moment there was no way I could follow him.

Instead I asked for the Black Pig's valley. The farmer teased his hay for a minute. 'I wouldn't believe all that old rubbish. If you want to see it there's a wee hole up where the Black Pig is meant to have gone aground. But it's not worth your trouble.' He seemed to be right ... an earth bank rising up in a field behind a bungalow – was this where the mythical pig rooted its furrow?

At Kiltyclogher I got a lift, a lucky chance since people do not easily give lifts to strangers in border areas. The driver of a small bread van was taking his vehicle among leafy lanes to the odd lonely farm house. The van smelt of warm bread with trays of cakes and pieces of apple tart in crinkly paper. At each stop there was time to talk – to a pensioner living with a dog, a girl with a kitten in her hands who took a loaf, an old man in a farmhouse that was an island in rushy fields. A lot of customers were elderly.

'There will soon be the county home,' the driver said, waiting for yet another old lady to stumble out and take her sliced pan. 'No one wants it, but it's coming for us all.'

He dropped me near Conagee National School before returning along a winding country road. I was near the Cuilcagh mountains, little brown and green hills under an overcast sky.

This was where the Chevalier de Latocnaye came walking, his jaunty tricorne and shabby black coat with silver buttons glistening with drizzle, the bundle on his stick heavy with wet. He was not to be put off by the rain. Throughout most of his trip around Ireland he was enthusiastic, energetic, the perfect traveller. When he reflected on his wanderings he wrote;

> The life of a wandering Jew agrees with me very well, that although I was wet to the skin nearly every day, and often much fatigued, I grew visibly fairer and fatter. If I met with good or ill I knew how to enjoy the one without becoming desperate of the other ... my whole baggage was slung over my shoulder or in my pocket, I walked, I ran, I searched ... nature appeared to me in many guises, new scenes occupied my attention and gave me instruction.

His purpose in coming here was to explore the source of the

Shannon, 'that venerable patriarch of Irish rivers' in whose waters he had bathed where it met the sea and had sailed using his umbrella to propel him. Now his effort in seeking its beginnings was faced with continual difficulties. Local guides tried to put him off. It would be six miles there and six miles back, they said ... Irish miles. 'This distance over peat-bogs simply to see the source of a river, was, they thought, a great labour for nothing.' However the Frenchman was obstinate. 'Mr Bruce, said I to myself, spent seven or eight years in searching for the source of another river [the Nile] – why should I not spend four or five hours in a similar search! and off I started across the mosses to find the source of the Shannon.'

He walked over unsignposted bog, dragging his reluctant guide with him. I had a road and sprightly tourist signs with the legend SHANNONPOT for every tourist to see. We arrived separately at the round pool which is the colour of Ireland's favourite drink. An American family had walked with many groans at the exertion from their car and were taking photographs. It began to rain, big drops falling on the small dark pool from which issued Ireland's greatest river.

De Latocnaye commented: 'As with all great personages, the approach to this one was difficult. As with them, too, access gained did not reveal anything very remarkable ... a stream of four or five feet wide by two or three deep flooding out of a round basin about twenty feet in diameter, and, they say, without bottom.' He decided that he must kneel down and drink the boggy waters. Later that evening, lying in whatever noble bed his address book provided him, he wrote down his experiences.

'After satisfying my curiosity and drinking a deep draught of the spring from the crown of my hat, I took leave of the Shannon and wished sincerely the happiness of seeing prosperous hospitable banks of the waters.' (He had been led to believe that the nearby land was full of coal and iron.) ' "It is very surprising," said I to my conductor, "that they have not made a holy well out of the source of the Shannon." "Only the saints can do that," said he. But why have the saints not thought of it? – that is what surprises me.'

AUTUMN

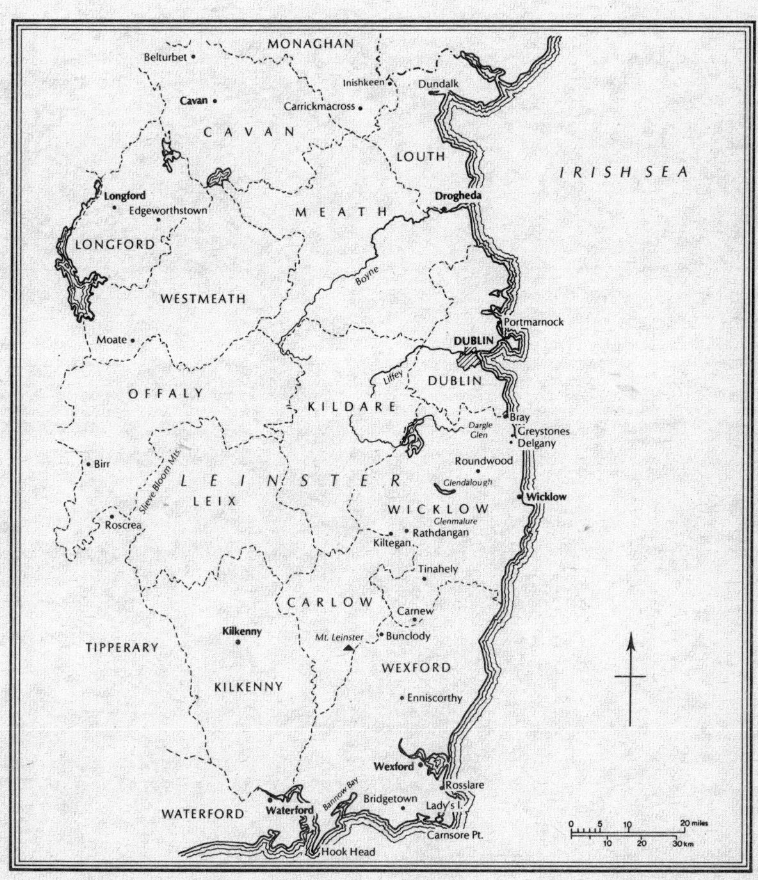
MONAGHAN
Belturbet
Cavan
Inishkeen
Dundalk
Carrickmacross
CAVAN
LOUTH
IRISH SEA
Longford
Edgeworthstown
Drogheda
MEATH
LONGFORD
Boyne
WESTMEATH
Portmarnock
Moate
DUBLIN
Liffey
DUBLIN
OFFALY
KILDARE
Bray
Dargle Glen
Greystones
Delgany
Roundwood
Birr
Slieve Bloom Mts.
LEINSTER
Glendalough
Wicklow
LEIX
WICKLOW
Glenmalure
Roscrea
Rathdangan
Kiltegan
Tinahely
CARLOW
Carnew
Kilkenny
Mt. Leinster
Bunclody
TIPPERARY
WEXFORD
KILKENNY
Enniscorthy
Wexford
Rosslare
Bannow Bay
Bridgetown
Lady's I.
WATERFORD
Waterford
Carnsore Pt.
Hook Head
0 5 10 20 miles
10 20 30 km

15
Moate · Edgeworthstown · Drumsna · Cavan

Moate was one big street through which the Dublin–Galway traffic raced day and night, a thin town clinging to the highway. Behind the narrow lines of houses fields took over quickly. Today there was a wedding party, and the street, commodious enough for old cattle markets, was choked with cars and guests. Fat men wearing carnations in the buttonholes of striped blue suits crowded the hotel bar, bridesmaids in pink ran around, music and sounds of tramping feet came through the glass doors.

'You should have seen the wedding last night,' the waitress said as I sat in the empty dining-room. 'Compared to that, this one is half dead.' By then most of the guests had gone and the roar of traffic had taken over again.

'It's great company,' she said bringing in the chips. 'The sound only lightens after three in the morning.'

Next morning I climbed the Moate, an ancient earthwork to the south-west of the town. From the top I looked down on the old grey houses bisected by the road, a warehouse or two, the courthouse with its curved stone front, the two churches and an old weighing scales like a gallows, a relic of the marts. Behind were the green fields and undulating drumlins like a dragon's back.

Although it was only the beginning of September summer had gone. It had been wet, but today there was a burst of sun on queues of children buying school books and on harvest scenes. I could see a combine trundling through Moate and it was too much even for that street, wide as a football pitch; impatient traffic piled up behind it.

I called on Mr Cox, a retired school teacher whose severe little house near the Carmelite church was crammed with material relating to Moate. 'You can't do it in just a few minutes,' he said, handing me a pile of books. Here was *Fraser's Handbook* for 1854 which mentioned a small inn with post horses and talked about Moate's Quaker colony. Did I know, Mr Cox asked, that the town used to be divided between two parishes, two dioceses and two landlords? The Handcocks owned one side of the street and the Quaker Clibborns the other. A Handcock was elevated to the peerage and became Lord Castlemaine. Had I heard of the blind poet Adam Scholes who was born four doors from here and emigrated to America in 1840? Did I know his poem 'Thoughts for Kind Hearts'? Did I know that John Wesley had considered Moate 'the pleasantest town he had seen in Ireland'?

I didn't know any of these things. I was seeking information about the author who called himself 'A. Atkinson Gent' who flourished in the early years of the nineteenth century in this 'clean, airy town' which he claimed was 'the centre of Ireland'. Had Mr Cox heard of him? Indeed he had . . . he wasn't generally remembered which was not surprising since some critics found him tedious and just a little mad. I disagreed – I found Atkinson's nuttiness charming and his observations on the Ireland of his time most valuable, provided the reader was selective about his rambling prose. We both agreed, however, that there was no information extant about him outside his few books.

Learning nothing more from Mr Cox I wandered around Moate searching for traces of Atkinson. He was a Quaker by origin, but the old Meeting House which he attended, built in 1692 by a man named John Clibborn, was demolished and nothing was left apart from some tombstones and pieces of wall. There are now no Quakers in Moate. But there is a Clibborn. I walked across the road from the old castle and site of the Meeting House to a small Georgian building with an inscription over the door. JAMES CLIBBORN BUILT THIS HOUSE IN 1776. Since then his descendants have gone on living there, and the current James Clibborn is in residence and farms the surrounding land. He showed me an old scrap of paper giving the original estimate for building Mountain View House.

£32	12.	3	
£ 2	13.	0	
			8 March 1762.
£35.	5.	3	Finished 16th September 1762.

This seems cheap, even for the time. I suspect that the Clibborns began with a humble sort of dwelling, possibly thatched, which thirteen years later James Clibborn enlarged and endowed with its Georgian elegance before setting his proud inscription over the door. I complimented the present owner on the industry of his ancestor and namesake.

Atkinson must have been acquainted with the generation of Clibborns who lived in this house at the beginning of the nineteenth century. It is extremely likely that he was on bad terms with them. After his education at Ballinator Quaker School he went into the linen trade. He was, he wrote, 'bred to the linen business'. But by the time he came to publish he was impecunious. When he privately printed his second book, *The Irish Tourist*, he could only afford the cheapest sort of paper for the printing and he could not pay for proof corrections. My copy has a despairing note written in his own hand: 'This work contains several errors of the Prefs, which are unavoidably refer'd for correction to the judgement of the reader.'

The reason for his destitution, he explained in his introduction, was his trust in the Quakers of Moate 'whose apparent wealth and moral integrity I supposed to be the best security in the world'. He invested a good deal of his capital with them, and through a nameless disaster the money was lost. He had a wife and six children and nothing coming in. But, like many authors, he was more concerned for his literary offspring. In his own words, 'the Quakers having procured from him [the author] the main chance, they left him to shift for himself, and by the abridgement of his finances, he has been obliged to send his Tourist into the world in garments which have nothing whatever to recommend them to the notice of the Irish people'.

Previously, before 1810, while engaged in unprofitable business, he had been immersed in theology and wrote a number of essays on Christian doctrine and philosophy. Publication became paramount, and he came to a decision. He would leave his family and tour Ireland seeking subscribers for his book which would be entitled *The Roll of a Tennis-Ball through the Moral World*.

He achieved his aim and in due course the *Tennis-Ball* was published. But meanwhile six thousand miles of travel – so he claimed – in search of financial support had resulted in enough material for a second book. This, too, needed subscribers to whom he owed the explanation about the bad quality of print and paper. He was able to collect fourteen pages of names and addresses of those who promised to support his new enterprise, which he entitled *The Irish Tourist; in a Series of Picturesque Views, Travelling Incidents and Observations Statistical, Political and Moral of the Character and Aspect of the Irish Nation.*

He divided his subscribers into four categories and placed a number beside each printed name. 'The figure One signified the first class or largest measure of subscription contributed to the expense of the work ... the figure 2, the second; and so on to the least measure of subscription.' It is easy for the reader of *The Irish Tourist* to compute the generosity or meanness of Atkinson's patrons. Lord Meath, the Primate of Ireland and Daniel O'Connell, were among those entered under Class One, while a number of impoverished or avaricious clergymen, farmers and gentlemen were subscribers under Class Four. A solitary Joseph Jacob, a merchant of Waterford and a Quaker from his name, was entered under Class Five. Only three citizens of his native Moate showed interest in a local author, all Class Three.

The Irish Tourist is a reflective travel book, serious, informative, garrulous, sermonizing and gossipy. 'Ballyconnell is a little village in the county of Cavan ... Here I obtained a few subscribers and some marks of civility from Mr Whitelaw, the curate, who is married to a daughter of the late valuable Mrs Angel Anna Slack of the county of Leitrim whose character and the remarkable termination of whose life have often been the subject of conversation in select parties ...'

His quest for subscribers began on a cold November day in 1810 when he set out from Moate on horseback, the pages of his *Tennis-Ball* wrapped in paper and packed in a saddlebag. A combination of necessity and impulse had driven him to start his tour at the beginning of winter. He had many bleak Irish miles and muddy roads to cover under what seems to have been a constant downpour.

The first stage of his journey took him seven miles from Moate to Athlone, the busy neighbouring town on the Shannon. 'Very dense population increased by it being a market day ... limbs and lives held very cheap in Ireland ... post boys push their horses without restraint through the masses in the street, and which do not move upon any argument except through the pressure of force.' He lodged with 'a respectable inhabitant of the town'. But he had not gone far enough away to shake off his responsibilities. That first evening he received an urgent message from his wife, as a consequence of which he had to sell his saddlehorse 'to pacify the feelings of my family who were alarmed at the pecuniary consequences of my undertaking'. He had, it seems, left little or nothing behind to feed his hungry dependants. Now he was forced to proceed on his journey on foot.

However, his little flock was dear to him. Six weeks later at some inconvenience he came rushing back to be with them for Christmas. 'Joined with a sick officer ... in a carriage to Athlone, from whence proceeding on the mail coach to Moate, I flew into the embraces of my family about five o'clock in the afternoon of Christmas, 1810.'

I traced Atkinson's route from Athlone to Ballymahon which still fitted his sweeping opinion – that it has little to invite description. He was unimpressed or ignorant of the fact that Oliver Goldsmith was born five miles from here and Ballymahon was his last home in Ireland. The modern town has a church at one end, a garage at the other and between them all the limitations of Irish provincial life.

I found the dank green lane at right angles to the main street down which Atkinson walked to Castlecor. A mile or so on was a large stone gateway, some trees and the old estate wall that surrounded what had once been the property of a sporting eighteenth-century dean named Cutts Harman. The dean built Castlecor as a hunting lodge, employing the Italian architect, Davis Ducart, who worked on a Sardinian model. The result was strange. Castlecor's main feature is a ballroom in the shape of an octagon in the midst of which is a square pillar with four fireplaces, one on each side. Even if they were all lit, the hall would be difficult to keep warm.

Atkinson wrote that Castlecor was a 'model of eccentricity' which would have been a very proper and consistent production of Dean Swift rather than Dean Harman. When he arrived, a Mr Peyton Johnson was tenant, who welcomed Atkinson hospitably and enabled him to spend two days in the neighbourhood seeking subscriptions.

Very likely it was only in the days of the dean, who was rich, that huntsmen had gathered round four big fires in four fireplaces fed by turf boys such as Violet Martin described, after a meet or shoot, and drank whiskey punch or consumed a vast hunt breakfast. The octagonal room has not quite sunk to dust. It looks dismal enough, the fireplaces gutted and the mirrors which Atkinson saw gracing them all ripped out. A carved sunburst and a gilt swag of roses invoke the sunlit Sardinian landscape that had been in Ducart's eye when he set about his design. Nuns took over Castlecor which has now become a nursing home. I saw the front room, where Atkinson retired in the evenings with the Johnson family, filled with old ladies in bed, the radio blaring above them. The four fireplaces remain, an unheatable nuisance during the Longford winters.

Rain poured down on Longford as I went along in a steaming bus still following Atkinson's trail. The sunshine at Moate had been a brief reprieve. Atkinson had walked past the same rushy fields I viewed from my window – 'the country between Athlone and Longford does not exhibit any very striking variety of scenery' – and surveyed Longford: 'the main street is roomy, the houses tall and the shops rather numerous ... in recent years the linen trade has declined and the fortunes of the people.' He could only pick up two Class Three and one Class Four subscriptions.

After his Christmas sojourn with his family he journeyed over similar landscape to Edgeworthstown which is also called Mostrim nowadays. Naturally he visited Mr Edgeworth.

The Edgeworths have left their mark on Mostrim. The hotel where I stayed was called after them and their framed crest brightened the bar. Another Edgeworth crest was inset into the wall between a butcher and grocer, another at the remains of the Courthouse and a sign pointed to Maria Edgeworth's House. I followed Atkinson up the avenue.

Most likely he was shown into the library which so many visitors admired. 'The library of Edgeworthstown,' wrote Mr and Mrs Hall in the summer of 1842, 'is by no means the reserved and solitary room that libraries are in general. It is large and spacious and lofty; well stored with books ... an oblong table in the centre is a sort of rallying point for the family who group around it ... reading, writing and working.'

At the time of Atkinson's visit in 1810 the Edgeworths were at the height of their fame – the firm of Edgeworth and Co. as Sydney Smith called them. By then old Richard Lovell Edgeworth had been through four wives and fathered seventeen children. Byron saw him two years later in 1812 and thought him 'a fine old fellow of a clarety elderly red complexion, but active, brisk and restless. He was seventy, but did not look fifty, no, not forty-eight even.' He had recently been engaged in designing carriage wheels, and also, in spite of poor health, directing the drainage of a large area of bog. He may have been too busy to pay much attention to Atkinson. He gave a solitary subscription for the *Tennis-Ball* and nothing for the *Irish Tourist*. Atkinson was ungrudging. 'Edgeworthstown is a little insignificant village on the road from Longford to Mullingar. I recant the word insignificant on account of the Edgeworth family who live there.' He had to avail himself of the village where he spent an uncomfortable night, and 'while endeavouring to obtain repose on a little pallet ... had ample opportunity of reflecting on the danger of those easy and luxurious habits which effeminate the character'.

Many more illustrious visitors than Atkinson had stopped at Edgeworthstown. They included William Wordsworth and Sir Walter Scott. In August 1825 Scott stayed here for a week during his Irish tour which had turned into something of a triumphal progress. Maria Edgeworth had been to Abbotsford two years before and this was a return visit. The arrival was vividly described in a letter by one of Maria's younger sisters.

> We were all happily dressed and in the library before half past six when a German barouche drove up to the door containing Sir Walter, Miss Scott and Mr Crampton, apologizing for the remainder of the party who would come in the evening ... the first sight was all dust, their coats and eyebrows all powdered over, Miss Scott's hair quite white. The first surprise I felt about Sir Walter was how very lame he is ...

At this time Maria was over fifty, and since her father's death had taken over the responsibility of running the Edgeworthstown estate and ruling her interminable family. She was 'a small, short, spare woman with an extremely frank and kind manner who looked at you with a pair of cold, deep grey eyes'. Characteristically she once said 'that she was the last ugly person left, the rest of the world were no longer anything but plain'. But her spirit gleamed from behind the spectacles she always wore. 'No one ever conversed with her for five minutes without forgetting the plainness of her features.'

Scott's party included Philip Crampton the Dublin physician who had entertained the bard of Abbotsford at his home in County Wicklow where my family lived a couple of centuries later. Maria wrote: 'I am glad that kind Crampton had the reward of this journey ... though frequently hid from each other by clouds of dust in their open carriage, they had, as they told us, never ceased talking. They liked each other as much as two men of so much genius and so much benevolence should, and we rejoice to be the bond of union.'

For the following week Scott and his companions were entertained by Maria. There were visits to the church and school, literary discussions and long earnest walks in the summer garden. The first night after dinner 'the whole party was attracted to the music of the school band and excited Miss Scott's and Crampton's spirit of dancing so much that they flew out on the grass plot and made Harriet join them in a reel'. The boys at a distance were playing leapfrog; Sir Walter stood benevolently looking on. After dancing by the light of the moon they all went into the library where they had a discussion on 'mad dogs and hydrophobia'. On another hot evening they sat in the library where the thermometer registered eighty degrees and talked and talked. 'It would be vain even if I could do them justice in the telling,' Maria's sister wrote, 'to attempt to repeat, as the tone of voice, manner and countenance would be still wanting.' The two authors conversed *tête à tête* while the others listened eagerly. Maria wrote afterwards: 'More delightful conversation I have seldom in my life heard than we have been blessed in these last three days. What a touch of sorrow must mix with the pleasures of all who have had great losses. Lovell, my mother and I, at twelve o'clock at night joined in exclaiming "How delightful! Oh that he had lived to see and hear this!"'

Edgeworthstown is turned into another old folks' home. I suppose it is no more grotesque a fate for a noble house than those imposed by damp, neglect, fire and ruin. As the kindly sisters showed me around, I tried to imagine the furniture so carefully detailed in Edgeworth memoirs and writings in and among the old women sitting huddled around the walls. Behind the hall where a religious statue has replaced the cases of stuffed birds and fish, Richard Lovell had his workshop where he was always making or designing things. Maria's bedroom had its special bow window and in the library near the great one-armed clock she sat at the little desk her father had made her. She was a person of routine and habit. An early morning rising with a cup of tea was followed by a walk before breakfast. In summer she always returned carrying roses. Writing until lunch undisturbed by the hubbub of her family around her was followed by a session of needlework, always a good exercise for active minds. Here where the old women watch television a dozen or so little Edgeworths had passed their noisy mornings. In this room Maria and her father had first read the Waverley novels, the volumes inscribed by the author.

There is more atmosphere in the little church of St John's nearby, the church where the ingenious Mr Edgeworth erected a spire that was lifted into place to the sound of a bugle. Inside, the Edgeworth memorials overlook the small inlaid marble table that Sir Walter gave to Maria and a touching small collection of mementoes – a crocheted purse, another with the initials M.E. garlanded in flowers, an early photograph of Maria in a ribboned bonnet taken a few years before her death, a family prayer book and letters signed 'affectionately yours'.

The Edgeworths were forerunners in educational theory and Richard Lovell started innovations which are radical in today's Ireland. In 1798 he published his *Practical Education* and set about putting his theories into practice, founding his own school where Catholics and Protestants, rich and poor, could be taught together.

> There were to be two peculiarities in the plan of the school. The pupils were to be admitted of all religions and sects ... and all ranks, gentlemen's sons, middlemen and the poorest day scholars were to be taught together in the same classroom ... And to avoid all distinction in their appearance, all were to wear over their own clothes or no-clothes a linen smock, something like an English carter's dress.

Scott was brought to see the classes on a Saturday when religious education was proceeding. 'The Catholics with their priest in one room, Protestants with Mr Keating in the other.' The present National School close to St John's church is Protestant. On the day I visited it Mrs Cunninghan told me only nineteen children attended it. Catholics go elsewhere.

The older school where Edgeworth made his educational experiments, which included the use of a Chinese Mongolian reckoning board, is now a small museum with more Edgeworth memorabilia, photographs, plans and elevations drawn out by Maria's father, her books and even her steel eyeglasses. But nothing in this dusty room captures the vitality and high spirits that sent her bounding through life – bowling along at the age of sixty-seven with the Cullen Smiths towards Connemara, taking up Spanish at seventy and always maintaining that perhaps at eighty she would arrive at the years of discretion. 'I really think that if my thoughts and feelings were shut up completely within me, I should burst in a week, like a steam engine without a snifting clack, now called by the grander name of safety valve.'

When she was really old she wrote to her sister: 'My dear Harriet, you can conceive yourself to be an old lamp at the point of extinction and dreading the smell you would make at going out, and the execrations which in your dying flickerings you might hear. And then you can conceive the sudden starting up again of the flame when fresh oil is poured into the lamp . . .' At eighty-one in 1848 she was sending out appeals in aid of victims of the famine. Contributions included a hundred and fifty barrels of flour and rice from the children of Boston labelled 'To Miss Edgeworth for her Poor'. The porters who carried up this assignment refused to be paid, so she knitted each one a comforter. She died in May 1849 having recently read and enjoyed Macaulay's *History*.

Around Edgeworthstown there were educated people with whom Maria and her family could converse, people more interesting than those whom she considered 'booby squires'. At Pakenham Hall and Castle Forbes one could discuss literature and other subjects that would stir the cultivated mind. Perhaps A. Atkinson's moral reflections afforded a brief moment of conversation.

After leaving Edgeworthstown he sent his 'veleise' to Granard with a sticker on which he wrote *Take care of the Tennis-ball* in strong legible letters. His search for subscribers had mixed results. The weather was harsh and the walk exhausting. 'I had never felt, in my own person, the hardships which our troops were suffering on the continent – twice or thrice I lay down on the margin of the road with fatigue; but this is a small portion of the hardships which I have had to endure in rolling that book styled "*The Tennis-Ball*" through this disjointed district of the moral world.'

However, around Granard he had a number of successes. His kindly hosts, Mr and Mrs M, proved most helpful, Mr M introducing him to Lady Ash who subscribed, and to 'promote my views had the complaisance to invite a party to her house'. Then he had a triumph. He went to Castle Forbes which is situated among tawny hills and lakes, small farms, empty roads with the waterway of the Shannon snaking by. ('The country is poor, bleak, ill-cultivated and in the present state very uninteresting.') There he encountered Lady Granard, whose mother, Lady Moira, was a particular friend of Maria Edgeworth. Lady Granard received him in the main hall with 'condescending politeness', and, he was proud to note, 'subscribed handsomely to my book and promised me her influence with the ladies of her acquaintance'. Against 'Earl of Granard' in his list of subscribers he could mark 'Four Copies'.

The current Lord Granard still owns Castle Forbes. Like Atkinson I walked up the gravel drive and stopped to look at an amazing sight – a large estate, immaculately kept up, the grass mown and numerous gardeners snipping, cutting and weeding. The house, a baronial hall full of towers with a courtyard alongside dominated by a clock tower as large as Big Ben, was glossy with careful maintenance. From the front door came a butler wearing a green baize apron as though he had just been cleaning silver.

I asked if I might see Lord Granard. I had hoped that I might find something about Atkinson's visit. But his Lordship was away in Paris, the shutters were drawn and only the staff was at home.

'Don't wander too far or you'll get lost,' a gardener advised me as I set off past the sunken garden. Pheasants walked among the flower-beds. Beyond the brown and golden trees was the silver light of the Shannon that cut through the estate. I came upon the crypt where the Forbes family was buried, the coffins stacked in shelves and covered in purple cloth. Outside were the tombstones of servants and employees.

'Of your charity pray for the repose of Thomas Hanna for many years Harper to the Earl and Countess of Granard. Died 3 November 1869 aged 67 years.'

He must have been just about the last of the harpers. Very likely Maria Edgeworth listened to his playing when she came over to Castle Forbes to drink tea and converse. When Atkinson walked up the drive Thomas Hanna was a boy of eight picking up tunes. Atkinson was in good heart as he went on his way thinking of his 'benevolent' reception by Lady Granard and 'contrasting the easy and unassuming manners of this distinguished personage with the low and insolent behaviour of several persons whose birth and employment might entitle them to rank with the servants of her hall'. The Quakers of Moate were never far from his thoughts.

I followed his route through land which he correctly called 'soft and spewy'. He stopped at Rooskey ('a wretchedly appointed village') from where he took the Drumsna coach, getting off 'and proceeding on foot nearly two miles across the country to the seat of Mathew Nesbitt of Derrycarn'. Derrycarn was marked on my map and next morning I left to find it. A man walking a herd of cows along the road had heard of it all right. 'Once it was a grand old place with a yard as big as the town of Longford and bells ringing to bring the men in to work.' When he was young it had belonged to people named Ormsby-Gore who cleared out during the civil war. Knocked down ten years ago because of the rates.

I crossed a bridge and turned down a side-road. A strong wind in my face, sedgy fields and the silky grey glimmer of the river. 'This gentleman's seat stands on rising ground three parts of which appear to be surrounded by the Shannon.' When Atkinson called Mr Nesbitt was out, but once again he was in luck. He was invited to stay by Mrs Nesbitt, 'a gracious lady ... a member of the primitive church ... in whose character the virtues of wisdom and benevolence are singularly conspicuous'. Both she and Mr Nesbitt were extremely hospitable, offering Atkinson ' a well aired bed, an object of no little importance to a stranger', the loan of Mr Nesbitt's horse and some introductory letters to people in the neighbourhood who provided six more subscriptions.

The laundry house, a small eighteenth-century building, is all that survives of Derrycarn. The Thorntons who live there are as hospitable as the Nesbitts. They fed me apple pie and cream and reminisced about the old house. Mr Thornton had an old photograph showing its sham-battlemented front; he regretted its passing although he had helped to take off the roof and its ten thousand slates. He showed me the remains of the Ladies' Walk, the Rose Garden, the broken-off stretch of pier and the focal point that Atkinson had admired from where the Shannon spread like a sea and Roscommon was just visible on the other side. Then the Thorntons gave me a lift down the road to the little church of Annduff which had an old square tower looking out over the river and stables in the front where in the days of old Mr Thornton put his horse and trap during Sunday service.

Among the brass and marble monuments I found the name of Nesbitt. Francis Nesbitt, died 1854, last of his line to live at Derrycarn, 'an affectionate husband, a tender father and the poor man's friend'. He would have been the son of Atkinson's host, a ten-year-old boy when Atkinson sat drinking tea in the new drawing-room overlooking the river. I wondered if the Nesbitts were buried in the dank graveyard at the back. Indeed they were, all in a stone vault under the Nesbitt crest. The man clipping the hedge brought me through weeds and briars. The stone doors had been broken off and lay in the grass.

'Do you want to go inside?' He went in himself. 'It's not that bad,' a muffled voice came up to where I stood hesitating. 'Which man are you looking for?'

'Mathew?'

'There's a good deal here all right and someone's been at them.' Now in the shadows I could make out broken coffins, bones and skulls. None of the old coffin plates bore Mathew's name. I quickly left the Nesbitts their broken solitude and went on to Drumsna.

'You are walking back into history,' Mr Daly at the garage said. He was considering the graceful old houses, the ruined gateway, the wall of the old church where John Wesley preached, the grave of Surgeon Major Parkes who had accompanied Livingstone to Africa and the vanishing mansions of the Rowleys and the Kings. He did not include Atkinson who stayed at what he called 'a house of entertainment' by which he meant an inn. I stayed in the same place and so did Drumsna's most distinguished visitor.

'In the autumn, 184— business took me into the West of Ireland and amongst the places to the quiet little village of Drumsna.' So Anthony Trollope began his first novel, *The MacDermots of Ballycloran*. He came here on behalf of his employer, the Post Office. He is not remembered. No signs, no notices, no Trollope Country information in the tourist guides.

'What sort of man was he altogether?' I was asked in the bar.

I said he was an English writer who liked Ireland. He wrote, 'The Irish people did not murder me, nor did they even break my head ... it was altogether a very jolly life that I had in Ireland.' He liked hunting. He married an Irish girl.

'Does anyone read his books?'

Although the pub had a recent face lift it closely resembled the establishment where Trollope and a friend had stayed that day in 1843. According to him there were two types of Irish lodgings, the dry, where no drink could be obtained, or the other, usually associated with mailcar stops where a drink was offered along with a bed. This place was one of the latter type. Behind the bar which Trollope wouldn't recognize was a small parlour which he would, and upstairs vast unchanged bedrooms. The one where I slept had bulging papered walls and a large brass bed that looked out on to a small yard, a sky threatening rain, three chimneys with grass growing out of them, a flight of crows and a field straddling the skyline. I went down the passage and the stairs with its holy shelf lined with religious statuettes topped by an oleograph – 'Pray to the Rosary' – into the parlour where the blank Sony television and the huge fry waited. Then, like Trollope and his friend John Merivale, I went for 'an aimless walk' in the direction of Headford where he was inspired to write *The MacDermots of Ballycloran.*

Down at the bridge which links Leitrim and Roscommon some tourist boats were moored at the marina. A giant chocolate meringue filled with Germans backing rapidly into the pier.

'They give them ten minutes' instruction and then they're on their own,' a Dubliner said watching them making for the wall. 'I told you so,' he added as we listened to the crunch.

Trollope and Merivale walked down 'as dusty, ugly and disagreeable a road as to be found in any country'. Within a few miles of Drumnsa I was on the same old vaulted bridge with two arches where they stood looking up the same forgotten avenue at the end of which was the same old mouldering castellated mansion. 'The usual story, thought I, of Connacht gentlemen; an extravagant landlord, reckless tenants, debt, embarrassment, despair and ruin.' The two friends wandered about the place suggesting to each other the causes of the misery, 'and while I was among the ruined walls and decayed leaves I fabricated the plot of *The MacDermots of Ballycloran*'. How many fictional Irish houses from *Castle Rackrent* to *The Big House of Inver* have been suggested by picturesque ruins? If I was to write a novel about a big house, it would be inspired by Castle Forbes. In due course Trollope changed his journal and opened the novel instead with a fallen ash tree, cut down years before. 'On this I sat, lighted a cigar and meditated on this characteristic specimen of Irish life.'

Enough time had passed for the big ruin to have a little ruin. The old castle or whatever, so smothered in ivy that you cannot tell what it was like, stands beside a farmhouse fallen to bits, but still showing domesticity in a waste of nettles – a broken chair, visible through the cobwebbed window, a pair of old boots, a mildewed coat and cap, a brush ready to sweep out the embers in the fire. 'He only bought it thirty years ago, but he let it become a wreck altogether.'

That evening I thought of Trollope and Atkinson in the rooms upstairs, Trollope writing away, and in the morning having to face the problems of bringing a postal service to this remote spot, dealing with weather, the Shannon flooding and the physical difficulties of communication with head office in Dublin. And at the back of his mind the plot of a possible novel. Atkinson checking his list of subscribers, the Earl of Granard, Mr Nesbitt, Messrs Simpson and Thompson, clergymen. He had failed with that 'rich poor man' who pleaded that 'the claims of the poor in these necessitous times were more imperious than literature'. Shivering under the cold sheets, his damp clothes and mud-spattered hat hanging on a chair, he reflected how Mr Simpson had observed that 'instead of *The Roll of a Tennis-ball*, I should have called it the *rolling snow-ball* which gathers as it goes'. Atkinson concluded sourly that snow-ball was an excellent title, 'for after the snow-ball had stopped gathering . . . it melts away; and the same may be truly said of my Tennis-ball, the subscriptions . . . with about one hundred pounds sterling of my own proper money, having been completely melted down in the propagation and publication of that work'.

Meanwhile I was being entertained by the girls in the inn who formed a musical group, one singing, another playing the guitar, while elderly patrons quaffing silent pints put down their glasses and danced.

Atkinson left for Mohill ('a filthy little village'), searching out subscribers, a young man in trade, a Methodist Minister and a Presbyterian of good breeding. I paused to view the big house outside Mohill which is Lough Rinn, once the seat of the Earls of Leitrim and home of that Lord Leitrim who was the landlord of Maam Cross. A snooty great place, said the farmer who directed me. I wandered round the empty courtyards with their scalloped slate roofs, the agent's house with the little window to which Lord Leitrim's tenants used to bring their rent, and past the shuttered Victorian mansion, fifty empty cold rooms looking over Lough Rinn. It was for sale. A few years ago there was a rumour that Howard Hughes would buy it. But Howard Hughes had died.

Lough Rinn is one of a group of lakes that make up this corner of Leitrim. Lough Erre, Lough Bofin, Lough Boderg, Lough Erril, Lough McHeigh, Drumbad Lake, Meeldra Lake and so forth, like a negative image of Clew Bay. I bypassed some of them on my way to Swanlinbar. This is a remote little place which owes its existence to some springs which during the eighteenth century made it famous as a spa: 'excellent for scurvy, nerves, low spirits and bad appetite'. Now it is a restless border town scratching the North, occasionally appearing in the news for evil reasons. Unapproved roads wind among the

Cuilcagh mountains, the customs post is burnt out, the Catholic church was burnt down and had to be replaced.

I picked up Atkinson's trail at the next town, Ballyconnell, where he arrived after Christmas to find snow three feet deep. For me it was the rain bucketing down that made me lose my way. 'It's a brave wee distance,' a woman told me when I mentioned Belturbet. I passed three lakes ribbed with reeds in three miles and a madman carrying a bucket. From beneath a mottled blue woman's felt hat a nose stuck out like a cherry and when I asked directions a guttural Northern voice answered. 'You're the smart one and I'm only the dummy. I couldn't tell you.'

Atkinson was having his own problems with the snow. He had acquired another horse for this stage of his trip, but it wasn't giving him much help. 'I was several times near buried in the drifts.' As he struggled along, his breath freezing in his mouth, he met a possible subscriber. His horse had stuck in a deep drift. 'Twice or thrice I had to obtain help to loose the saddle and restore him to his legs.' While this was taking place he caught sight of a man standing on a high bank who had been watching him go back and forth. Atkinson immediately made towards him through the drifts.

> I plunged into the gripe filled with snow, and stood there until he had read part of the prospectus of my first volume. Mr Erskine, for that was the gentleman's name, endeavoured to dissuade me from taking so cold a position but upon assuring him that my zeal for the promotion of that work could not be quenched by a heap of snow (I would have added unless I drowned in it) he observed that without seeing my prospectus he had already conceived a favourable opinion of my design.

'You'll get a wee spot of weather yet,' a woman passing on a bicycle observed as I tried to get shelter under dripping trees, among stained blackberry leaves. I noticed a small church beside the road and, after collecting the key, used it as a temporary refuge. Empty churches are a traveller's friend, and if the days of sanctuary are long gone, they provide a shelter. Over the pew where I sat was a plaque commemorating a chaplain in the Orange Order and by the door in a glass box hung a flute, undoubtedly old, presumably Orange. It had been played on by one Robert Pattyson before the advent of the organ, whistling the hymn tunes about the time Atkinson passed on his frozen steed.

Belturbet was only a stroll away. 'Arrived safely in Belturbet on Saturday 2 February 1811,' Atkinson wrote. 'That little village is in some sort rendered respectable by a weekly market and by two bleach yards . . .'

I crossed the flood water of the Erne and plunged into the first bar since Ballyconnell. Beware of the man who grabs you by the hand and says, 'I know your face.' He was a Northerner on his way from a wedding in Enniskillen where he had played the organ and spent three days drinking. A droll, dark face, puffed-up eyes. He lolled against the bar and bought me a drink.

'Have you heard the one about the two sisters? One day their grandmother noticed them all dressed up. "Where are you going, dears?" "Why, to work! We are two prostitutes." The grandmother faints. When she is revived she asks, "What's that you said you were?" "Prostitutes, granny." "Oh that's all right, I thought you said Protestants." '

I fled and walked down to the Erne that flowed impressively past a marina with craft tied up after the summer and beyond wooded green islands and Northern skies. On the bank a whole lot of men sat under striped golf umbrellas as the rain poured down. They were fishing. There were thirty-five of them and they came from Lancashire; they had travelled all the way over in a bus from Rochdale to Belturbet and now sat in great contentment ignoring rain and border politics. Each umbrella was like a small tent sheltering fishing tackle, thermos of coffee, sandwiches, tins of bait, lines and reels. The fishing was better here than it was in England as it had been for a long time. A hundred and fifty years ago the Sportsman could write:

> The English angler, who by due application has at length extracted leave for a day's fishing in some dull ditch or putrescent pond of an English landowner, exults in having captured a pike or two . . . but compare this to fishing in Ireland and fill your boat daily, without the mortification of having asked a favour from the selfish owners of the water from whence the supply comes.

Atkinson spent three days in Belturbet before riding over the hills to Cavan. 'A bleak and barren country . . . not one gentleman's seat, grove, lake or improvement of any kind enlivened the scene.' He arrived in Cavan town soaked through, but in spite of damp clothes set about calling on the gentry, with moderate success apart from the gentleman who turned him away from the door, 'having given a subscription to one of my vagabond tribe for a book, which, perhaps, never existed, but which, at all events, he never afterwards heard of . . .' Then he went off again into narrow Cavan lanes where I parted company with him. He had led me all over the black border counties and now had the rest of Ireland to cover. There were gentry in every county to persuade to take the *Tennis-Ball*. I would come across him again.

16
Cavan · Drogheda · Dublin · Glendalough

In Cavan I suffered almost as much as Atkinson in my hotel where my bedroom was what he would have called 'a garnished sepulchre'. All night water pipes rattled away beside the hard bed. The smell of fry and Jeyes fluid woke me. The fry was cold and the fruit juice fizzy.

A beggar with a tin whistle played to housewives outside a supermarket, two attendants in green smocks gazed from a window of the hospital and the gates of the Protestant church were locked. 'If we keep them open the dogs and people go to the toilet on the lawn.' The rain was beginning again. A helicopter flew overhead, a reminder of the nearby troubled border.

Patrick Kavanagh had nice things to say about the Cavan people. 'I passed through County Cavan, the best place in the world for a beggar . . . Generous are the Cavan folk. There is only one other place in Ireland that runs Cavan's generosity close, and that is South Armagh . . .'

I took the bus to his old home at Inishkeen and got off at Carrickmacross to find the road along which he travelled to the hiring fair. 'Carrick was a town of three streets and many nameless lanes . . .' The spire of the chapel still resembled 'a paling post on the top of a hill'. On the road I looked for the images in his poetry, the crows and the turnip fields and the mean hungry hills. They were there to be found unchanged, unlike Inishkeen itself which had been cleaned up for the Kavanagh industry. It was like Lourdes. Signposts directed you to every place where the poet had set foot. The school, his house, his grave and the bar were labelled with his name. Trollope was luckier to be forgotten at Drumsna.

From Inishkeen in the spring of 1931 Kavanagh left his home.

'I'm going on a journey,' he told his mother.

'Musha where?' she asked in surprise.

'As far as Dublin.'

'What nonsense are ye up to now? It would fit ye better to be cleaning the drain in the meadow and not have the flood drive us out of the place.'

He set out walking with three shillings fourpence halfpenny in his pocket. 'My jacket was down to beggar standard, my boots were a hobnailed pair of my own making.' He travelled the hard cold way, sleeping out in barns, begging for food, drawn to that hard capital city where most Irishmen come sooner or later.

Leaving Inishkeen and its stump of a round tower and poet's grave, I took the shorter, easier route to Dundalk to pick up the trail of William Brereton. Brereton had come to Ireland in 1635. He was thirty-one, a bon viveur who had already done the newly fashionable grand tour of Europe, a spoilt and greedy man. In late middle age he would be described as 'a notable man at a thanksgiving dinner having terrible long teeth and a prodigious stomach'. He was also a prominent parliamentary general during the Civil War. But meanwhile he had come over to Ireland where he had connections to make inquiries about profitable investments.

He was peevish by the time he reached Dundalk. After a bad crossing from Port Patrick to Carrickfergus, he had been ill for some days, before journeying southward over poor wild country to Dundalk. He noted that 'the greatest part of the town were popishly affected' and that his landlady, a Mrs Veasie, had the impudence to claim a relationship with him. 'A most mighty fat lady; so fat she is as she is so unwieldy she can scarce stand without crutches.' Later after a good meal he grew slightly better tempered. 'This is reported to be one of the best times in the north of Ireland ... ordinary 8d and 6d ... only the knave tapster overreckoned us in drink.'

I went to Drogheda and walked up the footpath beside the Boyne. A short distance from the old town the river meanders upstream among water meadows through russet and silver foliage. Behind herons and autumn leaves planters' houses look down on the placid scene of King William's victory.

The old Jacobite camp was above the river. Among the horsemen watching the Williamite army grouping on the other side had been John Stevens in his battledress carrying his gleaming musket – very different from that tattered figure flying over the Slieve Aughty mountains.

Here was an oak that must have witnessed the engagement. In a field where the battle had thundered two combine harvesters were parked like exotic war machines. A willow broke the surface of the river. It was hard to imagine battle, bloodshed and the sudden end. King William's cavalry charged through the Jacobites like a great wind.

> The horse came on so unexpectedly and with such speed, some firing their pistols, that we had no time to receive or shun them, but all supposing them to be the enemy took to their heels, no officer being able to stop the men even after they were broken and the horse past . . . looking back I wondered what madness possessed our men to run so violently nobody pursuing them . . . dispensing their arms, others even their shoes and coats to run the lighter.

In Drogheda Brereton, cheered up by his stay at Mrs Veasie's inn which settled his stomach, thought the town was fair, the largest and best built he had seen in Ireland. His master, Cromwell, was to visit fourteen years later. I took the Dublin train. When my mother was a child she and her parents, brother and sister and Scottish nanny came this way regularly. As the train reached the bridge over the Boyne the whole family would stand up as a mark of respect to King William and his famous victory.

I watched a holiday camp pass, then grey breakers on the beach to Gormanstown. Coming into Portmarnock there was a bang from a stone and the window beside me was shattered.

'I thought things like that only took place in Belfast,' the woman opposite me said as she watched small boys scuttle away from the line. The guard at Connolly Station appeared unconcerned when I reported the incident. 'It often happens.'

I breakfasted at the Busarus, the bus station from where people depart from all over Ireland. Why the place should have such an air of melancholy was hard to discover. There was nothing particularly tragic about the few passengers sitting on wooden benches waiting for the crackling loudspeaker announcement . . . an elderly priest, a student, nuns, a couple of girls returning to their country houses for the weekend. But they all looked sad. How much more full of life and energy had been the nineteenth-century departures of cars and coaches into the countryside.

Although trains gradually changed the process of travelling, for the greater part of the nineteenth century Bians and stage coaches carried people round Ireland. *Murray's Guide* for 1878 devotes a page to hints for those intending to use them. It informed its readers that since the death of Mr Bianconi the cars were better known as 'public cars' or 'mail cars'. It advised:

> Ascertain which way the wind is blowing if the weather is likely to be bad, and choose your seat accordingly, as the tourist will find it no slight comfort to hear the rain beating on the other side while the well and the luggage shelter him. Aprons are provided in the car; at the same time a private waterproof apron is a great convenience; added to which the traveller should obtain a strap by which he may buckle himself to the seat during the night journeys and thus go safely to sleep without fear of being jerked forward . . . the drivers of the Bianconi cars . . . are with scarcely an exception, steady, obliging and civil men, and pleasant companions to boot.

The old Mail Coach Hotel in Dawson Street was the departure spot for most road transport from Dublin to the south or west. Murray's gentle hint that the coaches and cars were not as comfortable as they might be is reinforced by travellers' tales. When Madame de Bovet climbed into a Bianconi she compared the passengers to a string of onions. 'Of course [the car] is always uncovered, as if the natives wished to make themselves believe it never rains in their country.' Asenath Nicholson sat in a coach unable to turn her head – 'The beautiful Vale of Avoca we entered, but my crampt position kept me from one solitary look at it . . .'

John Gamble commented on the tendency of Irish husbands to squash their wives inside the coach while they took the more airy top seats. Johannes Kohl wrote: 'It is in vain that [the traveller] seeks where to sit most comfortably on the coach. In the inside, which is as narrow as a herring barrel, he thinks himself in danger of suffocation and on the outside nothing but a single iron rail four inches high, separates him from the abyss of fifteen feet . . .'

At least the unhappy passengers at the Busarus shuffling towards their buses would have comfortable seats to themselves. I left them and went north to the Five Lamps. Someone had written under the Victorian candelabra ALL COPPERS ARE QUEERS and the water trough surmounted by grinning lion heads was filled with empty bottles. The Corporation had seized upon the usual half-solution to inner city decay and torn down a lot of buildings without replacing them. I walked down Seville Place under the railway bridge past Sherriff Street, New Wapping Street, Coburg Street, Oriel Street and a line of red brick houses with avenues leading off into the wilderness which appeared to be called merely One, Two, Three and Four. At the corner of Two, or was it Three, was a sign, the Welcome Stay, where the Conways dispensed Bed and Breakfast. They had the traditional good humour, that particular brand of raucous gaiety that has long sustained all the miseries that Dubliners have been subject to. And they were kind; nothing was too much trouble for the comfort of their guests. They seemed unaffected by the blitz that had shattered their neighbourhood and left stray dogs, boarded windows, weeds, half-crushed itinerant caravans and the windows of St Laurence O'Toole's protected from vandals by metal sashes. In Coburg Place one house still stood where an old woman refused to leave. Parts of Belfast look very like this.

I went down to the Liffey flowing under grey skies and seagulls. Under the portico of the Custom House an old man in a begrimed mackintosh nursed a bottle while high above his head the old Royal crests cut the Dublin sky. I took the ferry that charges ten pence to cross the river, a service that dates back more than three hundred years. There are two Dublins, the north and south side. I am a southsider, preferring to live with my back to the Wicklow hills. Landing at Ringsend after a five-minute trip brought me back to my home territory.

JESUS SAITH I AM THE WAY THE TRUTH AND THE LIFE was written on the board outside the Mission Hall. Down the cobbled quay two visiting Canadian destroyers were moored. I walked up to the final arm of the Liffey to where it reaches the sea. Here was the empty Grand Canal, a relic of a more leisurely age of travel that lasted to my childhood, leaving memories of slow-moving barges pulled by horses.

Beside the towering chimneys of the ESB station the old Pigeon House has survived, a graceful stone building with a staircase leading to the glass cupolas of the roof. In front of it is the old wharf where before the age of steam passengers disembarked after crossing the Irish Sea. This moment – their arrival in Ireland – has been more chronicled than any other. They would either land here or wait for another tide to take them up the Liffey. Most chose to land because they had had enough. Handel, John Wesley, Mrs Delany, Sir John Carr, Mrs Pilkington, the famous and the unknown, all had one thing in common – a perfectly terrible voyage to Ireland involving dangers, delays, hunger and seasickness. They tottered off their filthy sailing vessels with feelings akin to jet-lag. Contrary winds, rough seas, heaving decks and days of delay were the normally accepted hazards of the journey.

Let John Gamble speak for every traveller before the steam boat came into service, as he boards the Liverpool packet and finds it impossible to enter his cabin 'without feeling nausea and disgust, the air is so confined and suffocating'.

Gamble had his remedies for discomfort. 'When a person is compelled by seasickness to quit the deck and betake himself to his berth, he should stretch himself as much as possible, with his head low and firmly pressed to the pillow, endeavouring to lose all motion of his own to accommodate himself to the ship. Wine or spirits is bad ... the drink I would most recommend is bottled porter, soda or seltzer water.' At the beginning of the age of steam Sir Walter heard a story about a steward consoling a distressed lady passenger. 'The steward said that the best thing for seasickness was whiskey – the lady declined, saying it would not stay in her stomach. "And is that agin it?" asked the steward. "Surely your ladyship would have the same pleasure of taking it twice over." ' Violet Martin correctly defined seasickness as 'the pathetic in oneself ... the revolting in other people ...'

Going round the Pigeon House and down the East Wall I thought of new arrivals diverted from their misery by 'the rugged hill of Howth' and the undulating hills over south Dublin which made the Bay like the Bay of Naples with one or other of the Sugarloaves taking the place of Vesuvius. Then, shaken by the journey, but uplifted by the view, they would set out for Dublin through Ringsend. There was little to cheer them up. 'Nothing can be more filthy and disgusting than the town of Ringsend at which the pier terminates.' 'Ringsend ... the most horrible stink of filth ever beheld ...'

Leaving the Electricity Supply Board chimney striped like a barber's pole, I crossed Merrion Strand. The quality of garbage has changed since Stephen Dedalus observed it. He did not contemplate French letters and Harpic cartons in the wrack beside the snot-green sea. A couple of ducks flew off the Booterstown slob parallel with the traffic and a camel stuck its neck out of a trailer belonging to Fossett's circus parked at Booterstown for its autumn season. My route took me past the shell of Frescati House which Dubliners have watched for years crumbling like a snowman in a thaw. Past the pagan head on the ancient cross in the heart of Blackrock outside the chip shop where cars flew by within inches of it. Down beyond the station beside sea the colour of a stale mackerel stood the small Greek temple with the corrugated tin roof in which Lord Cloncurry gave tea to his friends.

At Dun Laoghaire I sat on a bench outside the Royal Irish Yacht Club and looked down on the harbour where the first autumn gales had swept through the neat lines of boats. Some had their sails clipped, others were hulls without masts, and all were about to undergo the indignity of winter and the long wait in the yard. An old man beside me clutching a carrier bag between his feet was drinking from a bottle of Guinness and talking to himself. 'How are you getting on? Holding on ... doing the best I can ... the same as everyone else ... What else can I do?'

I walked down the south pier built with granite from Dalkey to form an arm of the harbour that together with steam boats transformed the journey from England. By the time the Halls produced their guide books passengers no longer landed at the Pigeon House and no longer did they have to suffer the vagaries of sail. 'A voyage to Ireland is at present very different from what it was within our memory before the application of steam had made its duration a matter of uncertainty and enabled the traveller to calculate without reference to wind or tide.' When Prince von Pückler-Muskau made the crossing in an early steam packet in 1828 the journey had been reduced to ten hours. But it was scarcely more comfortable; he was 'tossed about sick to death, the disgusting smell of the steam boiler, the universal sickness ... a frightful night ...' Still, passengers were now spared the windy exposed pier of the Pigeon House. Kingstown 'made for the reception of ships in tempestuous weather' welcomed travellers with 'one of the most beautiful scenes the rich fancy of nature ever produced', a scene that still gives pleasure.

Below me two nuns were walking down to the bandstand in their drab post-Vatican II habits. I stood near the little filigree cast iron, all-purpose memorial to Queen Victoria. I believe there are similar ones in other parts of the old empire. Little iron owls gazed down under the lazy canopy and Queen Victoria's profile kept a regal eye on the busy road and harbour. In a few months this pretty folly would become a victim of statue politics and be blown to pieces. The pity is that, so far, the nearby monument commemorating George IV's departure from Ireland has proved too solid for patriots' destructive energies. No one ever liked it. When Thackeray landed in Kingstown in rain that all but extinguished the bright glow of his cigar he inspected 'a hideous obelisk stuck on four balls' (a contemporary guidebook described it as 'a remarkable erection'). Madame de Bovet agreed wholeheartedly. 'An ugly obelisk surmounted by a crown lying in a cushion . . . the emblem is not badly chosen to remind one of the idle and voluptuous monarch.' So far it survives, although someone succeeded in blowing away one of the balls, which has been replaced by a stump of concrete.

Along here the Walking Tourist walked his last bit of Ireland looking grubbier and more dishevelled than ever. He attracted attention; young men on foot stared . . . young men on the roofs of omnibuses stared, even the police stared. He stood for a moment on this same road and in a loud English voice proclaimed, 'I am not a Fenian but only a tourist.' After the ardours of his tour he was rather pleased with himself. 'My appearance and unshaven beard and carrying a rucksack certainly savoured more of a military career and that of a soldier.'

I left him for the Forty Foot where Buck Mulligan capered before Stephen and Haines, fluttering his winglike hands, leaping nimbly, uttering brief birdlike cries. That 16 June, 'warm sun merrying the sea', the elderly man who climbed beside him as he unlaced his boots wore a full-length Edwardian bathing suit, a 'black sagging loincloth'. Today in chilly October the middle-aged men frisking around the rocks were naked while two girls in bikinis stood under the sign marked Gentlemen's Bathing Place prepared to make a resolute swim for Women's Lib.

I continued along the coast past Bullock harbour and Dalkey, the line of Sorrento Terrace and Vico Road. And so on to Bray where I arrived in the evening. A cold wind blew across the harbour and promenade with unseasonal strings of coloured lights. Some old ladies were in the Amusement Arcade pulling the one-armed bandits. The hotels were closed.

'We have only an eight-week season,' said the landlady who finally gave me a room. 'October is very thin.' The chips had closed down, the ghost train was boarded up. It was not the time of year to visit 'the Brighton of Ireland', a place where the sun always shines brighter than in Howth or Dublin.

Until the middle of the nineteenth century Bray was a miserable little fishing village. Then William Dargan, the railway entrepreneur, turned it into a seaside resort. Visitors came and stayed at Quin's which was claimed to be one of the most comfortable and economical hotels in Ireland with its private rooms and pleasure grounds and flower gardens a full quarter of a mile in length.

Pleasures of Bray in those leisurely days included strolling on the front listening to one of five military bands, or swimming from bathing boxes or visiting the Turkish Baths topped with minarets. 'Hydro therapeutics and eclatic medicine to promote the recovery of health' were advertised. Charges were moderate: public baths 2s, private baths 5s, bathing dress, sheets, towels, shampooing if required 6d extra. Dr Baxter supervised in the special room where the heat brought on 'a slight faintness and quickness of the pulse . . . a gentle perspiration soon breaks out over the skin'.

'We cannot conceive,' a handbook for 1860 enthused, 'any more delightful day than a free one spent quietly at Bray.' The town was a magnet for Dubliners rather than for visitors from elsewhere. In 1891 Madame de Bovet decided Bray was Dublin's Vanity Fair, crowded with women in fashionable attire, 'a white linen frock with a saffron or orange sash, cinnamon coloured jacket, a sailor's hat with a broad stripe ribbon, black flowery chintz with a fur cape on their shoulders . . .'

Bray was a good place to start a tour of Wicklow. But before its development travellers had to set out for the Devil's Glen and neighbouring beauty spots from Dublin which meant long tiring journeys. However a number of privileged travellers began their sight-seeing in these parts with a stop at St Valory. This was a handsome romantic house with Gothic trimmings overlooking the Dargle and the Big and Little Sugarloaves. Behind it is the ruin of the old Pale castle of Fasseroe and an ancient twelfth-century cross removed by its owner from the glen and pattern route it once dominated.

My family lived at St Valory for a time, and the welcome it gave to Sir John Carr and Sir Walter Scott first stimulated my interest in travellers in Ireland. My father did not acquire the house for its Gothic charm and seclusion. When he bought it in 1946 he embarked with his usual energy on numerous self-sufficient schemes. We would have a home farm that would supply most of our needs and a dynamo harnessed to the Dargle so that the river provided us with our own electricity. The man whom we employed to milk the cows was taught to cut our hair so that we would have no need for barbers.

My father had little in common with Mr Joseph Cooper Walker, 'that elegant scholar, that man of refined classical taste' according to Ann Plumptre who gave the house its romantic gloss. He was an invalid who had lived in Italy where he indulged in gentlemanly classical enthusiasms until he retired home to Ireland and the Glen of the Dargle round about 1790. St Valory was a simple house which he improved; he built up the bow-fronted south-facing rooms, always filled with sunlight, stocked the library which became our kitchen, planted the cedars and other trees sketched by Sir John Carr, which are now way past their best, and diverted the river to become a lake full of swans, later the site for our swampy tennis court.

Mr Walker encouraged visitors. 'Stayed with Mr Walker,' de Latocnaye wrote at the beginning of his travels. He needed rest; the night before he had miscalculated the time it took to walk from Dublin to Bray and when dusk fell he had to solicit shelter. 'I passed the night on a three legged stool, my back leaning against the wall.'

When Sir John Carr called on Mr Walker he made a charming drawing of the avenue and grounds and wrote a lot about his host who was blessed with 'a variety of knowledge ancient and modern, a long residence in Italy, a correspondence with the most distinguished literary men of the age . . . a felicity of temper and a resignation to the hand of heaven'.

Miss Plumptre stayed five days at St Valory, 'a sweet spot, but it stands in a country where every spot is sweet'. She explored the grounds and the neighbourhood as Walter Scott did nearly ten years later. By that time, 1825, St Valory had changed hands and was owned by the well-known Dublin surgeon Philip Crampton (for years an odd little fountain in College Street in Dublin stood to his memory). When we lived at St Valory a hippopotamus skull, still resting under a glass balcony beneath a drawing-room window, was evidence of Crampton's interest in natural history and all that remained of his collection. Later, as we have seen, Crampton accompanied the Scott party on its tour of Ireland.

From Bray and St Valory visitors were in easy reach of the Dargle Glen and Powerscourt. Such beauty spots became increasingly popular; by the beginning of the nineteenth century the excitement of travelling to Wicklow's renowned sylvan shades was a little blighted by Dubliners out on picnics. Carr found the approach to the Glen blocked by coaches, sociables, gigs, jingles and jaunting cars from which the servants were unpacking food. He had seen Barrett's exaggerated painting and had expected something more on the grand romantic scale. However he dutifully wound his way up to Lovers' Leap above the narrow gorge. So did Miss Plumptre, resolutely climbing the rock high above the small rustic temple and seats provided by Lord Powerscourt, complaining that the picnics spoiled the wild poetry of the ravine.

Travellers went regularly to visit Tinnehinch, home of the patriot Henry Grattan, and Powerscourt where around the waterfall music was provided for effect just as it was at Killarney. 'The symphony of flutes, violins and voices lull the soul to softness and repose while the clamour of trumpets, drums and horns rouse the spirits to martial ardour.' Queen Victoria listened to the music.

No one went to Greystones which scarcely existed until the later part of the nineteenth century. It had communication problems. From the cliff path beneath Bray Head and Greystones you can see the remains of the old railway line far beneath. This was the brainchild of Isambard Kingdom Brunel who, although he never came to Ireland, took up the challenge of building a line that still hovers dramatically over the sea. He was dead by the time it became clear that he should have heeded local opinion of wind and storm. An engraving of the 1867 accident shows the train spilling out passengers into the sea like confetti. The broken old line is still known as Brunel's folly.

When Atkinson was in the neighbourhood there was nothing but a few hovels. But he noticed 'the native outline of a harbour' and expressed a fervent wish that it should be developed. The expansion of Greystones was always regarded as a curiosity; until the recent sprawl of new housing estates it was the only town in the Republic with a majority of Protestants. Their varied life-styles were reflected by evidence of fierce non-conformity. Bible classes held on the pebbly beach in July and the contrasting lavish Edwardian comfort of the red and white Burnaby estate. Times change and now it is inaccurate to associate Greystones with retired colonels and colonial officials and to describe it as the place where the elephants go to die.

Although Greystones was not on the fashionable Wicklow tour, at nearby Delgany the La Touche family, descendants of Huguenot bankers on their lavish estate, Bellevue, kept almost open house. They positively invited people to come and admire their philanthropy. The remarkable wall-sized monument to Peter La Touche in the parish church, showing him life-sized with his hand over his heart, states that 'his profusion was a disinterested liberality to the deserving, his luxury the relief and the protection of the poor and defenceless'. Carr was full of admiration for Mrs La Touche, 'a lady who in a country remarkable for its benevolence has distinguished herself for the great extent and variety of her goodness'. He was shown the schoolhouse where twenty-eight girls received a good liberal education. De Latocnaye saw them too and, like Carr, noted approvingly that when the girls married 'honest labourers' Mrs La Touche provided them with a dowry. 'This is one of the most noble amusements that I ever saw people of fortune occupied with.'

Besides philanthropy Bellevue was also remarkable for its glass house, said to be only equalled by Prince Potemkin's in St Petersburg. Carr thought that 'the palace of glass' could have been put up by Aladdin's lamp. It was a novelty, since it pre-dated the great nineteenth-century glass houses by half a century so that visitors were amazed by the grape house, peach house, orangery and vinery filled with 'the most precious and beautiful plants from the sultry regions of Asia, Africa and America'. Carr was shown a consignment of plants newly arrived from New South Wales.

Atkinson naturally came to Bellevue during his tour of Wicklow in search of subscribers. The glass house affected him less than the row of Bibles and the elegant simplicity of the La Touches' chapel where he knelt down 'and returned thanks for the favours of this terrestrial paradise'. When he rode through the Glen of the Downs, music came from a little cottage at the foot of the mountains where the La Touches were entertaining their friends à la Suisse. Atkinson was unimpressed: 'To the music which softly echoed through the mountains, and to which at another time I could have responded with pleasure, I now paid little attention; my passions being moved by a species of grandeur surpassing the charms of the finest concert.' For all their liberality the La Touches did not put their names down for a subscription to the *Tennis-Ball*.

I turned away from the rich coastland to go up on to Calary Bog, the desolate plateau that lies among hills more spectacular-looking than their size deserves, creating a scene that has a look of Tibet. Beyond Roundwood I picked up more memories of my childhood. I visited Derralossary and the austere eighteenth-century church where we used to sit in a high box pew listening to Canon Synge, a brother of the playwright, John Synge. Canon Synge had been in China as a missionary for many years and since his return was much given to declaiming against women wearing makeup and the evils of drink. He always seemed to be addressing my mother who wore an untidy dab of lipstick and had relations who worked in Guinness' Brewery. The mountain church has become a victim to the decline of the Protestant congregation, deserted, windows broken, rotting pews. Curled autumn leaves swept through the graveyard where President Childers was buried.

Down the road was the ruin of the mill at Annamoe which nearly killed Laurence Sterne when he was a small boy. He came here from the barracks at Wicklow where his father was an officer, to visit Mr Fetherston, the rector of 'Animo' who lived in the rectory just above. 'It was in this parish during my stay that I had a wonderful escape in falling through a mill race while the mill was going and of being taken up unhurt. The story is incredible, but known for the truth in all that part of Wicklow, where hundreds of the common people flocked to see me.' The granite wall, pieces of ancient machinery and the millwheel itself are plainly visible beside the humpbacked bridge where the shallow Avonmore runs through. Close by is the main road from Dublin, and even now buses full of tourists on their way to Glendalough thunder past. Could one start a tearoom here with Sterne souvenirs? Tristram Shandy Teas? The Sentimental Journey? and cream off just a percentage of those who flocked to visit the seven churches and St Kevin's Bed?

That was not a project that appealed to my father. But he did start a hotel near by. Laragh House had been his first empire. Between thirty and forty people ran it, including a man whose sole job was to catch rabbits, a full-time laundry maid and a French chef who went berserk and stabbed at the kitchen staff with a carving knife. In days when men were paid forty shillings a week such huge payrolls were possible for an affluent person. The place had something of the atmosphere of a maharajah's palace.

He bought the Victorian country house twenty miles from Dublin in the Wicklow Hills very cheaply in the thirties. Before that it had belonged to a man who gambled all his money away in Monte Carlo and then came home and hanged himself in the hall. The poor fellow's ghost never had a chance to haunt his old home when my father started to transform it, adding new wings, building a ballroom, constructing an eighteen-hole golf course on the hillside, and a nine-hole one for those who didn't want to go out that far.

On the avenue rhododendrons heralded ruin. Here was the riding field where we exercised horses retained for the pleasure of guests, the bog field for shooting snipe and the lake with its little islands that my father rimmed with diving boards and turned into a swimming pool. The main house was burned down except for the ballroom which has been turned into a little private house surrounded by the remains of the Dutch barn, the saw mill, the lines of stables and the laundry room with its big metal stove where a succession of maids ironed sheets and tablecloths.

In Glendalough I looked up Rodge and Sally Miley. While my father built up his surgical practice in Dublin and my mother vaguely supervised the indoor staff, Rodge ran the estate with panache. The farm flourished while the hotel subsided at the outbreak of the Second World War. Rodge showed me the farm books which he had carefully kept from 1936 to 1947, the accounts meticulously entered, the wages of the twenty-two men who worked on the farm, the prices of pigs and calves, the cost of bringing up a herd of Kerry cows from Kerry and a Kerryman to look after them, the cost of running the old reaper and binder, which also needed many men. Arthur Young would have been impressed.

Perhaps it was the constant presence of Glendalough and its tourists going by all summer long that turned my father's attention to hotel-keeping. Today the dark scowling valley and its enclosed lake were as unwelcoming as ever to those who have always flocked to the place where St Kevin pursued by the fair Kathleen sought peace under the dripping canopy of trees. It is a gloomy spot. Countless visitors have allowed themselves to be impressed or depressed by the combination of cauliflower oak trees, the finger of the round tower and the little lake enclosed by 'stupendous mountains' calling for precious peace but made raucous by beggars, guides and in our time transistors.

In the nineteenth century every tourist trap was rendered hideous by beggars. 'A curse . . . a string of ragged amateurs,' cried Thackeray about those who greeted him at Glendalough. Carr, who had been sitting in his chaise reading Dr Ledwiche's remarks on 'Old Legends and Foolish Superstitions', had to take cover. Kohl was followed all the way along the cliff to St Kevin's Bed by a party of idle women, girls, boys and children, together with a guide named George Irwin who boasted of having taken around the quality – Sir Walter Scott, Maria Edgeworth and Queen Victoria.

When Carlyle visited the 'fit *pot* among the black mountains for St Kevin to macerate himself in' he enumerated the 'hideous crowd of guides – no guides needed' – and beggars:

> Little black-eyed boy, beautiful orphan beggar, forces himself on us at last; ditto grey-eyed little girl, with fish her uncle had caught. Scarecrow boatman, his clothes hung on him like a tapestry; big mouth, rags, hunger and good humour . . . woman squirrel clambering on the rocks to show St Kevin's Bed; which needed no showing at all; husband had deserted her, children all dead in work house but one; shed under a cliff; food as the ravens.

This poor woman undoubtedly called herself Kathleen. There was always a Kathleen squatting at St Kevin's Bed; Kohl saw one of them 'like a bird on its nest and presented a very comical appearance'. Asenath Nicholson encountered 'an old barefooted Kathleen who . . . carried presumptuous visitors on her back up the steep and dangerous cliff'. Fifty years later Madame de Bovet was greeted by a young girl. 'I am Kathleen, your honour, Saint Kevin's Kathleen – you cannot see the ruins without me.'

Shades of the travellers linger among parked cars and litter bins – portly Mrs Nicholson trying to put her arms around the ancient cross to make a wish, Carr scraping away some of the mortar that bound the stones of the Round Tower to see how it was built. 'Your honour shall have the taste of it,' his guide said in a whining voice, and later told him that the burial ground was a snug little place. 'All the world loves to be buried here.' And Sir Walter Scott, determined to make the wearisome climb to St Kevin's Bed, 'the first lame man that ever tried it' his biographer admiringly remarked. Four years later, his son made the climb and scratched his father's initials on the rock, a plain W.S. for all the world to see.

17
Glenmalure · Bunclody · Wexford · Lady's Island

The chestnuts were already bald, the beeches scattering, the ash lustreless and the oaks preparing for the autumn display. Beyond the turn off for Glenmalure the plantation firs hung on grimly to their needles. They heralded 'the uninhabited mountains that lie so close to Dublin'. On weekdays at least this part of the Wicklow Hills is mostly silence and forestry.

At the bottom of Glenmalure there is a little hotel where Miss Plumptre lingered in 1816. She didn't want to, she wanted to get on. She had asked for dinner and been told there was only chicken, which would take two hours to cook.

'Get me some eggs, then, I won't wait for the chicken.'

'We have good beds here, you'll be very quiet and very comfortable,' the innkeeper, who was anxious for business, told her. So she stayed, feeling impatient.

Today in a misty autumn the rooms were closed and empty, waiting for spring. You felt you might glimpse the shade of Miss Plumptre among the lines of tables covered with white cloth in the dining-room and the empty bedrooms up the draughty stairs. Only in the small bar was there a stir of life around the fire. Outside, mist curled around the edges of 'the vast and gloomy den'. While waiting for her chicken to cook Miss Plumptre took a walk to see the lead mines at the end of the valley. Opposite the hotel was the shell of the old barracks which would have been full of troops when she was there in 1815. It was built after the Ninety-Eight, 'to keep the wilderness in check' as Kohl noted. A German, he was always on the lookout for military activity. Soldiers from these barracks went out to hunt Michael Dwyer whom Carr called Three Fingered Jack.

I climbed the track at the end of the valley which leads to the site of the last house at Glenmalure which Synge made the setting for *The*

Shadow of the Glen. Beyond was the pass that led down past Lugnaquilla, the highest mountain in the Wicklow Hills, to the Glen of Imaal, then the back road that curled past Spinans Hill down to Rathdangan. This was West Wicklow, where the Wicklow range tumbles down to the plains of Kildare and Kilkenny. Thickets of rowan, their branches bright with berries, hid small empty farms, rabbits abounded and the occasional roe deer jumped over the road.

At Rathdangan the autumn sheep fair was taking place in a field behind the houses. Sheep were moving into the small pens, breaking up and meeting again in a flow like mercury. Farmers with sticks and dogs followed the white-coated auctioneer taking bids from the air for hoggets, ewes, cheviots, black-faced mountain sheep and one pen of ancient ewes, now barren, with bad teeth, which would probably end up in the Middle East where the Arabs like their mutton old and greasy.

Rain poured down as I walked into Kiltegan to spend the night. Kiltegan's avenue of trees and air of refinement have been bestowed by the Victorian castle of Humewood, whose builder went broke because he underestimated the cost of constructing a castle the size of Windsor. Like Castle Forbes it is still meticulously maintained by its owner.

Next day rain was falling and I had the choice of a sojourn in a huge empty bar and hurrying down the road to Hacketstown. I chose the great outdoors where the country was an endless demonstration of farming techniques, wet fields, sedgy fields, good fields, bad fields. Here were patches of uncut barley and mounds of black hay that had been left by farmers cursing the 'English weather', for the wind was in the east.

'Will it ever stop?' I asked a man sheltering in a doorway in Hacketstown.

'Not this year, anyway.'

It was good to reach Ballinglen and seek shelter for the night with the Synges in their millhouse. John Synge was son to the old clergyman I remembered as a child in Derralossary. He had grown up in China among his father's converts and retired to Wicklow.

The millhouse was a hard place to leave for the same wandering Wicklow road on which John's uncle had walked in summer dust. Hanging in the porch was the playwright's blackthorn stick which had accompanied him on his wanderings.

Above Ballinglen was Croghan mountain which sailors used to use as a mark as they steered into Arklow harbour. A man walked in front of me wheeling an old-fashioned lady's Rudge bike up the hill. 'Heavy as hell,' he grunted. But he had the advantage of me when we reached the top of the hill and went on in front spinning down to Tinahely.

Tinahely was small and compact with a market house, hotel and drapery shop which served also as a post office. The menacing peace of winter was beginning to settle on the town.

'Only for the cow and a couple of hens I'd stay in bed,' a woman remarked as the wind whistled through the door.

Coolattin used to be remarkable for its situation in a native oak forest. The only other substantial stand of native oak is at Killarney. From a distance as you come towards Coolattin you can still see an impressive wall of oaks. But, recently, ownership had changed and much of the old forest has been mutilated.

'I've never seen anything like them,' said a man who had lived there all his life. 'They'll never be seen again.' He repeated the phrase and there was real grief in his voice. Swathes of the old trees had been cut down and sawn up in a haphazard way that suggested storm or catastrophe but was the result of convenience to a road or lane-way. Ragged clearings open to the sky were turning the ancient plain of trees into a wilderness. Here was the final act of the long episode of destruction that began four hundred years ago when all over Ireland the new settlers chopped down the forests and turned the wood into charcoal or ship's timbers. It seemed ironic that the Fitzwilliams of fierce planter stock who acquired Coolattin had taken trouble to preserve the last native forest of Wicklow and this new wave of destruction had taken place after they departed. Around the big house of Coolattin the specimen trees, a mere couple of hundred years old, still graced the lawns and parkland; while, beyond, the oaks were being felled, creating a tangle of broken branches lying in a swamp, pools of mud and huge sections of trunks among brambles.

William Brereton came riding through Coolattin in 1635 when these woods belonged to Sir Morgan Kavanagh. He had ridden down from Drogheda in his sweeping black hat and laced tunic accompanied by an escort of two armed men. The woods were 'troublesome and dangerous' and, the evening before he came through, it had been reported that 'there were lurking about sixteen stout rebels well appointed, every one of them with his pistol, skeen and darts; they also have four long pieces but we see no more'. Brereton and his companions sat down under the trees while he took out a flask of Irish whiskey which he had kept hidden in his bag. At that point one of his men noticed a man's partly hidden face gazing at them from among the bushes. But no shot was fired and they were able to have their sup of drink. 'We have had one lusty young fellow in jealousy in the wood,' Brereton wrote. The editor of his travels explained what he meant: 'jalousie ... tottice or grate from behind which you may peer unperceived'.

Coolattin village is still tidy and neat as the Fitzwilliams planned it and as Dr Forbes observed in 1852 when he sat in the window of the inn waiting for the horses to be changed. What could he write about the fostering efforts of the landlord? 'Coolattin Park is of small extent but contains some timber and is watered by a small river, the Derry, one of the feeders of the Slaney ...' He continued in an uncharacteristically florid passage to comment on 'one of those artificial villages that we see spring up at great men's gates, brand-new, stiff and staring, with no trace of the olden times'.

Down the hill towards the coast was Carnew, which used to be in the orbit of the Fitzwilliams. They filled the town with little houses but Carnew was so remote and out of the way that soon there were complaints that 'vigilance is required to prevent their being used as lodging houses for tramps'. Brereton came here riding from Coolattin. 'Carnew ... where Mr Chambers' castle is erected, and which is a neat rough-cast and well contrived convenient house. Here calling to drink a cup of beer (the weather being extreme hot) Mr Chambers overruled us to stay all night.'

Mr Chambers' castle stands behind its wall at the bend of the road, a square thick-walled keep with the daintiest of Gothic additions. Having protected Mr Chambers and his successors from surrounding enemies, it became a guard house during the Ninety-Eight where it was the scene of a cruel massacre, then a rectory, then a private house.

The walls in the drawing-room where no doubt Brereton drank his beer were three feet thick. The reception room close by, added two hundred years later with a bay curving round high Gothic windows, showed glistening walls that suffered from a leaking roof. Down in the kitchen where the cook was preparing a fry a burst pipe over the Aga sent a spurt of water spluttering into the sausages. It had been burst for two months. Plastic buckets, galvanized buckets, saucepans and jam jars were packed tight together in various parts of the underground room to catch leaks. Altogether the thuds and drips made quite a loud noise.

'Don't step there, Sir, or you'll go through.'

The timber on the floor was a mass of brown powder into which footprints sank like boots in snow. This was dry rot. Outside, a carefully tended garden was beautiful even in the autumn. A small castle, little bigger than a substantial suburban house, it was for sale. If you had funds in plenty you could save it.

In the yard where the Yeos slaughtered their prisoners I met Joe O'Toole tending his horses. He was in a gloomy mood.

'When God finished making the world the last place he made was Carnew. And he left the O'Tooles at the top of the town.' Later he took me around the bars to cheer up. Even in this rural backwater there was a new Golden Clipper where a discothèque was being held. Among the young couples and farmers drinking their pints was an Australian girl who was staying in Carnew to do an anthropological study of Irish male sexuality. I wished her luck.

The weather was fine the next day and I walked in sunshine the few rolling miles from Carnew to Bunclody tucked under Mount Leinster. An open market was being held at the end of the tree-lined Mall. I toured Bunclody with Paddy Fenlon and described to him a man who was trying on a jacket supplied by a Pakistani from an open van. 'You'd better be getting a new one. Buying one like that is like buying a second-hand coffin.' He should know because his father had been a tailor.

Paddy was blind, but could still sense and see in his mind's eye the life and bustle of the town. He had been working in Scotland until six years ago when he developed glaucoma. 'It was like taking an orange from a bowl of oranges, the one that happened to be bad.' He returned to Bunclody where he managed to look after himself and be entirely independent.

In his small house he produced an old biscuit tin full of memories. Here was a photograph of his father as a soldier in the British Army in the First World War. Here was another of his brother dressed in the uniform of the 21st Lancers. 'He was always daft on the army.' Blindness alerted Paddy's memory and he could recall every detail of each photograph with the briefest of prompting. He was familiar with every stone of Bunclody. When he was a young man it had been a strong town with a fair amount of prosperity. There were half a dozen bakers, the same amount of blacksmiths, not to mention the sixteen carpenters and all the tailors among whom was his father. Only one tailor was left now in Bunclody.

Paddy took me down to the shop with its discreet sign BOOTH'S SUITS. Inside the little room on a wooden dais, surrounded by a lapboard and goose iron, pieces of cloth, needles and big scissors, sat Mr Booth stitching the arm of a suit.

'It takes a long time to learn before you're master of it.' Mr Booth didn't mean the long tailor's apprenticeship he had served when he was young, but his difficult crosslegged sitting position like the Tailor of Gloucester. No one would go for it today, squatting indoors all your life. The old tramp tailors or beer sharks were a thing of the past. He had retired after thirty years' work, but he liked to keep his hand in by making just one single suit a week.

His shop was in a row of houses most of which were empty. Paddy had been to a wake in almost every one. Tap, tap. He didn't like people helping him across the street and there was no need for it. In his way he could see as well as I could. After his stick nosed out a child's toy in the middle of the pavement he expertly avoided some empty bottles before tackling the busy main street. He listened for the sound of traffic and then moved across to the lines of trees along the Mall. He pointed out the post office which was once Loudon's Hotel where all the gentry came to fish, and now they sorted out letters where people drank whiskey punch in the old days.

We continued around, Paddy tapping his stick, people calling out, 'Hello, Paddy!' There was the old millhouse where they had once ground corn. There was the barracks. When he was a child he had seen the picture of Michael Leary, the Tipperary V.C., in there, and as well as that a poster of Dan Breen wanted dead or alive for five hundred pounds reward. He could remember the days when Redmond's volunteers marched up and down the street with wooden rifles that cost two and six. It was a different world now, and the young didn't care. They were always in a hurry. He stopped outside the large windows of the commercial café for me to glance inside at a group of young men. Hearing that I had come from Carnew, Paddy gave me a rhyme. Had I heard of Biddy Dolan who worked for the Yeomanry in Carnew? The ballad? Part of it went: 'We've a warm spot for you, Biddy Dolan, in the lower part of hell ...' We parted soon after that, Paddy taking his time, walking home, a shopping bag in one hand, his stick in the other, feeling the familiar edges of the kerb.

On the bus to Enniscorthy a shabby half-drunk man was shouting, 'Do you know "Danny Boy"?' The lady sitting beside him stared stonily ahead to no avail. He obliged her and us by singing every refrain. When the driver came in he called out, 'I want some relief.'

'Make it quick!'

He bolted to the nearest pub for a pint and reeled back in under five minutes. The bus was packed with people out for the shopping.

'Drive on, drive on,' the same man shouted. 'Put your boot down ...' And the decent driver obliged.

Brereton rode into Enniscorthy after negotiating the woods of Shillelagh.

'We lodged ... at one Andrew Plumner's, a Scotchman, where we paid 1 shilling ordinary for ourselves and 6d for our servants ...'

Later travellers admired Enniscorthy. 'The approach is imposing,' Inglis wrote, 'there is an ancient look about it and some great towers and the navigable river and bridge and wooded banks form a rather striking assemblage of images.' But another image was the beggars 'collected here in greater numbers than we had yet seen in Ireland ... importunate and clamorous'. 'Hapless creatures standing under the torrents of rain,' wrote another traveller peering from the small buttoned-up window of his coach, 'strong able women with children in their arms ... jokes and vile ribaldry of both sexes ... this had more effect than the silent wants of infirmity or age.'

A tinker girl with a baby walking over the old stone bridge beneath the cap of Vinegar Hill evoked the past. The sun shone on the river, grey like the castle and the grey slated houses rising up the steep hill to the top. Here was County Wexford among the richer fatter greener lands. 'They give no challenge,' John Synge had told me, 'Wexford is duller after the hills.'

Thick bands of reeds and trees with tortoiseshell colouring lined the Slaney over which ducks were flying in scores. But their numbers were few in comparison to the newly arrived gathering of Greenland white-fronted geese on the North Slob. I stayed around there to watch them by night and by day – at night, lines and V formations against the moon, by day, the same with a sudden rush and beat of wings and honking as they flew in to feed.

A wall has held back the sea since 1847 when Dangan's pumping station drained the marshes and made the playground for geese that conflicts with the demands of farming. Where the embankment ended and the beach began was the bridge with its long string of lights shaking in the wind and a large notice WELCOME TO THE WEXFORD FESTIVAL.

This was the bridge over which de Latocnaye walked in 1798. He considered it 'the longest bridge that ever joined two pieces of land' and it took seven minutes to cross. He disliked Wexford. 'Without wishing it any harm, I may say that it is one of the ugliest and dirtiest towns in the whole of Ireland.'

Rebellion was in the air in 1635 when Brereton rode the eight weary miles from Enniscorthy to Wexford which made him hungry for a meal at the sign of the Windmill. He attended the Assizes and heard three rebels being sentenced. He caught sight of one followed by a group of women and supporters lamenting 'sometimes so violent as though they were distracted'. 'In this town are many Papists.' They had crowded to the Assizes.

> Some gentlewomen of good quality I observed clothed in good handsome gowns, petticoats and hats, who wore Irish rugs, which have handsome, comely, large fringes, which go about their necks and serve instead of bands. This ruggy fringe is joined to a garment which comes round about them and reacheth to the very ground, and this is an handsome comely vestment ... the most of the women are barenecked and clear-skinned, and wear a crucifix, tied in a black necklace, hanging between their breasts. It seems they are not ashamed of their religion, nor desire to conceal themselves.

The wind blew round the market place and the figure of the Pikeman, up Church Street, past Selskar Abbey where Strongbow's daughter married Raymond le Gros, through Keyser's Lane and Oyster Lane. In the foyer of White's Hotel opera buffs in evening dress were having coffee and warming themselves in front of a log fire. They had booked ahead for the privilege of staying at White's, an old place, established in 1779 as a lodging house for militia men. The doorman in his green uniform with red lapels looked on as they waited for the curtain to go up on one of the obscure operas which the Festival disinters each year, a Dublin business man, numerous musical enthusiasts from England, some gushing school teachers. Downstairs, more people in evening dress were touring an exhibition of shell pictures; upstairs in the Gents others were reading the sports pages of newspapers put up by the kindly management to read as they urinated.

'It's all very highfalutin,' a woman was saying in the foyer. 'That's why they can only draw it out for a week.' Her friend agreed. 'What's the use if you can't understand it?'

I felt I was swimming against the tide. The efforts of finding a place to stay at such a foolish time soured the place for me, and I was glad next day to be on the Rosslare train that ran through the town along the quays and then out by the South Slob. From the carriage window I could see waves of geese rising and falling against the sky.

Beyond Rosslare harbour the beach began where in the old days horse races were run on the sands under English rules. It had long returned to its wild state, the cliffs rising above the hard-packed glistening sand, the grass coated with heavy dew.

'There's a few wild dogs, but they won't harm you,' I was told as I walked towards Greenore Point. Slumbering farms overlooked the sea and Tuskar Rock in the distance. Twenty minutes from the bustle and crowds of Rosslare was the silence of the wilderness. This was a place that seemed as remote as it had been when Richard Pococke rode along the strand and saw seals lying on the rocks so placid they took no notice of the noise he made to frighten them.

Near a small pier and harbour beside a couple of fishing boats and lobster pots thrown on the grass were the walls of a small ruined church, and a solitary tombstone with words obscured by a century of coastal weather. The date was 1878 and the stone recorded the death of Peter Pendon and his crew of the *Emma of Scilly* drowned on this coast. A rock offshore is named after Captain Pendon.

Another long ribbon of sand led to Carne which looked so impressive and wavering in the distance like the mirage of a city, but at close quarters turned into a caravan park hostel and restaurant closed down for the winter. Inland towards Carne Head, a maze of lanes with thick hedgerows marked off with well-tilled fields and neat houses, a country of castles and long thatched cottages.

At Carnsore Point Ireland ended in a thick snout of grass and rock opposite Tuskar Rock and the Saltee islands, a peaceful wild place under threat while the government toys with the idea of fouling it with a nuclear power station. Pococke explored here. 'I went to the point which is covered with mussels that fix to it with their beards

... there are also whelks and limpets on these rocks, and a boy seeing me walk on them came and groped for crabs, and I observed he knew every hole tho' it was under water.'

Across a landscape of slob, reeds and waterbirds rose the tall church spire on Lady's Island. A thin isthmus of gravelly storm beach divided Lady's Island lake, which is a salt water lagoon, from the sea. The island that extends from one side of the lake contains the remains of an Augustinian monastery, a place of pilgrimage since Norman times when the Virgin appeared here in a shining light. I walked towards the huge massive redstone spire of the Puginesque church beyond wavering reeds, passing Castletown and a ruined castle. Was it worth looking at?

'Jesus Christ, it is not,' said the man I asked. 'There's nothing to see but old murder holes and they are now covered up.'

Further down the road I met Paddy Wall living opposite the family windmill in which he had worked as a child. He was eighty-six now, and his brother was ninety-nine. Although he had lived much of his life in Australia the old mill was nearest to his heart. He remembered times before the century when the carts of barley had come this way and the great sails turning were one of the sights. The mill, like so many of the old things, was killed in the First War. Now someone had taken the farmhouse beside it, made it smart and filled it with opera people.

On Sunday the big red church around which the mist and rain swirled was packed. There was a fine strain of people in these parts. Outside, facing Lady's Island, I met Niko Scanlan, ninety-four years old and looking half his great age. Niko rode a 75cc Honda. Earlier in his life he had been the first man to put steel strings on a fiddle and he had built his house for twenty-three pounds. All done without learning.

'If you go to school you will ruin your brains.'

But his most remarkable achievement was as a sculptor. From the church door you look down on Lady's Island at the Norman keep and gateway that guard the sanctuary and Niko's two concrete statues in front of them. One is of Christ the King and the other is the Queen of the Island, plump and smiling, standing among plastic flowers.

Niko had done the work with one tool – an old spoon. The Queen of the Island had taken six days to make. He could remember nothing of the six days, nothing of using the spoon on the wet concrete, only that before he was about to begin, just as he was leaving the small henhouse which he had turned into a makeshift studio, he had heard a voice. 'I'll bless your hands.' And here she stood smiling in the rain. It was part of the holiness that persisted in this place for the eight hundred years that pilgrims had been coming to Lady's Island.

Pococke rode here on an equally bad day and under a sluicing grey sky. He wrote of the old church with a niche for an alabaster virgin and saviour and an old brass cross with the four evangelists on either side. He admired the maiden tower 'which was settled on one side' like the leaning tower of Pisa (it still is), built on the site of an earlier castle founded by a stout Norman named Rudolf de Lamporte who went off on the Third Crusade and got killed. Pococke wrote without comment about the activities of pilgrims. 'They come to do penance here by walking once round the island barefooted and three times round the church, and sometimes they perform this three times over, and some on their knees . . . the tracks of their feet is seen all round the Island . . . and all the roads are exceeding fine in these parts.' It was the time of the Penal Laws and heavenly visions of the Virgin were not in favour. But official disapproval never stopped the pilgrims. The same pilgrims' path, worn by centuries of pious use, signposted by yet another Virgin placed here in Holy Year, guides the devout in their circle in the midst of the salt lake. They tour less extravagantly, being advised by a notice in the church to follow mild devotional practices like reciting three rosaries.

18
Clonmines · Tintern · Kilkenny · Roscrea · Birr

The same rain that Pococke endured poured down on the network of narrow lanes linking the wet country. I sheltered and drank coffee at Bargy Castle, now a hotel, where Cromwell was driven off by a swarm of bees and Bagenal Harvey planned rebellion. Another lane between high hedges. A rat ran in front of me and four wet black horses watched mournfully as I passed in the direction of Bridgetown.

Just outside Bridgetown was a railway station, which, given the vulnerability of rural rail services and the remoteness of Bargy seemed like a living ghost. It looked like a Meccano set – a grey metal bridge, two platforms, a ticket office which was closed, a 'mechanical snatcher' beside the tracks and a signal box that radiated warmth and comfort. Through the glass I could see in addition to the double line of levers for changing the points, an anthracite fire, some old car seats and a teapot. The signalman, an avuncular man, seeing me standing there, invited me to come in for a cup.

'There's no train till the evening.' The line wasn't too busy. The beet kept the trains going, but the days when passengers used them were almost gone. Just a few pensioners spending their time travelling free like the old man of seventy-nine who was here recently and did nothing but go up and down. The train was warmer and more cheery than his own place. That old fellow had stopped off at Bridgetown and missed the express and the signalman had to give him a bed.

I contemplated asking the same favour, but it was still early. Bridgetown was also enduring the rain. The Bargy Bar was closed and so was the shop, and the derelict house at the crossroads was boarded up. Only one bar was open with four sad men drinking pints and a child playing with bottletops. Here was a Protestant church and the weedy cemetery with a yew-tree and a holly-bush among the old headstones that Pococke explored. He found a stone that must be blank-faced now in the rank grass.

> Here lyes a jolly merry blade
> Who's gone; – but now he's but a shade
> To teach the ghosts a Masquerade:
> But Pluto likes not such a Guest
> Bids him depart and go to rest.
> William Hoskins, Dancing Master 1748.

Could Bridgetown ever have required the services of a dancing master? Riding on horseback among these lanes, Pococke took a great liking to Bargy and Forth which he called 'an enchanted country'. He was one of the earliest of travellers to be intrigued by the Normans of Forth. The Anglo-Normans, who settled here and stocked the flat country with castles, remained isolated, marrying amongst themselves and stubbornly following their own contrary ways. They rejected the Reformation and remained Catholic, at the same time largely loyal to the Crown – both disastrous decisions resulting in dispossession. They remained a distinctive tribe, speaking English, which by the eighteenth century was the most ancient English speech in Ireland. For Pococke this was the more noticeable in a country where the majority spoke Gaelic. He considered it archaic, and affirmed that it was 'the English of the time of Henry II and comes pretty near to Chaucer's'. They made use of some particular expressions and many of them talked very broad. He wrote down an ineffectual list of words and common idioms. The people of Forth said 'right well' instead of 'very well', 'broad way', instead of 'highway', and 'kine' for 'cows'. They talked of 'just before the downing' and sent departing travellers on their way with 'God Almighty keep thee saf upon zee and lone', which meant sea and land. It was not easy to collect and his list was short, 'and tho' the difference is little yet when I heard it spoken I could understand very little by reason of the different pronunciation'.

Arthur Young agreed that the people he met on Forth spoke 'a broken Saxon English'. A century later the Walking Tourist mentioned that the strange language 'was almost unknown to the other inhabitants of the country' although very likely he spoke from hearsay. An earlier traveller had found himself delighted with the community, quoting from a Statistical Survey of Wexford published in 1810 which talked of a 'superiority of peasantry, even equivalent to those of Great Britain ... and one never hears a general complaint of idleness and indolence'. There was nothing as good as Norman blood. He had concluded a homily on the excellence of Bargy and Forth by saying that the two baronies 'contained a superior order of things and a superior race of people'.

I spent the night at Carrick at a guesthouse near yet another old castle standing beside a farmhouse filled with cattle. Next morning Father Butler, an Augustinian priest, took me to Bannow, the lost Norman town beside the great sandy beach stretching for miles down the east side of Bannow Bay. A few grassy indents and the lovely ruin of St Mary's church looking out across the water to Hook are all that is left of nine good streets, twenty-seven gardens and a busy coastal port. The first Anglo-Norman corporate town in Ireland was ruined by shifting sand. In 1684 Robert Leigh wrote how 'on the east side towards the towne of Banno where by ancient passage was, shippes used to come in, is now a perfect dry strand and may be walked over from the island to the towne'. Drifting sand turned Bannow Island into a peninsula and almost within living memory eighty families inhabited this small area beside the scant Norman ruins.

In the shell of St Mary's effigies of a Norman knight and his wife lie gazing at the sky near a monument to a lady named Mrs Fielding. Earlier that day my landlady had quoted some lines of it:

> Formed of no common material
> Her failures were few and trifling
> And her virtues were true and great.

Mrs Fielding must have been a nice woman, like her daughter Mrs Hall, that charming, if gushing, travel writer. One suspects that her husband supplied the facts while she contributed the prose. Her father died when she was a child and her mother remarried a Mr Fielding who lived at nearby Craigie where Mrs Hall had spent her childhood. 'Dear Bannow,' she wrote, 'how mysterious and deep rooted are the feelings of our early days in its fairy land; we shall never see any earthly spot to love as well.' She called the lost town 'an Irish Herculaneum' and believed that the small piece of masonry sticking out of the ground was all that remained of the massive chimney of the medieval town hall.

From Bannow I took the road around Bannow Bay, a deep, almost landlocked estuary which is known as the Little Sea. Below Wellington Bridge I could see the towers of Clonmines, a town that suffered a similar fate to Bannow. If Bannow was Herculaneum you might think of the more substantial ruins of Clonmines as Pompeii, although its demise was the same slow encroachment of sand. Clonmines, the site of ancient silver and lead mines, was founded before the Normans by the Danes. The ruins at the end of the peninsula by the edge of the weedy estuary are dramatic, comprising an Augustinian monastery, the shell of four castles and three churches, one of which, St Nicholas, appears to be fortified, and could be a fifth castle by the look of it.

This is a place where you cannot get the Normans out of your mind. Into Bannow Bay Hervey de Marisco, uncle of Strongbow, sailed with Robert FitzStephen and a small force of four hundred men around May Day, 1169. They joined with Maurice de Prendegast and another group of archers on Bannow Island and waited for Diarmud McMurrough while the local people took no notice, or, according to the Four Masters, 'set no store by them'. Across the bay on its south-western point is Baginbun, where 'Ireland was lost and won'.

From Wellington Bridge I took the 'Military line', a long straight road to the west of the Bay which was full of charging beet lorries. Tintern Abbey was down a side-road. From a small arched bridge fringed with battlements made out of stones pillaged from the earlier structure of the abbey I looked up towards the old stone tower 'secluded upon a rising ground of rock . . .' and the house at 'a pistoll shot distance'.

The Augustinians at Clonmines controlled the ecclesiastical interest on the east side of the Bay, and the Cistercians on the west side, here at Tintern, a rich abbey whose possessions at the time of the dissolution included much of south Wexford. About 1200, William Marshall crossed from England in a bad storm and founded Tintern in thanksgiving for his safe landing. Known as Tintern de Voto or Tintern of the Vow, it was a daughter house of the abbey in Monmouthshire which is the subject of Wordsworth's poem. The first monks were Welshmen who came over from the parent abbey with an abbot named John Tyrrell to what was known as Little Tintern.

After the abbey was dissolved in 1538 and its last abbot, John Power, fled to France, it was pillaged by a local chieftain, 'a wild Irish man' named Cahir McArt Kavanagh. In 1562 the lands were vested in a soldier named Captain Anthony Colclough, whose family, originally from Staffordshire, had settled in Co. Carlow. He did some radical alterations to the abbey's buildings, converting the chancel and fifteenth-century tower into the 'fair, large stately house and of great receipt' seen by Brereton who visited his grandson in 1635. (As much as the house, Brereton admired Sir Adam Colclough's wife, 'a dainty, complete well-bred woman'.)

After Brereton came Pococke, to be shown into the small parlour overlooking the bay.

> The church was large with a great tower in the middle, the Chancel part was converted into a house with three floors and chimneys of which I never saw an instance before. I was informed that this family came over in Queen Elizabeth's time, that an Ancestor marrying a Papist went over to the Popish religion, but in the present is a convert who has fixed a Spinning School here and a Linnen Manufactory.

Then, the house was Gothicized with 'walls and battlements in the antient style . . . and so well executed that in a few years will give the appearance of being part of the original buildings'. The cost may have impoverished the family, since for a period Tintern became decrepit. When the artist, Gabriel Berenger, saw it at the end of the century, it must have been rather as I saw Carnew Castle, with rooms 'full of various vessels to catch the drips and parcels of rats and mice sat warming themselves before the fire'.

When Atkinson came to Tintern in 1810 in search of subscriptions, the family had abandoned full attempts to live in antique splendour and only used the abbey as a summer house. However, he thought 'the walls of this ancient edifice are, considering the antiquity of the structure, in tolerable preservation'. The inside was also passable. 'The adequately luminous and respectable appearance of those apartments which Lady Colclough had the politeness to show me were well deserving of regard.'

Whatever disadvantages the family suffered from the inadequate roof, the Colcloughs moved back on a permanent basis and stayed at Tintern until 1960. In Wexford I had visited Miss Marie Colclough, the last of her family to have lived in the old abbey. She had retired to a nursing home named after her neighbours at Bannow, the Elys. She was too old for memories or reminiscences of memories, but she showed me some albums of old photographs, the tennis court outside

Tintern full of romping children, a group arranged round the Gothick front door and Miss Marie herself standing by the conservatory in a stiff black dress. She had an old copybook in which was written in childish copperplate: 'England is the centre of the civilized world.'

Changes in Miss Marie's lifetime encompassing the end of her family at Tintern had been as sweeping as those four hundred years ago when her ancestor took over from the Cistercians. He is buried in the little church, built out of more surplus material from the substantial walls of the old abbey. I found his stone, Anthony Colclough, son of Richard Colclough who died in 1584.

It is said that this Tintern has architectural details similar to the Monmouthshire Tintern, but its present appearance of late Gothick wings held together by a rather squat tower seems totally unlike the soaring ruin in Wales. I met Jerry Cruise who worked for the Colcloughs for forty years like his father before him. He knew the place well when Miss Marie lived there, before she gave it to the nation. The nation hasn't treated it too well. Thirteen years ago Eric Newby wrote of Tintern Abbey: 'Hidden in a grove of fine trees ... the ruins are romantically sited and completely obscured from view when the great trees are in leaf.' Most of these have been chopped down, and only a few are left with the odd dispossessed crow cawing from the top branches. Jerry had seen the roof ripped off and the rooms inside destroyed and God knows what other destruction. Local people talked about the rape of Tintern.

Without Jerry's help it would have been impossible to visualize the layout of rooms in what is now, to quote a phrase of Atkinson's, a piece of grandeur in ruins. He pointed out the old hall, the drawing-room and the two kitchens that looked down into the empty crypt. In his time two maids were inside while an outside staff of seven men looked after the ground. He had worked in the small creamery. The terraces were so well kept that you wouldn't get an ounce of grass from them if you paid a man a hundred pounds. He showed me the stone heads of monks placed in a line on an outside wall. Did they look satisfied? Had justice been done? As Jerry said about the changes, 'That was the way of things.'

I spent the night with the Powers who own Tintern Farm above its more famous namesake. Mrs Power's family, the Laffans, had built the slender crenellated tower of Slade Castle down at Hook Head. Mr Power drove me down to Fethard where we stood above the pier and stared at the sea. 'There's no mercy in that place.' In spite of the Metal Man standing above Tramore Bay and the old Hook Tower that was once described as 'a mighty flail beating the darkness out of the waves', this was one of the most dangerous stretches of coastline round the country. Mr Power reeled off shipping disasters, the *Kinsale*, the gunboat *St Patrick*, the *Royal Arthur* which sank off the Hook with a cargo of ivory tusk, and the Norwegian three-masted schooner that ran aground in 1914. Seven of the local lifeboat men who went out to save the crew were drowned and their memorial stood in the centre of the village.

'The old ships mistook the Hook for the Tuskar, and then they couldn't get out again.' He told me that it used to be a boast that almost every family round here had a son in the British Navy and most of the men had rounded the Horn before they were twenty.

I could not resist a look at Loftus Hall. Big houses look bigger on those flat landscapes and Loftus Hall was an Irish copy of Buckingham Palace. Lord Ely demolished his previous and perfectly adequate house and erected this great three-storey building in the expectation that his son might marry one of Queen Victoria's daughters. No marriage took place.

The house resembles a stranded Grand Hotel. The situation overlooking Waterford Harbour is windswept. 'Here is Loftus Hall,' Pococke wrote of the earlier house, 'no tree will grow above the shelter of the walls.' The old house had a ghost that escaped through a hole in the roof. A year before Pococke's visit Henry Loftus became Baron Loftus, and four years later he was created Viscount Ely. The Loftuses were a greedy family, acquiring property all round the place, including Slade Castle and the lost town of Bannow which became Lord Ely's very own rotten borough. Both ghost towns of Bannow and Clonmines were rotten boroughs which continued to send two members each to the Irish Parliament, although all they represented was ruins in the sand. At the Act of Union, when Bannow was taken from Lord Ely, he was paid £15,000 in compensation for the loss of the representation.

Loftus Hall does not make the guide books because it is hideous. Ugly and imposing, its bulk dominates the view. Down the avenue, past the deer park wall with a pair of plaster eagles on a parapet I walked towards the inside porch where a nun sat reading a newspaper in the weak sun. I counted twenty-eight windows, but she told me there were forty rooms in all. 'Do you want to buy it?' She was Welsh. In 1917 her order, the Sisters of Providence, had rescued the house. (When you think of the buildings they might have rescued instead!) Now it was too big for the four nuns who remained. They did not need the ballroom and chapel, the great hall and the staircase made from thirty varieties of oak brought from Italy. A small parlour in front was known as the Devil's Room, a relic of the past; the devil must have been evicted. It was clean like all convents and it was cold. The cumbersome central heating radiators installed by the last Lord Ely were cold to the touch, and the ancient boiler had not been lit for years.

On the other side of Waterford Harbour bluffs of headlands rose and fell towards Tramore and above them the soft hills of south-east Munster were streaked with sunshine and autumn cloud. At Duncannon, looking back, I could see Loftus Hall like a haystack perched on the back of the Hook, and Hook lighthouse beyond it. Atkinson had ridden this way, observing 'oblique' views of the sea and various 'interesting elevations'. He hated the gorse and heather round about: 'the spectator's eye, from the proximity of this disgusting spectacle, cannot preserve itself from that shocking drawback to its enjoyment which this object produces.'

From Ballyhack I took the ferry to Passage. Pococke had been impressed by the fairs held there 'for tame fowl of all sorts which sell very cheap as also white coarse frieze at low prices'. Passage was also on de Latocnaye's tour; he had arrived here after crossing from Milford Haven ('an ugly hole', he called the Welsh port, 'where a traveller may spend every penny in his pocket waiting for a fair wind'). After leaving Passage he had visited the Geneva Barracks where soon afterwards the Croppy Boy would die. For Arthur Young, Passage was his departure point from Ireland. He was taking the *Countess of Tyrone* to Milford Haven. 'I soon found the difference of these private vessels and the Post Office Pacquets at Holyhead and Dublin. When the wind was fair the tide was foul; and when the tide was with them, the wind would not do; in English there was not a complement of passengers, and so I had the agreeableness of waiting with my horses in the hold, by way of rest, after a journey of 1,500 miles.'

The last souring note of his Irish experiences was heightened by the violent storm that shook the ship when it eventually left Passage.

Young said proudly that out of seven passengers he was the only one to escape being seasick.

Passage was my final stop in south-east Leinster. I left the coastline by getting a long sweeping lift that took me right up to Kilkenny.

I was dropped off at St John's bridge under the battlements of Kilkenny Castle. I looked for a meal and tried Dame Kytler's Inn. The patterned carpet, the leather chairs and the medieval menu card were intimidating. 'Full many a goodly wyne from abroad have wee in Kytler stored again ... the wench will list our store, an you question her.' I fled and ended up with chicken and chips.

I waited until next morning to find the 'queer old house', No. 8 William Street, where Carlyle stayed the night. He woke early on a hot morning of Wednesday, 11 July 1849. 'Sound of jackdaws, curious old room, two windows to street, one behind; tops of all come down (*not* bottoms up, of all); look out over the grey dilapidated town; smoke, to bed again, but sleep returns not.'

After writing a letter to his wife Jane, he did some desultory sight-seeing to the Cathedral and the round tower nearby which he climbed ('sat there, very high, view hungry looking parched, bare Sahara-looking') and to the Castle where he paid half a crown to view portraits he did not care about. But the greater part of that long hot day was spent viewing the poor-houses. He went only to two. 'Eheu! *omitted* other subsidiary poor-houses (I think).' In the aftermath of famine they were paramount to survival and were dreadfully overcrowded. The first, run by his friend, O'Shaughnessy, a Poor Law inspector, was a subsidiary poor-house, one of the many opened during the famine to accommodate the starving. This one, 'a converted brew house', contained an unbelievable 8,000 paupers. The women knitting, spinning and carding cotton, buttermilk pails which provided nourishment in such institutions throughout the country and the general cleanliness won his grudging approval. But in the official workhouse the atmosphere was nightmarish, and Carlyle, inveterate institution visitor though he was, felt himself 'quite shocked'.

It was a lot more crowded than the subsidiary poor-house.

> Huge chaos ... huge arrangements of eating, baking, stacks of Indian meal stirabout: 1,000 or 2,000 great hulks of men lying piled up within brick walls, in such a country, in such a day! Did a *greater* violence to the law of nature ever present itself to sight? ... Schools, for girls, rather goodish; for boys

clearly bad. Hospital; haggard ghastliness of some looks . . . literally their eyes grown 'colourless' (as Mahomet describes the horror of the Day of Judgment). 'Take me home!' one half-mad was urging; a deaf-man; ghastly *flattery* of us by another (*his* were the eyes): ah me! boys drilling men still piled within their walls; no hope but of stirabout; swine's meat, swine's *destiny* (I gradually saw) right glad to get away.

Here was one edifice it was good to see go to ruin. The workhouse became a hospital, and then, during the Emergency, the army took it over. 'And what would you expect to happen to it?'

Buses took me up to Roscrea. It is strange that one of the most detailed pictures of that town in the past has been supplied by that crusading teetotaller Asenath Nicholson, since Roscrea's prosperity came from its distillery. This has been true in Atkinson's time when the town supplied whiskey throughout Ireland. Atkinson had ponderous jokes about 'the advantages of the trade to the lower classes of our countrymen' and 'its tendency to maintain in due operation the *fire* and *talent* of the Irish nation'.

Mrs Nicholson walked in after her usual travelling troubles. 'I waded through darkness, mud and storm sometimes on the road, sometimes in the ditch; only once meeting a human being. I reached Roscrea about ten and everything in the town was still but for the loud pouring of the rain . . . my clothes were dripping with wet the rain was tremendous . . . I believed I am not to have a lodging in Ireland tonight.'

But never in all her wanderings in Erin did she fail to find a shelter, if not a bed. Her lodgings in Roscrea were far from ideal, 'a Protestant whiskey house'. She had to endure the perpetual babble of her landlady's conversation interspersed only when the lame old woman had to serve customers, hobbling to the whiskey room to fill a glass.

It was therefore with pleasure and fervour that she attended temperance meetings given by Father Mathew. 'At eight o'clock . . . and again at twelve Father Mathew gave a stirring discourse on the importance of temperance, proving from Scripture as well as from facts the sin of using ardent spirits.' The concourse was immense, 'so that they trod one upon another'. The next day she went to the Chapel, surrounded by children lisping the pledge and swearing to abstain from tobacco. There was every temptation to keep them to the drink. I found that even the old Temperance Hall, erected since Father Mathew's time, stood cheek by jowl with a defunct distillery. The most famous distillery in Ireland at the time of Mrs Nicholson's visit was Birches', located a couple of miles out of the town. It was so well known that in most places throughout the country if you wanted good Irish whiskey you would demand 'a drop of Roscrea'. No whiskey has been made in Roscrea for a long time.

Everyone Mrs Nicholson met was connected with drink. She called at the house of an Englishman who was a brewer. 'I found him in his parlour with a well-dressed sister from London, and was introduced to them as an American lady.'

'I never saw but one American lady,' said the sister, 'and she was very wealthy; but the most ignorant, unlearned creature that I ever saw that was well-dressed.'

Both Atkinson and Mrs Nicholson went out from Roscrea towards Birr, the Slieve Blooms hovering gently in the distance. For once this plucky American lady did not complain about the hardships of her walk. 'The grass was green, made young and fresh by the rain, and the morning bird had begun his song. I would be ungrateful to say I was not happy and commenced singing.'

Atkinson had made a diligent note on the gentlemen's seats around Roscrea. He turned off a side-road to Leap Castle standing high on a ridge. This was a former stout O'Carroll castle that came into the possession of the Darby family not by conquest, but by marriage – it was the marriage portion of an O'Carroll daughter. The Darby family lived here until 30 July 1922 when it was destroyed with thirty bombs and twenty cases of petrol. Crowds in donkey- and horse-carts came up and looted it for two days.

When Atkinson arrived he waited on old Admiral Darby. Everything about the estate was trim and neat, and the two new Gothick additions were smart. Jonathan Darby, whose wife was a cousin of the architect Sir Edward Lovett Pearce, had 'modernized' Leap with the aid of Batty Langley's ideas; the doorway, which is still there, was copied from *Gothic Architecture Improved.* The yard and its buildings, the offices and the deer park contributed to everything that was desirable in a gentleman's residence. When Atkinson was brought into the hall hung with flags and old weapons, the Admiral opened the back door which gave a prospect over the valley of the Slieve Blooms. In his irritating way Atkinson proposed that, if the view at the rear of the castle had comprehended a lake in the intervening valley, its beauty would have been complete. To which the Admiral, unusually for a sailor, replied that he preferred 'land scenery instead of water'.

The Admiral signed up as Class One, 'signifying the largest measure of subscription'. He had commanded the *Bellerophon* at the Battle of the Nile, and it may have been that he would more gladly have faced the French guns once more than another hour of his visitor's company.

Looking down the valley Atkinson noticed 'a glebe house and a little parish church on the declivity of one of these mountains' which are still there. In the church I found a memorial to his benefactor, Sir Henry D'Esterre Darby, Knight Companion of the Most Noble Order of the Bath, Admiral of the Blue Squadron. Died in the fullness of time, in 1832, thirteen years after Atkinson's visit.

There were other remarkable Darbys. John Nelson Darby founded the Plymouth Brethren in the early nineteenth century; then, when the sect split, he led his disciples to the formation of the Darbyites, and eventually to the Bethesda. Mrs Jonathan Darby wrote a series of solid and well-observed novels about the Irish peasantry under the name of Andrew Merry. The best known was *The Hunger*, which was set during the Famine and contained material taken from eye-witness accounts in the Leap area during those years. Her husband disapproved of her literary activities and forbade her to write any more after *The Hunger* was published in 1910.

I walked to Birr whose centre is frozen in its Georgian mould as the centre of Bruges remains forever medieval. Here I visited the grounds of Birr Castle as Mrs Nicholson did in 1844: 'the lawn containing Lord Rosse's telescope was open and the old lady who presided at the lodge asked me to go through the grounds which were free for all.' Nowadays you pay a pound.

The telescope which lies on the ground, its great eyepiece covered with a block of wood, was then projected upwards to the heavens. Old photographs show viewers climbing a ladder to the wooden balcony. Mrs Nicholson insisted on being helped up, but as usual the elements were against her. 'Clouds obscured the sky, so that not one gaze could I have through that magnificent instrument.' She made no mention of the formal gardens or the river walk and trees. For once she was not critical of the landlord's way of life. 'The Earl is mentioned as a man of great philanthropy and much loved by the gentry and poor.' Over the years the Parsons family had a reputation for benevolence which is one reason why their castle survived as a family home instead of becoming a fire-blackened ruin.

Next day, the Sabbath, Mrs Nicholson heard a Baptist minister preach, and on the Monday, the fourth of November, 1844, she set off on foot for Ballinasloe. 'The sun rose most beautifully; poor labourers were going to their work smoking and singing, their tattered garments but an apology for clothing.' This was the last time I would encounter her on her 'excursions through Ireland for the purpose of personally investigating the "Conditions of the Poor"'. I would miss her clear eye, her eccentricities, her compassion and her religious tolerance.

Here I would also part company with A. Atkinson Gent. He spent the days in Birr taking notes on the 'airy' square, the lines of gentlemen's houses and the 'well executed column of the famous Duke of Cumberland'. Near this column he made the momentous decision to produce two separate books rather than one. 'The author's theological Tennis-Ball would go out in the brave world, and his sophorsis of Irish Travelling would become the Irish Tourist.' He would continue on his tour, even though it had brought its toll of suffering. 'Let the reader take into account the hardships which must be endured in the long course of travels in all seasons, sometimes lodging in dry rooms and sometimes in damp rooms . . . nearly half of my time labouring under the effects of these extremes, having a constitution dependent on them, extremely tender.'

The Roll of a Tennis-Ball through the Moral World was published in 1812. Its long preface written by a 'Solitary traveller' was addressed to different readers: critical . . . choleric . . . liberal . . . the mere man of fashion. 'Any exertions of the author's friends to promote this work will be gratefully acknowledged, and any letters (prepaid) addressed to Mr Atkinson, General Post Office, Dublin, on this subject shall meet with respectful attention.'

Then followed a sonnet:

The earth's inclement shore was cast
Propell'd by some mysterious blast,
A tennis-ball endued with powers
Of mind and matter like to ours . . .

After *The Irish Tourist* appeared two years later he was sufficiently encouraged to consider a third book, because in the hasty printing process there had not been time for him to write up his notes about the neighbourhood of Dublin. His travels had not yet taken him to the northern counties of his country. He persevered; many years later, in 1824, his ambitious, wordy *Ireland Exhibited to England* was accepted by a London publisher. It is pleasant to know that he became moderately successful.

Today was Hallowe'en in Birr and children wearing grown-up coats and masks were walking along Oxmantown Mall, knocking on doors and rattling money-boxes. At Dooley's Hotel a group came into the foyer shaking a box in front of two old men sitting by the fire sipping whiskey. 'What sort of dress is that?' Giggles came from behind a tiger and a skull. The vampire and Donald Duck lifted their masks to play 'One Wheel on my Waggon' and 'Brown Girl in the Ring' on whistles, their companions intoning the words with not too much confidence.

I walked back towards Leap Castle. Just outside the town tinkers were camped along the side of the road, the shabby motorized caravans strung out and haphazard like the line of washing on a string and the blankets thrown on the bushes.

'Will it rain?' I asked a red-haired woman.

'It will,' she said. 'We prefer to be outside.' Wind was blowing the washing so that it snapped. 'It's fresher.'

By the time I came to Leap it was blowing something like a gale. Wind roared through the old tower and the shells of the Gothic additions. When I sought shelter in Mrs Neenan's house she told me that as a child she had seen the castle on fire in 1922. She could remember the plumes of black smoke pouring out of the roof and a large bearskin rug smouldering on the lawn. That had stuck in her mind.

In those days Leap was like Tintern, hidden in trees. (Like Tintern it is now denuded.) There was a time when travellers never passed the castle after midnight, for this was the most haunted house in Ireland. Altogether twenty-four ghosts lingered around here including those associated with the Bloody Chapel where Teighe O'Connor murdered his brother. One or two haunted the Hangman's Field which early Darbys used regularly. One Darby sent a bill to the Crown for 'ye hooks for hanging ye rebels'. They cost 1s 6d each. Eighty years ago one such hook was found embedded in a felled oak tree.

The most famous ghost at Leap is an elemental which Mrs Jonathan

Darby called The Thing. This was a nasty creature about the size of a sheep with a sickly human face covered with dirty brown hair and emitting a foul smell that sent maids screaming from their rooms. My family had dogs like that. The ghosts were driven off first by the installation of Mr Darby's new central heating, put in during 1920 so that the family had two winters of warmth, then by the fire that destroyed the house. It is a minor irony that the age of central heating coincided with the departure of so many landlords; however historic or beautiful their residences might have been, there was never a period when they were comfortable.

There are those who believe that ghosts still linger at Leap. When I was a boy I went to school with two members of the Darby family and, inspired by them, my brother and some friends spent a Hallowe'en night in Leap. They brought along a jar of holy water, a crucifix and rosary beads to discourage The Thing. Neither he nor his fellow ghosts put in an appearance. I climbed the old stone spiral staircase in the dusk to the empty room upstairs which was the Bloody Chapel. In one corner I knew there was an oubliette from which were cleared away three cartloads of bones. The chapel was chill and musty in the semi-darkness, and also noisy with the swish of wind rattling the corrugated sheets nailed to the roof. But tonight, another night when ghosts and witches walked abroad, those that haunted Leap failed to show up.

WINTER

Bunbeg
The Rosses
Errigal Mt.
L. Veagh
Glencolumbkille
Ardara
Slieve League
Carrick
Killybegs
Donegal
D O N E G A L
Lifford
Strabane
Derry
Lough Foyle
Ballyshannon
Portrush
Giant's Causeway
Bushmills
Rathlin I.
Dunluce Cas.
Coleraine
Ballycastle
Cushendun
D E R R Y
U L S T E R
Glenarm
A N T R I M
Larne
T Y R O N E
Antrim
Lough Neagh
Carrickfergus
Whitehead
BELFAST
FERMANAGH
Armagh
ARMAGH
Hillsborough
Ballynahinch
Spa
DOWN
Clough
Downpatrick
Castlewellan
Dundrum
Newry
0 5 10 20 40 miles
10 20 30 60 km

19
Ballyshannon · Glencolumbkille · Bunbeg

The bus swung into the North of Ireland. The border war has made the authorities confuse the crossings so that here vehicles have to take a couple of minor roads that turn the route into a zig-zag. Then came a stretch of good northern roadway smooth as velvet, so different from our own familiar potholes. At Enniskillen wreaths of poppies were lying at the base of the war memorial. As we left the town a patrol of English soldiers with guns and blackened faces stopped us.

'All right,' said the sergeant after a time, waving us on and giving us a wink. We stared at him stonily. The bus continued beside fields of cows and the tranquil waters of Lower Lough Erne. A few miles down the road we re-entered the Republic at Ballyshannon.

I went up the airy hill to the top of the town and the wonderful site of St Ann's church which looks across Sligo Bay to a monumental Benbulben. The dead never had a better view. William Allingham the poet is buried here.

High on the hill-top
The old King sits;
He's now so old and grey
He's nigh lost his wits.
With a bridge of white mist
Columkill he crosses
In his stately journeys
From Slieveleague to Rosses.

Allingham was born in Ballyshannon in 1824. 'An odd out of the way little town, ours,' he wrote, 'on the extreme western edge of Europe, our next neighbours sunset way, being citizens of the great new Republic which, indeed to our imagination seemed little, if at all, farther off than England in the opposite direction.' Ballyshannon, proud of its native son, runs the occasional William Allingham week and has put up a bust of him outside the bank.

I talked to a glazier who was working on the church window. 'You want to take care of Belfast,' he said when I told him I planned to go there, 'with a voice like yours they'll think you're a member of the SAS.'

In Allingham's time many tourists came to Ballyshannon to look at the falls which a dam has now destroyed. The waters used to tumble dramatically over a thirty-foot drop below the town where the Erne hurried to the sea. Because of the falls Ballyshannon was a place of drama.

'At low tide the salmon would jump as high as the top windows of the Imperial Hotel,' an old man told me. Wicker baskets used to be filled with fish that leapt into the sky and came down like falling angels. You could tell a Ballyshannon salmon by its great hump.

Dr Twiss, who stood by the cascade filling up his notebooks, thought that the jump was 'probably performed by a forcible spring with their tails bent'. He was told that 'they have often been shot or caught with strong barbed hooks fixed to a pole during their flight, as it may be termed, and instances have been known of women catching them in their aprons'.

Twiss was capable of being vivid and accurate. Unfortunately when his book was published in 1778 it caused great offence to the sensitive Irish public. No one seemed to like the doctor, neither the waiter who served his meal, the coachman or those whom he treated like delinquent children. In retaliation his readers behaved like delinquent children – for a while a popular item for sale in Ireland was a chamber pot with Dr Twiss's portrait on the bottom. His book is unread and forgotten unlike that of his contemporary, Arthur Young, who also came to watch the salmon leap. 'The water was alive with them.'

De Latocnaye put in a brief appearance, to watch the salmon caught in their funnel-shaped traps which were still being used a century later by Messrs Moor & Alexander who sent salmon all over Ireland. 'Great quantities are taken at this spot so that I think very few manage to reach the lake.' The Frenchman was wrong. Those were the days of abundance when fish tumbled in their thousands into Lough Erne.

Carlyle hadn't the time or interest for viewing salmon. He stopped the night, but was in a hurry and as usual his notes give the impression of being written jerkily as he was borne along in a carriage.

'Donegal mountains, blue-black over Donegal Bay ... moory raggedness with green patches near, all treeless ... nothing distinct till narrow street of Ballyshannon, mills, breweries, considerable confused much-whitewashed country town.'

At the Royal Hotel I was the only guest and the dazzling tablecloths in the dining-room were like shrouds. I sat and ate alone, thinking of other visitors. The Walking Tourist, jaundiced after a night sleeping in the open, too late in the year for the great display. 'I saw one small salmon or trout rise when I was there.' The American, Samuel Bayne, like the Irish Cousins chose a jaunting car for his travels and in Ballyshannnon he and his companion were exposed to rain. 'It came in at our collars and went out at our boots.'

'Make yourself breakfast,' said the lady in the bar. 'The people don't get up here till nine.' So I boiled an egg and made tea in silence before emerging in the main street where a cloud of rooks hovered over the Northern Bank. Rain began to fall on me as it had fallen on Sam Bayne. 'Had old Noah been with us he could not have bragged much about the flood.' The torrent did not prevent him from quoting William Allingham.

> Adieu to Ballyshannon! where I was bred and born;
> Go where I may, I'll think of you, as sure as night and morn;
> I leave my warm heart with you, 'tho my back I'm forced to turn,
> So adieu to Ballyshannon and the winding banks of Erne!

Mr Bayne continued to be exposed to the downpour, but I was soon snug in the steaming bus. The time of year emphasized the emptiness of the landscape. Peering through the rain I began to wonder how many people were left in the world. Towns were full of empty guesthouses and hotels and empty streets with empty milk bottles outside doors. Roads were empty – here was the turn-off for Lough Derg, and nothing could be more desolate. The road, made for busloads of pilgrims, was improved since Dr Twiss's coach had been manhandled over it and he complained that it 'was so badly constructed lest the devotions should be interrupted by too many heretics'.

Even in nervous Pettigo, the border town where a Garda car faced a British Army patrol, there was little action. Out on a boggy road scattered with rhododendron towards Donegal town and the sea. Westward, the emptiness continued. Occasionally we stopped and the driver threw out a bundle of sodden newspapers tied up with string at various doorways. No one appeared to collect them.

Killybegs showed its usual burst of prosperity with million-pound trawlers tied up alongside the quays. But a night spent there was full of tales of diminishing fish stocks and greedy foreign trawlers getting to them first. Next day I dropped off at Carrick, a little town dominated by the ruin of a large hotel in ironic imitation of Donegal town, dominated by its castle. Both ruins have their fireplaces, Donegal's famous and reproduced in many a tourist guide, Carrick's marbled and handsome, still in the wall of the burnt dining-room.

The rain had cleared by the time I bought sweets and biscuits and prepared to climb Slieve League. Hadn't Lloyd Praeger described County Donegal as 'the best walking country in Europe'? And I had not yet taken a step into it. Pat O'Donnell, the bus driver, encouraged me by saying that it was hardly a step from the other side of Slieve League to Glencolumbkille.

I reached Amharc Mor, the Great View – could that be translated as the Great Outdoors? – and struggled along One Man's Path above the highest sea cliff in Europe. Slieve League should be climbed in Donegal's rare summer sunshine when the slopes are strewn with Alpine flowers, not on a November day when the wind strives to hurl you off a two-foot ridge. Bat's wings, a curving scimitar, teeth of a gigantic saw, lips, horns – the cliffs have inspired many comparisons. It offered a great challenge to early hermits. Bishop Assicus and St Aodh Mac Bric claimed this mountain for their particular holy squat. Assicus had abandoned the religious community that St Patrick had put in his charge at a place called Racoon which is near Ballyshannon. He was discovered after seven years and induced to return to his post. But in despair at abandoning his hermitage he died on the journey back.

St Aodh Mac Bric built a little oratory here. I did not seek it out, nor the holy wells associated with the contemplatives. I was nervous of getting on. Was there truth in the story that Lord Leighton had climbed Slieve League to sketch the cliffs for background to his painting of Andromeda? I was down now in a dark valley, cursing Pat O'Donnell and his advice, since my map could not confirm whether the mountain opposite was Malinbeg. I was far from Glencolumbkille and the time was four o'clock. But I was luckier than I deserved when just before dark I stumbled into Peggy and Brian

O'Byrne's house. They had given hospitality to errant climbers before.

At Malinbeg the road stopped or began, taking your choice, at a group of houses, an old signal tower and a curving silver beach (no pub). The place had those rare qualities which we hungrily seek out – a fraction of what Aodh Mac Bric looked for at the top of Slieve League. But peace and beauty do not make for easy living – the cottages, their thatch held down with rope and stone, were witnesses to the old harsh life when fishing meant going out in eight-oar boats seeking herring around Rathlin O'Byrne Island. Life for the Killybegs trawlers is easier. 'Rich glow worms,' old Mr O'Byrne said as we watched their lights dotting the sea at night.

At Malinmore tourism gradually took over the landscape. Here was a large hotel and some chalets to be let out during the summer, part of Father MacDyer's cooperative development that had its headquarters in neighbouring Glencolumbkille. They sit oddly side by side with the remains of megalithic farmers, the first people to settle here more than three thousand years ago. A startling group of six tombs was situated awkwardly in a line up a boreen between two houses, and plenty of other evidence of ancient settlement stuck out of the bog. I walked over an old track to Glencolumbkille. If the saints were alive they would be working at the tourist board. They had unerring taste for location, and St Columcille, like the rest, chose well with his broad fertile valley, an oasis in the bare hills.

The valley has been somewhat tamed by Father MacDyer's false thatch and folk village. Sixty years ago Arthur Fox considered it 'one of the wildest spots in a singular wild country. Half the year it is said to be enveloped in mist and rain.' Father MacDyer's activities may have diminished the ancient grandeur of the valley, but they gave an immense uplift to a hard-pressed community. It is sad that in these harsh economic times his ideas have turned into financial problems. His efforts since his arrival in 1953 have increased the trickle of tourism and enabled others to make their living of their own volition. Among them is Pat O'Donnell, the same bus driver who had urged me up Slieve League. For years Pat worked in England before returning home to a job with the bus company. At the same time he had set up a small hostel that takes in hitchhikers. It is a steep place to get to, and after his day's work on the bus you see him running up the hill to be in time to open up to people from all over the world.

However in November it was peaceful – no twanging guitars, no hearty Germans, no Dubliners in orange rain gear.

The valley is scattered with ancient remains like chess pieces at the height of a game. They are not easy to find – I tracked down various ringforts, court cairns and pillar stones before going after something easier. Glen Tower is a specimen of English bureaucracy, uniformity and panic. After the French invasion of Bantry Bay and Killala, signal towers were hurriedly put up all around the Irish coast on nearly every exposed headland. They are very similar although there are variations according to date and to the architect who designed them. The machicolations on the tower here are similar to a type found along the north coast of County Mayo and have been dated to about 1800. If these towers were built in a hurry they were built well. I walked up a stone-paved path that cuts through the gorse and heather to the solid construction of Glen Tower with its blackened limestone windows and a gutted interior. Here a lonely group of men speaking a different language from the people of the crowded valley below them brought their provisions, gossiped about home, played cards and kept a futile look-out over the most spectacular coastline in Europe, on the remote chance that the French would be in the bay at Glencolumbkille.

The Sturrel Rock like a giant pillarstone, once a remote nesting place for eagles, stuck out of the unfriendly sea. Eagles used to infest Donegal, nesting under the cliffs of Slieve League and in other remote sites. Guns, not nest-robbers, put an end to them. And yet even out there on Sturrel their nests were not safe if the author of a short book called *Cliff Scenery of Donegal* published in 1867 is to be believed. He tells a tall story that around the time the tower was built a boy rose from his bed and rowed over to steal eagles' eggs.

'Now he fastens his toe in a little crevice, now holds on by a friendly crag. On, on they observed him going . . . heavens! see, his head hangs down as he looks into the eyrie, holding on by his knees. Look, his hands are in the nest; how softly he steals the eggs; see he gathered them into his night gown.' Later the lad claimed he had been sleepwalking. A nightmarish escapade like that would have provided a winter's conversation for the men in the tower.

From Glen Tower to Port stretches a line of craggy cliffs, and huge rocks beside them flung into the sea. No one lives there now, but people have tried. Port is an indent where the cliffs subside for a swift interval to a beach made up of smooth round pebbles. The empty cottages above the harbour are mostly roofless, but with walls intact. They have not been abandoned all that many years. The situation of Port among cliffs at the head of a long trackway twisting among mountains and lakes and scattered farms amounted to what Victorians called desolate savagery.

I trudged along for ten miles or so until I hit the main road leading through the wooded Glengesh Pass towards Ardara. Carlyle drove along this detestable road when people were still starving, grumbling to himself. 'Moor, moor, brown heather and peatpot, here and there a speck reclaimed into bright green and the poor cottier oftenest gone. Ragged sprawling bare farm-stead, bright green and black alternating abruptly on the grounds and no hedge or tree – ugly enough.'

Beyond Ardara a man had driven down by Glengesh and stopped to pray at the small shrine, his thoughts lulled by the sound of running water and the white virgin in her glass box. Glenties came swimming out of the bogland, an outpost of civilization with bank, cinema, supermarket, solicitor and no doubt the undertaker I felt I needed. I had walked too far.

A man driving a fish lorry to Dunglow gave me a lift and entertained me with stories of working in Scotland long ago when he was young. The mean Scots got up at four o'clock on the farm and worked your ass off all day. They made a single Woodbine give three smokes. After two years he hadn't been sorry to leave and return home. His last words to his employer had been: 'I'll stick the fork in you up to the maker's name.'

The Rosses were always full of people, one of the densest Congested Districts of the West. They used to be picturesque, like parts of Connemara, filled with little low thatched cottages and far from anywhere.

> To reach it even's a weary process!
> Toil awaits you ere you enter Rosses
> between tides and strands and river fosses . . .

It is a sweep of flat land beside the sea out of reach of the mountains, still with a healthy population – Donegal did not lose its people at the same rate as other parts of Western Ireland. Traditions of emigration were different and the annual migration to Scotland to some extent limited the appeal of America and other countries overseas.

Every owner of a thatched cottage must be glad to exchange it for a bungalow. In the modern Rosses bungalows of multicoloured brick, many villas on top of rocks and picture windows reflecting sea and lake make up a big urban wilderness that contrasts sharply with the surrounding rural wilderness. It's a fair exchange for the old picturesque discomfort still visible at places like Malinbeg.

The walk to Bunbeg was troublesome because there were no signposts in English. Instead there were regular scrawls on rocks BRITS GO HOME, H BLOCK. On one GOD BLESS THE IRA was printed in apple-green paint. The signposts had been sawn off, wrenched off, twisted off, or twisted upside down with great effort by patriots. There would have been no signposts here either for Carlyle or the Walking Tourist – they are a modern convenience in rural Ireland. In one of the 'Irish RM' stories Major Yates comments: 'The residents, very reasonably, consider them to be superfluous, even ridiculous, in view of the fact that everyone knows the way, and as for strangers "haven't they tongues in their heads as well as another?" It all tends to conversation and an increasing knowledge of human nature.'

Bunbeg was a seaside town with an industrial estate pinned to its belly. I ate in a seaside restaurant that showed no tendency to close for the winter – it catered for residents, and tourists and visitors were a bonus. There was great comfort in the restaurant with the dazzling multicoloured carpet. At the next table a nun in snowy white bodice and black headdress was tucking into a large plate of chips beyond two business men holding pints of stout and a harassed couple with many children listening to their cries for Coke.

I sought out information on Lord George Hill, the improving landlord of Gweedore. By nineteenth-century contemporaries his efforts were admired, not only as a contrast to absenteeism or despotism among landlords, but also as a positive good. A landlord owning thousands of acres, influencing the lives of thousands of people, had plenty of opportunity for carrying out his reforming ideas. One or two, Thompson of West Cork and Vandeleur of West Clare, tried unsuccessfully to run their territories on socialist principles laid down by Jeremy Bentham. But autocratic benevolence was more common among those landlords who took their responsibilities seriously. There was no more positive-thinking and energetic believer in practical charity than Lord George Hill.

In the Protestant church, where strong Donegal voices reverberated through the building, there was no resident clergyman, and someone, perhaps the lay preacher who had travelled down all the way from Derry (regarded as the capital of this part of Ulster) had chosen 'Jesus Loves Me' as the opening hymn. The church was small and plain with a stone tower erected at the beginning of the century. In recent years the interior had been redecorated with financial support from the Catholic parishioners of Bunbeg, a warm ecumenical gesture. Behind the altar spread a large stained-glass window in memory of Lord George, while near the pulpit a memorial told how 'A self-denying Christian, he dedicated his life and fortune to civilize Gweedore and raise the people to a higher social and moral level.'

'Strong words,' Jack Boyd commented as we left the church. Not everyone would agree with them. The word 'civilize' gave offence to many. You would have to be more careful today.

As I walked down with Jack to his house he pointed out the remains of Lord George's benevolence sited among the rocks and along the last run of the river Clady before it reached the sea.

'To Bunbeg,' Carlyle wrote, 'a village of perhaps 300 or more scattered distractedly among the crags sprinkled along, thickening towards Clady mouth where are the store house, mill, harbour all amid crags for evermore.' Jack's house was part of the colony located between the courthouse and the corn mill. Like his father, he had worked for Lord George's descendants and wouldn't hear a word against any of them.

Lord George Hill was a younger son of the Marquis of Downshire whose family had established the neatest tidiest landlord village in Ireland at Hillsborough in County Down. Gweedore offered a contrasting challenge. In 1838 Lord George retired from the British army with the rank of major and bought 23,000 acres in this wild part of Donegal. The area was isolated, almost totally outside English jurisdiction and law. Its Irish-speaking population held on to the traditions of the past which included the old communal strip system of farming known as rundale.

The penalty for holding on to tradition was poverty. A touching memorial to the Lord Lieutenant of Ireland by one Patrick M'Kye, schoolmaster, described the misery of the district. (Lord George reprinted this memorial in his book, *Facts from Gweedore.*) There were 4,000 people who between them possessed 'one cart, no wheel car . . .

one plough . . . eight saddles . . . eleven bridles . . . twenty shovels . . . seven table forks, ninety-three chairs . . . no bonnet, no clocks, three watches, eight brass candlesticks, no looking glasses above 3d in price, no boots, no spurs, no turnips, no parsnips, no carrots, no clover . . .' Most households could not afford a second bed, 'but whole families of sons and daughters of mature age are indiscriminately lying together with their parents, and all in the bare buff.'

Lord George set about changing everything. He abolished rundale, which was often an inconvenient system. A farm of four acres might be a mile long, and subdivision arising from inheritance reached extremes – one case was quoted of a horse shared by three men, each of whom claimed a leg but left the fourth unshod. He placed each tenant on his allotted piece of land. Opposition to this 'scattering' was 'vexatious and harassing'. On the new farms, in squares now, rather than strips, the new stone-built houses, still comfortless, though possessing a chimney, were several hundred yards from a neighbour's instead of cosily cheek by jowl. Nevertheless the changes were carried through. Roads were built where there had only been rough tracks, and signs of 'civilization' like a post office and schools were introduced. For the first time there was a proper harbour, and boats could trade with ports as far away as Glasgow, Liverpool and Dublin. Alongside the harbour was a store, something like the Hudson Bay Stores still found in remote parts of Canada. Commodities on sale included paint, sealing wax, fishhooks, scissors, Epsom salts and coffin nails. Premiums were awarded for the best and neatest cottages and the best farm animals on the estate.

Lord George Hill wrote his book *Facts from Gweedore*, describing the reforming experiments prior to the famine, and it was generally praised. Some disapproved, however, and there had been plenty of argument as to whether he was a far-sighted landlord moved by the highest motives or 'out to exterminate the Irish race'.

Carlyle considered the benefits brought to the people far outweighed any loss of tradition. His long uncomfortable journey to the far reaches of Donegal especially to view the estate was worth all the trouble. He noted the awful poverty: 'Black huts, bewildered rickety fences of crag; crag and heath, unsubdueable by this population, damp peat, black heather, grey stones and ragged desolation of men and things!' But Lord George Hill was continuing his endeavours. 'In all Ireland I saw no such beautiful soul.'

The majority of Lord George's buildings have long been ruins. One of the most imposing is the derelict three-storey store house beside the harbour, still with its quotation in Irish written over the doors which is taken from the Book of Psalms. 'A just weight is a pleasure to the Lord, but an unequal balance is an abomination in his sight.'

Another ruin is the hotel Lord George established at Gweedore six miles inland from Bunbeg. The Clady river ran past it, in those days 'fishy but unfished till now'. The idea of a hotel in such a desolate spot seems lunacy, but after Lord George built it the Gweedore Inn existed as a fishing lodge until 1965 when the destruction of the salmon river by an electricity dam ensured its demise. Jack Boyd worked there. Of the many ruins in Ireland hotels form a small category – with good luck and good location they stagger on from age to age. But hotels in Donegal are vulnerable and remote – and here was another shell, like the deceased hotel in Carrick.

Jack Boyd took me along the old road from Bunbeg to Errigal. As soon as the land begins to rise the urban glut and sprawl of houses fades into the bogland and what Carlyle called a 'black, dim, lonely valley'. You can see where the railway line went that once linked Gweedore to the rest of Ireland. The hotel stands alongside the diminished Clady.

'Gweedore Inn,' Carlyle wrote, 'two-storyed white *human* house with offices in square behind at the foot of the hills on right near the river; this is the only *quite* civilized-looking thing; we enter there thro' gateway into the clean little sheltered court, and then under the piazza at the back of the inn.' There was a signal tower with a flag flying from the mast showing when his Lordship was in residence. From the windows Carlyle and succeeding generations of visitors could watch anglers catching salmon and almost landing them in the dining-room.

After the hotel was sold in 1966, Jack remained here for some years as caretaker. When he left the vandals moved in. Now he toured sadly under falling plaster ceilings and among walls of rooms which he remembered full of satisfied guests. He showed me the hall where the Ulster manager used to smile his welcome, the smoking-room, the dining-room where Lord George Hill's portrait had hung, and some family rooms used by the Hills and their descendants. A vandal or a squatter or an Orangeman had written on a wall – 'warmed up a bit here ... does the sun never shine in Eire?' Behind the model farm which Lord George had reclaimed (Carlyle: 'the prettiest patch of "improvement" I have ever in my travels beheld') had all gone wild.

Above Lough Nacung Errigal's smoky white sides rose 2,466 feet above me. From here it was a most beautiful mountain, a perfect cone with quartzite facings dribbled down its side like snow. From other viewpoints it has been compared to a slag heap. It has not attracted reverence or legend like Croagh Patrick or Benbulben, and no legendary figure or early saint is associated with it ... only climbers.

I stayed with the Gallaghers whose house is beside Lough Dunlewy with Errigal right at the back. I could hardly avoid the climb.

'No matter which way I turned, my heart thrilled within me with a sense of awe blended with exquisite delight,' wrote another climber who neared the top wearing his Norfolk jacket. 'I shall see Derry the brave devoted city, the joy of the whole Protestant world under my feet! I ran, covered with perspiration and panting with heat to mount the topmost ridge ...' None of that leaping for me. I plodded up without any such enthusiasm on a day of sunshine that was unseasonably warm for November so that I too was covered with perspiration. The view was good – mountains to the North, Benbulben across the sea to the south and a blur that could be Derry, so delightful to my predecessor up here.

Next day was also unnaturally sunny when I set off to the Poisoned Glen. At the head of Lough Dunlewy the Glen is heralded by the ruin of a cold white Protestant church. The whiteness is quartzite from a quarry behind. This big lonely building topped with imposing finials like a crown, served a minute local population and those connected with the mine. 'I do not think I should be over-eager to worship in it,' wrote Arthur Fox, 'if it is true that it is only attended by three families.'

The Poisoned Glen is a dark cleft in the mountains. Perhaps a sense of claustrophobia and unease gave the valley its name rather than other suggested deprivations like the presence of Irish spurge (which is all over the west) or the poisoned dart of Balor of the Evil Eye. 'Detestable', one guide book described it. 'It looks uncanny and forbidding, and seems as though possessed, giving the visitor a creeping feeling,' Samuel Bayne considered in true American style without getting out of his jaunting car.

A small lizard like a little dragon sat in the unseasonable sunshine just before the turn-off into the glen and its deep shadow. Something a lot more spectacular greeted Arthur Fox as he walked up the valley in 1904, a sight that left him an exhilarating memory for the rest of his life. An eagle landed close to him, 'a male bird just emerged from the moulting season and in fine plumage, deeply brown, with his tail slightly white-barred beneath while his golden head and breast shone vividly'. As Fox crouched and watched the bird ate the hare he carried in his talons, dissecting it skilfully with his beak, devouring it to the skeleton and regurgitating the flesh, looking like 'an emperor ... under the incontrollable influence of seasickness'. When Fox came to write his memories of Donegal twenty years later he called his book *Haunts of the Eagle*. By then the eagles had gone from Donegal and from Ireland.

On the far side of the Poisoned Glen I looked down at Glenveagh, a gentleman's castle beside a long narrow lake named Lough Veagh. 'A modern abortion', a contemporary writer called it. 'It is singular what wretched attempts modern architects make when they are called upon to build a castle ... yes, I was glad to put Glenveagh behind me as soon as possible.' This comment is a little hard – the towers and turrets, kept in beautiful order beside a pleasant garden, are no worse than any other baronial exercise you can think of. The dream of Cruel John Adair and his American wife still flourishes.

You can see the traces of the Adairs' work, the deer fence erected by Mrs Adair holding thousands of wild acres to keep in the imported red deer and keep people out. You can see the deer; I glimpsed a herd on the slopes on the far side of Lough Veagh. In the Adairs' time they were shot by the quality. Lord Kitchener shot one. Details of society shoots survive in game books.

'1906 ... killed August 29th ... 1 stag shot by Earl of Eglington ... 17 stone, 3 lbs 10 points ... Lord Montgomerie ... Captain O'Neill ... Places shot ... Waterfall, Scallops, Lough Insgagh ... Bogles Cutting.' The waterfall was above me, falling down a shoulder of the Derryveagh mountains into the black lake.

For many years a battering ram manufactured for John Adair's evictions was visible at Falcarragh. When Arthur Fox viewed 'this monstrous monument of British respect for the rights of property, an imposing looking instrument fashioned after a strictly classical fashion and made of oak', the local man who accompanied him went silent with anger. The columnist of the *Derry Standard* saw another one at work on the Glenveagh estates in April 1861.

The first family evicted was a widow named Ward aged sixty years who had six daughters and one son ... Throwing themselves on the ground their Gaelic wails and terrifying cries resounded around the vale and mountainside for many miles ... while the male population bestirred themselves in clearing the furniture from the houses, the woman and children remained until they were forcibly removed from the scenes of happier days. One old man near four score and ten kissed the doorposts with all the fervour of an emigrant leaving his native land. In nearly every house there was someone far advanced in years, while the sobs of children ... took hold of every heart ... Passing along the base of the mountain the spectator might have observed near to each house, its former inmates crouching around a turf fire close by a hedge, and as a drizzling rain poured upon them they found no cover ...

The presence side by side of the good landlord and the bad landlord seems like a fable. While cruel John Adair tormented his people, Lord George Hill's zeal for reform declined somewhat during the later years of his life. His tenants stubbornly opposed his efforts and objected principally to his appropriation of mountain land which he planted according to that insensitive practice of rural landlords with sheep and Scottish shepherds. He could not abolish poverty and there were many times when the wretchedness of his tenants was compounded by famine and near-famine. Opposition to his programme of reform came to a head after his death in 1879 when his son, Captain Arthur Hill, succeeded him. This was the time of the Land League and the fierce zeal of Father James McFadden, 'the patriot priest of Gweedore', a redoubtable opponent of landlordism whose flock supported him with such passion that on one occasion they lynched a policeman sent to arrest him.

Undoubtedly Lord George Hill was moved by the highest motives. When he put up notices in Gweedore in 1844, announcing the restrictions that led to the abolition of rundale, he signed himself to his tenants as 'your sincere Friend and Landlord'. Carlyle who so approved 'the largest attempt at benevolence and beneficence on the modern system ever seen by me or like to be seen' saw the inevitable failure. 'Alas, how *can* it prosper except in the soul of the noble man himself? ...'

Across the mountain boundary the battering ram was at work. John Adair, a gentleman from Co. Offaly who bought the Glenveagh estate as a sporting property in 1858, was described as 'a gracious and upright man, but he contended that he owned the land and could do as he liked with it'. When trouble over black-faced mountain sheep and Scottish stewards resulted in sheep disappearing and the murder of a steward, he resolved to be firm. The most notorious of his evictions took place in 1861 and were conducted with the aid of two hundred policemen drafted in from other parts of Donegal, Leitrim and Roscommon. Forty-six families were evicted, a total of two hundred and forty-one people. The outcry resulted in a relief committee paying for the passage to Australia of every single one of his victims. In the state of Victoria they founded a settlement which they called Derryveagh.

Julian Burkitt, the agent of the present Glenveagh Estate, showed me letters he had received from their descendants. In one a poem was quoted:

> He brought the Sheriff to our doors
> He quenched our fires so bright
> My grandsire he is no more
> He died that fatal night.
> My mother weeps her youngest child
> A boy of beauty rare
> But four months old, so meek and mild;
> All done by John Adair.

20
Derry · Eglington · Portrush · Bushmills · Giant's Causeway

The emotive details of the siege of Derry slipped easily into folk memory. I was regaled with them as a child, the zeal of the apprentice boys, Lundy's treachery, Walker's unappetizing shopping list ('a dog's head 2.6, a cat 4.6, a rat 1s . . . a mouse 6d'). My mother possessed a small table reputed to have belonged to Governor Walker.

No symbolism could have been invented that was more potent than the myth of defiance of the overwhelming forces of Catholicism led by the shifty Pretender. The champions of Protestantism were, like William himself, irreproachably colourless. The clergyman, Walker, writing his diary and Michelburne with his bloody flag (whose scarlet colour is remembered in the uniform of the Apprentice Boys) are dim figures compared to James. The last Stuart king emerges as an easy villain for those who continue to find emotional sustenance in the conviction that the exertions of their forebears preserved a perpetual small corner of the earth for the Protestant faith.

Such thoughts occur without much prompting in Derry. So do ideas about its alien atmosphere. De Latocnaye felt that the city 'had no appearance of being an Irish city – a degree of industry and activity reigns there unknown in any other parts of the country'. Of course it appealed to Carlyle – 'The prettiest looking town I have seen in Ireland.' 'Everyman in it is "town proud",' wrote Samuel Bayne in 1904.

No one could be town proud about Derry today and the inroads which the IRA have made on the old civic arrogance have been a dubious achievement. Past walled-up houses, vanished houses and shuttered houses with security screens on the windows I made my way to St Columb's Cathedral, built in 1633 by the Irish Society in the design of a very large English parish church. Among the military monuments, the cannonball from the siege and other militaria that even more than usual in Protestant ecclesiastical buildings suggest the siege mentality, I found two monuments to members of my mother's family. They appeared to be average Establishment figures, a judge in Bengal and a general.

The Scott family has lived in the neighbourhood of Derry since around the time of the siege. An early Reverend Scott was a chaplain to King William and received a watch. King William seems to have given timepieces to a number of clergymen. I have an idea of him on that day at the Boyne mounted on his white charger surrounded by his chaplains in their robes like a flock of birds, all murmuring blessings. And later that evening they line up while he dips into the huge trunk full of watches.

The wind blew in cold gusts across the Foyle, scattering rubbish. There are no hotels in Derry at present; the violence has seen to that. I retired to a café in Ship Street darkened by steel grilles before going down below the Diamond and the city walls to the bus station. Two small boys were inside a bus breaking up the seats. It took time for Ulsterbus to find me an unvandalized vehicle and I was driven out of Derry along another smooth highway. Southerners tend to sneer at the splendid roads in the North and claim that some of the money spent on their upkeep could go on urban renewal. It is envy.

Near the turn-off for Eglington was the defunct Courtauld factory, a reminder of all that was wrong in Ulster. At Eglington the riots and burnings in Derry and the unemployment represented by the demise of Courtaulds could be easily forgotten. Many people who lived there worked in Derry. In the evenings they hurried out to the tree-lined Georgian village built by some London Livery Company in the days of plantation. The mock Tudor pub and the cricket ground where teams in white flannels play on summer weekends stressed the English connection. No bombs, no graffiti, no torn black gaps in the lines of pretty houses. And Derry less than eight miles away.

In the centre of Eglington was the old manor house, the home of the Davisons who had lived here for generations. After Colonel Davison gave me tea in a sitting-room filled with reminders of Peking and Tientsin he showed me round the village, pointing out oak trees, planted to commemorate coronations. His father had planted one for Edward VII, his mother another for George V. His sister had done George VI, while he had been responsible for the present queen. As for Charles, his wedding wouldn't count and he would have to wait for his own coronation before he was entitled to a tree at Eglington.

Beyond the commemorative trees was the church – the only one in this town. Right by the gate was a conspicuous memorial to a dozen or so Scotts, topped with a mention of my Aunt Hatta who died not so long ago at the age of a hundred and seven.

I spent the night in a mock Tudor farmhouse full of creature comforts – a corner cupboard containing toast-racks and shepherdesses, a sideboard with bright sporting trophies, the top of the lavatory covered with mauve mohair and antimacassars over the top of deep, cushioned sofas. At eleven at night when television was nearly over an extra meal was wheeled in described as 'dinner' – stacks of sandwiches, cakes and potato cakes. No wonder so many of the people I met were plump. Conversation was not about politics, but about money. As usual in the North the subject of our southern Mickey Mouse currency aroused hilarity.

In the morning I walked to the Scotts' old house which they had loyally called Willsboro. Curiously, the landscape here on the east bank of Lough Foyle is less an imitation of Old England than a Dutchman's dream. A dyke along the edge of the lough stretching from Derry has reclaimed the flat polder land that lies below sea level and allows the creation of even fenced fields. The neighbourhood was once filled with market gardens, but these have gone. The long plain reaches to the dyke behind which the Foyle bulges as an inland sea. On the far side of the Lough in dramatic contrast to the flat plain rise the mountains of Donegal.

Willsboro itself had a tinge of Holland – the family adoration of King William affected the architecture. The Scotts kept their own market garden. The snowdrops that grew in such profusion used to be sent to London to be sold, while later in the year strawberries, black cherries and other produce from the walled gardens were also disposed of commercially. My mother had a little gardening book given to her by Miss Archibald, the daughter of the last Archibald to be an agent to the Scotts. Published in 1793, entitled *Every Man his Own Gardener*, it was inscribed 'To David Archibald from W. R. Scott. 1827.'

Beyond the crested gate-lodge the trees under which the snowdrops had grown were cut down. Here was the house where the Scotts lived as gentlemen for more than two hundred years, occasionally exporting their sons. One became an ambassador to the Imperial Court in St Petersburg, another had attended the Emperor Maximilian in Mexico, another was sent to Canada in disgrace for seducing the cook. I remembered some of those who had stayed behind and had played hymns on the great organ in the hall beside the case of stuffed birds. Here was my first demonstration that ruin of old houses was not confined to the south of Ireland. Willsboro had become a potato store. The room where Uncle Jack had shown me a pair of duelling pistols was filled with potatoes; so was the study where Aunt Hatta's cockatoo had lived for almost as long as she did in its birdcage. More potatoes in the bow-fronted drawing-room, and more again in the dining-room where the silver épergne had stood on the long table, and stacks of them in the inner hall where the servants trooped in for prayers.

The flat land continued all along the shore, its monotony perpetually broken up by the views of mountains on the Donegal side. It missed Limavady, another Plantation town all trim and neat, where long ago Miss Jane Ross noted down the 'Londonderry Air' as it was played by a passing fiddler, and swept northwards to Magilligan Point where the mouth of the bottle-shaped Lough Foyle brings Derry so close to Donegal that it seems the two Irelands link hands. Ideas of friendship receive a setback by the presence of Magilligan prison camp which was used at the outset of internment. It is empty now, but in good order, its high concrete walls, towers and barbed wire ready for use. Beyond the notices – THIS IS A PROHIBITED PLACE WITHIN THE MEANING OF THE OFFICIAL SECRETS ACT – lies Magilligan Strand where a decade ago protesters marched along its magnificent eight miles to confront the military.

Magilligan, which for one reason or another connected with security remains unspoilt, is one of the most magnificent beaches in Europe. It heralds a series of striking landmarks on the north coast – the Temple of Mussenden, Downhill, Dunluce and the basalt mysteries of the Giant's Causeway. First at the end of Magilligan comes a cliff, rising very sharply, on which perches the Temple of Mussenden, built by Bishop Hervey for Mrs Frideswide Mussenden, a twenty-year-old girl he admired and who died before it was completed. Views from this folly include some of the western isles of Scotland. Around the dome is a Latin inscription from Lucretius which Dryden translated:

> Tis pleasant, safely to behold from shore
> The rolling ship, and hear the tempest roar.

Bishop Hervey, the eighteenth-century Bishop of Derry, was known for his liberal views and for his predilection for building – his nickname was the Edifying Bishop. The sites for his ambitious creations were in keeping with his eccentric nature, and he chose to build Downhill on this windblown cliff. 'It stands on a bold shore, but in a country where a tree is a rarity,' observed Arthur Young. Although the Bishop feverishly ordered the planting of thousands of trees, not one ever grew. It must have been a troublesome place to live – the Bishop didn't spend too much time there – and there may have been some feeling of relief when the draughty house filled with imported classical furniture burnt down in 1803, even though its art collection and library were destroyed. The ruin sits on the cliff, like a monstrous signal tower. Up the steep hill through the broken palace gate which has a pair of smiling lions, the shell contains scores of roofless rooms and empty courtyards. On a broken wall someone had coloured in a Union Jack and written: WE SHALL NOT FORSAKE THE BLUE SKIES OF ULSTER FOR THE GREY SKIES OF THE REPUBLIC.

Over the hill and down again was a caravan site and the suburbs of Coleraine. 'There is nothing very particular to arrest the attention of the tourist at Coleraine,' Sir Richard Colt Hoare wrote in 1806 in the careless manner whereby a traveller skips many towns on his journey. Few bothered to pause at this point on their way to the great sights of North Antrim. Before they built the tower of the new university, which looks like a rocket about to track into space, there was little to catch the eye. Thackeray was satirical about the town's dullness. 'Among the beauties of Coleraine may be mentioned the price of beef which a gentleman told me may be had for fourpence a pound, and I saw him purchase an excellent cod fish for a shilling.'

He went on to Portrush, already an established seaside town, another town exuding signs of Scottish virtue. 'The whole place has an air of comfort and neatness which is seldom seen in Ireland.' As a tourist resort Portrush's advantages include sweeping beaches, its vicinity to the Causeway, the right sort of land for golf courses. Against these is the climate, invigorating, but never great for sea bathing. In November I found it terrible. A wind from the Arctic whipped up a raging sea and swept through Braemar, Westward Ho and other guesthouses facing the North Atlantic.

'I wouldn't call it the coldest,' said the landlady whom I induced to give me a bed. 'We can expect it a lot worse. Ha, ha,' she added, that brief bantering Northern expression that hints something funny has been said. She made allowance for my weak southern blood by lighting a fire in the cavernous sitting-room. Her house must have been built at the time when Portrush was beginning to grow as a holiday place – presumably one of those observed by John Barrow in 1836, 'neat and comfortable'. The nineteenth-century proportions were too generous for warmth. I sat alone under a light too weak to read by, as the rain rattled the sash windows and stirred the air around three great sofas and a dozen armchairs waiting for summer.

Portrush was an early stop for the Walking Tourist who hiked here from Belfast. He had started to grow a beard which to his dismay was turning out to be a mangy red. The straw Leghorn hat he had brought from London had long been cast aside and his umbrella torn to shreds by strong winds. Portrush was a haven. 'Table d'hôte dinner consisting of two sorts of soup, fish, meat and pastry for the moderate charge of 3s.' After dinner he went to the smoking-room and filled the treasured pipe which he carried wrapped in a piece of black waterproof silk. 'Beyond the coffee- or dining-room there is a drawing-room for ladies and gentlemen . . . there is whist and some young ladies sang songs.' The evening sing-song after a day's promenade beside the sea must have had a leisured charm. Were the songs in 1865 sentimental? Young ladies still sang Tom Moore. The Walking Tourist would have liked 'Believe me if all those endearing young charms'.

In the morning I walked along the empty beach flanking the windy golf course. Ahead was a line of cliffs, pounding seas, the scattered Skerries rocks, and another big fenced-off caravan park. There was something austere about Portrush which was not entirely attributable to the weather. It may have been a feeling of remoteness that lingered from Pococke's time. In the mid-eighteenth century Portrush was almost inaccessible, cut off from the rest of Ireland by the lack of roads. In 1752 Pococke wrote that 'the little town is of so little consequence that there is not a publick house in it for the accommodation of travellers; they may have but one merchant in the town who deals chiefly in shipping of corn and kelp'. The coast of Antrim was so remote that the Giant's Causeway wasn't even noticed until 1692 when it was 'discovered' by a Bishop of Derry who reported its unusual qualities to the Royal Society.

Pococke, the energetic clerical traveller, liked nothing better than seeing and exploring remote places in Ireland and elsewhere. Already he had travelled in France, Italy, had climbed in the Alps and journeyed up the Nile as far as Philae. His successful ecclesiastical career is a puzzle or a disgrace – when did he have time for parish duties?

'I walked along on top of the sea cliffs half a mile to Dunluce and it was very curious to see the gulls in their nests, which they have made of clay in the sides of the perpendicular rocks, so that the nests overhang the rocks.' When he came to Dunluce he took his usual careful measurements and noted that the castle was old and irregular and roughly an eighth of a mile in circumference, and that it used to be inhabited by the Earls of Antrim. But the dull prelate failed to appreciate the magnificence of the sprawling ruin at the cliff's edge, a counterpart and contrast to the Bishop of Derry's classical temple faintly visible on another cliff twenty miles to the west.

'There is not another castle in the world in such an extraordinary situation,' mused Johannes Kohl. His guide whined after him correctly: 'Ah your honour! you will be sorry your whole life that you have not seen Dunluce and that you cannot return thither tomorrow.' For Thackeray, it was 'those grey towers of Dunluce standing upon a leaden rock and looking as if some old old princess of old old fairy times were dragon guarded within'. Tidiness is not always a virtue, and the ticket office, car park and stretch of cut grass do Dunluce no good. One of the pleasures of ruins is the drama of the approach – the barbed wire, gorse barriers, fences, bog, charging bull or irate farmer. Dunluce needs a bramble barrier through which a prince may hack his way.

Beyond the gatehouse with its corbelled turrets in the outer court are ruins of a Jacobean house – the one referred to by Pococke who was told how one of the Earls of Antrim's ladies could not stand the sound of crashing waves and had a house built at the entrance where it was quieter. The wind whistled through the bare windows of the north-east tower and battery. I peered a hundred feet down a latrine. The empty buildings looked right over the turbulent ocean. Just exactly where had been the servants' quarters which had collapsed into the sea in 1639 together with quite a number of servants?

The castle's position on top of an island of basaltic rock made it an easy place to defend. Originally a Viking stronghold, it was built up as a fortress by Richard de Burgh, Earl of Ulster around 1300. Fought over for centuries it came into the hands of the MacDonnells, Scots freebooters, who had crossed over from the Caledonian shores. These

MacDonnells, later Earls of Antrim, abandoned Dunluce after the 1641 rebellion and left it to the weather.

Don Cuellar, the shipwrecked Spanish captain, must have seen Dunluce during his flight.

> I reached the place where Alonso de Leyva and the Count de Parades and Don Tomas de Granvela were lost with many other gentlemen whose names would fill a quire of paper. I went to the huts of some savages who were there, who told me of the great misfortunes of our people who were drowned at that place and was shown many jewels and valuables belonging to them which caused me much distress.

This could only be a reference to the galleass, *Girona*, the last of the vessels in the Spanish Armada to sink off the Irish coast, which, overloaded with 1,500 shipwreck survivors, instead of its usual complement of 550 men, struck a rock called Lacada Point beside a steep inlet known as Port na Spaniagh, a few miles east of Dunluce. In spite of the clue afforded by the name, the location of the shipwreck was lost until 1967 when a Belgian archaeologist named Robert Sténuit began to dive for a glorious find of treasure.

Sorley Boy MacDonnell, Lord of Dunluce, managed to obtain three cannon from the *Girona* which he added to the defences of his castle. Since he offered a refuge to a number of Spaniards, including the five survivors of the *Girona*, it is a puzzle why Don Cuellar did not ask him for help. But he was directed eastward to the territory of another chieftain, O'Cahan of Derry at his stronghold at Castleroe near Coleraine. Then he was aided by Redmund O'Gallagher, Bishop of Derry, who arranged for his voyage in the company of seventy-eight other Spanish refugees towards Scotland.

Down the coast was Bushmills where monks have been brewing since 1273. But the real business of Bushmills began in 1609 when Sir Thomas Phillips was granted a licence to distil, and soon after the Bushmills whiskey was in production.

The gates of the distillery were beyond the War Memorial and the Orange Hall. I was the only visitor that day and after the briefest of guided tours I was brought down to the cellar. Three Blackbushes later the problems of finding a bed for the night receded.

'You've a way to go,' said my kindly guide. 'Have a freshener.' With pure Bushmills throbbing in my veins I set off for the Giant's Causeway although I knew there was very little prospect of finding the hotel open. Darkness had almost fallen when I arrived and sure enough, it was closed for the winter. The whiskey was wearing off. I have rarely felt more grateful to be directed up the hill to Mrs Lynch's farmhouse.

Next morning the rain streamed down and the world was still half-dark. The eggs in a massive nest of sausages and bacon fortified me, but it took an effort of will to abandon the Lynch farm for the Causeway.

'It looks like the beginning of the world,' Thackeray mused. 'The sea looks older than in other places, the hills and rocks strange and formed differently from other rocks and hills.' I thought it looked like the end. I was the latest of a long procession of visitors come to see the molten columns of basalt set in hexagons and pentagons of astonishing evenness. This almost unique natural wonder had given rise to observations that underpinned a whole philosophy which believed in nature combining with art.

Although the Giant's Causeway was in such a distant part of Ireland it had the good fortune to be in the vicinity of Bushmills. The whiskey had to be carried to the outside world and soon there was a two-way traffic as a fairly intrepid strain of travellers journeyed to Antrim to view this wonder of nature. Nothing like it had ever been seen before and no one knew how such a remarkable phenomenon could come about. It was not until 1771 that a Frenchman named Demarest suggested that the origin of the columns of the Causeway was volcanic.

Pococke was an inevitable visitor 'with equal pleasure and astonishment viewing this wonderful work of nature'. He went a number of times with his measure. 'I measured the three sides and took the bearings and measured the octagon with all the pillars around it.' At much the same time Susannah Drury painted her prize-winning gouaches which are the most famous pictures of the Causeway ever made and have saved Miss Drury from that oblivion which is the lot of so many women artists. Mrs Delany, the former Mrs Pendarves, also drew the Causeway, and her pencil sketches, a lot more feeble than the strong lines of Miss Drury, are none the less engaging.

Mrs Delany journeyed to the Causeway in 1749 from County Down. Like any party with which she was associated, the group that accompanied her 'walking and stumbling among the rocks' was out to enjoy itself. There were the two young Leslie boys, Mr Mathews, the curate, Sally Smith and others. When they were fatigued they chose a sheltered spot and baskets were produced containing cold mutton, tongue and other dainties. (Pococke also had a picnic with his friend Mr Duncane, salmon stuck on skewers and roasted before a turf fire.) Between slices of mutton Mrs Delany drew. 'I took an imperfect sketch of the place while we were at our repast . . . our attendants were differently grouped some distance to the left side . . . a little below were women and children that gathered seaweed and shells for us, about twelve in number with very little light drapery, guides of different ages seated on the points of the rocks whose figures were very droll, and I believe we ourselves no less so.'

Although visitors came regularly during the eighteenth century, as Mrs Delany's mention of guides indicates, the Giant's Causeway had yet to achieve its great popularity. For one thing it was still very difficult to reach. When Boswell tried to persuade Dr Johnson to visit Ireland (Johnson: 'It is the last place where I should wish to travel') and asked him, 'Is not the Giant's Causeway worth seeing?' the Doctor replied: 'Worth seeing? yes; but not worth going to see.'

This attitude changed abruptly with the discovery of Fingal's Cave on the island of Barra where a similar columnar structure produced even more dramatic results. The two landmarks provided ample evidence for current theories that nature was not only divine but could do as well as art. Causeway and Cave became powerful symbols of the sublimity of nature. While Barra really was inaccessible, North Antrim could be reached with a certain effort.

In 1837 the building of Sir Charles Lanyon's coast road between Larne and Portrush opened up an easy route for those who wished to see nature at her architectural best. Soon the Giant's Causeway vied in popularity with Killarney. Dozens of guides and sellers of geological specimens waited to pounce on visitors, cartloads of basalt were taken to decorate gardens. 'As for the fossils,' warned *Murray's Guide*, 'many of the specimens offered for sale were never obtained at the Causeway or even in the neighbourhood.' The guides were terrifying. Most of them were McMullens, and their activities got so out of hand that the Earl of Antrim who owned the Causeway (or thought he did – there was a grotesque century-long dispute with the Lecky family over possession) had to appoint a chief guide named Neil McMullen to keep them in order. He was not very effective, and visitors continued to record their importunities. '"Please your honour, take me wid you, I'll show you the curiosities" ... another bawls out, "Let me show your honour the mighty wonders of creation."' So John Barrow was escorted, spluttering, much against his will.

Thackeray described his awful experiences at length, the guides, the shrill beggar boys. '"I'm the guide Miss Henry recommends," shouts one. "I'm Mr Macdonald's guide," pushes in another. "This way," roars a third and drags his prey down a precipice.' Kohl tried to escape by taking a back route, but he was caught. 'They hunted me as dogs would a deer.'

In those days you could take a boat – you cannot do it now – and be rowed up and down the coast to see the deep caverns of Runkerry and Portcoon whose echoes were aroused by the boatmen firing off cannon, just as in Killarney. Thackeray was manhandled out into the sea on a rough day 'before I had leisure to ask myself why the deuce I was in the boat with four rowers hurrooing and bounding madly from one huge liquid mountain to another – four rowers whom I was bound to pay'. Meanwhile the guide bellowed in his ear, 'That is Port Noffer ... them rocks is the Stookawns ... and yonder – fire away, my boys – hurray, we're over it now: has it wet you much, sir?'

The actual pavement built by Finn MacCoul so that the Scottish giant, Benandonner, would not get his feet wet before they began their fight, is between two little bays, Port Ganny and Port Noffer. The collection of over thirty thousand even exact columns a foot and a half across sticks out like a tongue two hundred yards into the sea. It has tended to disappoint. John Gamble, a proud Ulsterman, tried to get himself in the mood to appreciate it by reading from a guide book which assured him that the viewer would be 'lost in wonder and admiration (his eye ranging from the base to the summit of this most magnificent amphitheatre) repeating to himself in substance "wonderful are the works of God"'. But, alas, Gamble felt that 'the sublimity of nature is in irregularity, and she seems downgraded when she counterfeits the trimness of art ... The Giant's Causeway inspires none of those indescribable feelings which we experience when we gaze on the wild glen or hearken to the foaming torrent.'

De Latocnaye found 'nothing more remarkable in the Causeway than in the other quarries of the country'. Kohl, chased by twenty ragged guides snatching at his hat and telescope, christened the famous natural feature 'the dwarf's Causeway; it is nothing more than the beginning of the Causeway which soon sinks beneath the waves'. Inglis read much tourist bombast and concluded, 'As for grandeur or sublimity, I saw nothing of either.' And Thackeray viewing it from his rowboat: 'Mon Dieu! and have I travelled a hundred miles to see that?'

The Walking Tourist had one adjective for the unusual hexagons, 'slippery'. He was more interested in eyeing 'a pretty young woman with flaxen hair and red petticoat who sells fossils and photographs. The guides warn you not to go near her ... she seems to be under some kind of spell.' By the time he walked here in 1865 the Causeway was at its height as a tourist attraction. It continued to flourish in the eighties when a tramway ran from Portrush to Bushmills and Causeway Head, the earliest system of hydro-electric traction in the British Isles. Souvenir shacks made their appearance and an admission was charged – a situation that did not change until the National Trust acquired the site.

I left the concrete shelter and followed the route trodden by Mrs Delany and the rest, round the coast with its carefully labelled points of interest – the Honey Comb, Lord Antrim's Seat, the Giant's Pulpit, the Chimney Tops and Harp. The third little bay past the Causeway is Port na Spaniagh where the *Girona* struck through a variety of circumstances – a north-west wind, poor visibility, bad seamanship arising from fatigue. Sorley Boy MacDonnell's people must have had difficulty manhandling the cannon up the cliff to be taken to Dunluce. At the Wishing Well an old woman used to sit selling whiskey mixed with water from the spring. (Thackeray: 'She has no change for a shilling; she never has, but her whiskey is good.') There are still plenty of visitors who come down in summer to view nature's sublime effort and to buy guide books and souvenirs from the little shop sanctioned by the Trust. But today rain drummed on the strange patterns of the Giant's Causeway and on the tarmac of the sequestered car park and there were only ghosts and echoes of the shouting guides of the past.

21
Ballycastle · Rathlin Island · Glenarm · Whitehead · Carrickfergus

At the corner of the Diamond in Ballycastle stands the Antrim Arms which has flourished ever since the Giant's Causeway became a tourist attraction. The stables behind used to be full of horses which the landlord hired to guests who wished to ride out to the Causeway. The old-fashioned comfort has one modern jarring intrusion, the buzzer at the locked front door which is a precaution against bombers.

Just before he set off through 'bleak wild and hilly country' towards his awful experiences at the Causeway, Thackeray paused to pay a particular compliment to the Antrim Arms, which I endorse. 'Ballycastle must not be left without recording one of the snuggest inns in the country.' Thirty-three years later the Walking Tourist was less satisfied. After complaining about the food, the prices and foolish questions from other guests he went to bed. As he lay back before gliding into refreshing sleep induced by exercise, his last thoughts were that 'chambermaids in Ireland don't know how to make beds properly'.

Johannes Kohl arrived as I did, in bad weather, or as he poetically put it, 'on the wings of the wind'. The Antrim Arms was very much to his taste. 'We found a right comfortable room, a cheerful tea-table and a homely warm fire.' Sitting beside it were two young ladies hoping to visit the neighbouring island of Rathlin where their uncle was the clergyman. The two young ladies were obliged to receive the wet, frozen, very pitiable-looking stranger and make room for him at the fire without asking leave of Papa or Mama ... an unusual state of affairs in 1842. He passed the evening with them 'pleasantly, conversing to my heart's content'. Did they get bored with the young German?

In the windy streets of Ballycastle the Chinese restaurant heralded by lanterns hung with tassels looked unusually exotic. Down at the pier I waited to see if a boat came in that would take me out to Rathlin. The island lying between the Antrim coast and the Mull of Kintyre, the largest off the Irish coast, can be cut off in winter for days and weeks. Among the hazards of the voyage over is the effect of an ebb tide meeting the Atlantic swell. Casualties of the crossing have included Brecain, son of King Niall, who in the fourth century was lost with his fleet of fifty curraghs. The antiquarian, Dr Drummond, who visited Rathlin in 1785 impelled by 'my natural curiosity and the wish I had to trace the whole extent of the basalts of this country', suffered from bad seasickness and wrote with emotion about the force of these waters 'violently agitating twice a day'. 'The moment that the ebb began to return to the ocean, rushing in opposite to this western swell, all was confusion and tumult. The long wave which had before rolled forward in silent majesty, was now fretted and broken into a tempestuous sea, which the stoutest boats dare not encounter and even the best ships wish to avoid.'

The vast majority of travellers in North Antrim gave Rathlin a miss. Thackeray was too aware of his creature comforts to contemplate the crossing – the hour's boat trip off the Giant's Causeway had almost finished him. The Walking Tourist continued walking. Kohl was at first mad keen to go out to 'this romantic wild place' together with the MacDonnell girls with whom he had passed such a pleasant evening at the Antrim Arms. But he had to give up the idea because of the storm that kept eight fishing boats tied up in the harbour at Ballycastle. He could only climb the hill and gaze through his telescope at the white line of cliffs that seemed so near. 'While contemplating Rathlin I thought of Shakespeare's *Tempest* and the island of the banished Duke Prospero.' When he came to write his travel book he filled half a dozen pages of closely lined text with information about the island culled from stories he had heard in Ballycastle, Dr Drummond's notes in the *Transactions of the Irish Academy* and Dr Hamilton's *Letters on the County of Armagh*. He wrote of the one thousand one hundred inhabitants and their Lilliputian cattle and horses – the sight of a full-sized horse had filled them with fear because they thought it was a monster. He wrote at length about Robert Bruce (nothing of the spider), the tides, the rats, the mice, the seabirds, the MacDonnells, the seaweed and other subjects of interest to his German readers. There was really no need to make the stormy crossing.

One traveller who did manage to get over to Rathlin was that intrepid spinster, Miss Anne Plumptre. In 1816, carrying a copy of Dr Hamilton's book, she embarked bravely in a small fishing boat on what seemed at first a calm sea. But after the boat began to tack over mountainous seas she regretted her impulse. When she staggered ashore again at Ballycastle she wrote, 'Though very desirous of visiting this island, and very glad when I was safe back again, yet I believe that if I had previously any idea of the sea I was to navigate I should have entirely relinquished the idea of venturing upon it.'

That was in the bad old days of sail. Could things be anything like as uncomfortable now? The uncertainty had not changed. No one at Ballycastle knew when and if there would be a boat from the island and no one cared. Communication was haphazard to the verge of being non-existent.

One moment the harbour was empty and the next a small boat full of cattle was bucketing up and down beside the pier.

'Are you going to Rathlin?'

'Aye.'

I stood and shivered as the frightened bellowing cattle were unloaded and the decks washed down. Then the *Iona* was loaded up again with bags of coal and crates of vodka.

From the deckhouse window a bottle was thrown into the sea. The crew inside were chatting amiably. 'Must get back in time for *Dallas*.' No move was made to cast off. More empty bottles followed the first skimming out into the turbulent harbour. Beer and stout mostly, no one was broaching the vodka. In the old days passengers paid their fare with half a guinea and a quart of whiskey. Now a burst of singing came from the deckhouse.

The departure was so sudden that, sauntering on the pier, I was almost left behind. A car tore up, screamed to a halt and a fat man, some vital crew member, leapt on board. I had just time to follow him and hang on to the heaving deck as ropes were cast off and the *Iona* pitched into the sea. The crossing was short – forty-five minutes – and very cold. I was the only passenger. All the way over a stream of bottles was hurled from the deckhouse into the sea.

It was pitch-dark when the *Iona* roared into the harbour, approaching with practised confidence the line of exposed rock that seemed to offer the only shelter. By the time I had collected myself the crew had vanished and I was alone in the darkness. The sea roared and lamented around me.

A few specks of light indicated houses. I groped towards them one at a time, but no one took in guests. Some people did not answer my knock but kept to their beds. I contemplated breaking into one of a line of caravans behind a sheltering wall before I set off for the last light. Beyond it must be cliffs and ocean. Heaven bless Mrs McCurdy whose house was the usual cocoon of Northern comfort. 'They built it in the morning and danced in it for the evening,' she told me. Such speed was possible because of the community spirit of the islanders.

Next morning I saw Rathlin for the first time, looking over Mill Bay and Church Harbour where the *Iona* kept her ceaseless movement. A line of cliffs looked like very white teeth. The sea had calmed down and winked in the sunlight. Everything was bare and bright.

The island is nine miles long and shaped like a boomerang. Most of it is perched on cliffs flecked with seabirds. There are few proper roads. In summer if you have great powers of persuasion you might get someone to haul you about on a tractor or an old Volkswagen.

Outside the shelter of Church Bay the wind was strong as it swept over the grassland and heath. A feature of the barren landscape was numerous little reedy lakes. The three lighthouses provided landmarks for walking. Going to the West Lighthouse I could count on one hand the houses that were occupied. Stone walls retaining a flake of thatch stood on screes of wild land, each with its stately views to the south of Scotland and the outlines of the Giant's Causeway and Fairhead. The cliffs fell four hundred feet. Seals gather at their base. Birds include all kinds of gull, guillemots, razorbills, puffins, shearwaters and stormy petrels. The wicked wind that scorches land and sea made climbing the steps of the lighthouse an ordeal. Inside, domesticity took over with plenty of burnished brass and cups of tea while the light above waited for nightfall to pierce the Atlantic.

The East Lighthouse overlooks Bruce's castle, a few wind-bitten pieces of broken wall facing Scotland. Somewhere in the cliffs below was the cavern where Robert Bruce had sat and bullied the spider. Anne Plumptre walked and took a prospect from Doon Point. Like her I marvelled at the nearness of the Scottish coast and like her I could distinguish without the aid of a glass the white foam dashing against the Scottish cliffs. She pondered the story of the enchanted green island that floated somewhere off the Antrim coast. Every seven years it came out of the sea, 'and it is crowded with people selling yarns and engaged in various occupations common to a fair'.

At Rue Point a smaller automatic lighthouse faced the Viking prow of Fairhead. All round were remnants of the time when Rathlin was filled with people – a lonely smuggler's house beside a rocky beach, a whole deserted settlement lying along a lake. Clumps of fuchsia and veronica planted scores of years ago surrounded broken cabins holding in two rooms, a fireplace and a couple of little windows looking out at the matted seed and vegetation. Lloyd Praeger noted a number of imported species of plants still flourishing here that had originally been brought over by the islanders for medicinal purposes – caraway, tansy, sweet cicely, soapwort, alexanders, hemlock, elecampane and green alkenet. Few flowers bloomed in November. Behind the houses the scars of potato ridges were covered with dead bracken. The only sign of life was hundreds of rabbits.

Dr Hamilton wrote at the end of the eighteenth century that the islanders 'possess a degree of affection for the island which may surprise the stranger ... they always talk of Ireland as a foreign kingdom ... a heavy curse among them is "May Ireland be your hinder end"'. Anne Plumptre agreed. 'The inhabitants are not less attached to their dreary and desolate home than those that dwell under the most auspicious and benign sun.' People still do not like leaving Rathlin. But the population has shrunk to a little over a hundred and the community is embattled. Every ruin of a house represents a tragedy of departure.

Because of the angled shape of Rathlin I kept coming back to the inside right angle which was Church Bay and the main settlement. Here were the post office, churches, manor house and a bar decorated with headboards from wrecks. 'May God be good and send a shipwreck,' the islanders used to say. I had a drink or two, rather furtively. 'You want to keep your mouth shut when you are listening to people,' I was told. Listening, I heard something about a life of sturdy independence vanishing. Summer vandals, bird watchers and television have brought about more changes in the last decade than in all the years since Dr Campbell arrived and watched the islanders' kelp drying. The future was not a subject discussed in the bar when the burning topic was who shot JR?

In the small cemetery of the church of St Thomas lie victims of shipwrecks, three nameless sailors who died in the First World War known only unto God, and Elizabeth Browning, wife of Easdale, drowned by the wreck of the *Cambria* and cast ashore on this island aged twenty-nine. 'Her sun went down while it was yet day ...' Inside the church the roar of the sea was audible. The flaking monuments were covered with epitaphs to the Gage family who leased the island from the Earls of Antrim.

Kohl thundered at the Gages who must have been some distant connections of the young ladies in the Antrim Arms. 'The rector ... who resides here throughout the year with his family has a good income and lives in the enjoyment of all imaginable comforts, is a Protestant. But his poor tenants and vassals from whom he draws his income, and who in order to pay it, fish, cultivate oats, navigate the stormy seas and eat seaweed, are poor taxed Catholics.' That situation was not confined to Rathlin. The old manor where the Gages lived still stands just outside the harbour, the most distinctive building on the island, long and Georgian in style with numerous outhouses which make it seem like a palace.

'People never want to leave,' Mrs McCurdy said smugly after I had been on the island three days. Finding a boat to depart was more difficult than finding one to arrive. Queries were answered vaguely, the weather wasn't too good, tomorrow maybe. I was lucky as I had been lucky in finding Mrs McCurdy's house. It appeared that the clergyman from Ballycastle wished to visit his few parishioners and someone had to go over and fetch him. The small ship heaved and tossed as it got away into Church Bay and the white line of cliffs showed for the last time. I could see the McCurdys' small farmhouse at the end of Mill Bay, the old wrack wall, the line of little houses, and the incongruous manor house beneath the bare hills. Forty-five minutes later we came into Ballycastle where the lonely figure of the clergyman could be seen waiting on the pier.

The Corrymeela Centre was a large white building on a cliff near Fairhead. Before the present troubles began a group of religious leaders bought this house to provide opportunities for people of different religions to meet. Groups came together to discuss mixed marriages, the stubborn problems of sectarian education and related subjects. People of different denominations shared their experiences.

Children from the backstreets of Belfast, women who have lost relatives through violence, continue to be brought here under the sheltering wing of Fairhead. Inspecting the lecture rooms and dormitories and the common chapel, I expressed admiration and tried not to feel cynical or overwhelmed. 'A candle light in the present darkness' is how Corrymeela thinks of itself. On a blackboard was written 'thank-you for a lovely weekend' and no one had rubbed it out. The blend of charismatic and gospel fervour and all those young volunteers tend to promote reservations in those who sneer at the idea of a clean-living holiday camp. To some the wholesomeness of the atmosphere verges on the oppressive. But it has survived and kept its ideals over all the unhappy years, while bigger, more bombastic peacemaking efforts have failed in tears.

A clean wind ruffled the whitecaps in the north channel and blew round the great stone columns that make up the bulk of Fairhead. Not far from this massive precipice I met Pat MacBride whose family had farmed sheep in this area for generations. Back at his house we sat and ate apple pie and put cream in our tea. Most of the people around here were Catholic, Pat said, but the religions got on well. Not like Belfast. A fence should be put around that place.

His grandfather had remembered ships coming round the coast from Dublin to ship coals from the fearsome old mines in the cliffs near Fairhead. These collieries yielded 'blind coals' that did not give out flames or smoke. When Anne Plumtre tried to visit them a surveyor prevented her: 'Madam ... I wouldn't for all the coals in the country have you abuse yourself in such a way.' They must have been grim. De Latocnaye penetrated the whole murky way, 'a mile underground in a horizontal direction'. 'It is one of those whims which (like matrimony) may be indulged for once. But I shall never venture again into one.'

'From Glenarm to Ballycastle the people are all Papists,' Pococke found, and that still holds true. A man's religion could be told instantly by language. 'On this side ... almost all the people speak Irish, but most of them understand English as well. But on that side from Ballycastle westward no one understands Irish.' Now, the Irish language has almost gone, differences are more subtle. Was it the hills around or the particular blend of Pat's hospitality that put me so much in mind of Wicklow?

From the MacBrides' farm I took the road that can be described as a roller-coaster in the most literal sense of the word. It twists down to Morlough Bay, skirts Tor Head and leads down a hair-raising route by the side of the sea to Cushendun on one of the most spectacular passages of the Antrim Coast Road. This sixty-mile stretch of road between Larne and Portrush was constructed partly with the intention of opening up the wilds and linking the seven glens of Antrim, and partly to provide employment during a period of famine. From the wall on the sea side an abyss of cliff falls down to the sea floor. At Culreeny a small lonely church, the Star of the Sea, was sited in front of the cliff face in a sunless dip of the road. In front was a view looking north-east that the hermit saints might have sought, where the sea sparkled far below and the hills of Scotland rose twelve close miles away. From the shadow of Culreeny the source of so many of Ulster's troubles shone in brilliant sunlight, the little white houses clearly visible. From there had come the first invaders into Ireland to settle on the beaches near Larne. Here, Thackeray had stopped his jaunting car and stretched his legs and looked across. 'If ever this book reaches a second edition . . . a sonnet shall be inserted in this place describing the author's feelings on his first view of Scotland. Meanwhile the Scottish mountains remain undisturbed, looking blue and solemn, far away in the placid sea.'

Cushendun is possibly the last landlord's village in Ireland, consisting of pretty houses built between 1912 and 1926 to the designs of Clough Williams Ellis for Ronald MacNeill. They combine in a soulless little place in a beautiful location, much admired and preserved as a kind of outdoor museum. Near Cushenden in the Glenarm valley stands Ossian's imposing grave that so impressed Johannes Kohl. 'Those glens are said to be, even now, full of songs and traditions which glorify the deeds of Fingal and Ossian who was himself converted by St Patrick.' It has not the slightest connection with St Patrick, but is a mighty impressive example of a segmented gallery grave, an Ulster 'horned' cairn unlike any remains that we have in the South. The situation above the little Glenarm river is enough to make the visitor go into similar reveries to Kohl's, and I stayed around there for rather too long. By the time I had taken the school bus to Carnlough, driving back and forth dumping children all around the glens as the lights of Scotland beckoned from across the sea, it was dusk and I was faced with the usual winter problem. Carnlough could offer me nothing.

'You won't find anywhere in Glenarm,' they called after me as I set out for the next village around the next high bluff of the Antrim coast. As darkness and cold increased the road straightened out beside a long pebbly beach. Near the RUC barracks, spotted with lights and enveloped in wire mesh, I found Glenarm's only hotel, another Antrim Arms. It was bombed and boarded up.

I retired to Margaret's Café and thought about going on to Larne. Over the door near the list of prices for tea, milk and soup a text proclaimed FOR ALL THY WAYS ACKNOWLEDGE HIM AND HE SHALL DIRECT THY PATH. He was good enough to direct my path towards Mrs Morrow who owned Margaret's and gave me accommodation and a substantial meal in her sitting-room.

Mrs Morrow's cousin was a famous man in Glenarm and elsewhere. He was known as Fernie the Magician. When he came to see his relative we were introduced, and he asked me at once for the date of my marriage.

I gave it to him, trying not to be vague in that smog of heat and television.

'It couldn't have been that,' he shook his wild mop of hair. 'That was Sunday.'

Next morning I met him outside his small terrace house in Vennell Street, which not so long ago, he said, used to be called the Stinking Vennell before they cleaned it up. Fernie was English and had come to Glenarm and married a local girl after the war. Today he was taking his motorbike, a large 400cc Honda, all the way to Drogheda in the Republic. There was scarcely a town or hall in the North or South which he hadn't visited on his motorbike in the last thirty years. He ignored political or religious divisions and had not yet found a Republican or Loyalist stronghold where he hadn't been made to feel welcome. No trouble at all – apart from one stray shot through the front wheel of the Honda – 'a trifling incident'. He specialized in giving shows for children and charity performances presented with a blend of enthusiasm and innocence.

I watched him load up with gear for his twelve-act Christmas show. The bike carried a burden that weighed something like sixteen stone, not to mention Fernie propped on top. His equipment included a complete set of Swiss bells, a ventriloquist doll, a Punch and Judy show and a fez. He gave me a poster printed locally in blue and red letters that were not always entirely clear: Fernie presents his novelty

ENTERTAINMENT at this school. A First-Class Novelty Programme: MAD CONJUROR, MAGIC & SCAPO VENTRILOQUISM, YOUR BELL BAND AND DUET CONCERTINA, CHAPEAUGRAPHY TROUBLEWIT, BA-LOONATIC & THE ROLLO, LAUGHS, SCREAMS, YELLS. Then he put on his waterproof suit, polythene wrappings taken from bread loaves over his hands to keep them warm and dry, a helmet squeezed down over his unruly hair, and he roared away. In Glenarm he was such a familiar figure that people scarcely noticed his loaded motor-bike passing by.

When Thackeray stayed in Glenarm he met some precursors of Fernie. After a good dinner at the Antrim Arms he heard the sound of music wafting up the street from near the pier. A small travelling theatre had been set up to attract customers. Prices were modest. 'Gallery 1d ... Pit 2d ... Bombastes Furiosa and the Comic valley of Glenarm in an uproar to an empty house.' He was not beguiled by the music or the promise of entertainment, preferring the comfort of the inn and a good bottle of wine.

Like other travellers to Glenarm, Thackeray sought out the castle which stands beside the town just over a wall with the valley of Glenarm tucked into the hills beyond. When I went up to have a look it was empty, the owner, Lord Dunluce, being away in England. When no one is about it is difficult to resist the temptation to peer within. Like Anne Plumptre who looked in at these windows and saw the vertebrae of a whale, I cast my eye into the porch and saw some deck chairs and a bike among the splendid furnishing. The Earls of Antrim possessed two fairy castles, totally different in style and setting. The enchanted fortress at Dunluce contrasts with this frivolity here at Glenarm which looks like a big toy or perhaps a cake. Thackeray compared its four corner towers to the Tower of London.

Antrim Castle was a keep built in the sixteenth century; since then, the fashion and the folly of a succession of rich earls has encrusted and topped the stone walls with gables, crests and cupolas. The tree-filled valley of the Arm provides a delightful setting for this ridiculous building. 'The most beautiful and romantik ground I ever beheld,' Pococke considered, a statement of true ecstasy coming from him. About thirty years after his visit Francis Wheatley, who spent some time in Ireland as an itinerant painter, came to Glenarm, and in one of his most pleasing compositions painted Lord and Lady

Antrim dressed in stylish sporting clothes sitting in their phaeton, a distant representation of the castle behind them.

Wind shook the trees in the glen and the Arm river raged as it flowed down through the village and empty harbour, a receptacle for heaving waves. Along the coast road waves spumed over the tarmac. At Whitehead there was nothing frivolous or fairylike about the seventeenth-century Chichester Castle above the sprawling suburbs of the newer railway town. Here I sought out references in the memoirs of the young Parliamentarian William Brereton. It was near here that he landed in Ireland for his quick visit in 1735, and put Whitehead on the map for literature. Whitehead carefully remembers Brereton's visit: his journal and the comments of a later traveller named Richard Dobbs are on display in the public library.

A short distance along the coast from Whitehead is Blackhead – there is a lighthouse and some caves which in Brereton's time contained 'a multitude of pigeons'. This was near what used to be the location of a little exposed harbour called Port Davey which has now completely vanished. It would be indistinguishable from the rest of the rocky shore except for two landmarks, a couple of big rocks sardonically christened the Wren's Eggs. Wooden chalets, picnic tables, chairs and a hedge of veronica combine to suggest the most forlorn of seaside holidays.

When Brereton set out from Portpatrick in Scotland to his destination at Carrickfergus, he ended up here. As usual the weather was the culprit, and his vessel ran into a storm worse than I was witnessing now. The little gaff-rigged open boat, crowded with horses as well as men, was battered by mountainous waves. This coast was 'a hard shore without a harbour or shelter for anything except fishing boats, and these must have fair weather'. Port Davey was just such an uncertain haven. Richard Dobbs wrote of it forty years later that 'many boats of 16 or 18 tons land here from Scotland but there is no getting in but at full sea ... and that is dangerous enough'.

However, any port is welcome in a storm. With great difficulty the master of this precarious passenger boat aided by his son whose name was David Dickie ('a dainty fine pretty boy, who will make a good sailor') steered the heaving boat, its hold full of sick passengers and plunging horses, under Blackhead. 'Hereby we were sheltered all night from most cruel, violent and tempestuous storms which did much affect and discourage us, though we lay at anchor under the shelter of a large hill.'

At dawn 'all the horses were first thrown into the sea, and did swim to land and climb a good steep rock'. The animals survived the experience in rather better form than the passengers who disembarked at the little jetty beside the Wren's Eggs among fishing boats with tattered sails and scoured woodwork. Brereton's clothes were soaked in spray and he felt 'a faintingness' for a few moments before being sick. Seasickness was an occupational hazard of seventeenth-century travel as fear of flying is now, but his description of his ordeal is peculiarly disgusting. 'The sea wrought effectually and plentifully with me and brought me more vomit only when I was at sea than ever formerly, so as my stomach was not only cleared and discharged of phlegm, but also of abundance of choler and green stuff.' He was to find there was more wrong with him than mere seasickness.

Not long ago the small railway station at Whitehead was lovingly tended with borders of flowers. There is not a daisy there now, and the vandals have done their work. On this bleak November day the ticket office and the waiting room were boarded up, the seats along the platform had all been torn up and the smell of urine lingered near walls which were closely covered with graffiti. There were comparatively little political graffiti apart from a few indications that the UDA or IRA flourished in these parts; the vast mass of this spread of outdoor literature was meaningless or obscene.

'What went wrong?' I asked another chilled passenger who stood in the wind waiting for the train (no chance of sitting).

'They savaged it. The young boys from Carrickfergus broke it up.' He averted his eyes from an unpleasant observation on the wall opposite. Until recently a clergyman used to come here regularly with a pot of grey paint and paint over the writing. The hooligans came back as regularly as clockwork. And then the poor man died. Soon there would be no place left for them to write on. 'They're quite right on the Isle of Man to keep using the cane.'

Carrickfergus, only a few stops down this melancholy little railway line, is dominated by yet another castle on a coastline of conquerors. This one is the biggest and the best, perhaps the finest military building in Ireland. It was erected overlooking Belfast Lough to guard the chief port in the North; among Norman strongholds in Ireland its strength was second only to Trim.

When Brereton arrived at the 'preattie little town' the castle loomed large beside a line of thatched cottages and Arthur Chichester's new mansion. This was Joymount, erected in 1618, its name an elegant compliment to Chichester's friend Lord Mountjoy. Brereton thought it pretentious.

'Lord Chichester's house, which is a very stately house or rather like a Prince's palace,' he wrote and went on immediately to mention the decayed furniture and the wasteful expense of keeping such a huge building in repair, 'which are a burden to the owners of them.' The house was less than twenty years old. Either it had special inconveniences that contributed to the problem of maintenance and made the furniture 'decayed' or every house of its size in Ireland was programmed to be a burden the instant it was built, or Brereton was feeling very sick. Joymount survived for over three hundred years until it was torn down in the present century. Behind the town hall a small conical tower survives, part of the old gateway, and the name is preserved in various streets and in a pub called the Joymount Arms.

The castle goes on looming over Belfast Lough, 'a real romantic looking castle' thought Thackeray, which was a careless observation since there was little romance in its eight hundred years of military occupation before it was turned into a museum full of guns. It was built on its promontory, that dominates the approaches to the town by land and sea, by John de Courcy around 1180 and was in constant military use until after the First World War. Its sieges included one by Bruce's army during which the defenders ate eight Scottish prisoners, and one by Schomberg who took it just before King William set his hallowed footsteps beside what is now a venue for yachts.

The church of St Nicholas was a Norman foundation of John de Courcy who was responsible for the founding of the town. Various rebuildings and alterations, including one by Sir Arthur Chichester who assumed de Courcy's role as conqueror and benefactor, have left a hotch-potch of styles. The most notable feature of St Nicholas is what Brereton called 'a showy new tomb' belonging to the Chichesters. This splendid Jacobean two-tiered monument has Arthur Chichester kneeling in alabaster and facing his wife, and down below another little kneeling figure of Sir John Chichester who was ambushed and killed by the MacDonnells in 1597. The monument was made in England and shipped over to be reassembled in sections. The inscription is in English, not the customary Latin that might present difficulties for rough soldiers and settlers.

> If that desire or chance
> thee hither lead, upon this
> marble monument to tread; let admiration
> thy thoughts still feed,
> while weeping through this epitaph dost read . . .

Did I hear ghostly laughter echoing in the aisles?

> For he did virtue and religion nourish
> And made this land, late rude, with peace to flourish.

Soon after inspecting St Nicholas's church Brereton found that his stomach began to trouble him again. He sought out lodgings from a Mrs Wharton who took him in for the night and then had to endure him for much longer. For three days and nights the unfortunate lady had this testy vomiting English visitor on her hands. Most of the time he lay in bed complaining loudly about the flux and the Irish ague, the malignant fever or looseness that was supposed to come from the dampness of the air. When he came to write about it he did not spare his readers. 'It brought a great weakness and indisposition upon me, the rather the more by reason my body was sufficiently purged by vomit at sea which wrought with me more effectively than formerly in my whole life.'

Mrs Wharton was kept running to and fro with remedies for her guest's bloody flux. She gave him cinnamon in burnt claret, and the syrup and conserve of sloes, well boiled. A pipe of tobacco was supplied in deference to Lord Mountjoy's theory that it 'combatted sickness and the foggy air' (but Lord Mountjoy himself had died of fever). Brereton recalled a remedy thought up by Sir Marmaduke Boyd, and Mrs Wharton was sent running off again to the kitchen. 'Barley boiled in a bag, as hot as it may be placed in your close stool or under you when you go to the stool.' It had not helped and Brereton gave a nauseous account of how 'a thin watery stuff came from me like a steam gushing'.

This is not the best point to talk of food and ale, but inns played an important role in a port like Carrickfergus where intending passengers could wait for days for appropriate weather. Fynes Moryson recommended 'there be some houses where the ordinary is kept for diet, and beds may be had, and the ordinary is common twelfth pence each meal'. Some inns advertised 'if a man be hungry here he may have meat free in calling for a pot or two of ale'.

Pococke had dined in Carrickfergus on a big plate of scallops. I went to Dobbins, which in Brereton's time was a small sixteenth-century castle, and was offered the usual lavish Northern High Tea with a stacked plate of chips and plaice half hidden in tartare sauce. It was very different to the place where Anne Plumptre sought accommodation. 'I found the inn such a deplorable, dirty disgusting place that I determined ... contrary to my usual practice of never risking in the dark ... to go on to Larne.' Fatal decision. Her coachmen had been drinking. From her small coach window she looked out anxiously and saw two Irish hags enveloped in cloaks that came down to their ankles. 'Oh by Jesus, no, my lady ... you are come quite the wrong way; and the clouds of the night will come over you entirely before you can get at all to Larne ...'

Brereton got up shakily from his sick bed and set off from Carrickfergus, his saddlebags filled with purgatives prepared by Mrs Wharton. A lonely figure on horseback, he passed the grey castle with the masts of shipping around its base.

I left Carrickfergus by train reading about Johannes Kohl's arrival in the town, as he came down by coach from Belfast. A full storm had been raging and Kohl, sitting on the roof with some other passengers, enjoyed the Wagnerian effects with something like elation and stored his impressions away very carefully. 'With our heads wrapped in our cloaks, we huddled close together in order to afford the less resistance to the force of the wind ... the autumn winds flew like snow on the blast; the trees on the shore bowed like twigs before the storm; the waves dashed against the strand; the seagulls screamed ... it was the first time that I ever heard the Irish allow that the weather was bad.'

I closed his book and peered from the carriage window. I would change at Belfast and make my way to County Down to search out the route of another early traveller. Meanwhile Belfast arrived slowly out of the mist. A glimpse of the Lough with the grey silhouette of a destroyer, rolling on the waves, lines of rooftops and small red terraces, an industrial estate with the Union Jack floating over a church tower. A mammoth derrick with the letters W & H pierced the sky; they puzzled me until I realized that I was looking at them backwards and they stood for Harland and Wolff.

22
Armagh · Newry · Castlewellan · Downpatrick

'It is Armagh that I love, my sweet thorp, my sweet hill,' St Patrick said, a preference that aroused controversy from the start. He claimed the hilltop named Ard Mhacha, the height of the goddess Macha, to be the headquarters of Christianity in Ireland. King Daire, whose hilltop it was, objected, and tried to fob him off with the site later occupied by the Bank of Ireland.

Today the Protestant St Patrick's Cathedral sits on top of Macha's hill by right of conquest while St Patrick's Catholic Cathedral crowns another hill-top. The Catholic St Patrick's is a lofty twin-towered exercise in the decorated style built out of Armagh limestone and Dungannon freestone. The work was supervised by J. J. McCarthy, 'the Irish Pugin', so popular among those who headed the triumphant nineteenth-century Catholic revival. Italian artists were called in to decorate the interior, particularly the ceiling, in a style which is not only of fashion but a source of embarrassment to those who approve the strictures of simplicity imposed by Vatican II. The flying angels have their charm; some may condemn their sentimental innocence, but others find endearing their efforts to represent the gaiety of the kingdom of heaven.

The Protestant St Patrick guards the hill of Macha like a tired sentinel. It is known that at least seventeen previous cathedrals stood on the site, all of them burned or destroyed. This regular dismantling of the fabric, like a circus tent, has contributed to the general air of weariness about the present edifice. But its uninspiring atmosphere is mainly the result of the work of a dismal English architect named Lewis Cottringham, a pioneer in restoration. Between 1834 and 1837 Cottringham destroyed most things of value in the structure including the majority of medieval carvings, and much that was good in the Georgian cathedral where Thomas Cooley had done some noble work. He also pulled down the fine tower erected by Francis Johnston. Perhaps it is too much to call them ugly, the two cathedrals glaring at each other from their rival hills, hackneyed symbols of discord.

I searched the interior that Mr Cottringham had ravaged for the Caulfield tombs. The Caulfields were a planter family who settled at the town of Charlemont seven miles from Armagh. The first member of the family in Ireland, a Captain Tobias Caulfield, was a soldier in these parts at the beginning of the seventeenth century. His military achievements were not outstanding. He built the star fort at Moy across the Blackwater river from Caulfield in support of Lord Mountjoy's campaign against Hugh O'Neill.

In December 1602 Tobias Caulfield took the opportunity of relieving the tedium of garrison duty at Armagh. Together with two fellow captains, Captain Josias Bodley and Captain Jephson, he rode out from Armagh on a journey of over sixty miles to spend Christmas with another army crony named Sir Richard Moryson, who had recently been appointed Governor of Lecale, a barony which included the town of Downpatrick.

A vivid account of this journey was written by Josias Bodley, another English adventurer in Ireland and a brother of Sir Thomas Bodley who founded the Bodleian library at Oxford. Bodley's career as a soldier included work as an engineer – a year after the Christmas trip he was trench-master at the Battle of Kinsale. In 1604 Lord Mountjoy knighted him. Meanwhile he was governor of Newry, a hard-drinking bucolic soldier, who wrote about the advantages of drink, and the occasional therapeutic bout of drunkenness as well as the advantages of tobacco smoking. His manuscript of the journey to Lecale with his two fellow captains, written in dog Latin, was included in the catalogue of Sir James Ware's manuscripts, dated to Dublin, 1648. It was first published in the *Ulster Journal of Archaeology* in 1854.

Cottringham seemed to have removed a good many tombs as well as everything else. So many memorials were late nineteenth century. Above them waved some old army colours, one to the 89th Regiment, presented by Queen Victoria, another a Queen's Colour of the 43rd Battalion Royal Irish Fusiliers. The military had always been around, since the time of Caulfield and Bodley. Down in the centre of Armagh along the strings of coloured lights near the Christmas tree in Market Square, soldiers were more wary than usual after one had been shot a few days before.

I found the old library a grand old building, one of Archbishop Robinson's contributions to Armagh when he set about transforming it into a Georgian town. Here, I asked the Dean of Armagh about Caulfield monuments. 'Yes, of course, they are in the Chapter House.' Certainly another example of Lewis Cottringham's clean sweep. 'We don't leave it open because of vandals. We're afraid they might get at the organ or even steal the hassocks' (or did he say cassocks?). He kindly brought me back up the hill. The Chapter House was a fine hall containing a long wooden table and a couple of chairs looking like thrones at one end. The north wall was almost covered with an impressive display of Caulfield monuments. The most prominent honoured James Caulfield, 1st Earl of Charlemont, a man remembered for his patriotism and also for his good taste. Here as you might expect it was his military achievements which were prominent – Captain of the 1st Armagh Regiment, Colonel of the Armagh Regiment and Commander-in-Chief of the Irish Volunteers. But no mention of his pioneering military ancestor who rode out from Armagh on a cold December day in 1600.

At that date Armagh was very small and had been repeatedly ravaged by war. A contemporary map shows the market square with its cross, some lines of thatched houses and two windmills. The cathedral was in the customary condition of ruin. Eleven years later it would be rebuilt by Archbishop Hampton only to be burned down again in 1642 by Phelim O'Neill. Another building of some consequence was a fort constructed the year before in 1599, which was like Charlemont and part of Lord Mountjoy's defences.

The first destination of the three Captains was Newry, along a difficult and dangerous road. 'Good God! What have I taken on me to do?' Bodley wrote. 'Truely I am an ass, otherwise I would never undertake such a heavy burden; but no matter. I shall do what I can, like Coppinger's female dog who always took her own way.'

South Armagh is called bandit country now, but it has bred discord, not only in Bodley's time. De Latocnaye observed how 'the country, which is certainly the most beautiful in Ireland, is also that in which the inhabitants are the least tractable – the animosity between the different sects certainly contributes to this savagery, and if this pretext for it were not available another would soon be found.' He, too, hesitated before travelling on the Newry road. 'The renewal of the religious disputes in Armagh was attended with dreadful assassinations and instances of cruel revenge on both sides . . . It is rather odd that, during these disturbances, a traveller might pursue his journey in perfect safety or, indeed, anyone might during the day. When I was sure of this I resolved to go on as usual, and set out for Newry.'

The helicopter above Armagh's steeply inclined Abbey Street was the latest manifestation of strife. Like the mesh caging on the government buildings and the screens against bombs on the windows of the Charlemont Hotel, named for Caulfield's descendant. Scattered throughout the Archbishop's Georgian town, the Mall, once a race-course, the lines of tall red houses, and the observatory and other churches huddled under St Patrick's Hill, exhorting the passer-by. SEEK YE THE LORD WHILE HE MAY BE FOUND, urged the Baptists; TRAIN UP A CHILD IN THE WAY HE SHOULD GO, advised the Presbyterians, while the Pentecostals gave a warning, KNOW THAT IN THE LAST DAYS PERILOUS TIMES SHALL COME.

When I asked a man directions for Newry a soldier who was standing nearby watching traffic came over.

'Where you from?'

'The Republic.'

'Carrying a gun?'

'No.'

'Put up your arms.'

After he frisked me and let me go, I went a couple of miles down the Newry road before a Land Rover screamed up beside me. It was full of RUC men. Name? Address? Purpose in coming here? It took time to explain about Captains Bodley, Caulfield and Jephson, and the sergeant looked bemused. In the end the Land Rover roared back to Armagh and I continued along the road, the traffic lashing by. I didn't have to walk for long before I was offered a lift. I hesitated momentarily before climbing into the warm interior beside a silent farmer.

At Newry I searched out the address I had been given by the Northern Ireland Tourist Board. When I found the house it had been broken up, or rather smashed up. Bombed? Presumably, although it looked more as if a team of people had stepped inside the shell with sledge hammers. I went back towards the High Street passing a patrol of soldiers with guns and blackened faces crouching in darkened doorways before moving on in hurried movements that were almost balletic. In a little street off the main shopping area I found the Citizens

Advice Bureau. The two ladies behind the desk regarded me with more suspicion than had the two RUC men in the Land Rover outside Armagh. No one stayed in Newry. The main hotel had been bombed twice. The Tourist Board was totally out of touch. It was true they had a list of names, pitifully small. But no one would take me.

I left the unease and ugliness rapidly, giving a thought to the three Captains who stopped here for a time a little longer than my own – long enough to sample the rations. 'That town produces nothing but lean beef, and very rarely mutton; the very worst wine nor was there any bread except biscuits, even in the Governor's House.' Since Bodley was governor of Newry, the remark may have been directed against himself and provides a clue as to why, with shortages at their garrison, the three went to so much trouble to go to Downpatrick. Beyond Newry they were obliged to experience a windy cold night in the open. There was nowhere to sleep and Toby Caulfield wanted to call off the whole venture. 'Before we had ridden three miles,' Bodley wrote, 'we lost our way and were compelled to go on foot, leading our horses through bogs and marshes which were troublesome to us; and some of us were not wanting who swore silently between our teeth and wished our guide a thousand deaths.'

I came upon Hilltown. The Province is scattered with landlord villages, well-maintained, their houses properly listed and documented by architectural trusts and societies. It is bombs not indifference as in the South that threatens them. Hilltown was just such a landlord town, carefully tended. The landlords were the familiar Hill family, Earls of Hillsborough and Marquesses of Downshire – from which had sprung Lord George Hill, the improver of Gweedore. The tameness of Hilltown may have instilled in him the challenge of Donegal – did he envisage recreating something of the atmosphere here created by the Market Place, St John's church and the line of early houses beside the river Bann? Best of all was the Downshire Arms Hotel which had been architect-built to suit fishermen around 1830. It was open – a miracle. Inside I signed the visitors' book and read a comment by a previous guest who wrote of Hilltown: 'The village is unassuming, unpretentious and as good and pleasing a typical Ulster village as can be found.' Quite right. All the more enjoyable was the contrast between rural perfection and the squalor of Newry eight miles away – the same distance as Eglington from Derry. Away from the border areas which have rules of terror of their own, conflict and destruction appear proportionate to urban streets, rather than to religious and class differences.

I was the only guest. There was a large fire and good dinner. I spared a thought for Bodley and his friends riding in the dark.

In the morning I took the Rathfriland road away from the Mourne mountains which were at my back. Touched with snow and cloud, they were very wild compared to the green lowland landscape that had developed into rich farmland in the years since Bodley had travelled over it. Rathfriland stood on a little hill above the plain like a Tuscan hill town. In the Captains' time the town was the seat of Hugh Maginnis, whose successor, Art Maginnis, became 1st Viscount Iveagh, the title a trade-in for his status as petty king. Art built the castle, whose broken walls are visible, after its destruction in the rebellion when Rathfriland was granted to an Alderman Hawkins of London. Roads descended straight down from the top of the town like rivers. In Church Square the Christmas tree was waiting for decorations and a couple of soldiers stood outside the Northern Bank. A market was going on. Cabbages, leeks, oriental rugs and Christmas tinsel and ornaments were on sale. The view of the mountains of Mourne was very fine. They may have inspired the Reverend Henry Cary who was rector here at the beginning of the nineteenth century, when between parish duties he spent years translating Dante. 'We get tired looking at them,' said a woman in the market selling pink and mauve ladies' nightdresses. 'It's almost like looking at your own face.'

In the Captains' time Rathfriland was known as Insula Maginnis, the Island of Maginnis, the only piece of civilization for miles. An observer found Hugh Maginnis 'very civille and Englishlike in his own house'. Nevertheless, although Bodley mentions Insula Maginnis, and he and his companions had just suffered a night in the open, they did not stop here, but went on. Downpatrick was twelve miles away according to Bodley, a distance more or less as the crow flies, making no allowance for detours imposed by the terrain.

Today a frost had covered the hawthorn berries in the hedges with a film of ice. I crossed the Bann, which does not feature in Bodley's account, although the Captains and their Irish guide must have urged their weary horses over it on that rough windy day. A hint of what the terrain was like nearly four hundred years ago survives in the name of the Theiradurth Inn on the Downpatrick road whose name means bogland.

The oak trees of Castlewellan were visible for miles down the road. The taming of Castlewellan, a major estate in the development of the neighbourhood, was witnessed by Mrs Delany. Another stronghold of the Maginnis family, it was purchased from them in 1741 by the Hon. William Annesley, MP for the Borough of Middleton in Yorkshire. In the same year Dean Delany was made Dean of Downpatrick, and the Delanys were obliged to come up here to the North to stay each summer. There was no Deanery at Downpatrick so that they leased a house from the Annesleys named Mount Panther. When William Annesley's father died leaving him a fortune, Mrs Delany proved a good source of advice to him when he used part of his inheritance on his estate. In 1751 she described to her sister how Mr Annesley had 'walled in, and planted with oak, etc. three hundred and fifty acres of ground for a park'. When in July he began building a house, she was there. 'Going to dine under a tent on cold meat about a mile from that place where they are going to build. They say it is a fine situation, has much majesty about it ... as mountains, wild rocks, woods and extensive view of the main ocean.'

That was the very same view that sent A. Atkinson Esq. into raptures. His *Ireland Exhibited to England*, published a decade after *The Irish Tourist*, presented his native land in the best possible light. Instead of the 'nothing of interest' comments he was so apt to use during his weary progress in search of subscriptions, Atkinson had taken to enthusing. He found the view from the little temple above the lake that had replaced the Maginnis castle 'fine beyond description'. He went on to describe how

> the sombre hue of these mighty mountains and the deep rich shade which they shed upon the scene (while bending over the beauties of the valley) give an air of solemn grandeur to the temple, the town, the lawn, lakes and lodges that can only be tasted with rapture by that eye through which the majesty of nature communicates itself in silent eloquence to the imagination ... To feel the beauty and majesty of nature, you must see her with your own eye, and in her presence the finest works of art tremble, and the poet and the painter conceal themselves in a cleft of her rock.

You can check whether Atkinson was right by following the notice that directs you to the viewpoint. The Castlewellan estate is now a national park run with Swiss thoroughness, full of litter bins and sign posts, RIDGE WALK, MOUNTAIN WALK, SHEEP WORRYING

STRICTLY PROHIBITED, SWIMMING STRICTLY PROHIBITED. The lake is still there, and the oak trees planted by Mr Annesley, which are cherished because stands of oak trees are rare in Ulster. Mrs Delany would have loved the arboretum with its clipped yew hedges and sandy paths (PLEASE DO NOT WALK ON THE ROCKERY), filled with plants she would not have known, a small rhododendron from South-Eastern Tibet, a pink viburnum from China. Mr Annesley's house was changed by a descendant in 1856 into a castle of eye-catching ugliness. Now it is a Christian Conference Centre. I peered through a gloomy window into what seemed to be a grandiose Church Hall.

Another night of comfort for me at the Chestnut Inn in the lower square of Castlewellan. Another night in the open for the three Captains. 'The weather was very cold, and it began to roar dreadfully with a strong wind in our faces when we were on the mountains where there was neither tree nor houses, but there was no remedy save patience. Captain Bodley alone had a long cloak with a hood into which he prudently thrust his head, and laughed somewhat into himself to see the others so badly armed against the storm.'

I searched out Mount Panther where the Delanys used to stay. The unusual name is thought to have come from the crest of the Mathews family who built the house. In 1750 it was owned by the Annesleys who lived in nearby Clough while their new residence at Castlewellan was being built. Mrs Delany's letters to her sister were full of comment about Lady Annesley, a daughter of the Earl of Tyrone. 'Such another slatternly ignorant hoyden [as she] never was, and the worst of it is that she is very good humoured but will be familiar; her husband is well enough.'

The road from Castlewellan followed the arc of the sea above the grey tower of Dundrum Castle. 'Monday evening,' wrote Mrs Delany at the end of July 1750, 'went to Dundrum, a pleasant nest of cabins by the seaside where may be had kitchen chairs, French white wine, vinegar, Hungary water and capers ... the French wine is fivepence per bottle – we have not yet tasted it.' Such variety of commodities in an unlikely area was most probably the fruits of smuggling.

I found the back avenue of Mount Panther and walked up towards a big grey house on the brow of a hill. When I got nearer I could see that the windows were broken and grass growing over the front steps.

In the rounded inner hall were still the alcoves which once held classical figures and the remains of the staircase leading up three storeys to floors whose wood was smashed, and at last to a roof open to the sky. Sections of broken plasterwork lay crumpled in corners. The ballroom clung to its remaining lovely pieces of stucco; fruit garlands and acanthus leaves and a bunch of musical instruments breaking away from the wall.

Outside was the same, the walled garden was a waste. Mrs Delany had found it stocked with 'excellent gooseberries, currants and potatoes' to eat with 'fine salmon, lobster, trout, crabs' which were brought every day to her door.

Mount Panther's descent into ruin is a familiar enough story, although a contrast to the care lavished on so many of County Down's old houses. Could not this have been a more suitable location for a Christian Conference Centre than Castlewellan? In 1784, long after the Delanys' tenure, Mount Panther was sold for a reason that was evident from an angry comment by the agent of the Annesley estate: 'The general dissipation of our nobility and gentry have qualified them much better to sell estates than to purchase.'

The last person to live in Mount Panther was Seamus Fitzpatrick who owns the surrounding farm. His father bought the place in 1934 when the house had been empty for ten years, and he and his brothers and sisters were brought up in the cavernous rooms. In 1963 he had built the modern bungalow beside it and moved house. He needed to escape from the leaking gutters, the slates that needed repair and the fabric that demanded constant supervision. His bungalow was everything that Mount Panther was not. He was a farmer, not a millionaire.

'Either I ruled it or it me.'

Near Clough, Bodley and his friends paused on the last leg of their Christmas journey and shivered over the small wood fire they managed to light. Jephson complained as always about the cold. In Clough was a hilltop fort which in their time was crowned with a castle. When Mrs Delany dined with the Annesleys she visited the 'Danish rath furnished by a deep fosse, and which is something singular, at the top of it is a plain strong castle of stone, the building of which is ascribed to the Danes'. Most of the walls are gone, but the site provides another vantage point looking across the green farmland towards Downpatrick, crowned with trees.

By now the Mourne mountains, lying to the south, had ceased to dominate the landscape. At Seaforde, yet another manorial village, an arched entrance leads to the estate of the Forde family which had settled here not long after Bodley's journey. On the road to Downpatrick almshouses preceded a scrapyard of old car bodies, green fields, trimmed hedges, some scattered rose bushes and a bog and small lake filled with duck lying in an area of farmland that in Bodley's time had been a flooded inlet of the sea.

After riding for three days over the bogs the Captains looked more like wild Irish than Elizabethan soldiers. Their clothes were soaked and their saddlebags which contained extra garments were full of water. Their arrival in Downpatrick was like a fête. Servants had been watching out for them with pinewood lights, and as soon as they had caught sight of them escorted them to a handsome stable where hay and oats were waiting for their horses.

Two years before, their host, Sir Richard Moryson, had captured the castle at Downpatrick from Shane O'Neill and been appointed governor. The arrival of his old army cronies who had accepted his invitation and had taken such trouble to journey to Lecale was an opportunity for him to provide lavish hospitality as well as providing a break in his duties.

In the great hall burned a massive wood fire, 'the height of our chins'. Having taken off their boots they sat down and began to talk, 'Captain Caulfield about supper and food, for he was very hungry, Captain Jephson about hounds ... Master Moryson ordered a cup of Spanish wine to be brought with burnt sugar, nutmeg and ginger and we all drank a draught of it.'

They were increasingly hungry. It was an hour before they heard someone down in the kitchen call out: 'To the dresser!' They then dined in style suitable to the occupants of a castle. 'Forthwith we see a long row of servants, decently dressed, each with dishes of the most select meats which they place on the table with the very best style. One presents us with a silver basin with the most limpid water, another hands us a white towel; others arrange chairs and seats in their upper places.'

Supper was brought in 'a variety of meats and dainties' which the company ate with gusto 'calling now and then for wine, now and then for attendance, everyone according to his whim'. When the travellers eventually retired to their rooms they were provided with roaring fires, tobacco and pipes. Refreshed by their feast, they settled back and discoursed on subjects political and philosophical.

Although he was a scarred soldier of fifty, Bodley detailed the Christmas festivities with the enthusiasm of a schoolboy home for the holidays. Like Mrs Delany he had a weakness for describing menus in detail. The variety of the food indicates that in this part of Ulster at least wars had been won and the governor of Lecale was able to live off the fat of the land.

On Christmas Eve after the company had played cards and dice they came down to the great hall, where before the giant fire on a long wooden table stood a wooden vassal bowl, something like the one belonging to the Chichester family which is now in the Ulster Museum. Its three compartments were filled with sugar, spices and ale. The Captains were fêted as special guests of the lonely governor. There were no women present, and the atmosphere must have been like that of an officers' mess.

> There was a large and beautiful collar of brawn, with its accompaniments, to wit, mustard and muscatel wine; there were stuffed geese (as the Lord Bishop is wont to eat at Ardbracon) the legs of which Captain Caulfield always laid hold of by himself; for which there was a piece of venison and of various kinds of game; pasties also, some of marrow, with innumerable plums; others of it with coagulated milk – such as the Lord Mayor and Aldermen of London almost always have at their feasts; others, which they call tars, of different shapes, materials and colours, made of beef, mutton and veal. I do not mention, because they are reckoned vulgar, other kinds of dishes which in France much abounds, and which they designate 'Quela choses', neither do I relate anything of the different delicacies which accompanied the cheese, because it would exceed all belief.

Sir Richard Moryson took great trouble to keep his guests amused. They toured the neighbourhood on their host's handsome horses and were visited by 'certain maskers of the Irish gentry' with whom they made merry and played dice. But after seven days the duties of the governorship of Armagh demanded their departure and their long return journey across the wilds of Down and Armagh. No wonder they left 'mournful and sad'. For part of the way back Moryson accompanied them, and when at last they had to part they shouted 'farewell, and again farewell, for a long way, their voices growing fainter, their caps raised above their heads'.

23
Downpatrick · Spa · Ballynahinch · Hillsborough

In Downpatrick I stayed at Denvirs at the bottom of English Street, which is one of the oldest hotels in Ireland. You can still see the names of the original proprietors, John and Ann McCreevy, inscribed on a post, together with a date – 1641, not an auspicious one for Scottish emigrants. Denvirs has had a face-lift since then, and its interior now is early nineteenth century. Small dark rooms, sloping floors, and a function room where Daniel O'Connell addressed a crowd from the window are signs of a respectable past.

Like Bodley and his companions nearby I woke with the first light of the winter's dawn. 'We now all jump quickly out of bed, put on our clothes and approach the fire, and when all is ready walk abroad to take the air, which in that region is most salubrious and delightful.'

The castle from where Sir Richard Moryson governed has long been demolished, replaced by handsome town buildings. When Pococke came to Downpatrick the four main streets, English Street, Irish Street, Saul Street (originally Scotch Street) and Barrack Street, were already laid out. He toured most local points of interest, the new jail, the Apartments for Clergymen's Widows, the school to teach the poor children of the town and the racecourse, which is the second oldest in Ireland, founded in 1685. He saw the elaborate brick Southwell Charity, dating from 1733, whose structure included an almshouse for six poor men and six poor women and a school for ten children. Mr Southwell was a prominent citizen; Pococke called him Lord of the Town. Just before his visit the first floodgates were installed to reclaim the great Bay of Down which had lain in the path of Bodley and his fellow Captains. These were swept away in 1794 and the painful task of reclaiming the land from the sea had to start once again.

In the mid eighteenth century Downpatrick was an important but neglected ecclesiastical centre. The Penal Laws ensured there was little activity in the Catholic Church. The Episcopal Church, in spite of buttressing by these same laws, was at a low ebb. Country parishes were run by ignorant underpaid clergy. Many churches had been destroyed in the wars of the previous century and the small numbers of churchgoers were too poor to rebuild them. Congregations must have been rather as they are now – two or three gathered together. Often the discouraged clergy became absentees. Pluralism was a problem.

'This is the proper place of residence for the Bishop and Dean of Down, but neither of them have houses here,' Pococke wrote. The Dean of Down in 1752 at the time of his visit was Dr Delany, who was obliged to perform his parish duties from rented Mount Panther several miles away from the town. When he first arrived, the new Dean found that his predecessor had only been there for two days in six years. He began his duties in the spirit of reform. He could travel to Downpatrick from Mount Panther because the Delanys brought from Dublin their coach and six horses (as well as their harper) when they came each summer to the Dean's northern diocese.

As always when considering Mrs Delany, the elegant enjoyment with which she and the Dean regulated their lives suggests frivolity. But the newly appointed Dean of Down had a serious and amiable side to his nature. She adored him. 'I could not have been so happy with any man in the world as the person I am now united to; his real benevolence of heart, the great delight he takes in making everyone happy about him, is a disposition so uncommon that I wouldn't change that one circumstance of happiness for all the riches of the world.'

Before the Delanys arrived parish visiting had been almost unknown and parishioners only saw their clergy when they went to church. Mrs Delany told her sister, 'Never did any flock want more the presence and assistance of a shepherd than this Deanery where there has been a most shameful neglect.' So the Dean began his duties, visiting everyone including Papists. 'I trust in God it will be a very happy thing for the poor people that D.D. is come among them,' his wife wrote. He planned a new Deanery, built an infirmary and contributed towards the improvement of the overcrowded new jail visited by Pococke, and arranged for Divine Service to take place there for the first time.

During Dr Delany's deanship the cathedral at the top of the hill was a ruin with a round tower. It had been destroyed two hundred years before by English forces in 1538. Besides a similarly turbulent history, Downpatrick like Armagh had a hill-top association with St Patrick. For centuries it was believed that he was buried here. This was convenient for John de Courcy who in 1183 used the alleged discovery of the graves of St Patrick, St Brighid and St Columcille to move the See of Down from Bangor to Downpatrick and replace the Augustinian Canons installed by St Malachy with English Benedictines.

After a good deal of dithering, at the end of the eighteenth century the Episcopal Church swept away the round tower and anything else lying around. The building of the new cathedral was entrusted to a man named Charles Lilly. 'New drossery' Mrs Delany would have described his Gothic ornamentations, but it is much more successful than Armagh. The site provides a good place for a prospect. I stood in the wind looking down over bare trees to the distant mountains of Mourne where Pococke noted: 'This spot commands a view of the lake beneath, now almost drained, and of all the country to the south and west.'

An historic place like Downpatrick with its ancient associations with the saint always provided opportunities for pilgrimage or sightseeing. With the three Captains it was sightseeing. After eating several gargantuan meals they set out from Lecale Castle while their host was busy on garrison duty. 'Visited the well and chair of St Patrick, the ancient fort and returned home,' Bodley jotted down in his atrocious Latin. Pococke spent a full hour investigating every inch of Struell's wells, going over the four bath houses and the ruined church lying in a green hollow. Someone has suggested that the humpty little bath houses looked Turkish; this would be true except for the Irish verdure of their surroundings.

After so many centuries you walk round the same rounded stone buildings and St Patrick's seat above on the hill. It is another of those high places with a great view of sea and mountains.

'A famous place for pilgrimages,' wrote Pococke. 'The water rises from a spring covered over, and runs into two baths, one public and one private; at the spring they wash their eyes, and in the baths people as part of their religion go in naked and dip themselves, near the well they go round a sort of altar, probably the side of an old chapel by way of penance, sometimes on their knees.' Pilgrims still come for a more subdued type of devotion and a dip of diseased eyes on Midsummer's Eve.

Back in town Dean Delany preached while his adoring wife sat and listened. 'Saturday we went to Downpatrick; D.D. preached as well as ever I heard him.' Since the cathedral was in ruins, he took services in Holy Trinity, the old parish church of Down. Parochial duties included entertaining parishioners. 'We had a dinner, as usual, for as many as filled a table for twelve people. Our dinner was a boiled leg of mutton, a sirloin of roast beef, six boiled chickens, bacon and greens; apple pies, a dish of potatoes – all set out at once; time between church and church does not allow for two courses; tea after we came home, and talking over our company was refreshing to us.' It seems that the Dean had to flit from one church to another giving a service in each, much as harried Church of Ireland clergy do today, in small cars instead of a coach and horses.

These parochial dinners took place in a public house kept by a former butler who served one of the Dean's predecessors. Perhaps it was Denvirs. You can imagine maids dashing up and down the old staircase to the function room, the smoke from the fires, the smell of food coming from the kitchen – 'very clean – 7 dishes, one at a time, and no second course'.

All that eating did the Delanys no harm. Everyone who could afford it ate like that. D.D. was in his eighties when he died in 1768, and Mrs Delany lived to be eighty-eight. Very likely she took a nibble here and there at the vast array of dishes and considered that their presentation was almost pleasure enough. Only once at Downpatrick did she admit, 'Too much, I might add of food.' In her portraits she looks slim enough, although a miniature of D.D. as a young man makes him look tubby as the result of self-indulgence.

The lavish meals described by Mrs Delany and by Captain Bodley were succeeded by the banquets of the Down Hunt. In the old Assembly Rooms a little further up the street from Denvirs the Hunt used to celebrate its sporting achievements.

John McRoberts, who practises as a solicitor in a Dickensian office that was once headquarters of the Down Militia, had the key to the Assembly Rooms which turned out to be located in the old jail visited by Dean Delany. In 1798 a new jail was built (just as bad, or even worse than the old) and this building was specially converted for members of the Down Hunt who have used it ever since. The thirty current members sit around a long baize-covered table for their twice-yearly dinners, while etchings and portraits relating to their predecessors and their sporting achievements hang thickly around them. Former members portrayed on the walls include Viscount Castlereagh, the Earl of Moira, Viscount Londonderry and a certain Nicholas Price, elected in 1773 when the club had other premises, who remained a member of the hunt for the next seventy years.

Records of the dining club go back to 1751, making it the oldest in the United Kingdom. A few weeks before I arrived it had eaten its final dinner for the current year. 'Oh yes, we had oysters, salmon, and pheasant . . . and the usual wines and champagne.' Their predecessors did better. A dinner in 1796 was celebrated by the Rev. Samuel Burdy with a long poem that listed the menu.

> . . . At the head was good roast hare
> food was decked with lobster rare . . .

Food mentioned included turbot, chicken, ham, beef, mutton, gurnet, tongue, jelly, mince pies and plum pudding.

> . . . Long they eat and without ceasing
> As the dinner was so pleasing . . .

The tradition of good living is characteristic of Down. John Gamble, an Ulsterman, called it 'a rough abundance' and admitted that 'what is often wasted or given away in charity would be nearly enough to support an English family of the same rank for life'. Today good living in Downpatrick is best exemplified by the restaurant Bon Appétit which offers its patrons seventy-six separate dishes which would have confounded the Reverend Burdy.

Chinese restaurants provide welcome havens in Ulster's troubles. They abound; most towns have one among some drab row of shops or houses, gleaming like a jewel on a string. Inscrutably neutral, the Chinese ignore any sense of conflict and work silently to provide a service that verges on a need. Mr Sung Luk Chan and his fiancée Lai Yong Ngan, a name which translates locally into Susan, had recently opened the Bon Appétit at the bottom of English Street opposite Denvirs, specializing in Pekingese and Cantonese cuisine. They regaled me with Dragon and Phoenix scallops, pancakes filled with bean shoots and Cantonese roast duck washed down with China tea ('It helps to take the grease away'). I felt no envy of the Delanys or the hearty eaters of the Down Dining Club.

I went back to Mount Panther for the start of a journey taken by

Mrs Delany to Hillsborough. From there she went to the Giant's Causeway where I had glimpsed her picknicking and sketching. The week before the departure there had been the usual festive round. Somehow D.D. found time for his duties and Mrs Delany for sewing shifts for the poor.

'All this neighbourhood was now in an uproar of diversions! They began last Wednesday and went on till Saturday ... each day a horse race, assembly and ball.' They had danced in the ballroom at Mount Panther where three long windows looked out over the front and broken plaster swags peel off the ceiling. 'When any of the dancers had a mind to rest themselves they sat in the little parlour and tea was brought to them. They began at six and ended at ten.' And no entertainment at Mount Panther was complete without the usual great dinner. 'First course consisted of turkeys, endive, boyled neck of mutton, greens etc, soup, plum pudding, roast loin of veal and venison. Second course consisted of partridge, sweetbreads, collared pig, creamed apple tart, crabs, fricaise of eggs, pigeon ...'

A few days later came the planned excursion northwards. Mrs Delany's only regret was leaving her garden. Even an hour taken away from it, she declared, was an hour taken from life. The party came out from Mount Panther's curved inner hall to the steps now covered with grass and weed. The benign D.D. stood under the fanlight in his black robes, waving farewell. 'Sweet Mr Leslie' was hurriedly sent back to find some important luggage. Early morning sunshine drifted through the trees and on the chaises drawn by high-stepping horses whose gleaming harness was stamped with the Delany crest. Baskets of provisions and valises were packed in. What about her favourite dog? No, the Dean was firm. What about her maid, poor Polly? No, she was too young.

'We left Mount Panther on Tuesday the 26th at nine o'clock, a train of two chaises and two cars with us. Mr Bayly and Mr Mathews, one of D.D.'s curates on horseback, and our sumpter-car.'

It seems probable that the first stop was Seaforde House, home of the Fordes who lived there and still live there now. The Fordes and the Delanys were good friends. We get a brief glimpse of some Fordes from a letter to Arthur Annesley by his sardonic agent, John Moore, who was so shocked later on when the Annesleys sold Mount Panther. 'Our neighbour, young Forde, has brought home his bride.

Nancy is now at Seaforde where the hounds circulate briskly in the morning and the bottle in the afternoon.'

This couple was post-Delany. 'Young Forde's' grandparents would have been the Fordes that greeted her. The present house is also more recent – an early nineteenth-century mansion built in the grand manner. When I arrived I was shown through the outer hall full of flowers, the huge central hall hung with limp military honours, to the library. Here the current Fordes were entertaining a large house party which appeared to be just recovering from a heavy lunch. People came in and out before the big log fire, others lounged waiting for a maid to bring in a heavy tea. Maxwells, Fordes, Brownlows; many were descendants of friends and acquaintances of the Delanys. The entertainment was of a style associated with the past – there was an Edwardian luxury to the scene.

The house itself was the antithesis of poor Mount Panther which was the more beautiful building. I was taken in a car to see the walled garden whose maze and pavilion were in perfect order; the wooded ground beside the lake covered with birds was kept carefully. Seaforde had better luck than Mount Panther.

'From Mount Panther to Ballynahinch is the rudest country I ever saw – rough hills, mountains and bogs, but some of them covered in blossom, heath and thyme.'

The bus to Ballynahinch gave a ride that compared badly to Mrs Delany's 'mannerly' progress. It was filled with a pack of children releasing their venom after being liberated from school.

'Stop it or I'll tell my mother.'

'You're getting romantic,' a spotty girl cried out while two boys tussled around her, pulling each other's hair. Another child was yelling with the pain of being prodded with a ruler. We all got out at Harmony Lane on the outskirts of Ballynahinch and shivered in the raw December air. Winking plastic snowmen in tall black hats hung over the streets, alternating with bushy-bearded Santa Clauses. A lay preacher in a shrunken raincoat had parked his car near the courthouse and was shouting through a loudspeaker. 'Listen my friends, God came into the world to save sinners.' His words were noisy and not easy to understand. A different sort of religion was that expressed on a monument in a nearby church to a member of the Kerr family. 'He seemed imbued with the fruit of the spirit, love, joy, peace, long suffering, gentleness, goodness, faith, meekness, temperance . . . and being ripe for immortality, God took him to himself.'

Next morning the good weather had returned when I joined the Delany party at Spa near McAuley's Lake under the bare slopes of Slieve Croob. In the mid eighteenth century Spa was already becoming fashionable. In 1760 when Mrs Delany called upon Mrs Price, who was a daughter of the Fordes of Seaforde, she noticed how 'Master Price is much better from drinking the Ballynahinch waters, a chalybeate spring in the neighbourhood.'

People flocked to Spa from May to October. 'The company assembles on the walks about eight o'clock, and again, one and three, for the purpose of drinking the waters.' Amusements were provided, assemblies and fêtes and special archery contests in which ladies took part. There was a regular procession in which a cow garlanded with flowers figured largely, from whose milk syllabub was made. The very air itself 'sharp and cold in winter' was considered healthy. It encouraged longevity. Mary Crowly who lived near here died in 1743 aged 113, the venerable Prudence Barnett survived to 111 and Mary Duffield lived to 108.

Today 'Ulster's Aix-la-Chapelle' had returned to nature, the old maze nearly lost in weeds, the surviving pumphouse a small wooden octagonal building in a nest of wild vegetation. Mrs McLeland – long life to her! – lives in one of the few surviving buildings, a little Gothic lodge. She could remember the days before the war when Spa was still used. I quoted some of the miraculous cures that had been effected on 'leprous-like eruptions' and other unpleasant ailments. 'Pen and paper refuse nothing,' she said. She blamed Spa's demise on the American soldiers who had been stationed here during the war and had contaminated the waters. I did not like to ask how.

Like Mrs Delany and her friends I did not stay long. An old axiom about Spa proposed that it was unwise for delicate people 'that included most women' to take the waters too soon after abdominal relaxation. Chalybeate and sulphur tastes nasty.

From Spa the party drove back to Ballynahinch through the Montalto estate which had recently been acquired by Mrs Delany's friends the Rawdons. Sir John Rawdon, soon to become the Earl of Moira, had moved to this congenial neighbourhood from Moira, and like so many of Mrs Delany's acquaintances was bent on improvement. The town of Ballynahinch would be built to his specifications, his mansion would be erected and the estate at Montalto stocked with a herd of deer and tender plants transported from his hot houses at Moira. The oak trees he planted have provided a fruitful source of supply to the Belfast timber firm which possesses the estate now. Only a few survive like remainders after a sale.

The original house was destroyed in the rebellion and the fine house still standing is of a later date. In the summer of 1798 the United Irish army swarmed over the wall of Lord Moira's demesne and pitched camp. The commander-in-chief was a young illiterate Scottish immigrant named Hector Monroe. In glorious weather the rebels lay down under the shade of the oak trees. Parties of ladies were escorted round on tours to be shown the arms of the insurgents – pikes, pitchforks, steel pikes with an extra hook for cutting through a horseman's bridle and the occasional musket owned by the better class of rebel. The United officers wore green belts, green coats and patriotic tokens – an Irish harp entwined with a shamrock instead of a crown, the lion and the unicorn in disarray or a French cap of Liberty. Soon they would all be routed and Ballynahinch left a smoking ruin. The steward of the Bishop of Dromore would take away a couple of bloodstained pikes 'for to be put along with your Lordship's other curiosities'. The Bishop was also given the white plume Monroe had worn in his helmet before the rebel leader was taken to Lisburn to be hanged outside his draper's shop. Among the dead was gallant Betsy Grey who fought beside her brother and lover until they were all killed, and two beautiful young women who were known as the Goddess of Reason and the Goddess of Liberty, and who were the town prostitutes. Their bodies were found dressed in green silk beside the rebel standards they carried.

A mist enveloped me until I came to Hillsborough, a pickled eighteenth-century town which revealed itself as one more manifestation of the unreal beauty of Down. This Georgian toytown is much the same as the one that welcomed Mrs Delany's party in 1758 although no doubt many of the little red-brick shops and houses with the familiar fanlights and doorways curling up the street are of a later date. When Mrs Delany arrived Wills Hill, Lord Hillsborough was in the process of building them. He lived at the top of the town in a house that was replaced in 1795 by the present Government House, the residence of the Secretary of State for Northern Ireland.

Mrs Delany got a splendid welcome.

> The house is not extraordinary, but prettily fitted up and furnished – and Lord Hillsborough is very well bred, sensible and entertaining, and nothing could be more polite than he was to all the company . . . Lord Hillsborough was very merry, and said a great many lively and comical things . . . after the ladies had given their toasts they were desired to 'command the house' the hint was taken, and they said upon that liberty 'go and prepare the tea table for the gentlemen'. Sally and I took a little step out into the gardens . . . candles lighted, tea table and gentlemen came together . . . I made the tea . . . cribbage was proposed . . . and I consented to be one of the party.

Among the topics discussed was the reconstruction of the fort which Lord Hillsborough's ancestor, Colonel Arthur Hill, had built a century before when he founded the town.

'The old castle is fallen into decay. But as it is a testimony of the antiquity of his family he is determined to keep it up. The castle consists of one large room with small ones in the turret, the court behind it measures just an English acre and is laid down as a bowling green.' Not only did Lord Hillsborough restore the fort and a seventeenth-century gatehouse, but he revived the garrison which the family had been allowed to retain since the days of Charles II. The Marquess of Downshire – for such he became a few years later – and his descendants retained their little private army for another century and a half. In 1890, the year when it was disbanded, it consisted of a sergeant and twenty men.

One officer of this force has survived in hereditary and honorary capacity. General Silcock is bugler for what he calls the smallest army in the world. It is a position he inherited from his uncle in 1971. His uniform is believed to derive from that of the Dutch guards of William of Orange. He dressed up while his wife filled me with cake and tea. After half an hour the transformed husband came stiffly downstairs in a red jacket with silver buttons that cost £50 each, tight buckskin breeches and red plumed hat. He carried an old sword and a bugle.

We walked up Hillsborough's steep main street.

'Do I look all right?'

Outside Wills Hill's restored fort he raised the bugle to his lips. When the Governors-General of Northern Ireland had been in residence in the Marquess of Downshire's mansion, they had been woken each Sunday morning by 'Dress Call'. Today the worried Secretaries of State are mostly left to their uneasy sleep. This Sunday afternoon no one took any notice of the resolute figure standing outside the old walls.

Two years before Mrs Delany's visit her host had begun his most ambitious project, the rebuilding of St Malachi's church, which took him thirteen years. Since Downpatrick was in ruin he hoped that the church of Hillsborough would eventually be designated a cathedral. But the pull of St Patrick was too much, which was a great pity, since Hillsborough is not only a more suitable site for the headquarters of the Ascendancy religion, but the church is one of the most beautiful eighteenth-century buildings in Ireland. The name of the architect is lost. 'The church was a one-off,' the Dean of Hillsborough told me.

Although it almost seems to have been designed under angelic inspiration, Wills Hill took a passionate interest in its progress. 'I languish to have this church finished,' he wrote in 1772. 'Is it not time to fix upon the Shape, height etc of the Pinnacles of the great tower? I request that you will keep men constantly at the polishing of the spire that not any roughness may remain . . .'

The result is heavenly. C. E. B. Brett writing for the Ulster Architectural Heritage Society: 'The church comprises an octagonal porch below the principal tower, whose front wall incorporates armorial plaques with the dates of 1636 and 1774; a long and tall nave with ribbed and vaulted ceiling; transepts leading to pinnacled transeptal towers; chancel; and sanctuary . . . It is particularly notable for the high quality of its woodwork.'

From the floodlit tower a musical peal of eight bells installed in 1772 and now electrically operated summoned me to evensong along the avenue of alternate limes and rhododendrons. Inside, I entered a shoulder-high pew beneath the pulpit whose sounding board is crowned with a graceful Gothic pinnacle which seems to lift it so that it floats over the congregation. The Dean giving his sermon might be about to take off in a flying machine. The Hill pew is elevated so that the noble family was able to look down on the congregation. To achieve this, it had to be placed in an unusual position as John Gamble noted. 'The family vault runs under the family seat and the living lord sits on the ashes of the dead one.' No living lord this evening, only the Secretary of State sitting on a thick red cushion on dead Hills.

The Snetzler organ playing the 'Nunc Dimittis' was the work of one of the most famous organ-builders of the eighteenth century. In the chancel was a smaller organ – which had been in Hillsborough Castle.

Lady Arthur Hill had strummed on it as she composed 'In the Gloaming'. Where the wooden Gothic panelling was absent, the place was encrusted with memorials. The Rev. John Leaths, obit 1737, the inscription stated, 'really did leave half his goods to the poor'. Henrietta Hariwell was commemorated beneath a marble urn: 'Lovely was her form her manners fascinating and artless, her mind the seat of purity. She sparkled, was exhaled and went to heaven.' Best known of the memorials is a Nollekens cherub leaning on an urn commemorating Henry and Peter Leslie, no doubt connections of the 'sweet faced young man' whose antics had so often relieved the tedium of Mrs Delany's journey. It seemed inappropriate that Mrs Delany never sat in one of these rich wooden pews listening to her own Dean preaching under that Gothic tracery. Like the houses outside, surveyed by the benevolent statue of the 4th Marquess holding his blackthorn stick, this great church is a reflection of that ordered world of which she was a well-mannered representative.

24
Strabane · Antrim · Belfast

In Strabane a man had been shot and there was an air of agitation as if someone had poured boiling water on an ant heap. Policemen in flak jackets stood in desecrated Abercorn Square while the townspeople faced up to Christmas. A line of decayed Regency houses with lace curtains and flaking walls led down to the bowling green and the bridge over the river whose name echoed the sadness of the place – Mourne. On the other side was Lifford in the Republic. Fears and miseries came with the bridge and border. Soldiers watched cars from the green hills of Ireland bearing different lives, different currencies and ancient antagonisms.

It was an unhappy moment to be looking for traces of a native son of Strabane. In 1820, John Gamble returned to his home town after spending many years out of the country as an army doctor. From his reports of his youth at the end of the eighteenth century Strabane was already an uneasy place. In those days it was Protestant and the descendants of planters had taken on a grim individuality of their own. 'The people of Strabane were worse than Catholics. They had Protestant faces (in this country a man's religion is seen in his face as well as his actions) but they were mere renegades who had deserted the old cause and cared no more about King William than King Priam.'

Today Strabane is a largely Catholic town, a far outpost of the United Kingdom. Since the border was created its position at the western edge of the Province has not helped it. The old Stormont politics further isolated it when Catholic enclaves west of the Bann were deprived of development. Like other isolated rural communities Strabane had hiring fairs until the 1930s when a man could hire himself and his labour for ten shillings a day. Half the men in the town are now on the dole, which gives it the unhappy distinction of having the highest unemployment rate of any town in the EEC. Britain has as little inclination for putting investment into Northern Ireland as into her prisons.

There was always a streak of misery in Strabane from Plantation days when imported labourers trembling from the fury of dispossessed Catholics feared that nothing 'could save their throats from cutting or their heads being taken from their shoulders'. Two hundred years later John Gamble, after visiting his widowed mother 'bent with age', wandered around trying to recapture the springs of youth. 'I should never advise him who quits in early life the place of his birth to come back in matured age in expectation of enjoyment.' Everything was changed, and changed for the worse. The town was going through its perpetual economic degradation. The houses he had remembered were derelict in a state of 'mouldering decay'. (But was this, perhaps, true of most provincial Irish towns?) What seemed from a distance almost like Venice in miniature 'dissolved on entering the town into mean and dingy streets and houses'. They recalled bitter memories of Sunday as a child in a non-conformist household; 'in a day of gloom and mortification ... the morning was passed in listening to long sermons, and in the evenings to long prayers ... to smile was criminal.'

I crossed the Mourne into Lifford where a couple of Garda cars were listlessly parked. That Lifford is less depressing than Strabane is not because it is in the green fields of the Republic – it is smaller, and the atmosphere is a rural contrast to the decayed attempts of industrialization in Strabane and the spread of housing estates full of unemployed.

Both Lifford and Strabane were founded by planters – they started off on each side of the river, friendly rivals, strategically placed. Strabane was granted to a man named Hamilton while Lifford belonged to Sir Richard Hanson whose effigy, together with his wife's, both kneeling and facing each other in polychrome colours, brightens Lifford church. I did not stay long because a funeral was about to take place. Although the old lady was a Protestant, the mourners were mostly Catholic.

Edward McIntyre, the librarian in Lifford's public library, told me this but the day's news had sickened him. 'The IRA have knocked the heart out of Strabane and they're killing people for Christmas.'

The library was formerly the courthouse and jail (another extremely bad old jail). Among the collection of books I found Gamble's *Views and Manners in the North of Ireland*, published in 1818.

But there were none of his other books, and nothing which contained his views of his native town.

Strabane was the home of Mrs Cecil Alexander who wrote her *Hymns for Little Children* which included three that refuse to be forgotten: 'All Things Bright and Beautiful', 'Once in Royal David's City' and 'There is a Green Hill Far Away'. In a culture influenced by non-conformist traditions of hymn-singing she was stoutly Church of Ireland. Hymns are still powerful means of expression that take up political significance in the North of Ireland; 'O God Our Help in Ages Past' is almost secularized as a Protestant battle hymn. In pagan England the most stirring hymn of all is left to the Women's Institute. What if William Blake had written 'In Ulster's green and pleasant land'?

Today, Strabane would not inspire 'All Things Bright and Beautiful'. Probably it never did. Camus House where Mrs Alexander lived beside the river Mourne with a view of purple-headed mountains was outside the gloom of the town where Gamble walked disconsolately. 'I know nothing more calculated to draw forth sad and mournful reflections than a return after a long absence to the place where we passed our youthful days.' He had come to stay. 'I am no longer a stranger but a dweller here. I have received and returned all my visits, welcomes and congratulations are ended, and life flows in the usual muddy stream . . . I read, I walk and sleep again.' And the final sleep of forgetfulness. No memorial nor fountain or even an animal watering trough records his name. Just as A. Atkinson Esq. has been forgotten by Moate, John Gamble is unremembered in Strabane.

I walked down the main street of Antrim to Lough Neagh and then to the ruins of Antrim Castle on the outskirts of the town. 'Neat but boring', an early traveller described Antrim town – still a correct description of the single street and round tower surrounded by houses and factories. Its misfortune is to be situated beside the biggest lake to be found in either Ireland or England, which is also the dullest. A vacuous grey stretch of water is set in a flat grey desert. No hills, nothing to enliven the landscape. Information about eel fishing, folk traditions, recreational areas, the O'Neills, associations with St Patrick and water supplies cannot infuse Lough Neagh with interest.

The barren shore by this lake was the home of one of Ireland's most vivid eccentrics, Lord Masserene. Among the odd happenings in his life he endured twenty years of imprisonment in the Bastille rather than pay a small debt which he considered unjustified. When his dog died he arranged a funeral procession of fifty other dogs all wearing mourning scarves. There are scores of other stories about this eccentric peer.

The Masserenes are still associated with Lough Neagh. A neighbour is Lord O'Neill who lives in Shane Castle. You cannot call him eccentric, but he is a man of passion. He is mad about model railways. Since childhood he has wanted to be an engine driver. His three-foot gauge Shane Castle Railway runs little engines and carriages up and down beside the Lough. Overgrown schoolboys can ride behind the Tyrone and Shane which are engines straight out of Emmet drawings, and inspect the two diesels named Nippy and Nancy and other delights. Lord O'Neill kindly took me for a ride past the trees, through the nature reserve and past the shell of his family castle which was accidentally burnt down in 1816. This is where Arthur Young had been filled with ecstasy at the sight of four men hoeing a field of turnips. 'These were the first turnips I had seen in Ireland and I was more pleased than if I had seen four emperors.' Even the subject of agriculture becomes dull when associated with Lough Neagh.

The passenger in the carriage pulled along by the Tyrone can enthuse about the huge conservatory beside the ruined castle which was designed by Nash as an exact copy of one he built for himself. It houses one of the finest collections of camellias in the United Kingdom which are over a hundred years old. Even on a cold winter's day there were scarlet flowers behind Nash's curved windows. Chewing a cigar, Lord O'Neill talked of two-foot gauges and three-foot gauges and maintenance of diesels and the Londonderry and Lough Swilly Line and other related topics. As a tourist enterprise his railway had been unfortunate – it started in 1971, an unpropitious year. Still, it continued to give him great amusement. Perhaps his hobby, like the eccentricities of Lord Masserene, was compensatory for a dull environment. Here was another member of the landed gentry continuing a tradition that seems to have vanished elsewhere except perhaps in remote parts of Spain or Sicily. Such people have a little more chance of being affected by the hazards of politics than the majority of fellow citizens – their lives may be proportionally more dangerous rather as motor cyclists are more apt to be involved in road accidents than motorists.

Belfast approached in a stream of coloured lights that heralded the mean terraces with their blocked-up windows and doors. Quite suddenly the street opened to reveal Belfast Town Hall, as inappropriate a focus to the troubled city as a wedding cake in a rubbish pit. Black flags and graffiti were more prominent decorations than Christmas illuminations.

I found lodgings in a street behind Botanic Road, a house that turned its back on the troubles. The kindly widow who ran it had the brave optimism that rises from Blitz conditions. She spoiled her guests – both of them. I received constant motherly attention, lavish suppers and breakfasts and plates of scones brought up in case I felt peckish while watching television. I became like Oblomov.

'Are you warm, dear? have another . . . that'll never be enough for a big man like yourself . . . don't forget to turn off the electric blanket before you get into bed.' She seldom mentioned local problems. When she did she looked tired. A few days before I arrived someone had been killed near her front door and the gunmen had vanished.

'At least they are making an effort for Christmas with all the decorations.'

The other guest was an old lady who had arrived unexpectedly one morning and asked for a bed.

'She hasn't confided in you?'

'Confided?'

'Told you about herself? I'm afraid she might cause trouble.'

'Trouble?'

'I don't like elderly people coming here without recommendation. I could fill my house up a thousand times with people like that. They come to avoid being sent to an old people's home. She may have even escaped from such a place. That bag she is carrying . . . it was very small. It didn't have much in it.'

'Does it matter?'

'What happens if she retires to her room and gets sick? Who's supposed to do the nursing?'

No one ever called to see the old lady and her background continued to be a mystery. Two months later when I returned to Belfast she was still staying there in the same unobtrusive way. In the cruelty of Belfast the vulnerability of the old is more pronounced than elsewhere. It was easy enough to get in the frame of mind when these pleasant middle-class areas of the city seem to be a refuge. I lunched in a pleasant hotel near Malone Road which some weeks later I saw again on television in flames. In Sandy Row a florist was selling little baskets of orange lilies. Behind, there were little streets with boarded-up houses except for one here and there where the old or the obstinate had not moved. In the occasional little front window were brave Christmas trees. A helicopter hovered like a yo-yo over the Falls Road, over the tricolour on the Carnegie flats. The liveliness of the graffiti lifted the eye from the filth and black bags and bottles crammed into empty sites. Black and white lettering covered walls like lace. The content of the slogans and initials was tense and posters of starving men were arranged in the form of the letter H. Down the street crowded black London taxis drove fast towards the city centre. One backfired and the silence assumed menace.

When de Latocnaye came to Belfast in 1796, a green ribbon tied at the end of his umbrella, the small town had been rife with old tensions. The illuminations for the King's birthday resulted in a riot. 'The soldiers ran through the streets with sticks in their hands and broke the windows of all those who did not illuminate and of many who did . . . the noise they made was really terrifying.'

I walked down the Falls past Divis Street flats into Castle Street where the giant wire cage enclosed the shopping area like the inner keep of a castle. Women in uniform searched shopping bags, FUCK THE RUC and NO RUC HERE were scrawled on a wall in muddy letters. The long line of black taxis was disgorging people from the stricken Falls. Here was a small street market selling bargain decorations, a repository shop, a small Catholic chapel where women passed with their shopping bags to pray before guttering candles and two Bingo Halls where others played, the numbers called out by the hard-faced women tellers in shrill Northern voices. The Abercorn Restaurant blasted out crackling carols as it had been doing continuously for the last fortnight. A queue waited for hamburgers and a crowd listened to today's religious maniac. While a card was pressed into my hand by his associate telling me that he had been brought back to God by conversion, he was bellowing through a loudspeaker. 'Jesus friend of sinners . . . a person with 256 names. If you desire to know the Lord Jesus, send us your name and address in block capitals.'

They were putting up a belated Christmas tree at the junction between Great Victoria Street and the University Road. Traffic whirled past and children were happily bursting balloons. More taped carols came from the Chinese Takeaway. A few hundred yards on, the world was different, and in Britannic Street and Wesley Street only a few lights glimmered in the darkness.

'Belfast is only a cemetery at night . . . no one goes out.'

'Northern wounds are self-inflicted.'

'If the North want to join up with the Republic she has to be wooed – not raped.'

'The bomb won't go off so long as you are sitting there,' said the security man searching the bus.

The prospect of Christmas in Belfast was daunting. How would I spend it? A visit perhaps to the newly restored opera house decorated with gilded elephants to see a performance of *Cinderella*? Attending church services? Drinking hot whiskey behind the wired enclosure surrounding the Europa Hotel or in one of the pubs draped in flowers and grapes beloved by John Betjeman?

I went to the Morning Star Hostel opposite the Divis Street flats and asked if they needed voluntary help over Christmas. The three-storey building with the framed picture of the Virgin of the Morning Star has long welcomed vagrants. Upstairs, old men spent the night in dormitories. The atmosphere is humane, comfortable and old-fashioned. Put in an application in writing, they said; come back after we have discussed the matter in a meeting.

I went to the Salvation Army where in a big hall a party of the over-sixties club was being held. There was a dais with strident banners, copies of the *War Cry*, lines of wooden seats and a piano.

'Who'd like to choose our first carol?' Captain Kennedy asked.

'"Little town of Bethlehem".'

'I can't see the print.'

'"Away in a manger" . . .'

Between hymns sung to Mrs Kennedy's accompaniment on the piano, Captain Kennedy was telling jokes and keeping people happy. Like most members of the Salvation Army in Northern Ireland they were English. An elderly lady from nearby Lilliput Street showed me the card they left when they visited and she was out. We called to see you today and were sorry to find you were not in. We trust you are well and pray God's blessing on you. Usually she was at home, though. Her house was one of the few left in Lilliput Street. It had glass in the windows, a welcoming kitchen and a fire. All the neighbours were gone. But her condition was balmy compared to some of the other people who had lost children in the violence.

After the carols we had tea and cakes and Captain Kennedy asked me to distribute the prizes.

'A Milky Way for Mrs Foster . . . Who's having the Mars Bar?'

'Are you enjoying yourselves?'

'Yes, Captain,' chorused the old voices.

I was taken to the new hostel in York Road, a big modern building that could accommodate up to 134 people for under £3 a night each. Although many old people complained that this was too much, most were paid for by welfare organizations. Captain and Mrs Hardy ran the place with firmness and tact. Men were known by their Christian names or collectively were formally addressed as 'Gentlemen'. There was no question about a man's religion. In Belfast the only people less sectarian than the Salvation Army are the Chinese.

I spent Christmas in the York Road Hostel. The old men, their faces bored and listless, watched an Elvis Presley film. In the washroom an elderly pensioner was combing his hair and muttering to himself. 'It's all falling out.' Behind him two others were discussing the day's news. 'He spewed it up all over the bath . . .'

In the office beside the main stairs Captain Hardy was opening his mail. 'In thanksgiving for the safe return of a beloved son and the hope that the enclosed will help some other mother's son. Joyful Christmas to all.'

I helped to decorate the window with fake snow. On Christmas morning after breakfast everyone assisted in washing down the floor and setting the long table for dinner with crackers, paper napkins and bottles of mineral water. No alcohol. A short service was held but only a few of the guests at the hostel bothered to turn up. Some carols were followed by a duet by Captain Hardy and Bill Craig on trumpet and trombone. The proceedings were concluded by a resolute Major and 'Silent Night'. In the kitchen the woman beside me made mince pies, supervised three turkeys, peeled potatoes and left me with a giant net of brussels sprouts to be peeled and chopped.

'Like a bloody lot of hens,' an old inmate remarked looking in.

The food went out in a production line, a hundred and twenty plates of turkey and ham and a hundred and twenty plates of

Christmas pudding. Like the regular army on ceremonial occasions the officers served the mess – Captain Hardy, with his small black beard, Mrs Hardy and the others. The men regarded their heaped plates and bottles of lemonade as the Captain said a few words in his English voice. They sat at long lines of tables eating their Christmas dinner, an interlude, before retiring to the television room. After the meal presents were handed round – socks, soap and other useful things. I got them too. The man who was deaf and mute, the two German sailors who had missed their ship and others cast adrift from society unwrapped the Christmas paper around their little parcels. To many of them the hostel had become their one steady home through the years.

Television was an easy way to pass the time, the steadying tranquillizer for those who had no money and were allowed no drink. The old men sat before it during the long Christmas afternoon, occupied by its very presence. They dozed, or watched the strident technicolour programmes with steady stares – occasionally one of them would get up and flick irritably to another station but none of the other glazed sleepy faces reacted.

Over at the Star Hostel under the protective Republican bulk of the Divis Street flats where another soldier had recently died an elderly man lay down in front of the fire while another beside him shared a bag of crisps with his terrier dog. The white Virgin guarding the television set looked amused.

Someone from the kitchen looked in and said, 'Those two are enjoying themselves more than any rich man.'

Rain fell on the red-brick mansions of the Malone Road as their inmates recovered from too much eating and drinking. The Lord Mayors of Dublin and Belfast, their gold chains strung round their necks, went on a goodwill visit of the Falls and Shankill. The rain drenched a Negro soldier, red pompom sticking gaily out of his beret, who guarded the now empty canyons of Belfast. The blankets and black flags dripped hate. '13 dead and not forgotten, we got 18 plus Mountbatten.'

Rain fell on the Dean of Belfast standing outside his cathedral as he had done over the years. 'For needy children . . . for everything.' Cars stopped continuously as people climbed out and stuffed notes into the slit of his box; an RUC constable went over and shook hands.

'This is my whole remembrance, or nearly so, of the Irish Tour,'

Carlyle wrote in 1849, 'plucked up, a good deal of it, from the threat of fast-advancing oblivion (as I went along), but quite certain to me once it is recalled. Done now, mainly because I had beforehand bound myself to it; worth nothing that I know of, otherwise, ended at any rate this Wednesday . . . And now tomorrow.'

Bibliography

Travellers

ATKINSON, A., *The Irish Tourist in a series of Picturesque Views. Travelling Incidents and Observations Statistical, Political and Moral on the Character and Aspect of the Irish Nation.* Dublin, 1815

BARROW, JOHN, *A Tour of Ireland.* London, 1836

BARRY, WILLIAM W., *A Walking Tour around Ireland in 1865 by an Englishman.* London, 1860

BAYNE, SAMUEL G., *On an Irish Jaunting Car.* New York, 1902

BODLEY, CAPTAIN JOSIAS, *A Christmas Journey*, 1600. Printed in *The Ulster Journal of Archaeology.* Belfast, 1854

BOVET, MADAME DE, *Three months Tour in Ireland.* London, 1891

BRERETON, SIR WILLIAM, *Travels 1634–35.* Edited by E. Hawkins. London, 1844

CARR, SIR JOHN, *The Stranger in Ireland.* London, 1806

CARLYLE, THOMAS, *Reminiscences of my Irish Journey in 1849.* London, 1882

CUELLAR, DON, *Captain Cuellar's Adventures in Ulster and Connacht.* Edited and translated by H. Allingham and R. Crawford. London, 1897

DELANY, MRS, *The Autobiography and Correspondence of Mary Granville, Mrs Delany.* 6 vols. Edited by Lady Llanover. London, 1861

EDGEWORTH, MARIA, *Connemara ... A letter to Pakenham Edgeworth. Life and Letters of Maria Edgeworth*, by Augustus Hare. London, 1894

FORBES, JOHN, M.D., *Memorandum made in Ireland in the Autumn of 1852.* London, 1852

FOX, ARTHUR W., *Haunts of the Eagle.* London, 1924

GAMBLE, JOHN, *A View of Society and Manners in the North of Ireland in the Summer and Autumn of 1812.* London, 1813

Sketches of History and Politics taken in Dublin and the North in the Autumn of 1810. London, 1811

HALL, MR and MRS S. C., *Ireland: its Scenery, character etc.* 3 vols. London, 1841, 1842, 1843

INGLIS, HENRY DAVID, *Ireland in 1834.* London, 1834

KOHL, J. G., *Travels in Ireland.* London, 1844

LATOCNAYE, CHEVALIER DE, *A Frenchman's Walk through Ireland.* Translated by John Stevenson. London, 1917

NICHOLSON, ASENATH, *The Bible in Ireland, Excursions through Ireland in 1844 & 1845.* Edited by Alfred Tressider Sheppard. London, 1925

POCOCKE, RICHARD, *Tours in Ireland in 1754 and 1758.* London, 1898

PLUMPTRE, ANNE, *Narrative of a residence in Ireland during the summer of 1814 and that of 1815.* London, 1817

SOMERVILLE, EDITH and MARTIN ROSS, *Through Connemara in a Governess Cart.* London, 1893

Sportsman in Ireland, The, by a Cosmopolite. London, 1840

STEVENS, JOHN, *A Journal of my Travels since the Revolution.* Edited by Rev. R. H. Murray. Oxford, 1912

THACKERAY, WILLIAM MAKEPEACE, *The Irish Sketch Book.* London, 1847

TROLLOPE, ANTHONY, *The Macdermots of Ballycloran.* London, 1847
An Autobiography. London, 1883

YOUNG, ARTHUR, *A Tour of Ireland 1776–1779.* London, 1780

Residents

BLAKE, HENRY, *Letters from the Irish Highlands.* London, 1825

FOGARTY, MARY (SISSIE O'BRIEN), *The Farm by Lough Gur,* by Mary Carbery. London, 1937

HERBERT, DOROTHEA, *Retrospections of an Outcast or the Life of Dorothea Herbert.* London, 1929 and 1930

HILL, LORD GEORGE, *Facts from Gweedore.* 5th edition, reprinted Belfast, 1971

HOUSTON, MRS M. C., *Twenty Years in the Wild West or Life in Connaught.* London, 1879

MAXWELL, WILLIAM HAMILTON, *Wild Sports of the West.* London, 1832

SOMERVILLE, EDITH and MARTIN ROSS, *Some Irish Yesterdays*. London, 1906
Irish Memories. London, 1917

General

BUTLER, HARRIET JESSIE & EDGEWORTH, HAROLD, *The Black Book of Edgeworthstown*. London, 1927

DANAGHER, KEVIN, *The Year in Ireland*. London, 1972

PACKENHAM, THOMAS, *The Year of Liberty*. London, 1969.

PRAEGER, ROBERT LLOYD, *The Way that I Went*. Dublin, 1937

ZIMMERN, HELEN, *Maria Edgeworth*. London, 1883

Murray's Handbook for Travellers in Ireland (4th edition), 1878

Post Chaise Companion Through Ireland. Dublin, 1786

'Provincial Town Life in Munster'. Article by Rosemary ffolliott in the *Irish Ancestor*, No. 1. 1973.

Ulster Architectural Heritage Society. Surveys: Glens of Antrim · Carrickfergus · Mid-Down · Mourne · Downpatrick

Index

MORE ABOUT PENGUINS, PELICANS AND PUFFINS

For further information about books available from Penguins please write to Dept EP, Penguin Books Ltd, Harmondsworth, Middlesex UB7 0DA.

In the U.S.A.: For a complete list of books available from Penguins in the United States write to Dept DG, Penguin Books, 299 Murray Hill Parkway, East Rutherford, New Jersey 07073.

In Canada: For a complete list of books available from Penguins in Canada write to Penguin Books Canada Ltd, 2801 John Street, Markham, Ontario L3R 1B4.

In Australia: For a complete list of books available from Penguins in Australia write to the Marketing Department, Penguin Books Australia Ltd, P.O. Box 257, Ringwood, Victoria 3134.

In New Zealand: For a complete list of books available from Penguins in New Zealand write to the Marketing Department, Penguin Books (N.Z.) Ltd, Private Bag, Takapuna 9, Auckland.

In India: For a complete list of books available from Penguins in India write to Penguin Overseas Ltd, 706 Eros Apartments, 56 Nehru Place, New Delhi 110019.

PENGUIN TRAVEL LIBRARY

Labels

EVELYN WAUGH

Evelyn Waugh chose the name *Labels* for his first travel book because, he said, the places he visited were already 'fully labelled' in people's minds.

But even the most seasoned traveller could not fail to be inspired by Waugh's quintessentially English attitude and by his eloquent and frequently outrageous wit. From Europe to the Middle East to North Africa, from Egyptian porters and Italian priests to Maltese sailors and Moroccan merchants – as he cruises around the Mediterranean his pen cuts through the local colour to give a highly entertaining portrait of the Englishman abroad.

Written in 1929, *Labels* is a splendid example of the genius that was to make its author the greatest writer of his generation.

'He will be admired as long as there are people who can read' – *Daily Telegraph*

They Went to Portugal

ROSE MACAULAY

Henry Fielding sailed there with his household – at an all-in cost of £30 – in search of a cure for dropsy, jaundice and asthma. Later on, William Beckford anticipated orange-scented, wine-soaked afternoons and a fanfare from Lisbon society, while the Portuguese sent Byron into one of his inexplicable black rages, and Palgrave and Tennyson, both thickly bearded, found the climate rather too hot . . .

Rose Macaulay's wonderful book rambles down the centuries like a kind of Cook's Tour, from the pirate-crusaders, through sailors, poets, aesthetes and ambassadors, to Anglican, Roman and non-conformist clergymen, the port wine trading pioneers and the new wave of romantic travellers. The result is one of the most fascinating and unusual travel books ever compiled – a wonderful mixture of literature, history and adventure, by one of our most stylish and seductive writers.

PENGUIN TRAVEL BOOKS

☐ ***A Time of Gifts*** **Patrick Leigh Fermor** £2.95

In 1933 the author set out to walk to Constantinople. This award-winning book carries him as far as Hungary and is, to Philip Toynbee, 'more than just a Super-travel-book' and, according to Jan Morris, 'a masterpiece'.

☐ ***A Reed Shaken by the Wind*** **Gavin Maxwell** £2.95

Staying in reed houses on tiny man-made islands, Maxwell journeyed through the strange, unexplored marshlands of Iraq. His unusual book is 'a delight' – *Observer*

☐ ***Third-Class Ticket*** **Heather Wood** £3.95

A rich landowner left enough money for forty Bengali villagers to set off, third-class, and 'see all of India'. This wonderful account is 'wholly original, fantastic, but true' – *Daily Telegraph*

☐ ***Slow Boats to China*** **Gavin Young** £3.50

On an ancient steamer, a cargo dhow, a Filipino kumpit and twenty more agreeably cranky boats, Young sailed from Piraeus to Canton in seven crowded and colourful months. 'A pleasure to read' – Paul Theroux

☐ ***Granite Island*** **Dorothy Carrington** £3.95

The award-winning portrait of Corsica that magnificently evokes the granite villages, the beautiful mountains and olive trees as well as the history, beliefs, culture and personality of its highly individualistic island people.

☐ ***Venture to the Interior*** **Laurens van der Post** £2.95

A trek on foot through the breathtaking scenery and secret places of Central Africa, described by one of the great explorers and travellers of our time.

PENGUIN TRAVEL BOOKS

☐ ***Brazilian Adventure*** **Peter Fleming** £2.95

'. . . To explore rivers Central Brazil, if possible ascertain fate Colonel Fawcett . . .' – this is the exciting account of what happened when Fleming answered this advertisement in *The Times.*

☐ ***Mani*** **Patrick Leigh Fermor** £2.95

Part travelogue, part inspired evocation of the people and culture of the Greek Peloponnese, this is 'the masterpiece of a traveller and scholar' – *Illustrated London News*

☐ ***As I Walked Out One Midsummer Morning***
Laurie Lee £1.95

How he tramped from the Cotswolds to London, and on to Spain just before the Civil War, recalled with a young man's vision and exuberance. 'A beautiful piece of writing' – *Observer*

☐ ***The Light Garden of the Angel King*** **Peter Levi** £2.95

Afghanistan has been a wild rocky highway for nomads and merchants, Alexander the Great, Buddhist monks, great Moghul conquerors and the armies of the Raj. Here, brilliantly, Levi discusses their journeys and his own.

☐ ***The Worst Journey in the World***
Apsley Cherry-Garrard £5.95

An account of Scott's last Antarctic Expedition, 1910–13. 'It is – what few travellers' tales are – absolutely and convincingly credible' – George Bernard Shaw

☐ ***The Old Patagonian Express*** **Paul Theroux** £2.50

From blizzard-stricken Boston down through South America, railroading by luxury express and squalid local trains, to Argentina – a journey of vivid contrasts described in 'one of the most entrancing travel books' – C. P. Snow